Y0-CAF-895

The Riddle of St. Leonard's

An Owen Archer Mystery

R02034 89180

LT FIC ROBB

Candace Robb

Thorndike Press • Thorndike, Maine

PASADENA PUBLIC LIBRARY
1201 Jeff Ginn Memorial Drive
Pasadena, TX 77506-4895

Copyright © 1997 by Candace M. Robb

All right reserved.

Published in 1997 by arrangement with St. Martin's Press, Inc.

Thorndike Large Print ® Cloak & Dagger Series.

The tree indicium is a trademark of Thorndike Press.

The text of this Large Print edition is unabridged.
Other aspects of the book may vary from the original edition.

Set in 16 pt. Plantin by Juanita Macdonald.

Printed in the United States on permanent paper.

Library of Congress Cataloging in Publication Data

Robb, Candace M.
The riddle of St. Leonard's : an Owen Archer mystery / Candace M. Robb.
p. cm.
ISBN 0-7862-1246-2 (lg. print : hc : alk. paper)
1. Large type books. 2. Archer, Owen (Fictitious character) — Fiction. 3. Great Britain — History — Edward III, 1327–1377 — Fiction. 4. Civilization, Medieval — 14th century — Fiction. 5. Government investigators — England — Fiction. I. Title.
[PS3568.O198R5 1997b]
813′.54—dc21 97-36728

The Riddle of St. Leonard's

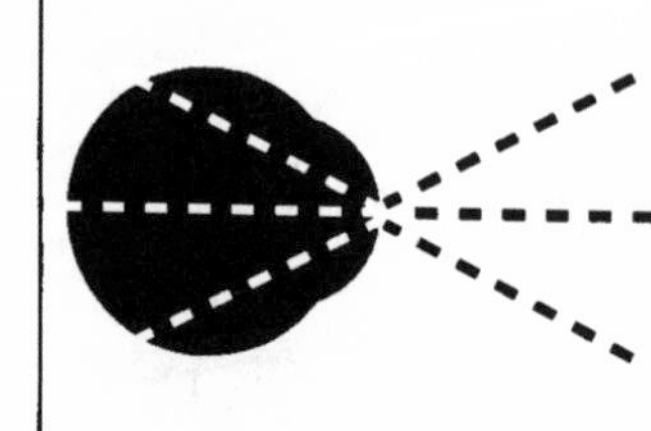

This Large Print Book carries the Seal of Approval of N.A.V.H.

For Aunt Mae,
who has ever been much more
than an aunt to me.

Table of Contents

Acknowledgements

I wish to thank Lynne Drew and Evan Marshall for nursing me along in the writing of this book during a difficult year. Charles Robb for patient systems support; painstaking work on the map; careful, detailed photography of key sites; and questions that led me deeper into my research. Lynne, Evan, and Victoria Hipps for thorough and thoughtful edits.

I owe a huge debt of gratitude to Patricia H. Cullum for her extensive work on St Leonard's Hospital, and her patience with my questions. Jeremy Goldberg, Joe Nigota, Carol Shenton, and the knowledgeable and generous members of Mediev-l, Chaucernet, and H-Albion for responding to my queries with facts and bibliographies. Any mistakes are my own.

Research for this book was conducted on location in York and at the University of York's Morrell Library, the British Library, and the libraries of the University of Washington, with additional critical materials from the York Archaeological Trust and my colleagues on the internet.

wen rcher's Fourteenth Century ork

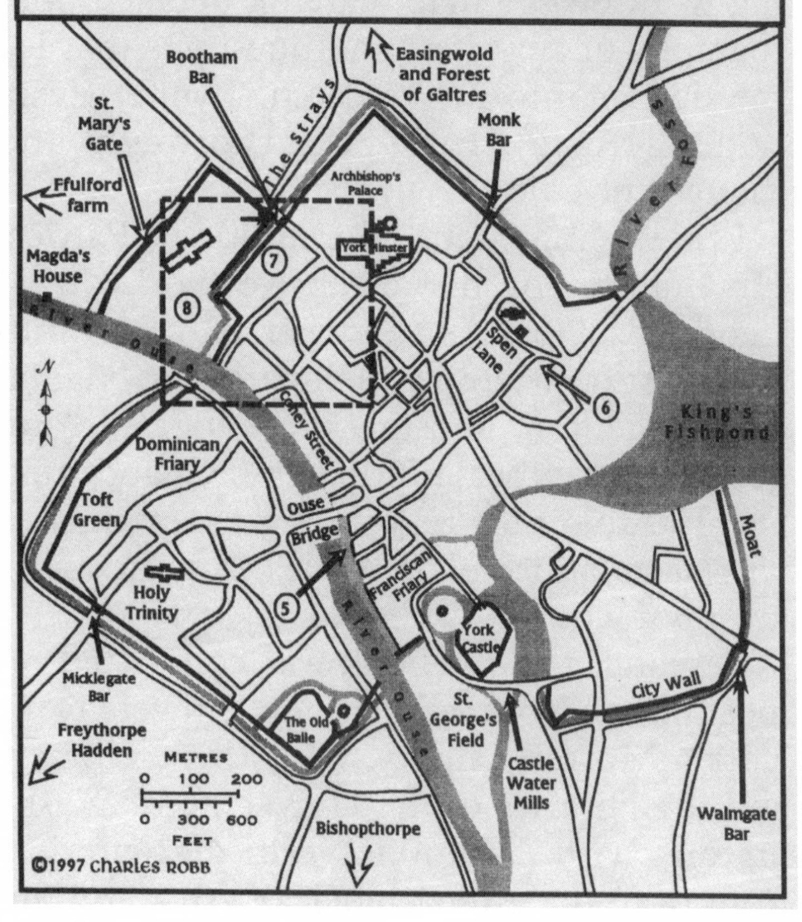

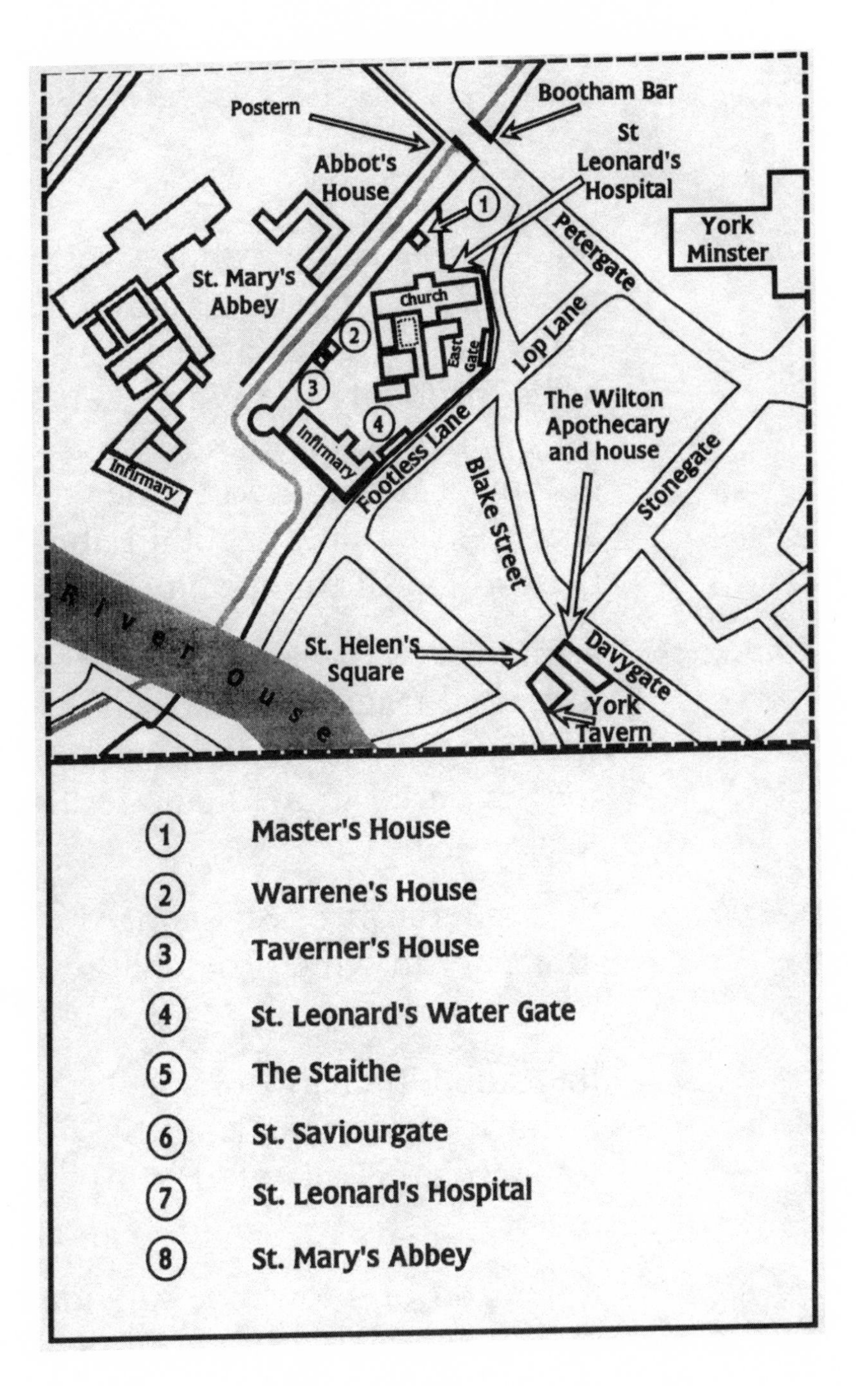
Postern
Bootham Bar
Abbot's House
St Leonard's Hospital
1
York Minster
Petergate
St. Mary's Abbey
Church
2
East Gate
Lop Lane
3
4
The Wilton Apothecary and house
Infirmary
Footless Lane
Infirmary
Blake Street
Stonegate
River Ouse
St. Helen's Square
Davygate
York Tavern
1 Master's House
2 Warrene's House
3 Taverner's House
4 St. Leonard's Water Gate
5 The Staithe
6 St. Saviourgate
7 St. Leonard's Hospital
8 St. Mary's Abbey

Glossary

almoner	one of the canons, whose work was to give alms (food and drink) at the gate (at St Leonard's, probably the Water Gate on Footless Lane), and also to go out of the house in order to visit the sick, infirm, blind and bed-ridden of the locality
ambergris	a fragrant waxy secretion of the intestinal tract of the sperm whale, often found floating in the sea, used in medicine for its aroma
Barnhous	the undercroft of St Leonard's infirmary in which the children were housed
cellarer	the canon in charge of supplies of meats and victuals; at St Leonard's he was often sub-master
corrody	a pension or allowance provided by a religious house permitting the holder to retire into the

house as a boarder; purchased for cash or by a donation of land or property

Gog and Magog biblical reference; Gog and the land of Magog were the enemies of Israel; it was believed that the reign of the Antichrist would be heralded by the return of Gog and Magog

grammar school a school in which the emphasis was on the *Trivium* (grammar, rhetoric and dialectic), or the analysis and use of language, preparing the student for university; St Leonard's operated a grammar school

grandame grandmother

houppelande men's attire; a flowing gown, often floor-length and slit up to thigh level to ease walking, but sometimes knee-length; sleeves large and open

jongleur a minstrel who sang, juggled and tumbled

Keeper of the Hanaper — head of the department within Chancery that received fees paid on charters and letters under the great seal, paid the wages of the Chancery staff and bought materials for the office, and accounted for the whole proceeds annually at the exchequer; also received payments of fines by recipients of chancery writs; called the hanaper because the documents waiting to be sealed were kept in a hamper (hanaper)

Lammas — first of August, when the Archbishop of York held an annual fair

lay sister — a woman who takes the habit and vows of a religious order, but is employed mostly in manual labour and is exempt from any studies or choir-duties

leman — mistress

manqualm — an Anglo-Saxon word for plague, pestilence

Martinmas	feast of St Martin, 11 November
mazer	a large wooden cup
messuage	a plot of land occupied by or intended for a dwelling house
Petercorn	income supporting St Leonard's Hospital, dependent on the harvest (Peter's corn)
prebend	the portion of the revenues of a cathedral or collegiate church granted to a canon or member of the chapter as his stipend
rood	cross
Queen's Receiver	officer in the Queen's household who gathered in revenue which he then disbursed at the Queen's order in lump sum, paid over to her treasurer; Ravenser had power to act as the Queen's attorney in any court in England
sext	noon
spital	early English word for hospital, later 'spitalhouse' and 'hospital'
staithe	wharf

strays	common grazing area
sweetwater	a medicinal bath of mallow and sweet-scented herbs
swine gall	exactly what it says; medieval medicine was not without its oddities
trencher	a thick slice of brown bread a few days old with a slight hollow in the centre, used as a platter
vespers	the sixth of the canonical hours, towards sunset

Prologue

York, July 1369

The elderly man took tentative steps out of the door of the infirmary. He favoured his right leg for a few steps, then, when the shooting pains of the day before did not attack his efforts, he tried a bolder gait, letting his right leg swing out. He felt a twinge in the knee, but at his age a twinge was to be expected in any joint. Walter de Hotter crossed the yard from the infirmary to the East Gate once, back, twice, back, then continued out on to Blake Street. It was a happy journey. He was to sleep in his own bed that night. Not that the infirmary bed at St Leonard's Hospital had been uncomfortable. Or unclean. Truth be told, it was cleaner than his own. But a man's bed is a special thing, and Walter looked forward to a night in his.

Each time Walter entered the hospital because of an injury he wondered whether he would return to his own bed. His days were numbered, he knew. Three-score and nine he was: a goodly age, a venerable age. And for a clumsy man prone to accidents, a quite remarkable age. It was fortunate that he had married well and improved the business left to him by his father, accumulated several valuable messuages in the city, more property than his children could claim a need for, and had promised the one in which he dwelt to St Leonard's in return for a corrody. He had made this arrangement after his wife had died; while she had lived she had seen to his injuries, and a commendable job she had done. But without her, Walter had been uneasy. Who would soak his sprained ankles, smooth soothing unguents on his burns, wrap them? His fellows in the merchants' guild had assured him they would see to him. And so they would have, for the guild took care of its own. But he did not want to be a burden. He was not feeble, merely clumsy. It was Tom Merchet, proprietor of the York Tavern, who had suggested the corrody. Walter would always be grateful to Tom for that. As a corrodian of St Leonard's Hospital he was given his food, clothing and a bed should he need it — which was the best part for him, for he needed a bed quite often. Not for long. Never for long. But he *would* break bones and twist ankles, wrists — an elbow recently. The swollen knee had been the latest injury. And he had received all the care from St Leonard's because, once he was dead, the hospital would have his property to lease and would make a nice sum. To Walter it seemed more than fair.

And he was still alive and ambulatory, praise God, and happy to be headed home. He was going to an empty house, which was not as he would have liked it, but it would not be so for long, God willing. His eldest son and heir to the business had taken his family to their small house in Easingwold, saying he was opening a shop there. Peter was fearful of pestilence, truth be told. And who could blame him? One Sunday, Walter had heard at Mass that a child had died of pestilence the night before, and by the following Sunday five had died within the city walls, one of them a fellow corrodian of St Leonard's, poor old John Rudby. Walter did not begrudge his son such precautions. Nor, for his part, had Peter protested his father's trading the townhouse on Blake Street for a corrody.

Evening had settled on the city and the streets were dark, although the sky, visible if one craned one's neck to peer at it between the buildings, was still blue. Walter picked his way with care, even though he travelled such a familiar route. Filthy streets offered tumbles at every step, and the sisters had warned him that the bandage on his knee would not protect him from a severe twist. But his belly was full and his heart light on this return home. Once more he had lived through a frightening fall. God was merciful.

At the door to his house, Walter fumbled with his key. At last the door swung wide. He stepped into the darkness, pleased to find it not too stuffy. But on second thought it concerned him. Perhaps he had left some windows unshuttered at the back of the house. He had been in much pain when he had gone to the hospital.

As he felt his way across the room, Walter could see the evening light through the chinks in the shutters. He had closed them then. But his relief was short-lived. The door to the garden was ajar, letting silvery evening light spill through. He did not think he could have been quite so careless as to leave that open. Which meant someone might have broken in. Perhaps thinking he had abandoned the house. It was happening all over the city; Peter was not the only one hoping to run faster than the pestilence. Empty houses became repositories for the dying. That frightened Walter. If a plague corpse had poisoned the air in the house, he would soon succumb. He fumbled for the pouch of sweet-smelling herbs that he had purchased at the Wilton apothecary the week before and held it to his nose as he moved forward. But he stumbled over something and dropped the pouch. He groped on the floor, found instead a stool that should not have been there. Thank God he had been moving slowly, though he should have been looking down, not towards the open door. But he thought he had just perceived a movement out there.

An intruder would know of his presence by now — the rattling key, the stool. He would be ready. Walter picked up the stool, crept towards the open door. He had indeed seen movement. There was a man in Walter's kitchen garden.

'Here now. What are you about?'

The man spun round, took a few menacing steps towards the door. 'Who goes there?'

'I am the one should ask that. I am Walter de Hotter and this is my house, that is my garden, and —' As Walter raised the stool above his head, he exposed his chest, which was just where the intruder had aimed the knife. 'Sweet *Jesu!*' Walter dropped the stool, clutched his heart, felt the sticky blood pumping out. And then strong hands were round his neck, pressing, pressing . . .

* * *

On the night after Walter de Hotter's body was found, the York Tavern overflowed with folk hungry for gossip to distract them from their fears. Bess Merchet considered it a mixed blessing.

Old Bede mumbled the oft-repeated numbers. 'Two corrodians of St Leonard's dead in three weeks. Both with town messuages going to spital on their deaths. Spital's in trouble, needs corn and suddenly the canons have rents, don't they?'

Bess found Bede's inaccuracy irritating. 'John Rudby died of pestilence, old man. And poor Walter was ever stumbling over his own feet.'

'Oh, aye? Poor Walter stumbled on a knife and strangled hisself, eh?' Old Bede laughed until he collapsed in a coughing fit.

Bess flicked a cloth at him. But in faith he was not the only one talking of it tonight. She did not like such rumours. Her own uncle was a corrodian of St Leonard's, and his best friend also. Perhaps it would not hurt to say a prayer for them this evening.

One

A Reputation at Stake

With pestilence in the south, most government officials had fled to the country a fortnight before. Nothing of substance would be accomplished in Westminster until the death count returned to a less terrifying level. The poor, the merchants who could not afford to close up shop for a season, and those who served them were left to live in sweltering fear behind shuttered doors or masked against the pestilential air.

There were also some whose duties delayed their flight. As Keeper of the Hanaper and the Queen's Receiver, Richard de Ravenser was one such, and even he hoped to depart for the north by the week's end in order to deal with disquieting matters concerning St Leonard's in York, which had been relayed to him in a letter from one of his canons. Ravenser was master of the great hospital.

Equally unnerving was the summons to London that he had just received from his uncle, John Thoresby, Archbishop of York.

It seemed an odd time for his uncle to choose to journey to London when he might have remained secluded and relatively safe at Bishopthorpe. Ravenser did not mind the short ride from Westminster to London, but he wished he knew his uncle's purpose. Presumably he had arrived recently, for Ravenser had heard nothing of his uncle's presence in the city. Which meant Thoresby's business with Ravenser had some urgency. He was to attend Thoresby at his house at sext, which gave him little more time to prepare than it would take to arrange for a horse to be brought round.

Juniper wood burned in a brazier near John Thoresby's chair. In his hand he held a ball of ambergris. The window to his small garden was closed. And this morning he had forgone the bath for which he yearned. He was determined to survive the pestilence and fulfil his oath to complete the Lady Chapel at York Minster.

Thoresby was in London examining the deeds to his palace at Sherburne so that he could ascertain whether he had the right to tear it down for its stones, with which he might complete the chapel. But this morning a missive had arrived that he must discuss with his nephew, Richard de Ravenser.

It was well for Ravenser that he arrived at the prescribed time. Thoresby already felt impatient with his nephew. What was not so clever was Ravenser's choice of garb: a costly blue silk houppelande and bright green leggings. The silk would be ruined by the man's sweat, which Thoresby thought considerable. Remarkable that such a slender man could work up such a lather on the brief ride from Westminster.

'You would rival the peacocks in any garden,' Thoresby said. It was impossible to tell whether Ravenser blushed, he was already so red. Red, sweaty, dressed like a peacock — and looking with every season more like Thoresby himself, though more pinched in the mouth and desperate round the eyes.

'Your Grace.' Ravenser bowed. 'I came as quickly as I might.'

'No time to change into something more elegant?'

A surprised look. 'I confess I dressed whilst awaiting my steed and escort.' Ravenser frowned down at his clothes. 'A poor choice?'

'They tell me that you aspire to my position. Do they speak true, Richard?'

Ravenser glanced at a chair. 'May I?'

'You are weary from your ride. Of course.' Thoresby watched his nephew smooth the back of his garment, flutter the sleeves so they might drape over the arms of the chair. His taste for finery was more suited to court than to chancery or the Church. 'Wine?'

The Queen's Receiver glanced up with a guileless smile. 'That would be a great comfort.' Thoresby guessed it was the quality of Ravenser's smile, so unexpected in a man of his status, that pleased the Queen. It made him seem an innocent in a world of ministers cynical from experience.

'If it is true that your ambitions lie in the Church, I would recommend that you adopt a more clerical look,' Thoresby said.

Ravenser looked stricken. 'Your comment about peacocks was not in jest?'

'Hardly.'

A servant slipped from the corner of the room, poured watered wine into two Italian glass cups, offered one to Ravenser from the tray. He took it, drank thirstily. The servant stood by, ready to refill the cup. After the second, Ravenser sighed happily and drew out a linen cloth to dab at his lips.

Thoresby lifted the offending missive with the tip of his finger, nodded for the servant to hand it to Ravenser. 'I received this today. I thought you might wish to discuss it.'

Ravenser's eyes fell to the bottom of the missive, and he frowned. 'Roger Selby, the mayor? But what of William Savage?'

'He died in late May. You had not heard? Selby was sworn in on the feast of St Barnabas.'

'God be thanked,' Ravenser muttered.

'Oh? I always found Savage a reasonable man.'

'The office had gone to his head.'

'No, it was his heart gave out.' Thoresby allowed a brief smile.

Ravenser winced.

Thoresby wondered what had transpired between the dead man and his nephew. But he must see to the matter for which he had summoned Ravenser. 'Read the letter, Richard. We must discuss it.'

As Ravenser read Selby's letter, he coloured. Thoresby saw it quite clearly now that his nephew had caught his second wind. At last Ravenser dropped the letter on the small table beside him, leaned on one elbow, chin in hand. Not so elegant now.

'The reputation of York's religious houses is precious to me, Richard. What do you know of this Honoria de Staines?'

'Sweet *Jesu*, uncle, she is a lay sister, no more than a servant to the sisters who tend the sick.'

'And she has been allowed to carry on her earlier profession in her hours away from the hospital?'

'No! Savage slandered the hospital without cause. The lay sisters live together under one roof in a house belonging to the hospital. A sinner amongst them would be reported, I am certain.'

'Tell me about this woman.'

'Fair and fond of men they say. Her husband went to fight for the King and has not returned.'

'How did she come to the hospital?'

Ravenser rose, moved behind his chair, leaned his elbows on its back, shook his head. 'This is all unnecessary. But if anyone is to blame it is my cellarer, Don Cuthbert, he who is in charge when I am away. He believes it his mission to give sinners a second chance. When Mistress Staines came to him and expressed her vocation, he thought it his Christian duty to accept her. I commended him for it.'

Was Ravenser so naïve? 'I suppose she made a small donation to convince him?'

'To Cuthbert that would not matter.'

'I do not recall this saintly man.'

'You would have no reason. He is rarely away from St Leonard's.'

'And there is nothing in this accusation that she still invites men to her bed?'

'Not unless she shares them with the other lay sisters at their house, no, Your Grace.'

Ravenser's voice rose slightly.

'You feel bullied. But you did not consider the potential gossip, did you? Have you encouraged Cuthbert to be so bold with other choices?'

'No others have come to my attention.'

Someone else's duty to notice. An ill-advised attitude. 'What of the comment about the hospital's financial straits?'

Ravenser wiped his brow. 'You know of that problem, Your Grace. But how it has become common knowledge . . .' he shook his head.

Thoresby considered his nephew. Should he give him advice or let him swim upriver on his own?

Ravenser cleared his throat. 'I have sent a request to the Queen for an audience. I will ask her permission to ride north to see what I might do to quiet this talk.'

Excellent. There might yet be a higher post for the man.

Ravenser drew out a letter. 'There is more. My almoner, a man I trust, has told me of another rumour.' He handed the item to Thoresby.

The archbishop read Don Erkenwald's missive in which he warned Ravenser of talk of deaths that conveniently eased the hospital's expenses. Thoresby gave his nephew his sternest look. 'You swear this is merely a rumour?'

Ravenser put his head in his hands. 'Christ's rood, if even you can believe it, I am without hope.'

'Enough. I go to Windsor myself on the morrow. If you receive an invitation, you are welcome to share my barge.'

Ravenser peered up through his fingers.

Thoresby nodded to him.

Ravenser lifted his head and smiled. 'You are kind to extend such an offer. How can I thank you?'

'You will thank me by resolving this business before other reputations are jeopardised, nephew.'

Ravenser bowed, still with a polite smile, but Thoresby had seen discomfort in the man's eyes. Good. He understood that Thoresby looked after his own interests in this. He would not want his nephew to think him an unconditional ally.

Don Erkenwald, almoner of St Leonard's, heard the whispers about Walter de Hotter's death. He did not like them. The rumour of the hospital's financial troubles had been circulating through the city for several months, and now someone had attached a juicier titbit to it. No one had thought twice about

John Rudby's death, but the death of Walter de Hotter was clearly murder. And though Walter had lived out in the city, he had just returned from the hospital when attacked. His death further risked the hospital's already tarnished reputation.

The situation deserved more attention than his brother in charge of the hospital gave it. How had his fellows elected Don Cuthbert to the position of cellarer over him? The puny canon had been content with the bailiff's suggestion that Walter had surprised a burglar, and he refused to speak of it further. He had been particularly deaf to Erkenwald's suggestion that Richard de Ravenser, Master of St Leonard's, be informed of the rumours.

As to informing him, Don Erkenwald had already seen to that, writing to Sir Richard about the hospital's financial troubles being made public. Ravenser might be busy in Westminster as Keeper of the Hanaper and Queen's Receiver, but surely not too busy to care about the reputation of his hospital. Erkenwald hoped that the master might even now be planning a journey north to mingle with the important families of the city and convince them that all was well. It was not the time to allow such lies to poison the people's opinion of the good works St Leonard's accomplished, not now, when the merchant guilds were building elegant halls and housing their own sick and elderly in the undercrofts. These were the very merchants on whom they depended for generous gifts to support St Leonard's.

On his almoner's rounds among the poor, Erkenwald now made it his business to ask whether anyone had seen aught, or heard aught about Walter de Hotter's death that seemed more than rumour. On one of the afternoons when he stole some time to practise at the butts on St George's Field — his vows had not obliterated his training as a soldier — Erkenwald asked the advice of one said to be the best spy in the north.

While he unstrung his bow, Owen Archer listened with interest — until Erkenwald came to the motivation.

'Murdering a respected merchant to ruin a rival hospital's reputation?' The tall, one-eyed man grinned. 'You should go back to soldiering. All that prayer has softened your wits.'

Erkenwald laughed at that. 'Prayer. There are those in my house who would say I pray too little. 'Tis why they chose Cuthbert over me. Prayer is ever his response. Every time another treasure disappears he flies to church and prays. I suppose he believes the good

Lord has decided to redistribute the wealth of St Leonard's.'

'I had not heard of any thefts.'

'Well, and that is as it should be. In that I agree with Cuthbert. I suppose a thief in our midst is not a story merchants would care to use, being thieves themselves, eh?'

'What is missing?'

Erkenwald needed no coaxing. He knew the story would go no further, and perhaps Archer would see a pattern in it. 'Riches, to be sure. A gold chalice finely wrought, a delicate silver missal cover, goblets of Italian glass. Such things.'

'And Don Cuthbert's response to such a loss is to pray?'

'He does little else.' But Erkenwald saw that Owen's attention wandered: he fidgeted with his quiver of arrows. No matter. The information was his to use. 'I thank you for listening, Captain.'

'Forgive my haste. My children leave for the country on the morrow. I have much to do.'

'You send them to Mistress Wilton's father?'

'We do.'

'To keep them from the pestilence?'

Owen pressed the scar below his eye-patch. 'Foolish, eh? As if Death did not walk all the countryside.'

'Still, a wise precaution.'

'God go with you, Don Erkenwald.'

As Owen walked away, the canon noticed a slump in the archer's shoulders, which was not in character. To send his children away must have been a difficult decision.

John Thoresby and Richard de Ravenser sat quietly on the barge travelling up the Thames. The afternoon sun had warmed the river water to an unpleasantly pungent degree, but at least a breeze stirred their rich garments where they sat beneath the awning. Their men-at-arms were not so fortunate; they stood in their own sweat in the sunlight. Thoresby watched the swans on the river, ghostly shadows amidst the reeds and grass along the bank. He felt his nephew studying him. Did he think to find his future in his uncle's face? Folk often commented on the two men's appearance: outwardly so similar, they seemed the same man at two stages in life, prime and, well, it must be said, old age. But it was an illusion. In soul they were nothing alike. Ravenser was enjoying the journey; he smiled now and waved at a lady on a passing barge who was being serenaded by a lute-plucking lover. Thoresby could not so enjoy himself this day, on his way to what might be his last audience with Queen Phillippa.

Windsor Castle shimmered in the summer heat but, within, the thick stone sweated and gave off a damp chill. Aromatic fires burned everywhere to ward off the pestilence, creating a fog in some of the passageways. Continuous Masses were said for the people, and once a day a procession wound from St George's Chapel around the lower ward, through the Norman Gate, and around the upper ward, with a benediction said at the royal apartments before the procession returned to the chapel. Servants with any signs of fever were sent to wait out their illness outside the castle. Only those necessary to or summoned by the King or Queen and who appeared in good health were allowed into the royal apartments.

Ravenser entered the Queen's chamber with trepidation. He had always come here on the Queen's business, at her bidding. This was different. This was his business, instigated by his missive to the Queen explaining his situation. The worst of it was that now it seemed a trivial matter to put to a dying Queen.

But she had graciously invited him. And now she waved him to her side with a red, swollen hand.

'Your Grace,' Ravenser knelt at her side.

'Come. I have little time for ceremony at present, my good Receiver.'

'Forgive me for intruding . . .'

She grunted to silence him. 'I have little head for state affairs at present. I have prayed over this and believe it is God's will that you go north and put your house in order. You are best away from the city and court at such a time.'

'Your Grace, you are most kind. I shall entrust the purse to my best clerk in my absence.'

The Queen lay her head back on the silky mound of pillows. A lady-in-waiting made herself known and showed Ravenser out.

Tears shimmered in the Queen's eyes. 'My dear John, old friend.' She pressed Thoresby's hand, released it. 'Pray for me.'

'I beg the same of you.'

'Help Edward when I am gone. He will need you.'

Thoresby did not say that the King had not called upon him for anything outside his duties as archbishop in a long while. This was neither the time nor the place. But he did have a request. 'I would be your confessor. Stay beside you until . . .' He could not say it.

Phillippa's rheumy eyes glistened with tears. 'No. I could not bear it. With Wykeham I do not feel this pain.'

So it was true. William of Wykeham, Lord Chancellor and Bishop of Winchester, was the Queen's confessor in her last days. Thoresby had not believed it. To hide his dismay, he told Queen Phillippa of his plan to complete the Lady Chapel.

'Alas, Sherburne. Is it not a lovely house?'

'I have many such houses. But the minster does not have a complete Lady Chapel. The quarries near York are depleted of the stone I need. And I wish to complete it now. So that you may come north to see it.'

Phillippa patted his hand. 'That will not be, my friend. Too many who were too young to die have gone. It is my turn. God may let Richard recover if I go quietly.' Her eldest son, the Black Prince, had suffered a wasting sickness for two years. Her second son Lionel, Duke of Clarence, had died the previous year, and her third son's wife, the lovely Blanche, Duchess of Lancaster, had died in the autumn. Many said it was the weight of sorrow that had finally broken the Queen's spirit.

'I would stay with you, confessor or no.'

Phillippa closed her eyes, gave one imperious shake of her swollen head. 'You must go north. Complete your Lady Chapel. Perhaps it may yet save York from the pestilence.'

Thoresby and Ravenser dined at the King's table on the evening before their departure. As the roast was set before them, a messenger hurried into the hall. He went straight to the King and knelt behind his chair. Edward turned stiffly, leaned, nodded. The messenger gave his news softly. But Edward evidently saw no need for discretion. He threw up his hands and shouted, 'Well done! Well done! There is some gold in this for you, by God.' As the messenger was escorted to a seat at a lower table, Edward turned to his puzzled company. 'She is safe delivered of a daughter. Mistress Alice has this night been safe delivered of a daughter.' The King rose to his feet unsteadily. Clutching the back of his chair with one hand, he raised his cup in the other and shouted, 'Let us drink to Mistress Alice.' His eyes were locked with Thoresby's.

The archbishop raised his cup. 'God be thanked for a safe delivery,' he managed to say without choking on bile.

All drank to Alice Perrers and her daughter.

Two

Manqualm

The two laboured through the high grass along the riverbank, sweating in the hazy sunshine. There was no breeze to ease them once they left the river. They were chided by frogs and bees disturbed by their passage and that of the boat they pulled up on to the bank behind them. When they had tethered the boat to a sapling, they set off across the fallow field leading to the cottage. Nettles caught at his leggings, her skirt, as if urging a retreat. Gnats and flies hovered close, tasting their sweat, then followed along in a noisy cloud. Crickets warned of their approach. Close by a horse whinnied and stomped.

Owen Archer and Magda Digby exchanged uneasy looks; they found the farm too silent. Absent were the sounds they strained to hear: those of a family going about its daily work — a scythe whistling through the tall grass, a bucket clanking against the side of the well as the groaning rope lifted it, children squealing in play.

Though Owen and Magda had been told that they would be greeted with silence, they had hoped to find Duncan Ffulford and his family hard at work, proving the fisherman's tale to have been fermented in a bottle.

Owen paused at the edge of the field, swatting flies from his face as he swept his head from side to side to study the yard; he had the use of only his right eye, his left scarred, blind, and patched, and thus he must compensate for half the range of vision with which he had once been blessed. His sweep took in a thatch-roofed cottage, its door yawning wide, no smoke drifting from the hole in the roof's centre; a dusty yard with a horseless cart sitting as if being prepared for use; a barn and other outbuildings behind the cottage, quiet but for the impatient horse, likely in the barn.

Owen turned to his companion. 'Where's the child gone to, I wonder?' The fisherman had claimed a girl crouched on the riverbank, calling to him as he drifted by that her mother and the babies were dead, and her father too sick to help her bury them.

Magda shaded her eyes with a gnarled, sun-browned hand. She faced the barn. 'Thou hearest the beast, Bird-eye?'

'Aye. 'Tis little noise to mask it.'

'Likely the child keeps it company.'

'Should we first go to her, then?'

'Nay. 'Tis best Magda and thee know the worst. Into the house with thee. But first attend thy protection. There is no wind to carry off the vapours.' From a pouch at her waist Magda drew two cloth bags filled with scent, handed one to Owen, held the other over her mouth and nose. These would protect them from the noxious vapours that spread disease.

Owen looked down at the bag with doubt. 'And who holds these to our faces whilst we bury the dead?'

Magda met his argument with a sniff. 'Cover thy face, thou contentious Welshman. Provident care when thou canst take it is better than none at all.' Without more ado, the tiny midwife strode across the dusty yard and stepped into the cottage.

Owen lifted the bag to his face and followed, having found it wise in the past to take Magda's advice. He ducked through the low doorway.

Within, the cot was dark, the only light coming from chinks in the thatch and walls, illuminating the dust that swirled with their every movement and the flies that swarmed round the four bodies, two children lovingly tucked in the wooden-framed bed beside a woman, and a man lying on the floor near the remnants of a fire. Magda crouched down by the bed, lifted the covers with a stick to examine the bodies. Even through the scented bag Owen smelled the putrefaction, gagged, retreated to the yard to catch his breath.

Magda joined him. ' 'Tis the manqualm, Bird-eye.'

Owen crossed himself. 'Let us find the child. She might tell us where to find a priest.'

Magda, hands on hips, squinted up into Owen's good eye. 'Thou thinkst to find a priest will say the proper prayers? Thou wouldst take such time with this?'

'They died unshriven, I've no doubt. And they should be buried in consecrated ground. 'Tis my duty as a Christian man to do what I may to help them to Heaven. I know it is not your way, Magda, but it is mine. And theirs. I must try.'

Magda did not argue, perhaps in thanks for his agreeing to accompany her on this mission. Heading towards the barn, she paused at the cart. 'Duncan thought to load his family into the cart and bury them? Take them to the priest? Or had he thought to flee it with them?' Magda grasped the side of the cart, touched her forehead to it, as if suddenly weary. 'And the worst of it still to come, Bird-eye. Thy Lucie will work from dawn to dusk, as will Magda, and what availeth it?'

'Come, Magda. Let us find the child.' Owen walked past the cart, across the rutted yard to the barn. The horse began once more to whinny and stomp. One ear to the door, Owen sought the sound of another living thing within. He heard the rustle of straw. Perhaps the horse, perhaps the child.

The barn door was warped by the river damp. Owen used his strength to lift it and swing it wide. Peering in, he saw an old nag in a stall. He approached it slowly, calming the uneasy creature with murmured reassurances. As Owen reached the nag, he picked up a cloth, rubbed the horse gently until it quieted.

Magda had followed him.

Owen patted the nag. 'Duncan Ffulford was better off than I had thought, to own a horse.'

'Aye, and he was proud of her. She carries her years lightly thanks to their tender care. Now, be quiet, Bird-eye.' Magda stood in the middle of the barn, listening. Her multicoloured gown seemed to flicker in the pied light. 'She is above.' Magda motioned for Owen to precede her. 'Her name is Alisoun.'

As Owen stepped away from the horse, it

nipped him gently on the arm, calling him back. Even the beast feared the unnatural quiet of the farm. Owen crept up the ladder to the hayloft, tucking his head down to avoid a pitchfork or knife. In times like this, a child on her own would do well to protect herself. As Owen was about to clear the ladder with his head, he said softly, 'Peace, Alisoun. I come in peace.' He held his hands up to show the child he had no weapon. 'A fisherman told us you needed help.' He prayed God it was indeed Alisoun up there.

'Who are you?' a child's voice demanded.

Much comforted by the high timbre, Owen said, 'Owen Archer, captain of the archbishop's retainers and husband of Mistress Wilton, master apothecary in York.' He was not sure which might prove more reassuring.

'Climb up slowly.'

'May I use my hands on the ladder?'

'Slowly.'

Owen obeyed, easing his head up, then moving up one rung, two, and stopping there, at eye level with the girl, who stood sideways, skirt hitched up into her girdle, bare, dirty feet planted firmly apart, her upper body expertly poised with a small bow and arrow read to shoot. 'Turn so I can see the left side of your face.'

Owen turned towards the light coming from a hole in the thatch, giving the girl a full view of his scarred left cheek and eye, the leather patch.

With no relaxation of her stance, the child demanded, 'Who accompanies you?'

'Magda Digby, the Riverwoman.'

Alisoun stepped to the edge of the loft, glanced down. 'What do you want here?'

Owen was about to chide the child for her disrespectful tone, but Magda spoke before he could. 'Magda comes to bury thy family and take thee back where she will find a home for thee.'

'This is my home.'

'Aye, that it is. But thou must have a mother's care, eh? Thou art but eleven years.'

'I would not have you for a mother, you old hag.'

'You should watch your tongue,' Owen warned.

Magda again did not react to the discourtesy. 'Thou blamest Magda for thy mother's poor state after Tom's birth, aye. Thou needst not worry. Magda does not yearn to play thy mother.'

Alisoun let the bow slacken. She stared down at the straw. 'My father is dead then?'

'Aye, God grant him grace,' Owen said.

'So we're needing to take them to consecrated ground and find a priest. Can you show me the way?'

The child shrugged her bony shoulders. 'The priest wouldn't come when Father tried to fetch him.'

Owen was not surprised; it was a common tale in times of pestilence. 'If you take me to him, I will persuade him to do his duty.'

'I would not have your wife for a mother, either.'

Tempted to give the unpleasant, dun-coloured child a lashing with his tongue, Owen controlled himself. He must do his duty and be done with her. 'We shall discuss your future once we've buried your family. Now take us to the priest.' He descended the ladder.

After a few minutes, Alisoun followed. At the bottom of the ladder she let down her skirt and shook out the hay and dust, smoothed back her braided hair, then fixed Owen with a steely glare. 'My future is my own concern.'

A matter to be discussed later. 'Come, child, we have much work to do.'

Alisoun rolled her eyes and sullenly headed for the door. As Owen watched her depart, he noted how thin she was, realised she might be hungry. 'Shall we try to feed her first?' he asked Magda.

'Do not waste thy time fretting about that child, Bird-eye. She will not hesitate to demand what she wants.'

'She is always so wayward, then?'

'Oh aye. Watch thy back with that one.'

Owen made for the nag. 'I shall hitch her to the cart.'

'Magda will prepare the bodies.'

When Owen led the nag from the barn, Alisoun stood halfway across the yard, waiting with an impatient look. Owen noted how the child averted her eyes from the abandoned cart and from the house. She had tender feelings, then, though she hid them well. As he worked with the cart, he tried to talk to her. 'I would wager you not only hold the bow as a trained archer does, but shoot it well, too?'

'I can fell coneys and squirrels. Why do you want to know?'

Owen decided to echo her lack of courtesy. 'Who taught you?'

'I asked you a question.'

'I choose not to answer.'

Silence. Then, without preamble, Alisoun said, 'My father taught me.'

'For protection?'

'What else?'

'There had been trouble?'

Hands on hips, Alisoun squinted up at Owen. 'You're nosy.'

'You are rude. We are quite a pair.'

The child ducked her head, turned, sat down in the dirt. Owen found her silence refreshing. He led the nag closer to the house, so he might more easily shift the bodies.

At first Owen thought the stone church empty, but as he moved to the centre he discovered a prostrate form before the altar. He turned to Alisoun. 'What is his name?'

'Father John.'

Owen approached the priest. 'Father John?' The figure stirred, but did not rise or respond. Owen knelt beside him, whispered into his fleshy neck, 'I pray you forgive me for intruding on your prayers, but I've come to fetch you to say prayers at the gravesides of four of your parishioners.'

The head turned, an eye peered at Owen, then the priest began to push himself up, but he was lifted to his feet instead. Owen grinned down at the short, corpulent man, filthy and stinking of onions and ale. 'Gather what you need. We must waste no time.'

Father John glanced at Alisoun. 'They are dead?'

'You know they are.'

'May God have mercy on them.' Father John crossed himself. 'How long ago did they perish, my child?'

'I am not your child.'

'She says you refused to go to them when her father requested your presence, Father John. Why was that?' Owen asked.

The fleshy face crinkled round the eyes and mouth as the priest raised his folded hands to his breast and cringed. 'Whence come you to this place?'

'York.'

'Ah. Then surely you noted the portents? The wind that came up from the south. The days the sky was dark, but the rain did not come. And the great multitude of flies. I have felt it my duty to pray. When Duncan Ffulford came, stinking of the pestilence, bringing it into this sacred place, I prayed for his soul and those of his family. But I could not touch them or I might be struck down, unable to pray for the other souls in my care.'

Owen gathered the fabric on the priest's chest and lifted him off his feet. 'You have found a convenient way to satisfy your conscience, priest. You do not deserve to wear this gown. But as you are all we have to hand, we must make do.'

Father John's face was purple. His eyes

bulged out. 'It is a sin to attack a priest,' he gasped.

Owen let him go.

The priest began to crumple, then caught the pillar beside him and raised himself upright, breathing hard.

'What you have experienced so far is hardly an attack,' Owen said. 'But you might wish to avoid learning the difference. 'Tis a small thing we ask, that you perform your priestly duties.'

Later, as Owen dug, he wondered what had come over him. He was not wont to treat a priest so. Had the child so irritated him? Or was it the madness that came with the pestilence? Might he be infected with it already? He prayed God that if so he died before he carried it to his family. As the priest stepped forward to say his prayers over the graves, Owen found himself praying as much for his own family as for the Ffulfords. Magda stood quietly, eyes closed, one gnarled hand clutching the opposite wrist. She did not pray, so she always said, and yet her stillness suggested a state, if not of devotion, then of concentration. On what?

And what of the child? Owen felt a twinge of guilt about his lack of concern for her. Her obstinacy was no reason to forget she was a child who had just lost her entire family. He glanced over to the foot of the graves where Alisoun had stood. Gone. He looked round, did not see her.

Soon all three were hurrying about, calling the child's name.

But she had vanished. And the sun was the gold of late afternoon.

'The river calls,' Magda said. 'Has the child any kin nearby?'

Father John frowned down at his feet. 'There are many Ffulfords in the parish.'

Owen could see no point to another search. The child had expressed her desire to choose her own accommodations. 'I shall trust you to go among her kin and let them know the child's situation, Father John.'

The priest frowned at the task, but nodded. 'It is my duty, of course.' He glanced at the horse and cart. 'I can see to them.'

Owen could well imagine. 'Tell her kin the horse and cart are at the farm, priest.' He began to move away, turned back for a final warning. 'I will return to check on the child's safety. And her horse.'

'You'll find naught to anger you, Captain.'

In the boat, Magda seemed to nod in slumber. Owen rowed downriver silently, squinting against the afternoon sun that glinted on the brown water of the Ouse. He was thinking about the Ffulfords. So far most of the half a hundred deaths in York had been among the aged or the very young. But today he had seen a couple struck down who looked his wife's age. They had been very thin, a result of last summer's failed harvest, perhaps.

'Winds from the south. Flies. The priest named them harbingers of the pestilence. But what of the bad harvest?' Owen wondered aloud. 'Might hunger so weaken the people that they succumb to the pestilence?'

Magda opened one eye. 'The girl shows no sign of illness.' She drew a small bottle from the wallet at her waist, opened it, handed it to Owen, who paused in his rowing long enough to take one drink. Then Magda drank. 'Was a time thou wouldst accept naught from Magda, Bird-eye.'

And not so long ago at that. Owen grinned. 'Perhaps I was not so thirsty then.'

The Riverwoman gave one of her barking laughs. 'Aye. Mayhap.' She took another drink, put the bottle away. 'Magda would give much to know what calls back the man-qualm from time to time, Bird-eye. A bad harvest?' She tilted her head, thinking. 'Each time it has followed one, 'tis a fact. But not every bad harvest summons it. Thy priests say 'tis the scourge of thy god, punishing thee for thy unholy ways. Mayhap 'tis why Magda survives. She is invisible to thy god.' She grinned, showing her teeth, white against her tanned leather skin.

So ancient and still she had all her teeth but one, and that one she had lost as a child. No one knew how long ago that had been. Magda was not inclined to say. But folk round York spoke of her as having lived on her rock in the mud flats of the Ouse just north of the city since the time of King Canute, hence the Viking ship turned upside-down that served as her roof. Owen knew Magda was too mortal for such a life span, but there was no doubt she was old. And rich with the wisdom of a life spent healing the sick and bringing children into the world. And thinking for herself: though she lived as saintly a life as a good Christian, she was not a Christian and found the Church's teachings poor, superstitious excuses for common sense. A dangerous opinion, but strongly held. Owen valued in her friendship her clear mind, common sense and a fresh perspective, free of fear.

'But how do thy priests explain the deaths of infants, Bird-eye?' Magda no longer smiled.

'To my mind it is the parents who are punished by such a death, Magda, not the child. I have heard it said that such a child was too good to live; God chooses to take such children directly to Heaven so that the world might not taint their souls.'

A snort. 'So thy god leaves only the unworthy on earth? Bah!'

Owen felt uneasily like agreeing with Magda. But was that not blasphemy? 'We cannot always know the Lord's purpose.'

Magda wagged her head. 'Thou art not taken in by such nonsense. Thou wast wise to send thy children off to Freythorpe Hadden.'

'Was I?' Since the first rumours of pestilence, Owen's wife, Lucie, had wished to get their children out of the city. Eight years earlier she had lost her first child to the plague — Martin, her only child with Nicholas Wilton, her first husband. So Lucie had conceived a plan to send Hugh and Gwenllian to her father's manor in the countryside, where his efficient sister Phillippa was also in residence. But there was one problem: Lucie had still nursed their son Hugh, born the past winter, and as master apothecary she could not leave the city at such a time. How was one to find a reliable wet nurse in the midst of pestilence?

And then Magda's granddaughter Tola had come down from the moors with her infant, Emma, and her two-year-old, Nym, grieving for her husband, who had been savaged by a wild boar. Lucie had befriended the young widow and asked her to be Hugh's wet nurse.

Owen had not been easily persuaded that Tola should take his only son out of the city. It was true that when Death stalked a city, people changed, grew wild in their despair, unpredictable in their deeds. Perhaps the children would be safer in all respects in the country. But . . . 'The country did not save the Ffulfords,' he thought aloud.

Magda, who had let her chin drop to her chest again, opened one eye, squinted up at Owen and grunted in sympathy. 'Tola and her young ones are best away from Magda's house, where the sick are wont to come. 'Tis not so different at an apothecary.'

'The sick are not brought to the apothecary.'

'Nay. But those who care for them . . . Oft they succumb. Why dost thou yet debate thy decision? 'Tis done.'

It was difficult for any parent, this pestilence that seemed most fatal to children. But for Lucie it was doubly hard because of the loss of her first to the plague. The hope that her family was protected by God's grace could not buoy her.

How much worse would it ever be for Alisoun Ffulford, having lost both parents and siblings?

'Are there any more in Alisoun's family, Magda?'

The Riverwoman jerked awake. 'Eh?' She shaded her sleepy eyes with a hand.

Owen repeated the question.

'Nay. Parents, three children, 'tis all.' Magda shifted, began to lay her head back down.

'So what does she guard in the barn?'

Magda grumbled and rubbed her eyes. 'Herself. Her valuable horse.'

'Why did she run from us?'

'Why should she trust strangers, eh? Be patient, Bird-eye. The child will come to Magda or thee in her own time.'

'How do you know?'

Magda lay down her head, closed her eyes. 'Some things cannot be otherwise, Bird-eye.'

As Owen rowed towards home, the fly-ridden farmhouse haunted his thoughts.

The boat rocked dangerously as Magda suddenly sat forward, eyes scouring the sky downstream. 'Fire in the city. Dost thou smell it on the wind, Bird-eye?'

Owen was breathing deeply with the effort of rowing. But he smelled no more smoke than usual. ‘Even in summer folk tend their fires, Magda.’

The Riverwoman frowned up at the air. ‘Nay. ’Tis more than that, Bird-eye.’

Three

Things Fall Apart

Throwing the shutters wide, Bess Merchet stood with eyes closed, head back, hoping for a breeze to refresh her and clear the dust from her nose. Hardly more air than in her bedchamber. How was a woman to revive her spirit while cleaning? 'May the Lord grant us an early autumn,' she muttered as she moved away from the window.

But what was that? She paused, listened. There. She heard it again. Over the usual din of carts on cobbles, children screaming in play, hawkers crying out to the passers-by, a smithy's clatter, over all these common sounds of a summer's day in York, and, down below, the maids noisily cleaning the tavern kitchen, over all this were shouts and shrieks and the clanging of a bell signalling an emergency.

Bess returned to the window. And now, as she breathed deeply, she noted how dense with smoke the air was, more like the air in the dead of winter than in July. Squinting and shifting from foot to foot, making good use of her vantage point three full storeys above the ground, Bess at last saw, round the chimneys and gables of her neighbours' houses, a plume of smoke rising over St Leonard's Hospital.

Her immediate thought was that it was a funeral pyre. She remembered how in the time of the first pestilence, even on the windy coast of the North Sea, the air over Scarborough had some days been thick with smoke from the burning of the plague corpses. She had been heavy with her son Peter and fearful that the stench would turn him to a monster in her womb. But the deaths so far had been few compared with that time.

Her second thought was for her Uncle Julian, who had a small house within the hospital walls. He was a careless man with a lamp or a candle, especially when in his cups, which might be at any time of day or night now he no longer did an honest day's work.

Bess glanced at her half-cleaned chamber and judged it tidy enough for tonight. Dirty it was not. She did not tolerate dirt in bedchambers, be they the guest chambers or her own. But organising the clutter must wait until she confirmed her uncle's safety. With an impatient tug, she removed the scarf that protected her thick hair, the red dulled with the passing years, but still a full head of hair of which she was quite proud, and replaced the scarf with one of her starched and beribboned caps.

St Leonard's Hospital stretched over a large area within the north corner of York's city walls, bordered by Footless Lane, St Mary's Abbey, and Lop Lane, and reaching almost to Petergate. The East Gatehouse stood at the top of Blake Street, with a high arch over the lane in which was set a statue of St Leonard. The church and the claustral buildings of Austin canons filled the north-east half of the precinct; the other half held the infirmary with two chapels, and extensive additional buildings for a grammar school, guest hall, tannery, malthouse, stables, workshops, kitchens, and dwellings of staff and corrodians. It seemed almost a self-contained town. St Leonard's had been founded by Athelstan before William the Norman harried the north, and it was said by many to be the largest hospital outside London.

As Bess passed under the arch, she encountered a scene of chaos: people swarmed like frantic bees smoked from a hive, running hither and yon, bumping into each other as if blinded by the smoke; buckets and pots clanked and sloshed with water. Bess pushed through the crowd towards the infirmary, shaking herself loose from those who clutched at her and shouted gibberish. But she realised in short order that the infirmary and its chapels were intact; the smoke came from the north wall, from either the grammar school or one of the small houses for corrodians — which included her uncle's dwelling.

With renewed urgency she pushed through the crowd, using her left shoulder as a battering ram, and was soon past the grammar school and forcing her way through an even louder throng. She was rewarded by the sight of Julian's house, scorched on the left side, but intact. The house beside it, however, was a burned-out shell. Before it lay two bodies, one writhing beneath the ministering hands of two women, one of whom Bess recognised as Honoria de Staines, once her uncle's servant and now a lay sister. The other man lay quietly beneath the bowed head of an Austin canon.

As Bess approached, she saw that much of the clothing on the motionless man had been burned away, and his body scorched — his face beyond recognition. Don Erkenwald solemnly prayed for his soul. Bess crossed herself, moved over to the one struggling to stand to escape the two women. 'Uncle Julian! Praise God!' She almost laughed, thinking how like him to be surrounded by fawning women. But when he turned to Bess and she saw his face bruised and cut, his mass of white hair singed on one side, both hands bandaged from fingertips to wrists, she saw how close he must have come to being the one lying still beneath the priest. 'What happened, uncle?'

'Tell Anneys and Honoria to see to Laurence.' Julian's voice was hoarse. He struggled to rise, pushing the two women aside.

'Don Erkenwald is with him,' Bess said. And glad she was, too, as she realised the dead man must be her uncle's oldest friend, Laurence de Warrene. Erkenwald was a former soldier and knew death when he saw it. He would have found help for Laurence if there had been any hope.

'Erkenwald knows nothing of physicks,' Julian said, taking a step towards Bess. As he put his weight on his left foot he stumbled with a cry of pain.

Bess caught him, and with the help of the one called Anneys managed to lower him gently to the ground. 'Sit and keep your peace, uncle.' Bess shook her head at his singed sleeves, hem, and hair. 'Were you in that house as it burned?'

Julian closed his eyes and put a bandaged hand to his forehead. 'Laurence's house.'

Bess caught sight of two men pushing their way through the crowd with a stretcher, motioned them over. 'Get him to the infirmary at once.'

Julian growled at them. 'See to Laurence.'

Honoria touched Julian's cheek. He pushed her away.

'Let the men lift him,' Bess said, grabbing the woman by the shoulder and pulling her up. Hearing her uncle groan, Bess turned, shouted to the stretcher-bearers, 'Be gentle with him.'

Honoria grabbed Bess's arm. 'I am a lay sister of this spital and not accustomed to such treatment.'

'I know your station,' Bess said. 'And your previous calling.' Folk said her husband had left her rather than compete with her lovers.

'I took good care of Master Taverner when I served him.'

'I am sure you did.' Bess turned to the other woman, who was dressed in a similar dark, simple gown and white wimple. 'You are a lay sister also?'

The woman nodded. She was older than Honoria — by her greying eyebrows and the lines around her eyes, Bess guessed her beyond her child-bearing days — and had a competent air about her.

But she was still a mere servant. 'Where are your superiors?' Bess demanded. 'Does my uncle not deserve to have one of the nuns tending him?' He had paid good money for his corrody at the spital, he deserved the best they had to offer.

'We were near,' Anneys said. 'Dame Constance has gone before us to the infirmary to prepare Master Taverner's bed.'

'Ah.' The Mother Superior. That was better. Bess watched as Honoria picked up her skirts and hurried after the stretcher. Even in her drab gown she managed to provoke stares from the men in the crowd.

Another stretcher had been brought for Laurence de Warrene. Don Erkenwald, relieved of his charge, joined Bess and Anneys. He was a muscular canon with the scars of his former life on his face. Bess had always thought him an odd one to be an almoner. 'Both women have been trained by the sisters and are trusted with our patients, Mistress Merchet.'

'Laurence was dead when you found him?'

Erkenwald gave a brief nod. 'I believe he was so when your uncle pulled him from the house.'

'He knows, then?'

'It is difficult for him to accept that God has taken his friend and spared him.'

He did not wish to know was more like. 'What happened here?'

'You know that Master Warrene's wife died of pestilence several days ago?'

Bess nodded.

'It was recommended that he burn aught that had touched her in her illness — clothes, bedding . . .'

'A simple task gone terribly wrong,' Anneys said.

Bess ignored the woman. 'Was he ordered to burn her things in the house?' she asked the almoner.

He smiled at the suggestion. 'We are not fools, Mistress Merchet. The fire had been built here, in the yard, before the door. How the house caught, or how the two men came to be within, I do not know.' He was suddenly distracted by someone in the crowd. '*Domine,*' he muttered under his breath. 'Here comes little Cuthbert.'

The crowd had parted to allow the passage of a tiny canon who strode forward, hands in sleeves, his face puckered in an expression of disgust as his eyes swept back and forth over the charred scene.

'What has happened here, Erkenwald?' the

newcomer demanded in a high, penetrating voice.

Anneys took the opportunity to leave. Bess did not blame her. Don Cuthbert was the type of small, delicate man who became a tyrant when given power.

'Master Warrene was your responsibility, Don Cuthbert,' Bess said.

Cuthbert jerked as if slapped and turned towards Bess with an expression that proclaimed him surprised to learn she could speak.

Well, she would let him hear more. 'Was it your idea to give him such a task, unaided, though he was so recently bereaved?'

The canon peered at her as if trying to identify her. 'What had bereavement to do with the fire, goodwife? And how is it your concern?'

'Her uncle, Master Taverner, was injured trying to save Master Warrene,' Erkenwald explained.

'Ah.' The cellarer closed his eyes and gave Bess a slight bow. 'Forgive me, I did not realise. We shall do everything we can for your uncle.'

And so he thought to dismiss her. Bess paused to ensure enough breath that she did not sputter, then drew herself up to stand taller than the canon. 'I find little comfort in your words after seeing how you cared for my uncle's grieving friend. Of course, it is impossible for you to imagine what one feels when deprived of one's life mate. But if you are to accept substantial sums of money from lay folk to see them easy through their last days, you ought to make it your business to learn about such things.' And with that, Bess turned and swept out of the hospital grounds.

As she turned down Blake Street, she paused at Walter de Hotter's house, its windows and doors boarded up to prevent trespassing. Now another corrodian's property had come to the hospital. She was not easy in her mind as she headed back to the York Tavern.

Nor was Don Erkenwald easy in his mind. He thanked the Lord for his foresight in writing to Sir Richard. He had lately received a message from the master of the hospital in which he agreed that it was time for him to come north and set his house in order. Pray God he arrived soon.

Four

An Unnatural Mother?

Magda had shooed Owen away when he'd offered to help her pull the boat up on to her rock in the Ouse. 'Hurry home, see to thy household, Bird-eye.'

The gatekeeper at Bootham Bar confirmed Magda's pronouncement of a fire.

'Aye, Captain Archer. They say 'twas near the great spital.'

That would be St Leonard's. But how near was near?

Owen ran down Stonegate. Once in St Helen's Square, whence he could see the apothecary, he paused to catch his breath and calm himself. The smoke was to the north. The queue of folk spilling out of the shop was waiting for service, not moving pails of water. God was merciful.

As his worry faded, Owen grew more conscious of his filthy clothes; his tunic and leggings reeked of the grave. He turned down Davygate. Next to the shop, the narrow end of his large house gave on to the street, with only a tiny window facing out from the jettied second storey. He could tell nothing of his household's welfare from the street.

'Captain Owen, welcome home. Did you find the little girl?'

Owen squinted, his eye not yet adjusted to the gloom in the entryway. At the end of the little passage stood a vague form, lit from behind by the windows of the hall. By her voice, he knew it was Kate, their new serving girl, a younger sister to their housekeeper and nurse, Tildy, who was at Freythorpe with Gwenllian and Hugh. Kate was learning her job well, but she had no talent for silence. Owen already wearied of her continual chatter. 'Aye, Kate, we found the girl, buried her family. The household is fine? No one was injured in the fire?'

Kate shook her head. ' 'Twas a fire at St Leonard's. The house of a corrodian caught fire. He is dead, his house ruined.'

'Who?'

'Master Warrene.'

'So soon after his wife. It seems a heavy burden on one family.' And on St Leonard's. John Rudby, Walter de Hotter, Laurence and Matilda de Warrene — four corrodians now dead. More fuel for the rumours. 'Mistress Lucie and Jasper are in the shop?'

'Aye, Captain.'

'Thank God we are all safe.' Owen crossed himself, as did Kate. 'Now I must make myself presentable for Mistress Lucie. Can you bring water up to the solar?'

'At once, Captain!' Kate bobbed away, appearing for a moment clearly lit by the hall casements. She was a short, round, muscular young woman, yet light and quick on her feet, with rosy cheeks, unruly blonde hair, and an almost comically wide mouth that seemed to smile even when in repose.

As Owen climbed to the solar he realised that her cheeriness jarred for the very reason he should appreciate it: few folk found cause to smile or laugh at present. A gloom hung over the city with the return of the Great Mortality. Kate was not ignorant of it — she had wept with relief a few days before when she'd returned from visiting her siblings, the little ones left at home. 'They are all well, Mistress Lucie,' she had cried, and collapsed on her mistress's shoulder. Lucie had commented that evening that she felt they had adopted a daughter; not hired another servant. Owen had smiled at her ambivalent tone. And then they had grown silent, thinking of their own absent daughter.

Owen found the shop crowded. Lucie and her young apprentice, Jasper, worked together behind the counter. A half-dozen customers waited in various tempers. The air was heavy with warring scents. It had been so the previous day when Owen had spent the afternoon dispensing the confused assortment of protections from the pestilence that folk wanted. There were the fragrant sachets such as Magda had given him; balls of ambergris for the wealthy, held to the nose to prevent the intrusion of infectious vapours; foul-smelling herbs to be strewn in doorways and beneath windows; sweet herbs to be strewn in bedchambers to ward off the devil; vinegar-soaked sponges to hold to the nose — and those were only the most common requests. Each day brought new recipes.

Lucie's voice was calm, her hands steady, but her face was ashen, her temples damp. She had just finished with a customer and was about to greet Mistress Miller. Slipping behind the counter, Owen drew Lucie aside and quietly asked her to step into the back room with him for a moment.

'I have customers, as you can see,' she said in a soft but firm voice as she blotted her damp forehead with her sleeve.

'Jasper can take them for a moment. We have matters to discuss.'

A flash of interest, but still Lucie hesitated.

'We are falling behind even with both of us working.'

'Then I shall help him while you rest in the garden,' Owen said.

Lucie glanced at him, frowned, then turned back to Mistress Miller, who looked so forlorn that Owen felt guilty for interrupting.

'Is it Master Miller's trouble?' Lucie asked.

The pale woman nodded, leaned forward to say softly, 'Aye, still bladder-stones, Mistress Wilton. Harry's been soaking in sweet-water baths, and they do ease his pain nights so he might sleep.'

'It is a long, painful process, I fear.'

The miller's wife shook her head. 'Oh, I've not come to complain, Mistress Wilton. Harry sits there nights and says "God bless Apothecary" over and over. I've come for more mallow, is what. Lot fell off shelf and dog ate it.'

As Lucie turned to fetch the mallow jar; Owen saw her bite back a smile.

He leaned over the counter. 'How is the dog?'

'Empty!' Mistress Miller said with a loud guffaw, then covered her mouth to hide her rotten teeth as she continued to shake with laughter.

'He would be that,' Owen said.

Lucie nudged him out of the way. 'Do you need something for the dog?'

'Nay, Mistress Wilton. She'll be better for it.'

As Lucie wrapped the mallow, Mistress Miller leaned forward again. 'Two dead at Fosters',' she whispered, 'little 'uns.'

Lucie crossed herself. 'Are you burning juniper wood or rosemary?'

Mistress Miller nodded. 'Rosemary. But I wondered. I see folk with pouches to noses . . .'

'Many think it effectual, but I can promise naught.'

'I don't want to cure him of stones to lose him to that, eh? Two pouches. And a stop at minster for a good, long prayer.'

When Lucie had wrapped Mistress Miller's purchases, she whispered something to Jasper, who nodded, never looking up from his work. Then Lucie led Owen through the beaded curtain. In the workroom which had once been their kitchen, she spun round with a look of irritation. 'Now what was —' She clutched at the table, put her other hand to her head. '*Jesu.* I am dizzy.'

Owen was beside her at once, steadying her. 'You began the day early, sewing the pouches. It is warm, the odours in the shop are overpowering. Come.' He led her out into the garden and to a shaded bench. 'Sit there while I fetch water.'

Lucie held on to Owen for a moment, then sank down on the bench. 'You had no news.'

'None of consequence.'

She took a deep breath, dabbed her forehead. 'You caught me just in time.'

'You forget yourself when you are in the shop.'

Lucie pressed her fingertips to her forehead. 'You must help Jasper.'

'I shall bring Kate to you, then join Jasper.'

Lucie touched Owen's cheek gently with the back of her hand. 'You found the child, and her family?'

'Aye.'

'Pestilence?'

Owen nodded. 'It took four of them. The child is the only one left.'

Lucie crossed herself. 'I shall be fine now.' She began to rise.

Owen pressed her back down. 'At least take some water, wait until you are no longer dizzy.'

'In faith, I am weary.' Lucie leaned back against the tree. 'They are all mad. Every day new remedies to try. And someone like Mistress Miller must wait among them.'

'She bought scented pouches.'

'Aye. She listened to the chatter whilst she waited.' Lucie closed her eyes. 'Poor Harry Miller.' She chuckled. 'Poor dog!'

They laughed so hard that Kate came running to see what was the matter.

Late that night Lucie and Owen sat up in bed, their glazed window open to the garden. A breeze stirred Lucie's hair and chilled her shoulders, a relief after the heat of the day. But Owen's body still radiated heat. Most evenings, Lucie was grateful for her husband's warmth, but not tonight. She slid away from him.

'Do I smell of the grave?'

'I am warm.'

'I smell of the grave.'

Lucie turned back to her husband. He was naked, with a light cover on his legs, and he smelled of the lavender and mint bath that she had prescribed to rid all trace of the odours that seemed to haunt him. 'You smell sweet as the night air in the garden, my love. You are hot is all.'

Owen took her hand, kissed the palm. 'What you said this afternoon, about everyone being mad . . .'

Lucie slipped down beside him, rested her head on his shoulder. 'Um.'

'I met a priest today who was as desperate

as those waiting in your shop.'

Lucie stiffened. 'Out in the country, you mean.'

'Aye.'

'The country is still safer.'

'I did not mean to question that.'

'Remember the strangers who came down Coney Street last week, crying that the end of the world was at hand? You saw how folk reacted, beating their breasts, some hopping about and howling as if possessed by demons.' Though the Pope had condemned the flagellants twenty years before, such people quickly gathered a crowd wherever they went, and drew many into their frenzy — and into their despair; which was not easily shaken off. 'It is like the other times. The madness lingers long after they have passed. Tom says a fight broke out in the tavern that evening. The city is no place for children in such times.'

'I did not say it was.'

'There was no need. You found a family in the country dead of the pestilence, a priest too frightened to do his duty.'

'Fear is everywhere.'

'It is worse in the city.'

'Such folk might pass by Freythorpe Hadden.'

'They might. But they are more likely to

come through a city. They want an audience.'

'But still —'

Lucie turned from Owen, sank down on her pillow.

'I had not meant to begin another argument about the children,' Owen said.

Lucie reached back, touched his hand.

Owen kissed her hand and leaned over her.

She felt the change in his mood, a sudden urgency. She twisted her neck to see him. 'Your eye is glinting.'

'Glinting, eh?' Owen reached up her shift, but Lucie caught his hand. 'I forgot,' Owen whispered. 'I'm too hot.'

But Lucie had already twisted back towards him. 'I was not suggesting celibacy for the summer. Though they do say that lying as man and wife opens one's pores to the pestilential vapours.'

'You believe that?'

She began to run her hands lightly up and down his chest, his back . . . 'I do not know what to think, but I must believe that God does not wish to destroy all our joy or I shall go mad.'

At dawn, Owen woke to find Lucie sitting up staring at the opposite wall. He wondered whether she thought about her first-born,

Martin. But for the pestilence, he would be nine years old now, older than Jasper had been when they'd taken him in.

Lucie glanced over, saw that Owen was awake. 'Hugh is so like you.'

'But for the fiery hair. That's from my brother, Dafydd.' Owen gathered her in his arms, kissed her forehead. 'Pray that he has your heart and wit.'

Lucie pushed him away. 'I cannot sleep for all my doubts.' Her voice trembled.

Owen smoothed her hair from her forehead, kissed it. 'Naught is certain, my love. But we did what we thought best.'

Not we, Lucie thought, but I. That haunted her. That and a dream that kept returning. She had had it first on the night before the children had departed. It was of her first husband, Nicholas, and once awake she had not been able to return to sleep. She had peered down into Hugh's basket. His fine hair was a fiery halo in the moonlight. What she had most wished to do was lift him from his crib and hold him close, whisper how she prayed to see him grow to manhood. But that would have wakened him, and he needed his sleep before the ordeal of travel. How she wished now that she had allowed herself that moment with him.

The dream was of Nicholas's terrible silence after their son had died of the pestilence. Night after night after Martin's death, Nicholas had sat in the garden, beneath the linden tree, with his pale eyes staring at nothing. At such times Nicholas would neither speak to Lucie nor look at her. During the day he was merely civil. And then suddenly, one morning, he had put down his cup of ale and looked Lucie in the eye. 'I will never forgive you for sleeping the night after Martin died. What made you such an unnatural mother?'

Lucie had been stunned. Had he forgotten how for three nights while Martin had suffered she had managed little sleep, continually sponging the child's painful pustules with mallow, trying to draw out the poison, cooling him with cold compresses on his forehead and neck when he'd burned with fever? She had been so weary that she had collapsed when Martin had gone and she had been able to do no more.

Had Nicholas forgotten that?

Later he had apologised. Over and over. He had not meant it. It was his grief speaking such hateful things. They were so untrue. She had been the best mother she'd known how to be.

But what sort of mother would send her

children away while she remained in the city to see to her business? Gwenllian and Hugh would be frightened. They needed her. How could she have done this? *Was* she an unnatural mother?

Owen broke into her thoughts. 'They are my children, too, Lucie. If I had been certain that keeping them here was the best thing to do, I would have fought for it.'

Lucie took a deep breath. In a steadier voice she asked, 'Have you heard aught from Archbishop Thoresby?'

'Not a word. I imagine him spending the whole day praying in the Queen's chambers. And praying in his own chamber at night. He has no time to write to his steward.' Owen was the steward of Bishopthorpe, the archbishop's manor south of York.

'He will take the Queen's passing very hard, should it come to that,' Lucie said.

'There was a time when I would have found a sinful pleasure in that. But now I pity him.'

'. . . Until you are the butt of his foul humour.'

'Oh aye.'

'You heard about the fire yesterday?'

'Magda smelled it. I feared for you.'

Lucie touched the back of Owen's neck. 'I worried about you on the river.'

Five

An Uneasy Conscience

Comrades on the road, because they are thrown in such intimate company, are away from their regular business, and have time to while away, will oft talk of things they might not otherwise. As Richard de Ravenser dined with his uncle, Archbishop Thoresby, at an inn on their journey to York, the nephew plucked up the courage to ask, 'What is the trouble between you and Mistress Alice Perrers? Do you — Had you hoped —' The chill in his uncle's eyes silenced Ravenser.

Thoresby speared a piece of meat, chewed, washed it down with wine, then at last leaned on the table with one elbow and looked his nephew in the eye. 'As the Queen's man, how can you ask? Every breath Perrers takes near the Queen poisons the air. It has killed her.'

'But surely it is the King who —'

'Hush, you foolish man! That is treasonous talk.'

Ravenser nervously looked round. 'That is not in my heart.'

Thoresby pushed his trencher aside, handed his knife to the servant who stood behind him, and took in turn a linen cloth with which he thoughtfully wiped his lips. 'Let us turn our minds to something more pleasant. Your troubles in York.'

'I hardly consider them pleasant.'

'Ah. But one might resolve them.'

'How? The revenues from the Petercorn diminish every year. It is not only the bad harvests. The King releases more and more people from the debt.' Ravenser felt his supper curdling in his stomach just thinking of the nightmare. 'And then this year you had so generously offered the revenue from the Lammas Fair. Alas. The pestilence has killed that hope.' He wiped his brow. 'But worst of it are the corrodians. You know how long I have argued against the sale of corrodies. A quick and fatal source of money. And now my warnings are turned against me.'

'An irony, to be sure. I fear you cannot count on the canons to assure people that you had warned them against corrodies.'

'Hardly.'

'How did such a rumour begin, Richard? Who spread the news of your financial troubles?'

The very question Ravenser dreaded. Not that he knew the original source, but he had a suspicion about who had kept the rumour alive. He did not find it easy to lie to his uncle. But he thought it best in the circumstances: the man was dead now; it was best forgotten. 'Only the canons should have such knowledge.'

'Indeed.' Thoresby let the word resonate for a moment. Ravenser detected doubt in his tone. 'Do you trust your canons? You have disagreed with them over the years.'

A deep breath, steady now. Ravenser would speak only truth. 'I trust them to understand the importance of St Leonard's good name. But tongues wag. A servant overhears. Or a corrodian. I have turned people away who wished to purchase corrodies. They do not always understand my position. But you know as well as I that if the people wish to believe rumours, no matter how absurd, there is little one can do to dissuade them.'

Thoresby signalled his servant to pour wine. 'I thought perhaps this malicious rumour might have politics as its purpose. But you think not?' He asked the question in a coaxing tone.

'I wish I knew.'

'Yes.'

Ravenser stared down at his cup. How did his uncle know he had not told him all? He wondered whether his uncle could hear his stomach churning.

He did not know why he was so hesitant to voice his suspicions, particularly to his uncle, a man of much more experience. The archbishop might suggest a remedy. Or reassure him that his sense of guilt was unfounded. Ravenser lifted his cup, drank. Unwise. He felt his bowels loosen. 'You must excuse me.' He rose.

Thoresby nodded towards the remnants of their meal. 'Greasy meat. Do you wish for an escort? One of my men —'

'There is no need,' Ravenser said, and hurried out the back way.

The episode was enough to convince him he must tell his uncle about a ridiculous argument with William Savage, the late mayor.

Savage had arrived at their meeting dressed too warmly for the April day, in heavy mayoral robes and hat. A foolish formality in such weather, Ravenser had thought, so no doubt considered necessary to press some point.

'Sir Richard.' Savage bowed slightly. He was a fair-haired, blue-eyed man with a sanguine complexion, always looking as if he had stayed too long in the sun, even in winter. He was large, but not portly; a man who did justice to the elegant mayoral robes. Ravenser noticed that he clutched a linen cloth in his hand; it would be needed at his brow. 'God bless you for agreeing to this meeting,' Savage said. 'I am most grateful.'

Had Ravenser had a choice? He had not considered the possibility. 'Please, put yourself at ease.' Ravenser indicated a chair by the window. 'Sit and share some wine.'

With a flourish of musty robes, Savage sat and dabbed at his forehead.

When the wine had been poured and the servant dismissed and still the mayor had not declared his purpose, Ravenser inclined his head. 'Do you come on official business, my lord mayor?'

Savage set down his cup, his hand and eyes lingering on it momentarily as he collected his thoughts. Then he met Ravenser's curious gaze. 'I come on a private matter, Sir Richard. My wife's mother has recently been widowed, and although we are much concerned for her and wish to ease her through this difficult time, she is in need of more attention than we can give her from day to day.' The mayor's expression changed subtly, a raising of the eyebrows, lowering of the corners of the mouth, as if pleading. 'We hope, indeed we pray that you will accept her as a corrodian of St Leonard's —' He held up his gloved hand as Ravenser opened his mouth to speak. 'We shall pay a fair price, Sir Richard. We should not think of asking favours.'

Not asking favours. And yet Ravenser knew full well that the Savage house could accommodate another person, and its considerable staff could see to the dowager's needs. The mayor simply did not wish his wife's mother to burden them with a long illness. 'Forgive me, Master Savage, but I must disappoint you. St Leonard's is no longer selling corrodies.'

The mayor's blue eyes narrowed even as his mouth expanded in a smile. He lifted his hands, palms upwards in supplication. 'But surely, Sir Richard, in certain cases —'

'Again, I must disappoint you. Even His Grace Our King has been refused corrodies for his retainers.' Ravenser nodded at the surprise registered on his guest's face. 'Indeed, you see the firmness of my resolve. It is a matter of survival. The selling of corrodies once seemed a sound financial scheme, but it has proved disastrous. The quality of our care appears to prolong life, you see. And with a corrody being a fixed sum . . . Well, to be blunt, the corrodians outlive their subsidies and become a burden on the house.' Even as Ravenser spelled this out he heard his uncle Thoresby's voice warning him against explaining oneself. *Thus is an argument twisted and prolonged.*

Savage sat back, scratched a temple, all the while studying Ravenser with a hardened glint in his eyes.

Ravenser tried to recoup his loss of ground by declaring the discussion closed. 'I am pleased that you understand. Was there anything else on your mind?'

A polite snort. Savage leaned forward. 'But you are mistaken, Sir Richard, I do not understand. It seems to me there is ample room for one elderly widow who shows no signs of living so long as to burden you, God help her. And as I have said, I am willing to pay reasonably.'

Ravenser considered what to say. Were he to complete the explanation, and say that accepting one corrodian would open the door to petitions from all over, and, worst of all, would anger the King, and the only way to mend that would be to accept one of his ageing retainers as a corrodian, for which the King rarely paid a fee, though he often promised one, Savage would argue that the King would understand that the needs of the mayor of York should be met. William Savage had never met the King.

'Sir Richard?' Savage was waiting for more discussion.

Ravenser shook his head. 'I cannot make an exception, Master Savage, even for you.' And each year another mayor. The thought sickened him.

The mayor's colour deepened. The musky scent intensified. His chin tilted up, he gazed down his long, bony nose at Ravenser. 'I suspect that your reasons are not those you offer me.'

'My reasons are not —' Ravenser heard himself sputtering and shut up. But the audacity of the man! He fought to regain his calm, and in a much softer voice asked, 'Surely you do not suggest that I am lying?'

Savage had the grace to squirm — slightly. 'No. No, I could not in good conscience accuse you of that. But there is another matter that I had hoped to avoid discussing.'

'And what might that be?'

Savage glanced round the room as if making sure he would not be overheard. 'It is the matter of a woman you employ as a lay sister. A woman of questionable character. Honoria de Staines.'

A low blow. 'Mistress Staines has performed much penance and is one of our best servants.'

'Some would be quite puzzled by that

claim, Sir Richard. Quite puzzled.'

'You have reports of her?'

The mayor smirked. 'In faith, you cannot be surprised. She has been seen. Even with some of your select number of corrodians.' He rose, filling the air with musk, bowed slightly to Ravenser, who rose also.

'Can you provide me with proof?'

Savage sniffed. 'I shall not betray confidences.'

'Lies, more like.'

Savage bristled. 'Have a care, Sir Richard. I know that the hospital is in financial straits because of a shortfall in the Petercorn. If you seek the goodwill of the freemen of the city, you must earn it. By choosing those who work in the hospital with caution. By being a valuable member of the community.'

Ravenser was finding it difficult to control himself. 'Would you be so kind as to tell me how you know about our finances?'

'It is all over the city. One need only stand on the street and open one's ears. I thought it common knowledge.'

'I see.'

Savage shook his head. 'I am left to conclude that your rejection of my mother-in-law has more to do with your dread that I might be privy to what happens at St Leonard's.'

Ravenser could take no more. 'Master Savage, it is widely reported that your mother-in-law is a tyrant. You wish to prevent her taking over your household, that is your motivation in trying to bully me into accepting her here.'

Savage had turned a frightening shade of crimson. 'That is not my purpose in asking you to take her in!'

Ravenser had wagged his head. 'Master Savage, now who is tripping on the truth?'

With a flourish of his mayoral robes, Savage had stormed from the room.

Thoresby listened to his nephew's story in growing despair. 'For pity's sake, Richard, Savage was right. You are dependent on the freemen of the city. And you made an enemy of the man who might have defended you to them. Have you no control of your temper?'

A startled expression told him that Ravenser had expected sympathy.

'And now the new mayor, Roger Selby, asks about her. What is so important about this lay sister? Why must you defend her? Why keep her?'

'Did not Mary Magdalen find redemption as a follower of Christ?'

'You would compare yourself with Christ?'

Ravenser groaned. 'You are a man of God,

uncle. Do you not see the goodness in what Cuthbert did?'

'Cuthbert has earned his place in Heaven by his desire to do good, Richard, but he has done nothing for your career. You must see to it if you wish to climb any higher.'

Thoresby found his nephew a puzzle. His elaborate, colourful attire contradicted the naïve simplicity of his faith.

Six

Disturbing Developments

Bess Merchet arrived early at the infirmary and sat watching her uncle sleep. Julian Taverner seemed old and frail. A network of veins crept across his cheeks, nose and eyelids. The skin of his neck was wrinkled. His hair was still abundant, a family trait, but it was now pure white. It curled tightly, as if someone had washed it the night before, and the singed ends had been trimmed away. That was commendable. Smoke was impossible to get out of hair any other way. A woman cried out in a bed tucked away somewhere in the forest of partitions. A dark-robed sister hurried past, rubbing the sleep from her eyes. Did they sleep on their watches? Bess did not like to think that. Nor did she approve of the cobwebs in the rafters or the strong scent of urine and sweat all about, though her uncle's bed and person smelled fresh. Once, as she'd kept her vigil, Bess had caught Don Cuthbert in the doorway and had sent him off with a hissed 'Can you not see he is sleeping?' Perhaps it would be best to take her uncle from here, let him recover at the York Tavern. She had an extra bedchamber for kin up above, across from her own. He would be quite comfortable there.

Julian Taverner rocked his head back and forth on the pillow in sleep, then woke with a groan, clutching his neck with a bandaged hand. His eyes were red. He blinked, trying to focus on Bess. 'Honoria?'

'Nay, 'tis only your niece, Bess.' Honoria indeed.

Don Erkenwald poked his head through the doorway. 'God go with you, Master Taverner, Mistress Merchet. May I come in?'

Bess liked the solid bulk of the canon, and his courtesy. But she preferred to speak to her uncle alone. 'I do not mean to be discourteous, but we have had no chance to speak since the fire. I hoped to have some private speech with my uncle.'

Julian, his eyes still slightly unfocused from sleep, was fumbling with his bandaged hands. 'I cannot feel with all this wrapping. Is there still a cloth over the wound at the back of my head, niece?'

Bess straightened. 'This is the first I've heard of a head wound, uncle.'

Erkenwald stepped closer. 'That wound is of interest to me.'

'Oh aye? You are the first to care,' Julian said, his tone petulant.

Bess leaned over her uncle. 'There is still a cloth round your head. Let me see the wound, uncle.'

' 'Tis enough to feel it.' Julian guided Bess's fingers to a considerable knot on the base of his skull.

'Holy Mary, Mother of God! How did this happen?'

'It bled so, I thought it would kill me,' Julian said.

'I see that you have suffered indeed, uncle. Answer me now — how did this happen?'

'I was attacked from behind as I bent to drag poor Laurence from the burning house.'

'No one told me of an attack.'

Erkenwald leaned close, felt the wound. 'Who hit you?'

Julian closed his eyes and dropped his head back on the pillow, wincing as the knot compressed. 'If I knew that, I would not be lying here.'

Bess crossed her arms over her chest. 'Oh? You would be steady on your feet and clear in your head? How would your burned hands feel as they met his jaw?' She shook her head. 'I am decided now. You will come home with me.'

'Nonsense.'

'It will take no time to prepare.' Her mind full of her plans, Bess did not notice her uncle's wet cheeks, the moisture seeping from beneath his closed lids, until he gulped, suppressing a sob. 'Uncle?'

Erkenwald had retreated to a bench away from the bed.

Julian swiped at his eyes with a bandaged hand, cursed. Bess knelt on the bed, dabbed his eyes with a cloth. 'What is this, uncle?'

Julian batted her away. 'I could not save him. The murderer was too quick.'

Bess's hand paused over her uncle. 'Murderer? I thought the fire an accident.'

Julian glared at her as best he could through his red eyes. 'Of course it was no accident, you foolish woman.'

Foolish? And she had thought to take him home, the ungrateful man. But his certainty was disturbing. She settled down next to him. 'Tell me what happened, uncle.'

'You'll not listen.'

'I am not such an idle person to ask for what I do not wish to hear.'

Julian looked uncertain, but he said, 'Fix my pillows so I might sit up and speak with ease, then.'

Bess did as requested, with more energy than Julian might have liked. But he sank back on the pillows and thanked her.

'When Laurence said he would burn his wife's belongings, I offered to help him. He did not say nay. He was to come for me when he was ready. I was down with the orphans, telling them stories, when I noticed smoke. More than the usual smoke. I ran out, found the fire untended, spreading to brush that had been dropped outside the fire circle. That was worrying. Laurence was a careful man. I stepped into his house thinking he might have thought of something else that must go.' Julian paused, a bandaged hand pressed to his forehead. He took a deep breath, dropped the hand, stared down at the floor beside his bed. 'He lay on the ground, face down, a bloody gash in his head — bloodier than the one I was soon to receive.'

Bess already had doubts about the story. 'You noticed all this with the fire spreading round you?'

'The fire was without, not inside,' Julian said impatiently. 'I knelt over Laurence to lift him and help him breathe. I was hit from behind. Not as hard as Laurence must have been hit, but it dizzied me. I fell over Laurence and rolled off him, spent a moment getting my breath back. That is when I smelled smoke inside. I looked round, the house was ablaze. So suddenly. Someone rushed out of the door, but the smoke made it impossible to tell anything about him. I dragged Laurence out, but his clothes —' Julian's voice broke. He shook his head.

'And no one has listened to your story?' Bess glanced over at Erkenwald, who stared thoughtfully at the floor.

'They say I am confused,' Julian said.

'Who says that?'

'Don Cuthbert.'

'That snivelling — I'll confuse him —'

Julian put a bandaged hand on Bess's arm to quiet her. 'You would help me, niece?'

'Of course.'

'They mean to bury Laurence quickly. For fear of the pestilence. Idiots. He died by fire. But that is their aim. You must convince Don Cuthbert or someone here at the hospital, someone respected, to examine Laurence before he is buried.'

Bess hesitated. The task did not appeal. 'Why?'

'Someone else must see his wound. Stand as my witness. Someone who would not otherwise listen to me.'

And what if there is no such wound, Bess wondered. Julian had been knocked hard — he might have imagined it all. Still, there was sense in his request. She glanced over at Erkenwald, who watched her with interest.

'Will you be his witness?'
'Gladly.'

Honoria de Staines crossed herself and shook her head when Erkenwald ordered her to untie Laurence de Warrene's shroud.

'It is not as if we had asked you to open a grave,' Bess said.

The lay sister clenched her hands. 'I do not like it.' She had turned pale.

Bess thought her pitifully squeamish for one who worked in an infirmary.

' 'Tis much the same as opening a grave,' the woman said. 'It is disturbing the dead.'

'To prove that he was attacked. His spirit will not rest otherwise,' Bess said.

Honoria sank down on a bench beside the shrouded corpse, pressed the heels of her palms to her forehead.

Don Cuthbert chose the moment to flutter into the room and demand an explanation. Erkenwald patiently told him why they were there.

To Bess's surprise, the cellarer pressed a linen cloth to his nose and waved them on.

'We cannot convince this sister to co-operate,' Bess said. 'Do I have your permission to open the shroud?'

'Make haste!' Cuthbert gasped.

Erkenwald nodded at the tiny canon. 'It is

not a pleasant odour. But better now than once in the ground.'

Bess made short work of the knot, then bent over the corpse, gingerly turning the head. The odour was indeed unpleasant.

Erkenwald leaned close, touched the wound. 'Someone knew where to aim it.'

'God help us,' Cuthbert said.

Bess glanced over at the cellarer. 'Come here. Feel this.'

Instead of approaching, Cuthbert took a step backwards. 'Pray, there is no need for me to feel it. I shall gladly take Don Erkenwald's word for it.'

Bess did not like it. There was something between the two men, some animosity that might work against her uncle. 'I wish you both to witness it. I want there to be no suspicion that I am protecting my uncle, or accepting the words of a confused man, as you called him. You must feel the back of the head.'

The cellarer looked to Erkenwald.

'You are the master in Sir Richard's absence. I think he would expect you to have examined Master Warrene,' Erkenwald said.

Cuthbert crossed himself and, muttering a prayer, stepped forward and allowed his hand to be guided to the wound, though he tried to jerk it away at once. 'It bleeds!'

Erkenwald held him still a moment. 'The man is dead. He no longer bleeds. You feel that there is a wound there?'

'Yes, I feel it.'

Erkenwald released Cuthbert.

The cellarer took out a cloth and wiped his hand. 'And yet what does it prove save he was hit? Perhaps by Master Taverner.'

'Then come with me and feel another knobbly wound,' Bess said.

Cuthbert sighed. 'It is my duty.'

When Bess turned to ask Honoria to summon someone to replace the shroud, she discovered that the lay sister had disappeared.

Satisfied that both Cuthbert and Erkenwald had now heard Julian's story, noted the serious and similar wounds, and that Cuthbert had promised to write to the master of the hospital about it, Bess took herself off to Lucie Wilton's apothecary. She wished to consult with Owen. He had dealt with suspicious deaths before. Cuthbert had asked that she remain silent about the wounds and her uncle's story, but he would never know she had spoken to Owen.

The streets were quiet for mid-morning. A house in Lop Lane was marked with a cross: a poor soul dead or dying of pestilence within. Bess crossed herself and hurried past.

The shop was empty but for Lucie, who sat on a stool behind the counter mixing dried herbs in a large bowl.

'What is this?' Bess said by way of greeting. 'Only yesterday I could not see the floor for the customers.'

Lucie pushed the bowl aside, wiped her hands in her apron. 'While the river mist lingers in the alleyways it is often quiet. A friar who passed through the city a few days ago said that it was the vapours that seep beneath the skin and raise the buboes.'

Bess sniffed. 'Nonsense. 'Tis the bodily fluids in the boils. Why else would the dying thirst so?'

Lucie shook her head. 'I envy you, Bess. I wish I could be so certain of the cause.'

Bess noted a sadness in her friend's voice. She knew Lucie was beset with doubts now that she had sent the children to the country. And there was no consoling her, for there was no remedy. 'Is Owen about?'

'He and Jasper went to St George's Field to practise at the butts. Why? What is amiss?'

There was no need to add to Lucie's worries. ' 'Twas but a passing thought.' Bess went on to her other business in the shop. 'Would you mix me a soothing poultice for my uncle's burned hands?'

'Gladly.' Lucie turned towards the jars that lined the wall behind her, then turned back with a quizzical look. 'But do the sisters not attend him at St Leonard's?'

'I would rather they used your medicines on him.'

'I should not interfere.'

'Not you. Me. His niece.'

'You do not trust them?'

'I do not wish to test them is all. Particularly Honoria de Staines. What could that idle creature know of healing such wounds?'

With a nod, Lucie turned back to the jars. 'Is there aught else you need for him?'

'Something for a painful knob on the back of his head.'

Lucie frowned at the detail as she eased a large jar on to the counter. 'How did that happen?'

Bess had walked right into that one. She thought fast. 'I imagine a falling beam. The roof collapsed, you know.'

Lucie bent to the task.

Erkenwald wished to go somewhere to be alone to think; or, better yet, find Owen Archer. But Cuthbert had asked him to accompany him to the cellarer's garden. There was no avoiding it. Erkenwald was himself to blame for involving the man.

The little cellarer stood in front of a cluster of comfrey heavy with bloom. He trembled with rage. 'Have I not instructed you to keep still to the world at large about our problems?'

'God help me, but you do begin far into the matter,' Erkenwald said. 'Of what do you accuse me?'

'Now Mistress Merchet has heard her uncle's tale.'

'She is his niece. She has a right to know.'

'You —'

'I told her nothing. Master Taverner told her. How did you hope to hide it? She might have thought little of it, but your secrecy made it a discovery. What are you doing about it, eh? Have you spoken with people who might have seen aught? Do you realise how dangerous it is to have a murderer loose?'

'Murderer.' Cuthbert spat out the word. 'You do not believe his story?'

'And why not? Do you have a better explanation for the knot on his head? And the one that felled Master Warrene?'

'We have never had such problems before.'

'Oh? What of Walter de Hotter?'

'That had naught to do with the hospital.'

'And the thefts?'

Cuthbert blanched. 'Those I cannot explain.'

'Do you know what folk are saying? That your reformed sinner Honoria de Staines wears underskirts of linen. That when away from the hospital her wimple is of silk.'

'Mistress Staines is not a thief.'

Erkenwald shook his head. The time had come to rattle the cellarer's complacency. 'You will have much to explain to Sir Richard.'

'I pray that all will be quiet once more before his next visitation.'

'I doubt it. He has sent word that he is on his way from the south.'

Cuthbert pressed his hands to his stomach, closed his eyes. 'You betrayed me.'

'I did what I thought best.'

Seven

A Vow to Heal

Owen questioned his wisdom in bringing Jasper out this morning. The wind was from the south and the sky a sickly grey, neither stormy nor fair; the sort of weather some said brought pestilence. Owen was not inclined to believe it, or the new fear of river mist. Such weather was common and far more often than not brought nothing more horrible than a lack of sunshine. But the quiet streets made him wonder whether he was being foolhardy. Jasper, too, seemed disturbed, gazing about with a worried frown.

The gate of Davy Hall was latched and chained as if the family had fled to the country. The few folk in the streets scurried about their business, heads low, many holding scented bags close to their faces. Near the Franciscan friary the street was almost deserted. A friar made the sign of the cross as he hurried past them and slipped into the friary, from which came a familiar smell.

'Juniper wood,' Jasper said.

'Aye. 'Tis a pleasant scent, though I do not know whether I believe burning it can save a man from the poisoned air.' They headed down to the staithe and walked along the jetty that would bring them quickly to St George's Field.

'Mistress Baker wondered whether smoke from the hospital fire carried pestilence.'

'Alice Baker discovers new causes and cures each day. I would not pay her much heed, Jasper.'

But the boy was not so easily dissuaded. 'What did Mistress Merchet say? Were they burning the dead?'

Thus began a rumour founded on naught. 'Mistress Baker should not speak of what she does not know. They were not burning the dead at the hospital. A house caught fire.' Owen did not add that Laurence de Warrene had been burning the clothing of a plague victim.

'Mistress Merchet seemed most upset.'

'Oh, aye, she was that. Her uncle's friend died in the fire. And her uncle, who tried to save him, has burns and injuries that will take long to mend.'

'How did it happen?'

'They say Laurence de Warrene had collected some clothes, bedding, and such to burn. The fire flared up in his face and caught his clothes. He fled to the house and set it alight before anyone could help.'

'Was no one tending the fire?'

'Warrene was.'

'It was an accident?'

Owen found that a curious question. 'As far as anyone knows. Though I heard it suggested at the tavern that he wished to follow his wife.'

'But to take his life . . .' Jasper shook his head.

'It is passing strange.'

They passed the castle mills. Jasper turned to Owen as they reached St George's Field. 'Does Mistress Merchet wish you to find out what happened?'

'Nay, lad. And you can be sure that if Bess decides there is cause for concern she will be the one to poke and prod.' Owen disappeared into a small building and emerged with a straw butt, which he set down in the middle of the cleared area. Jasper had a talent for the longbow, as had his father. And as a former captain of archers, Owen enjoyed training the lad. 'Now. Today we work on your aim.'

Jasper readied his longbow, took his stance.

Owen adjusted the lad's right elbow, nudging it up, pulled back on the left shoulder. 'Can you feel the difference?'

Jasper had been squinting, ready to fire. Now he closed his eyes, opened them. 'Moving my left shoulder like that feels odd. Like the bow is aiming left now.'

Owen got behind him, sighted, shook his head. 'Sighting with my right eye might make a difference, though I thought I knew how to judge that. Try it like this.'

Jasper squinted, let go the arrow. It landed true. He turned towards Owen with a look of wonder. 'You aim better with one eye than I do with two.'

'Eyes and body work together. 'Tis part of why we practise. Over and over until you know how it feels. Now, again.'

They worked at it for a while, then Owen suggested they walk down to the bank where the Foss and Ouse converged. His purpose in bringing Jasper to the field today had been to talk to him, convince him that Lucie would not rest easy unless the lad followed Hugh and Gwenllian to Freythorpe Hadden. But how to begin?

'Is that why you still shoot so well, Captain? Because you *feel* how to adjust your aim?'

'Somewhat. And days, weeks, months of training myself over again after I lost my eye.'

'So you meant to continue as captain of archers?'

'Nay, lad. I meant to sail to Italy and offer my services as a mercenary. Over there, a man might make enough to live in such service.'

'You wanted to become a mercenary?'

'A dark, devilish secret, eh? I lusted for blood.' Owen laughed to see the surprise on Jasper's face. He patted the boy on the back. 'Nay, 'twas nothing so terrible. I could think of naught else to do. My lord was dead. I believed he had kept me in his service after I'd lost my eye out of Christian duty. Henry of Grosmont was a devout man, a man of honour and grace. His successor was the son of the King. He had a retinue. What need would he have of a half-blind archer? Or a spy? So I planned, worked, then found myself taken up by the archbishop.'

'God watched over you.'

'Most days I think that. I would not be Lucie's husband were it not for His Grace.' Owen shifted so that he might see Jasper's face more clearly. The boy sat with legs bent, knees high, hands behind propping him up at an angle, his bony shoulders hunched. An age of angles and long limbs. 'Which brings me to something that is weighing on my mind.'

Jasper clenched his jaw, shook his head once so his straight flaxen locks fell across his eyes. 'I know. You wish to send me away.'

'For Lucie's sake, Jasper, not mine. I would lief have you here. You are a fine apprentice, and she needs you in the shop. But she is thinking of the last time, when the pestilence took her son Martin. She believes it is the children who are in the most danger. And it does seem so. Even with all their care, the sisters of St Leonard's have lost several orphans, but only Matilda de Warrene and John Rudby among the grown men and women.'

Jasper sat up, turned to Owen. 'Mistress Warrene? So they *were* plague things burned at the hospital.' His eyes were earnest. A little too earnest for the subject matter.

'Do not try to change the direction of this conversation, Jasper.'

The boy slumped again, head down, hair in his eyes. 'I must stay in the city, Captain. I am Mistress Lucie's apprentice. I am bound to stay, I am bound to do what I can to help the people of York against the pestilence.'

'But if Lucie is right you are one of those in greatest danger.'

Jasper's head shot up again. 'I am not a child.'

'Aye, 'tis true. You are thirteen, not a babe. But not yet so far from it.'

Jasper leaned forward, elbows on knees, looking out at the water. 'What would I do all day?'

Ah. More to the heart of the matter. 'Sir Robert would find occupation for you. You would not tend the children.'

The lad was silent for a time. Owen thought perhaps he had run out of arguments. But when Jasper spoke, that hope evaporated.

'Mistress Lucie spoke of Brother Wulfstan the other day, how he is risking his life to go among the sick in the city because so many of the priests are fearful to go near those with the pestilence.' Brother Wulfstan was the infirmarian of St Mary's Abbey. 'She said it is dangerous for him, far more so than for others, because he is so old. But she spoke of him with admiration.' He glanced at Owen to see his reaction.

Owen could not help but smile. The lad was bright, and a good debater. 'Lucie is worried for him, Jasper. She prays for him.' Lucie and Wulfstan were old friends.

'But she believes he is fulfilling his vow. I, too, have such a vow.'

Owen gazed on the flaxen-haired, gangly youth and found himself loath to argue further. 'I always said you grew so fast, one day I would look on you and think you a stranger. And there you sit, suddenly a young man.'

'Then I can stay?'

'How are we to reassure Lucie?'

'I do not mean to cause her pain.'

'The pain is not your fault, lad. It comes from memories. I see her suddenly turn pale, or her eyes grow dark, and I cannot understand what brought the memory, the pain. A scent? A sound? And even with all of you gone to the country I cannot say that would cease. Such pain dulls with time, but never disappears.'

Jasper had grown quiet, and Owen realised how thoughtless he had been. Jasper had painful memories of his own — by his ninth year he had lost both parents, and the man who was to become his foster father. 'Come. Let me see whether your shoulder remembers what I taught it today.'

The novice Gervase showed Jasper into the infirmary at St Mary's Abbey. Brother Henry glanced up from his prayers with a worried frown. 'I pray you do not seek Brother Wulfstan for someone in your household?'

'No,' Jasper said. 'I need to speak with

him. I need advice.'

The subinfirmarian got to his feet. 'I need advice myself. How do I stop him? How do I protect him?'

'From tending the sick in the city?'

Henry's eyes were wild. 'Night and day. He comes but to eat and gather more physicks, then he goes forth again. He says he sleeps at their bedsides.'

'What does Abbot Campian say?'

'My lord abbot says, "One does not stop a saint from his work." ' Henry stuffed his hands up his sleeves, shook his head. 'I have tried sending novices with Brother Wulfstan, but he convinces them to return alone. He is impossible.'

'Do you think he will be back today?'

'Oh yes, yes. You are welcome to wait. Pray for him whilst you do, lad. Pray for him.'

Jasper chose to wait in the abbey garden, among Brother Wulfstan's lovingly tended beds of medicinal plants. This garden gave him solace, for it was here that Jasper had first understood he might love someone as much as he had loved the parents he had lost. It was Wulfstan who had helped him see that. Jasper knelt, pinched off some spent blossoms, watched a pollen-laden bee in slow, awkward flight among the flowers. He noticed a lop-sided lavender. Someone must have assisted Brother Wulfstan with the pruning, someone clumsy with a clipper. It made Jasper's stomach ache to think of someone other than Brother Wulfstan tending the garden.

'You are sad, my child?' Wulfstan smiled and spread his arms wide as Jasper looked up, startled, then threw himself into the old monk's embrace, suddenly a child once more. Wulfstan patted him, let him cling until his heart stopped racing. Then the old monk dropped his arms, stepped back, lifted Jasper's chin. 'No tears, so it is not a loss that brings you here.'

Jasper was glad he had stayed the tears. Brother Wulfstan did not need reminders of his age. 'Mistress Lucie wants to send me to Freythorpe Hadden. Gwenllian and Hugh are already there.'

Wulfstan tilted his bald head, sucked in his wrinkled cheeks, nodded. 'Ah. Lucie thinks to protect you from the pestilence. And who would blame her? Have you yet seen a victim, Jasper?'

'Not this time, but when I was very young I had a sister die of it.'

The old monk rested a hand on Jasper's head. 'I did not know you had a sister.'

When Jasper thought back to that frightening time he could smell the horrible sickness again. 'Her name was Anne. She would scream when anyone tried to clean the swelling in her armpits and on her neck. My mother tried to heat them so they would burst, but she could not bring herself to lance them.'

'If your mother were here now, would she not be frightened for you, remembering her loss?'

'But my place is here. I am Mistress Lucie's apprentice.'

Wulfstan's pale eyes were sympathetic. 'Come. Let us sit on the bench. My legs ache.' Wulfstan shuffled over to a stone bench beneath a linden tree. He settled down on it with a grunt and drew a cloth from beneath his scapula, shook it out, blotted his forehead and upper lip and the back of his neck. 'Winter is the curse of old age, but summer this year does not feel much kinder. The Lord slows me down. Perhaps He means me to retire to the chapel and contemplation.'

Jasper joined the aged infirmarian on the bench. It was cool in the shade, and the air seemed sweet in the garden, yet Wulfstan's breath was laboured and sweat stood out once more on his face. The boy was worried about his friend. 'Mistress Lucie says you are taking too much on yourself, going out among the sick in the city.'

Wulfstan patted Jasper's arm, then stretched his wrinkled, age-spotted hand out beside the lad's. 'I am old, Jasper. Nothing that I do will change that fact. I have been infirmarian at St Mary's since long before God first purged His children with the pestilence. Always before I respected my abbot's wishes, stayed within to be at hand if any of my brethren succumbed. During the first visitation, I was wise to do so. Many fell, many died. During the second I was not so necessary, and I felt a guilt that has stayed with me these eight years. Now I must go forth. Who better than I? Our Lord cannot mean for me to stay in this mortal shell much longer. And Brother Henry is skilled in healing. Why not let him have the experience that will stand him in good stead when I am gone? Still, I thank you for your concern. And Mistress Lucie, too.'

'But what about me? Should I go to the country or stay here where I might help?'

'Has your mistress ordered you to go?'

Jasper shook his head. 'She says she will not order me.'

'Then she is leaving it to your conscience. What does your conscience tell you?'

Turning on the bench so he might face

Wulfstan, Jasper took the old monk's hands in his. 'How do I know whether it is my conscience or my pride speaking?'

Wulfstan's eyes twinkled. 'You worry that pride drives you to stay? So that you might brag of your courage to your friends?'

Did Wulfstan intentionally misunderstand? 'I don't mean to brag. They are all in danger, too.'

The reminder dulled Wulfstan's eyes. He dropped his head, murmured, 'God watch over all of you' and crossed himself. Jasper followed suit, and was quiet until Wulfstan spoke again. Which was a long time. Time enough for Jasper to wonder whether the old monk had fallen asleep. But at last Wulfstan lifted his head, his eyes pools of sorrow. 'I have seen such suffering these past weeks, Jasper, such unbearable suffering. I speak not only of the scourge of the flesh. So many are abandoned in their suffering and weakness. Their families flee, hoping to save themselves. They flee from children, Jasper. I sat last night with a boy of no more than five who had been left for dead near the King's Fishpond. God knows what his parents thought, exposing him to the night, dead or no. But he lived, he knew of my presence, he heard my prayers for him. He did not die alone, thanks be to God.'

'My mother did not abandon my sister.'

'Nor did Lucie Wilton her son. But not all have such courage, Jasper. And I am there to help those they leave behind.' Wulfstan mopped his forehead, his eyes, blew his nose. 'Now. You fear that pride leads you rather than conscience. I do not think pride stands up against the pestilence, Jasper. You might find other things to brag about. But what is in your heart?'

'I am not a child.'

'You prove that in your work, my son.'

'I do not wish to worry Mistress Lucie. But she needs me in the shop.'

'What do you judge to be worse for her — the worry or the lack of help?'

'How can I know that?'

'What of Owen? Can he not work in the shop?'

'He is steward of Bishopthorpe and captain of the archbishop's retainers, so he is busy.'

Wulfstan pressed Jasper's hands, let them go, pushed himself off the bench and stood. 'Let God guide you.'

'How do I do that?'

The white eyebrows lifted. 'How? Through prayer, of course, my son. Come. We shall kneel before Our Lady's altar and pray for her advice. And then I must go out again into the city.'

Eight

Julian Taverner

The sun had appeared in mid-afternoon and by evening the city was warmed and humid. Sweat trickled down Bess's neck as she made her way among the tables. The York Tavern was far from bustling, but not empty. Though many stayed out of crowds for fear that someone's breath or clothes might carry plague, there were those who believed that ale and wine fortified them. A group of the determined souls was huddled close at a long table, speaking in low voices of the latest plague victim, William Franklin. But their voices were not so low that Bess could not hear.

'They say he brought it from St Leonard's,' Jack Crum said.

'Aye. He should have stayed there.' Old Bede slumped in his chair, his greasy white hair sticking out in all directions from running his hands through it in his agitation.

'Why should he die at the spital? A man wants to die at home. Will's house was in the city, not in the liberty of St Leonard's,' said another.

'Aye. He sickened at home,' said a third. 'But he did come and go from spital, all the same. And when he fell sick, two lay sisters from spital stayed at his bedside.'

'With the pestilence upon us the corrodians should stay put. Or give up their allotment till it passes,' Old Bede growled. 'They carry it with them.'

'You're daft,' John Cooper said, rising. His face was flushed with ale and emotion. 'We have lost seventy-odd folk to the pestilence in the city and only ten of those at St Leonard's. How can you say the folk from the spital carry it?'

'We'd have none of it without them,' Bede insisted.

'It was a child in the city died first, you ignorant old man. A tanner's daughter.'

'Watch your tongue, Cooper,' one of Bede's elderly supporters growled.

John Cooper shoved past Old Bede, paused for a parting shot. 'You hate the corrodians for their comfortable situations, old man, but mayhap you should thank God you could not find the coin to buy a corrody — though pestilence be not the danger.'

Old Bede spat on the floor at Cooper's feet. 'You've a mouth on you, John Cooper.

I'll thank you to keep it shut.'

Cooper sneered and made his way towards the door.

Bess Merchet hurried after him. Cooper's last comment intrigued her. She caught his elbow as he reached the door. He shrugged her off roughly. 'Have a care, John,' Bess murmured, ' 'tis the hand that pours your ale.'

He glanced round, shamefaced. 'I thought you were one of Old Bede's fellows, aching for trouble. Did I hurt you?'

'Whist! It takes more than a nudge to knock me down. But to make amends you might tell me what you meant when you said the old man should thank God.'

Cooper hesitated, glanced round, obviously wishing to make a quick escape. But he motioned for Bess to step outside with him. Cooper stood beneath the lantern beside the door. He was a solemn, quiet man, with a face that Bess had often thought might be pleasant if ever lit by a smile.

'You are thinking of your uncle,' Cooper said.

'I am.'

'I heard he was burned trying to save Laurence de Warrene.'

'He is healing. Why should Old Bede be thankful?'

'I am not one to listen to rumours — or spread them, Mistress Merchet. But that old man put me in mind of something I heard. There's talk that too many corrodians are dying of a sudden. Just when the spital is short of funds . . .'

'I have heard those rumours, and more. Old Bede is fond of them. But there is no question three of the corrodians died of pestilence.' Still, Bess shivered. The night had grown chilly and the river mist was damp on her skin.

'Matilda de Warrene, mayhap, too many saw her suffering, though she was a frail one. But Will Franklin and John Rudby' — Cooper cocked his head to one side — 'who saw them but lay sisters and brothers from St Leonard's? And Laurence de Warrene — now there's something passing strange about his accident. How many times in a man's life does he light a fire and not even singe a hair on his head? Why did that fire take him? That's what folk are wondering. And poor, stumbling Walter de Hotter. *He* did not die of pestilence.'

Bess studied the man's eyes. He believed what he said, though she doubted he knew her uncle had been attacked. 'Why corrodians?'

'Living too long.' The blunt reply made

Cooper uneasy. 'What I say is not how I feel, Mistress Merchet. You understand that?'

'I do. But I pray you, explain yourself.'

'The corrodians pay a sum, reckoned on some assumptions: they are elderly, they have decided to retire from active life, and so they will likely soon sicken and die. The sum is set high, hoping that they die before it is used up in supporting them. Else why take them in? But some folk are too long-lived.'

Bess felt a queer chill down her spine. Certainly her Uncle Julian had outlived his fee. As no doubt had Laurence and Matilda. 'Where did you hear this?'

'It is whispered all about town.'

'God bless you for telling me what you have heard, John.'

'God go with you.' John moved away from the wall. 'I'll be on my way, then. Forgive me if I've worried you. Julian Taverner is a clever man. More so than his friend. You've naught to worry about with him.'

Bess found that comment surprisingly naïve. No one, no matter how cunning, was ever safe from all harm.

Flexing his fingers in the looser bandages, Julian Taverner wondered at the difference two days of the new ointment had made. His fingers were tender, but not so tight. His aching shoulder was much improved by Mistress Wilton's mustard ointment. And the tisane his niece brought him several times a day eased his headache miraculously. He must think of a way to show his gratitude. They had traded harsh words the previous day, and he was sorry for that. Bess thought it best that Honoria kept her distance. But Julian saw no harm in enjoying a pretty face.

Not that Honoria's devotion to him was without its problems. Julian liked Anneys — he found her crisp competence reassuring and she was comely despite her lined face — and he did not wish to antagonise her. But there it was. Honoria's cheery visits inspired frowns of disapproval from Anneys. Then again, he did not know whether pursuit of Anneys would prove rewarding.

That morning Julian had found Anneys a disturbing presence. He had been haunted by painful memories and had been trying to push them aside with prayer when Anneys had arrived. Setting her trays of medicines down on his bedside table, Anneys had stood back and shaken her head. 'You pray in such earnest this morning, Master Taverner.'

'I would be away from that coughing.'

Anneys cocked her head, listened. 'Mistress Catherine. She cannot help it.'

'My mother had such a cough.'

Anneys sat down beside him. 'And you do not like to remember her?'

'She died of such a cough.'

'Ah.' Anneys shook out a linen cloth, draped it on the bed, began to arrange the medicines. 'What of your wife? Is it true she was lost at sea?'

Sweet Heaven, how had she touched the ache so accurately? 'My wife and my only child.'

'You speak of it as if you still feel pain. Yet it must have happened long ago. They tell me you have been a corrodian of St Leonard's for nineteen years.'

Some pain took longer to lessen. Yet it was true, they had died a few years before the first visitation of the plague. Julian turned away. He did not like this conversation.

'I do not believe in remembering only the good, Master Taverner. God brought us suffering to cleanse us. We must not shrink from it.'

'I have done more penance than you can imagine. And Laurence with me. Now I wish to be left in peace.' Julian felt his eyes burning. Now look what her prying had done. He would embarrass himself with tears.

Anneys opened his shift at the shoulder, applied the warm mustard ointment. As she worked it into the stiff joint, she asked, 'Penance? Both of you? For what sin?'

'I would rather not speak of it.'

'There was a strong bond between you and Master Warrene. Were you comrades-in-arms?'

'Nay. Neither of us were for soldiering. We grew up side by side in Scarborough, went into business together.'

'The tavern?'

Why must she ask so many questions? 'No, Laurence was never a taverner. This is unfair, you know. You have told me nothing of your past.'

'There is little to tell. I married, raised three children, I was widowed and offered my services here.'

'Three children. Did you not wish to live with any of them?'

'No.' Anneys closed up his shift, helped him sit up so she might examine the bandage on his head wound. 'Now I have told you of my life. I thought you were a taverner.'

'I was.'

'And yet you say you went into business with Master Warrene, a business that was not a tavern.'

'You do not wish to go into detail, neither do I.'

'Why is that, Master Taverner?'

He winced as she probed the wound. 'Why do you not wish to tell me more of your life?'

'There is little joy in the tale. And you? Why do you not wish to speak of the business?'

'Because I lived to regret it and did great penance for it. I have told you how I worked among abandoned victims when the pestilence first came to the north.'

'Ah, yes. I remember.' She moved to his hands, completing her ministrations in silence.

For that Julian was truly grateful. Perhaps he did not like her looks so much. Honoria was far more comforting.

Lucie had gone out into the garden to work before opening the shop. Owen sat up above watching her, wondering what he might do to cheer her.

Kate knocked on the door. 'Mistress Merchet begs a word with you, Captain.'

'She is here?'

'Below, Captain. Whatever it is, it is not good news.'

Owen found Bess down in the hall pacing, arms bent and pumping, hands clenched into fists, her eyes blazing and colour high.

'They have accused Julian of setting the fire, have they?' Owen asked when Bess turned towards him. He leaned against the doorjamb, arms folded across his chest.

Bess paused. 'Who is spreading such an untruth?'

Owen pointed at his visitor. ' 'Tis you put the thought in my head, by your foul mood. Why else would you be so angry?'

'Angry?'

'That is how you appear to me.'

'I was but thinking.'

Owen pushed himself off the wall and, taking Bess by the elbow, escorted her to the table set up beneath the south windows. 'Come, sit down and tell me what thoughts make you pump the air.'

Bess sat down, clutching her hands before her. 'Forgive me for intruding. I know it is a difficult time.'

Owen leaned across the table, slipped one hand under Bess's and laid his other on top. He levelled his good eye at her.

Bess grinned down at her hands cradled in Owen's. 'If you meant to distract me, you have succeeded, you handsome rogue.'

'Good. I want no eruptions in my hall, just quiet talk. What is troubling you?'

'Bless you for asking. I need your advice. I've quite a tale to tell.' Bess recounted her uncle's description of the events surrounding the fire at St Leonard's and described the wounds she had seen on the two friends.

'It does not sound like an accident.'

Bess pounded her fist on the table with satisfaction, sat back. 'No more than Walter de Hotter's death. Indeed. Do you know what John Cooper said last night?' She told Owen.

'Rumours. You must pay them no heed. They will send you down the wrong path for certain.'

Bess threw up her hands. 'Then how do I find the right path?'

'Find out if anyone witnessed the accident, Bess. That is the only certain way to know the truth.'

'Cuthbert has me watched at the spital. I am herded to my uncle's bed. I cannot go elsewhere.'

'He is worried about the very rumours you repeated, Bess.'

'Oh, aye. He is right to worry.' She suddenly tossed her head, letting her ribbons bob merrily and gave him her most engaging smile. 'You would not . . .'

'No, Bess. I want no part of it. You would soon grow impatient with me anyway. My skill as a spy is naught compared to yours.'

Bess's expressive face was caught between a smile and a frown.

Owen had no intention of being drawn

into Bess's concerns. He had worries enough with the children away, Lucie's melancholy, the pestilence, Thoresby's absence and the constant stream of frightened customers begging for plague cures. Bess had time to spare at present — pestilence meant few travellers, and many folk avoiding public places as much as possible. But she was a good friend. Perhaps a suggestion.

'Don Erkenwald is also uneasy. You might speak to him.'

'I doubt Cuthbert will let me.'

'I have never known anyone strong enough to stop you when you are determined, my friend.'

Barker the gatekeeper bowed stiffly and gingerly placed two Italian glass goblets on the cellarer's table.

Cuthbert recognised them as part of the set missing from the guesthouse. 'You found these in your search?' He had ordered a search of all the spital and the houses in the city belonging to St Leonard's.

'In the room of Mistress Staines, *Domine*.' Barker wiped his hands on his doublet. 'And other items I did not care to bring. Personal, you see. But not of a sort should belong to a lay sister.'

Cuthbert closed his eyes, pressed his

hands together, rocked on his feet. Honoria de Staines. So he had been a fool to trust her. 'What other items, Barker?'

A pause.

The cellarer glanced at the gatekeeper, noted his red face. 'Personal items, you said. Shifts, perhaps?'

Barker nodded with grateful enthusiasm. 'Aye, *Domine.* Of finest silk they are. And a wimple of heavy silk. I thought to tell you. To my mind 'tis not fitting a lay sister should own such things.'

Indeed not. But a whore might. Or a thief. 'You were quite right, Barker. And these goblets, where in her room did you find them?'

'Hidden in a chest. Wrapped in some old cloths.'

'I see. Did you find anything else? Naught in any other rooms or elsewhere within St Leonard's liberty?'

'Naught, *Domine.*'

Only the woman who had so fooled him. His fellow Austins would be much amused. 'God go with you, Barker. You have done a good day's work.'

Cuthbert sent for Honoria.

She entered his parlour, hands folded meekly, eyes downcast. 'Don Cuthbert. They have told me what you found.' She was a small woman with a soft, caressing voice, even now when she must be fearful.

'Can you explain yourself?'

'It is not what you think. I am guilty of betraying your trust, yes, I admit to that. But I did not steal the goblets.'

'Why then did you hide them away?'

'Italian glass goblets were mentioned as missing from the guesthouse. I worried lest my fellow sisters might think mine were those goblets.'

'They are of the set.'

Only now did Honoria lift her eyes to meet Cuthbert's. They were wide set, round, like a doe's. 'Of the set? But that cannot be.'

'Whence came the goblets?'

She returned to her study of the floor. 'They were a gift.'

'From whom?'

'I would rather not say, *Domine,*' she said quietly but firmly.

'He may be the thief of St Leonard's, Honoria. You will tell me.'

'He cannot be. They were his to give. He swore that they were.'

'You would protect this man, though your own salvation be forfeit for him? Excommunication is the punishment for one who enters the hospital to do violence or to steal. Did you know that?' Cuthbert thought he detected a shiver.

But Honoria's voice was still calm as she said, 'God will not so punish me for something of which I am innocent, *Domine*.'

'You deny that you stole the goblets. Yet you confess you have betrayed my trust. Have you lain with men since taking your vows?'

She dropped to her knees, touched her forehead to Cuthbert's feet. 'I am innocent of what you accuse me.'

Cuthbert backed away from her. 'You have made a fool of me once, Mistress Staines. You shall not a second time.' He walked to the door with purposeful strides that made him feel tall. 'Barker!' he shouted.

Nine

The Master's Cares

Ravenser allowed himself only one night at his uncle's manor of Bishopthorpe, then headed towards his duty in York.

On the road, his company encountered a group of pilgrims making their way to the shrine of St John of Beverley, tattered folk with the smell of death upon them. Ravenser's squire moved to block their access to his master. But Ravenser ordered Topas to stand aside while he blessed the pilgrims. It was not that he approved; he wished such folk would stay at home, not spread the pestilence abroad and particularly to his beloved city of Beverley. For surely they carried the poisonous air about them, these folk who had lived among the victims, sat with them at their death beds, buried or burned their corpses. But he would not deny them his blessing. Still, when he was finished, Ravenser held a ball of ambergris close to his nose as protection and rode on; all in his company appeared discomfited by the encounter, especially his clerk Douglas, who gazed about him with haunted eyes, one hand protectively covering his broad middle.

Just outside the gates of York, the company came upon a man, wrapped in animal skins and clutching a shepherd's crook, who stood upon a rock warning all who passed of the coming of the Antichrist, made manifest in the form of healers. 'Seek ye not asylum from the Lord's wrath!'

Ravenser had never been so relieved to see Micklegate Bar. The gatekeeper smiled with surprise at the hearty greeting from the Master of St Leonard's. But once within, Ravenser saw that the city, too, was changed with the fear that hung over the people. The pillory at Holy Trinity stood empty, folk hustled along with heads down, the fishmongers on Ouse Bridge protected themselves with cloths covering their faces, though they still shouted their wares.

Their muffled voices brought a memory that startled and unnerved Ravenser, a vivid vision of his mother hurrying him past a leper who cried out for alms. His mother had gripped Ravenser's hand tightly and pulled him along. He did not know where the incident had occurred, but he remembered how frightened he had been when he'd recognised his mother's fear. Had it happened during the visitation of the plague when he was a child? Is that why he remembered it? Or was it simply the fishmongers' cloth masks that brought back the moment so clearly? God brought on such visions; what was Ravenser to make of it? Exceedingly uneasy, he crossed himself and trudged on with his men towards St Leonard's, trying to keep his eyes on his feet. He wanted no more visions.

Topas stayed close, sensing his master's discomfort. And he was shortly needed. As the company passed along the west corner of St Helen's Square, a man came rushing towards them, his eyes fixed on Ravenser. Topas moved quickly to block his way.

But Ravenser noted the goldsmith's emblem on the man's vest and cap. His guild was wealthy, much given to charitable gifts. Ravenser stepped from behind Topas.

'Sir Richard, these are dangerous times,' Topas warned under his breath. 'Trust no one.'

But Ravenser had his priorities. 'You have business with me, Master Goldsmith?'

The man took off his cap, bowed with respect. 'Sir Richard. I am much relieved to see you in the city.'

'You are kind to say so.' Ravenser cursed his poor memory for names. He recognised the odd slurring of words caused by the crooked jaw that twisted the man's mouth, but he could not remember the man's name, nor what his dealings with him had been.

'It is no flattery, Sir Richard. I am much relieved to see you, and I pray that I might have a word with you.'

Who was he and what might he want?

The goldsmith saw his confusion. 'Forgive me. Of course you cannot remember me after so long. Edward Munkton. My shop is in Stonegate, and you once . . .'

'Ah. Master Munkton. The necklace.' The goldsmith had designed a necklace for Ravenser, a gift for his mother. It seemed such a long time ago. And indeed, the man had aged, his once round face chiselled with years, his hair grey and wispy. 'Confer with my clerk, Douglas, to find a time convenient for both of us to talk. At my house in St Leonard's.'

Munkton's smile faded. He kneaded his felt hat with nervous hands. 'If I might have a word now, I should be most grateful.'

Ravenser glanced round. 'In the street? It affords us little privacy.'

'God forgive me, but I would stay away from the sick at present, Sir Richard.' Munkton's eyes danced away in embarrassment.

But Ravenser understood. 'Then briefly.'

He took the man aside, beneath the eaves of a closed shop, and held his ambergris down to show his trust in the man.

'It is about Don Cuthbert,' Munkton began, his breath sweet with fennel, 'he came to me a few days past and asked to see my account books.'

Ravenser blinked in disbelief. 'To see what?' Had the goldsmith gone mad? Cuthbert?

Munkton, studying Ravenser's face, smiled. 'I had hoped to see such surprise, Sir Richard. I did not want to think that you had ordered your cellarer to insult me so.'

'Of course I did not. Did he explain himself?'

'He did indeed. He thought I might have purchased a chalice stolen from the spital. I told him that I am a goldsmith, not a trader, and that I have no need for chalices, as he might see if he took the time to look round the shop.'

A stolen chalice? Ravenser had heard nothing of this. But then, one chalice . . . 'What possible reason did he have to suspect you, Master Munkton?'

'The very thing that makes it ridiculous. My reputation for fine chalices.'

Don Cuthbert had gone mad. 'Forgive me. I had no idea.' Ravenser had a dreadful thought. 'Has he so insulted any other members of your guild?'

'Several. But I was his first victim. Not an honour I welcome.'

'To be sure. I shall reprimand him, Master Munkton. You will receive an apology, I promise you.'

'That is all I ask, Sir Richard.'

It was with weary mind and body that Ravenser at last passed under the statue of St Leonard and into the hospital liberty. Here the mood felt more normal, with folk going about their business and the orphans shouting at play. Ravenser's servants had been summoned and quickly surrounded the travellers, seeing to their horses and baggage. As Ravenser crossed the yard towards the master's house behind the church, his eyes were drawn to the blackened remains of a small building against the north wall. The roof of the house beside it had been singed. All about was the pungent odour of damp ashes.

'There was a fire?' Ravenser paused, trying to remember what had stood there. A house, he thought.

Topas conferred with a servant. 'Aye, Sir Richard. It was the house of the corrodian, Laurence de Warrene. Your chess partner. He died in the fire.'

'Laurence de Warrene.' Ravenser frowned as he paced round the remains of the house, taking care to keep his hem away from the charred fragments. Behind the burned out shell lay the garden, dappled with ashes, waterlogged, the plants wilted, some trampled. The ruined garden, with its warring scents of life and death, struck Ravenser as more piteous than the destroyed house. 'This was Mistress Warrene's garden. She took great pride in it.'

'She was taken by the pestilence,' Topas said. 'A fortnight ago.'

'So I heard at Bishopthorpe. But I had not heard about the fire.' Ravenser turned away. 'Bring Don Cuthbert to me at once, Topas.' He headed to his house.

In his bedchamber, Ravenser stripped off his travel clothes and sponged off the dirt of the road and, he hoped, the stench of death he must carry on his person. Then he retired to his parlour, where a servant had set out brandywine and fruit. He settled into his favourite chair with a full cup, gazing round with satisfaction. It was a pleasant room, not as lovely as his parlour in Beverley, but comfortable, with good light. The brandywine soon eased the muscles cramped by the day's hot ride. But he did not have long to rest. A servant announced the arrival of Don Cuthbert.

'Send for Douglas and show them in together.'

In a few moments, the tiny, beak-nosed cellarer floated into the room, hands tucked in his sleeves. He bowed to Ravenser. '*Benedicte,* Sir Richard. God is merciful to send you to us at this difficult time. Your presence will be a comfort to all at St Leonard's.' Cuthbert carried with him the scent of damp, charred timber. Ravenser reminded himself to give orders to keep a rosemary wood fire going in his rooms to protect him from unpleasant odours.

Douglas settled himself behind Ravenser to record the meeting.

'I have had disturbing news of your activities, Cuthbert.'

Beneath apologetically furrowed brows, an ingratiating smile flickered, baring oddly pointed teeth. 'My activities?'

'Accusing freemen of the city of accepting stolen goods.'

Cuthbert's cheeks reddened. 'I wished to be of service. To reclaim a few of the stolen items before you returned.'

Ravenser's head began to pound, but he ignored the warning signals, sitting forward with an icy, 'A few?'

The cellarer's protruding eyes were suddenly expressionless, though his hands fluttered in his sleeves and he rocked up on to the balls of his feet. 'I had hoped to spare you the worry until I had completed my investigation, Sir Richard.'

But why had Erkenwald written nothing of this? 'Tell me about your investigation.'

Cuthbert glanced down at a chair nearby.

'Be seated,' Ravenser snapped. He disliked the cellarer's false humility.

Cuthbert's slender hands swept out from his sleeves, gracefully smoothing the habit beneath him as he slid on to the chair. '*Deo gratias.* It has been a long day.'

The cellarer's movement stirred the scent of damp embers. Where did the man sleep?

'Where to begin?' the cellarer muttered to himself.

'I should first like to hear the list of missing items.'

'A list. Ah.' Cuthbert glanced round, found no one to release him from this query. 'The list.'

'Are you not the one to ask, Don Cuthbert? Have you relinquished your post to another worthy canon?'

'No. No, Sir Richard. The list.' Cuthbert composed himself, hands returning to their comfortable nests within his sleeves. 'Two tapestries, a golden chalice, a silver filigree missal cover with precious stones, a silver and pearl crucifix, several Italian glass goblets, an embroidered altar cloth, three blankets, and a tooled saddle.' The canon's attention was now on his sandalled feet.

'Sweet *Jesu*. How could a thief walk off with so much and not be caught? There are so many of us here, we trip over one another.'

Red splotches spread on the cellarer's pale neck. 'In truth, I cannot say.'

In the ensuing silence, the scratching of Douglas's quill attested to the length of the list. Cuthbert, for all his unpleasant qualities, had a keen mind and was excellent at detail.

'Do you need anything repeated, Douglas?' Ravenser asked, the scraping of quill against parchment reminding him of his clerk's presence.

A further scratching, then Douglas asked, 'How many goblets?'

'Four,' Cuthbert said softly, then cleared his throat. 'I have retrieved two of them.'

'Indeed! So you have found the thief?'

'No, Sir Richard.' Cuthbert pressed a pale hand to his blotchy neck. 'But I have Honoria de Staines in custody as the recipient of stolen goods.'

'*Jesu!* Your repentant Magdalen?' How had his uncle known she would be involved?

'She has told you from whom she received the goblets?'

'She will not. In faith, she insists they are not the stolen ones.'

Had he been mistaken? Made a fool of himself as he had with the goldsmiths? 'Are they at all similar, Cuthbert?'

The cellarer's mouth pinched at the insult. 'Sir Richard, I am no fool. They are of the set, I am certain.'

Ravenser groaned. 'Perhaps it needs a gentler hand in questioning the young woman.' He studied the uncomfortable cellarer. 'In custody, you say?'

'In the gaol.'

That meant all the inmates of St Leonard's knew by now. 'So you were wrong to trust her.'

Cuthbert straightened. 'Nothing is yet proved against her.'

Why was the man so stubborn? 'I shall have one of the sisters speak to her. When did these items disappear?'

'The first we noticed was on the feast of St John of Beverley. The golden chalice.'

Early May. And had Erkenwald not summoned him, Ravenser might still have been unaware of it. Ravenser rose, paced to the window, stared out at the church, noting that work had begun on a small stained glass window. Why did benefactors choose such impractical gifts? 'And why have you been questioning the goldsmiths? How might they help you?'

'It is said that goldsmiths will sometimes take stolen items, melt them down, and make them into something new that cannot be identified as stolen.'

Ravenser turned to study his cellarer. 'Are you suddenly mad or simple, Cuthbert? The goldsmiths of York are members of a guild. They would be cast out if caught thieving.'

Cuthbert lifted his hands, imploring. 'Sir —'

'Your theory is nonsense, Cuthbert. You will apologise.'

Cuthbert bowed. 'Sir Richard, I —'

Ravenser silenced him with a stern look. 'We will speak no more of it.'

'There is one more item . . .' Cuthbert dabbed his upper lip.

'Dear Lord, what else?'

The cellarer told him of the condition of Laurence de Warrene's corpse, and Julian Taverner's similar head wound.

Ravenser sank into his chair, put his forehead in his hands. 'Leave me, both of you.'

'But Sir Richard,' Cuthbert said, 'we have not spoken of the finances.'

'Discuss them with Douglas.'

Ravenser's head felt as if a cooper were beating bands down around it. The thefts, Laurence de Warrene's suspicious death, Julian Taverner's wound, and a thieving and whoring lay sister in gaol. Sweet Heaven. If word of these scandals spread throughout the city he would never gain the support of the wealthier freemen. And how was he to sort out the hospital's debts if he was so distracted by other concerns? He needed assistance. Not Cuthbert. He was indiscreet and too busy working on the accounts. Perhaps Erkenwald. But a tight-lipped outsider would be better. Archer. Owen Archer. His uncle's spy. He would follow the threads to the culprits discreetly and quickly. And a woman like Mistress Staines might find him a more pleasing confessor. Indeed. It might be necessary to borrow Archer. Ravenser would send a request to his uncle at Bishopthorpe.

As Ravenser sat in his parlour waiting for Lucie Wilton's physick to work on his head, his thoughts strayed to the burned shell across the yard. Laurence and Matilda de Warrene, both dead. God grant them peace. He had thought them a pleasant couple, devoted to one another and seemingly content with their lot in life. Ravenser had often enjoyed a game of chess with Laurence on quiet evenings. Matilda would sit by the fire dozing. Occasionally, Julian Taverner would be invited to keep her company, though his loud conversation broke Ravenser's concentration.

Laurence and Julian. Had Ravenser met them separately, he never would have guessed them to be friends. Laurence had been a quiet, dignified man; Julian was boisterous, though he had another side. Laurence had spoken of Julian's work among the sick in the first visitation of the plague, following the death of his wife. Julian had believed it to be his penance to go among the sick who had been abandoned by their families and give them succour.

'Why penance?' Ravenser remembered asking. 'Was he responsible for his wife's death?'

'Goodness no. He was a devoted husband. No, his penance was for an older sin.' Suddenly silent, Laurence had stared down at the board. Then, so softly he might not have meant Ravenser to hear, he had murmured, 'But was it a sin?' His eyes had appeared to be focused not on the chessmen, but on something far away.

'You sit across from an expert on the topic of sin, Laurence.'

Laurence had looked startled. 'Forgive me, Sir Richard. I was babbling.'

'You seemed quite serious.'

Laurence had withdrawn his hand from the pawn he had been about to move, sat back in his chair.

'Come. Ask me,' Ravenser had urged.

Laurence had folded his hands, studied them, then brought his eyes up to meet Ravenser's. 'How might one unwittingly commit a sin?' he said softly. 'If none suffer but the guilty, has a wrong been done?'

'Is it a riddle? I delight in riddles. Is there more?'

Laurence had glanced over to Julian, who perched on the edge of his seat, as if about to pounce on his friend. 'Oh, if you could see your face, old friend,' Laurence had exclaimed. 'You see, Sir Richard, Julian is so weary of my mystical babbling he is horrified to hear it.'

'Mystical? Then your questions were in earnest? Not riddles?' Ravenser was disappointed, but willing to pursue such an interesting line.

Alas, Julian had joined them and, bowing to Ravenser, he had said, 'We must get him home now, Sir Richard, else he shall make a fool of himself with more riddles. Too much of your fine wine this evening.'

Obviously a joke between two friends, for Laurence had gone good-naturedly.

But Matilda de Warrene had seemed as perplexed by the incident as Ravenser had been.

Ravenser drained his cup. It was disquieting that the Warrenes were both gone. It was strange to think that he would not see them again until he, too, was dead. And how soon might that be? Did God mean to give him time to rise to one of the high offices his uncle had taught him to covet — Keeper of the Privy Seal, Lord Chancellor, Archbishop? Or was Queen's Receiver and Keeper of the Hanaper the best he was to do? Not that Queen's Receiver was a lowly position, but with the Queen dying and the King besotted with his mistress, his work in that capacity would soon be at an end. For a time at least.

Ravenser rose to refill his cup. His last game of chess with Laurence had been interrupted, as he recalled; Matilda had been taken ill. He wandered over to the corner table on which he kept the chess set, curious whether the pieces had been moved. To his annoyance the set was not there. Cursed servants. He must tell Douglas to instruct them not to move things round when they cleaned. So where was it? Ravenser searched the room but did not find the chess set. In the process he also noted the absence of a pair of silver candlesticks that had stood on a chest by the door. Why was he able to find good help in Beverley but not in York? Was it the hospital environment? Were servants afraid they might be ordered to work among the sick?

Whatever the matter, the servants must be better trained. Ravenser sent for Douglas.

Douglas, shoulders hunched forward, as always, to hide the paunch so emphasised by his straight-cut gown, frowned with distress at the empty table-tops. 'I shall call the servants together and lecture them sternly, Sir Richard.'

'Good. Meanwhile, find the chess set and the candlesticks.'

Douglas bowed and headed for the door. Ravenser noticed he carried the account books.

'Stay a moment, Douglas. How did you fare with Cuthbert?'

The clerk turned, his face solemn. 'It is worse than we thought, Sir Richard.'

'God's blood, how is that possible? Leave the accounts here.'

Douglas looked uncertain. 'Your headache, Sir Richard?'

'Can be no worse. Go. The chess set and candlesticks.'

After depositing the books on the table beside Ravenser's favourite chair, Douglas departed.

Ravenser returned to his seat and tried to quiet his mind by reading through the hospital accounts line by line. He must have dozed off, for he woke to find Douglas bending over him, a servant at his elbow.

'What is it?' Ravenser demanded curtly to cover his sleepy confusion.

'The servants swear they have not touched the missing items, Sir Richard, though none can say when they last saw them.'

Ah. The chess set and candlesticks. Now Ravenser remembered. He glanced at the servant. 'Who has been cleaning this room?'

'I do most days, sir. But some days 'tis Mary cleans here.' The servant stood stiffly, his eyes focused on Douglas's shoulder.

'And neither of you noticed the set and the candlesticks were missing.'

'Go on, Peter,' Douglas said gently. 'Show Sir Richard what you found.'

'I —' Peter coughed, cleared his throat. 'I did notice at last, sir, because I found this' — he held out an ocre-stained knight — ' 'twas fallen behind the chest, you see. Then I remembered the set. But I could not find it. Nowhere in the house, sir.'

Ravenser took the ivory piece, turned it

round in his hand. 'I do not like this.'

'Mayhap they, too, have been stolen, my lord.' Peter's face was pinched with distaste for the words.

They, too. So the servants knew of the other thefts. Of course they did. God help him, as if he did not have troubles enough. Servants had no discretion. 'You may go, Peter.'

When the servant had departed, Ravenser dictated his request to Archbishop Thoresby to Douglas.

'Captain Archer, Sir Richard? The one who helped you with Dame Joanna Calverley?'

'The very one. Send Topas to Bishopthorpe with the note, Douglas. Tell him to wait for an answer.'

Ten

Alisoun's Plight

Lame John Ffulford had decided to give up the search for his niece Alisoun. A week had passed since the priest had come to him, and for all his efforts, John had seen no sign of the child, save that she had managed to sneak away with the nag before he had reached his brother's farm. Who knew how far she might have wandered? But she had left the cart, and one or two items his wife might fancy. So this morning he had brought his donkey to pull the loaded cart home.

And who should he have found in the barn but Alisoun, tending to a wound on her nag's shoulder. God tested him sorely.

Now the girl stood beside the cart, arms folded, eyes cast down. She looked like some wild thing, shoeless, her gown in tatters, her hair a snarl of knots and debris.

Lame John shook his head. 'God help me, but if you were not my brother's daughter, and all that's left of his family, I would leave you here, you stubborn child. For a week you have led us a merry chase.' He tossed the bag of clothes and sundry items on to the cart, then grabbed his niece by the shoulder. 'Climb up or I'll toss you up, you changeling.' She was like her mother, she was. His brother Duncan's wife Judith had ever been a sullen, secretive woman. Duncan had oft complained about her. And he had feared she put strange ideas into her children's heads about how they had been born to better than what they had and someday would move up to a grander life. But John's immediate problem was how to reconcile his wife to Alisoun's presence. When the priest had come with the news that they must do something for the girl, Colet had agreed, but she had been very uncomfortable with the idea of Alisoun actually living with them.

'How did she survive when they did not, husband? A pact with the Devil, is how. Traded their lives for hers. And she will do the same with us.'

Now that was Colet's family, always ready to blame trouble on the Devil, or, at the least, spells and curses. John had demanded her co-operation in God's name.

But the child was difficult. 'My horse,' she reminded him.

'We shall send Rich for her as soon as he is able. She has plenty feed.'

The eyes in the child's dirty face looked forlorn.

'For pity's sake, we would not let the creature die. A horse is too valuable.'

'Pull her behind the cart.'

'Nay, child, the going is quicker without pulling a wounded nag behind, and I have much work to do in the fields. From which you have kept me these seven days.'

'I shall help you.'

'You might have helped more by coming to me on your own. And now this nag. What if she pulls away? With my bad leg, I cannot chase her.'

'I can.'

'I said she stays behind.'

'Send Rich for me and my horse.'

'I shall not leave you here alone another night, child.'

'Someone will steal her.'

'The nag belonging to a family dead of pestilence? Nay, child. Folk will fear it. And they will fear you, now I think of it.'

The girl squinted up at him. 'Why don't you?'

'You must put on a pleasant face, child, else your aunt will curse me.'

'So let me stay here.'

'You have no flesh on you. You've not been eating.'

'I eat.'

'Not enough.'

'Whoever has enough?'

'Aye, you have felt the hunger. Come now. Rich will come for your prize horse in a day or so.'

'Or so?'

'Tomorrow.'

'God will smite you if you do not.'

Lame John frowned. She was so small, yet so determined to have her way. And evidently thought God meant her to have it, too. 'Smite me, will He? Does the Lord oft do your bidding?'

Her head dropped, bony shoulders lifted. A tear worked its way down the muddy face, leaving a pale trail.

'Nay, He has not, child. He has tested you sorely of late. Come. Let Colet and Lame John give you some good food and company, eh?'

Alisoun met his gaze, her chin jutting forward. 'Tomorrow? He will come tomorrow?'

'Aye, child, tomorrow.'

'You swear?'

'I swear.'

Ravenser crossed the yard to the infirmary.

He wished to express his condolences to Julian Taverner and discuss the need for silence. The morning was chilly though the fog had lifted. Clouds gathered to the north, promising rain. Rain would be a relief, Ravenser thought. It would settle the dust, perhaps wash away some of the pestilential vapours.

As he passed the ugly remains of Warrene's house, Ravenser paused, remembering the couple. Matilda had been a quiet woman, happiest, it seemed, in her garden. Laurence had been a fussy husband, always reminding her to dress warmly, eat as much as she could. Had they been so when they first married? He wandered back to the ruined garden. A neat row of feathery carrot crowns bobbed in the breeze. Not such a wasteland, then. He would ask Douglas to find someone to tend the garden. It would be a fitting memorial to a gentle woman and would provide the kitchen with fresh vegetables.

In the infirmary, Ravenser found Julian Taverner sitting up in bed, frowning at the opposite wall. His white hair framed his face like a pale lion's mane, though lopsided. Ravenser realised Julian's hair must have been singed on one side and the burned ends removed. On his forehead and chin were angry patches of healing flesh and a thick dressing protected the wound on the back of his skull. His hands were awkward with bandages. But even so, Julian did not look like a victim. His dark eyes were fierce in his lined face.

'What is amiss, Master Taverner?' Ravenser asked quietly. 'Do you have a complaint about the care you are receiving?'

The angry eyes moved up, softened. 'Sir Richard.' Julian leaned forward, nodded to the stool against the wall. 'Pray, sit yourself down,' he said in his loud voice. 'God bless you for coming.'

Ravenser moved the stool closer to the bed.

'Nay,' Julian continued, 'I cannot complain about the care.'

'But you looked so angry.'

' 'Twas naught.'

'Come now. Tell me what angers you.'

The elderly man hesitated. 'I make much of naught.'

'You paid a goodly sum to lodge here. You deserve to be heard.'

Julian's eyes softened more. 'It is Mistress Catherine's cough. Do you hear it?'

Ravenser had indeed noticed the incessant coughing down the corridor. 'It keeps you awake?'

'I merely asked whether I or Mistress

Catherine might be moved so that I might escape the sound. It was a simple request. And Don Cuthbert behaved as if I were demanding my meals were served on golden platters with dancing women for my entertainment.'

'Ah.' Ravenser did not wish to become embroiled in such mundane problems. 'The hospital is very busy at the moment. You must forgive short tempers. I shall see what can be done.'

'I would be most grateful, Sir Richard.'

Ravenser considered the man's bandages, noted that they looked clean. 'With all else you are satisfied?'

'Aye.'

Thanks be to God his complaint was so slight. 'I have thought much about Laurence since I learned of his death. I shall miss him.'

Julian averted his eyes. 'Oh, aye. There's none to replace Laurence.'

'And to happen so soon after Matilda's passing. You have suffered much sorrow of late.'

Julian said nothing.

'I should be cheering you.' But in faith, Ravenser could think of nothing jolly to mention.

The uneasy silence was broken by Julian. 'I do have one other request, Sir Richard.

My niece has proved to be considerate and efficient in this trying time. I should like to change my will. Might your secretary assist me?'

A will? So he had more than what he had paid for his corrody and donated to the hospital? Ravenser wondered whether St Leonard's was remembered in the will. 'I shall be happy to send Douglas to you. Do I know your niece?'

'Bess Merchet. She and her husband run the York Tavern.'

Ravenser closed his eyes to hide his dismay. Bess Merchet. He had forgotten. A woman with her nose in everything in the city.

'It was my niece who convinced Cuthbert and Erkenwald to examine Laurence before he was buried. She wished them to see the wound on the back of his head. I believe that is what killed him, not the fire.'

Cuthbert had not mentioned Bess Merchet. 'I trust that Mistress Merchet will not speak of the wounds to anyone.'

Julian's head jerked up. 'You think she does not understand the need for silence during an investigation? She is a canny woman, Sir Richard.'

'Do you have any idea who might have attacked you?'

Julian studied Ravenser's face. 'It happened too quickly.'

'Ah. Of course.' Ravenser paused, trying to think of a more neutral subject. He must not forget the will. 'I was thinking about our chess games. A clever strategist, Laurence. And yet cautious. I remember that riddle he posed me one night . . .'

Julian's brows met in a bushy frown. 'Riddle?'

' "How might one unwittingly commit a sin? If none suffer but the guilty, has a wrong been done?" You dragged him away saying he would make a fool of himself with riddles.'

Julian's eyes latched on to Ravenser's with an intensity the latter found uncomfortable.

'You do remember?'

Julian nodded slowly. 'Did you — Have you spoken of that to any here in the hospital?'

He thought him a chattering jay like his niece? 'I had no occasion to. But should I not talk of it?'

Julian leaned back, pressed his bandaged hands to his forehead. ' 'Tis naught, Sir Richard.'

A soft noise in the doorway made Ravenser turn round. A tall, comely woman appeared, carrying a tray of unguents and bandages. 'God be with you, sir,' she said, her voice low. Though she wore the dark, plain gown and starched wimple of a lay sister, she commanded attention. Ravenser searched his memory. Anneys. Yes. The widow.

'Am I in the way?' Ravenser asked.

'Forgive me, sir. It is time Master Taverner's bandages were changed.'

'Where is Honoria?' Julian asked. 'I have not seen her in more than a day.'

Anneys dropped her head, as if uncertain what to say.

'She is detained by other matters,' Ravenser said.

Anneys looked grateful. Ravenser instructed her to send for Douglas when Julian was ready to see him, then took his leave.

Outside, the morning had turned misty. Ravenser lifted his face to the heavens and let them freshen him. A bell tolled somewhere in the city. Ravenser bowed his head, crossed himself and prayed for another dead of the pestilence. He caught himself. One might die from other causes, even in times of pestilence. Look at Laurence de Warrene.

He made his way slowly through the yard, noting the poorly patched areas in the surrounding wall, dangerous pits in the mud of the yard. In one, a rat swam happily. Ravenser was appalled by how shabby his hospital had become. Their financial situation was not so dire as this.

Coppery hair beneath a starched, beribboned cap caught his eye. He recognised Bess Merchet, chatting with one of the lay sisters. She must be here to see her uncle. He wondered what news she shared with the woman.

'Mistress Merchet!' he called in a friendly voice as he approached. 'God be with you both.'

The sister dropped her eyes and murmured a greeting.

Bess kept her gaze steady. 'God go with you, Sir Richard. I should like to speak with you by and by.'

Ravenser spread his hands. 'Will this do?'

'Oh, not today. Later. And in a less public place.' Bess glanced at the other woman. ' 'Tis not for distrust of you, but there are too many about.'

Complaints about her uncle's care, Ravenser guessed. He would rather not have any such grievances aired in public. 'Come to my house when you wish to talk.' He blessed the two women and took his way homeward, hoping that a cool cloth on his forehead might stave off the headache that had not entirely diminished. Clearly he could not count on rest to restore his health.

He was almost to the door when Don Cuthbert stepped into his path. 'Sir Richard, I beg a word.'

A convenient meeting. 'I understand Julian Taverner requested to be moved.'

Cuthbert coloured, rose on his toes. 'He summoned you?'

'No, I asked what had discomfited him. Is his request impossible to grant?'

'The infirmary is crowded, Sir Richard, and threatens to become even more so.'

'Then explain it to him with courtesy, Cuthbert.'

'Perhaps that will not be necessary. I have thought of a solution that might please everyone — he will escape the noise, the other lay sisters will stop complaining that Honoria and Anneys devote too much time to him, and none of the other patients need be disturbed.'

'This plan?'

'Move Taverner to his home. His niece is here every day nursing him. Let her take over completely.'

'She is here every day?'

Cuthbert bristled. 'She believes our medicines are inferior, our food does not promote good health.' He sniffed. 'She has destroyed the harmony in the infirmary.'

'Taverner is sufficiently recovered to be left alone?'

'He is well enough to complain about someone else's cough.'

Why did Cuthbert make so much of this? 'If he agrees, let him go home. He has a servant, does he not?'

'Of course.'

'Instruct the servant to call for one of the lay sisters if anything seems amiss. Anneys. She seems competent.'

'Anneys, Sir Richard? But she is our best —'

'You heard me, Cuthbert. I want Julian Taverner to feel he is getting the best care possible.'

Cuthbert made a submissive gesture. 'I wished to speak with you about Mistress Staines.'

'What about her?'

'She asks to speak with Taverner.'

'Why?'

'She will not say.'

'What is between the two of them, I wonder?'

'He was once her employer, Sir Richard. Perhaps she seeks his advice.'

Ravenser considered. 'Move her to the windowed room in the gaol. It is less like a cell.'

'Yes, Sir Richard.'

'Let her go about her work by day, return to her cell by night. We may learn something by her movements.'

Cuthbert's pinched face registered disapproval. 'As you wish.' He tucked his hands up his sleeves, bowed to Ravenser.

'And now, I pray you, leave me in peace.' Ravenser retreated into the comforting shadows of his own house. But his step was lighter than before. He was proud of his inspiration for easing Honoria de Staine's defensive silence.

Eleven

The Stones of Sherburne

Alisoun and her Aunt Colet circled round each other warily. Neither felt comfortable turning her back on the other.

'How did you come to be spared?' Colet asked the child as soon as she stepped from the cart.

Alisoun turned back to her uncle. 'I told you I should stay at the farm. She does not want me here.'

'Do not turn from me when I am speaking to you!' Colet said in an imperious voice.

Lame John pushed Alisoun forward. 'Pay your respects to your aunt, child.'

She turned to face Colet. Fair and fat she was, with eyebrows and lashes so blonde they were transparent and made her face look naked. She had large, prominent teeth and a sneer that lingered even on the rare occasions when she smiled. Alisoun thought her disgusting. It was at that moment that she took a vow to remain silent so long as she stayed in her aunt's house.

Three days of her silence drove Colet mad. 'I cannot have this impertinence in my house!'

'What is your complaint, wife? She has obeyed you in everything.'

'Except to speak. I cannot know her mind if she will not speak.'

'You did not much like her mind.'

' 'Tis the Devil's work. No natural child could keep still so long. And what of that longbow? Who taught her to use it?'

'My brother Duncan. A foolish idea, I admit.'

'You must take it from her.'

'If she aims it at one of us, I will do so, wife. But not before.'

'You are not only lame, but weak, husband.'

'And a fool for wedding such an ill-natured woman.'

Alisoun listened to the argument as she sat just outside the doorway, keeping an eye on her two young cousins while she stirred a sickening mixture of honey, oats and milk for her aunt's complexion. Aunt Colet had sneered at what she called Alisoun's mother's airs, but what farmer's wife pampered herself so with plasters to whiten and soften the skin? Did she ready herself for court? And while she lay napping in the late afternoon with the concoction on her face, Alisoun must sit and fan away the flies that fancied the honey.

Her little cousins began to shriek as they pulled each other's hair. Alisoun put the bowl aside and yanked the two apart. A shooting pain travelled up her right arm. Her hand was sore from stirring the thickening mixture. And who could blame the children for fighting? They were sweaty and irritable from playing in the sun. Even Alisoun, sitting in the shade of a spindly tree, felt lightheaded from the heat. And queasy from the sweet scent of her aunt's concoction. She drew the two girls over by the house and allowed them each to dip one fingertip into the mixture. That would quiet them for a while.

Alisoun settled back on the bench, shaded her eyes, stared off into the distance. But no clouds of dust heralded her cousin's approach. Three days she had been here, and there had been no sign of her cousin. That morning Lame John had read the anxiety in her furtive glances out of the door and had assured her that Rich would be back from market this day: he had been delayed, but surely by mid-morning he would appear, and he would fetch her horse as soon as he returned. It was now past midday and still there was no sign of him. Alisoun did not think it at all likely that he would agree to turn round on arrival and go to her farm for the horse.

So she planned to leave as soon as the sun set. It would be easy then. Her bed was in an outlying shed. No one would miss her till morning.

On the road to Bishopthorpe, Alfred, one of the archbishop's retainers, compensated for his sullen captain's silence by babbling statistics about the dead and dying in York. Owen did not listen long enough to be bothered by it. He knew that Alfred was nervous about a rash under his arm that he was certain foretold pestilence, despite Lucie's assurances that it was a heat rash. Alfred had seen a star falling from the sky the night before the rash had appeared, and that was enough to convince him that he was doomed. In the circumstances, Owen thought it best to let Alfred chatter and jaw if it eased his mind, though he could not imagine how talk of the plague comforted him.

As they rode through the gates of Bishopthorpe, Alfred pointed towards a figure standing by the door to the hall.

Owen was amazed. 'Brother Michaelo.

Out in the yard, sitting in the sunlight? How unlike him.' The archbishop's secretary was not fond of fresh air.

As grooms helped Owen and Alfred from their horses, Brother Michaelo rose and approached them slowly, his usually inexpressive face a mask of grief.

'*Benedicte,* Brother Michaelo,' Owen said. 'I pray all are well in the house?'

'*Benedicte,* Captain Archer, Alfred.' Michaelo bowed his head towards each in turn. 'I am sad to say Death has visited the household. Maeve, the cook, has this morning lost her youngest daughter to the pestilence.'

Alfred crossed himself and coughed nervously.

'May God grant her eternal rest,' Owen murmured. 'I hope that everyone else in the household is well?' He was not in the mood to linger on the death of a child. Their maid, Kate, had that morning learned of the death of her youngest brother, another victim of the pestilence. Her grief was hard to bear. Kate's sister, Tildy, at Freythorpe Hadden with Gwenllian and Hugh, had yet to hear the sad news.

'So far God has taken no others,' Michaelo said, 'but two of the gardener's children are ailing.' He crossed himself. 'His Grace hopes you can concoct something from our stores to calm Maeve. She will let no one comfort her.'

'A few cups of His Grace's brandywine should suffice. A scattering of balm leaves in the cup will lighten her heart. And if you have any valerian root, a pinch would hasten drowsiness. Sleep is the best remedy for grief.'

Michaelo glanced at the pouch Alfred held to his nose. 'I see that you carry the scented bags. We have been using balls of ambergris. Which do you recommend, Captain?'

Even in his grief, Michaelo's obsession with his own well-being remained strong. For once Owen found it refreshing. 'I cannot in all honesty swear to any of the remedies or preventatives, Michaelo. We worry about being in crowds. But what crowd would Maeve's child have been in out here?'

'She took the child into York to collect some items from the archbishop's palace,' Michaelo said darkly. 'And took the child to Mass in the minster.'

Alfred pressed one hand over the rash under his arm. As one of the archbishop's retainers, he lived in the barracks near the palace.

Owen cursed himself for getting caught in this pointless conversation. 'You have been a long time from York, Brother Michaelo. There are no crowds round the palace or the minster. Folk keep to themselves. Would you inform His Grace that I am here?'

Michaelo studied Owen for a moment. 'You are looking well enough.' He glanced at Alfred. 'But you have discomfort. You do not bring plague to Bishopthorpe?'

Alfred paled.

'For pity's sake, the pestilence is already here,' Owen grumbled. 'Alfred has but a rash from the heat if you are so fascinated with the health of others. Mistress Wilton has given him a lotion to soothe it.'

Michaelo's eyes said he did not believe Owen's explanation. Neither did Alfred, of course. But the archbishop's secretary merely sniffed and led them into the house.

Thoresby received Owen in his parlour, usually a cool room in summer, with the windows opening on to the garden and beyond it the river. But today the room was stuffy, with the shutters latched and a brazier aglow with rosemary wood. Ambergris, rosemary wood — Thoresby was not counting on prayers to protect him from the pestilence. The archbishop bent over some work. His hair had grown dusty with age in the past year. When he glanced up to nod to

Owen, his eyes seemed even more deeply sunken than usual, his lips pinched.

'*Benedicte,* Archer.' His eyes returned to the documents on the table before him.

Owen was accustomed to the archbishop. '*Benedicte,* Your Grace. I hope you find all to your liking at Bishopthorpe.'

'As ever.'

Thoresby did not make it easy to be pleasant. 'How fares Queen Phillippa, Your Grace?'

'Not well. The end is near.'

'May God bless her and keep her,' Owen said, crossing himself.

Thoresby sighed, waved Owen to a chair on the other side of the small table at which he sat. 'You have seen to Maeve?'

Owen settled in the chair, crossed his arms, nodded. 'I have given Michaelo instructions, Your Grace.' He glanced at the documents. They appeared to be petitions, letters.

'Maeve is a good Christian woman,' Thoresby said. He clapped for a servant, who silently emerged from the shadowy corner. 'Move these to my work table.' While the young man scooped up the parchments and carried them across the room, the archbishop said, 'I pray God the rest of her children do not succumb.' He motioned to the servant to pour wine, then settled back in his thronelike chair, resting his hands on the rounded armrests. 'And your family, Archer? Are they well?'

'Aye, thanks be to God. We have been spared so far.' Owen noted that the servant's hands shook as he poured the wine. It was no surprise. Pestilence had come to the manor. All would be wondering who would be the next to fall ill. 'We have sent the children to Lucie's father in the country.'

Thoresby picked up his cup, gazed into its depths. 'A laudable move, though the country has not saved the folk at this manor. Simon, the gardener, has two children ill. Who knows whether they would have been safer in York? But I seldom use the palace in the city. It made sense for Simon to be here. And with all those children . . .'

Owen glanced out the window at the garden. 'It matters not how many one has, each child is precious.'

'Simon bears it well.'

'So quickly the deaths follow, one on the other.'

'Is it not the way?' Thoresby examined his cup in the light. 'As Master Apothecary, Lucie must be busy.'

'Aye, that she is. With each visitation of the pestilence folk have become more inventive with their precautions. A wealthy merchant asked yesterday for enough crushed diamonds to strew round his bed and cut Death's feet to shreds.'

'Odd. I have ever thought of Death booted.'

'And I in sandals.'

Thoresby drank deeply.

Owen found the archbishop's idle babble disturbing. It was unlike him and it delayed the inevitable bad news or tirade. But he might be wise to play along with it. 'I trust Your Grace is well?'

'Well enough, Archer.'

Owen thought not. The archbishop's eyes had none of their customary fire. 'I have come to the manor as often as I could manage,' Owen said. In addition to being captain of the archbishop's retainers in York and keeping the peace in the minster liberty, Owen was responsible for the smooth running of Bishopthorpe in Thoresby's absence. Perhaps he might ease the conversation towards the business of the day.

'You have done well, Archer. You have proved yourself worthy of the trust I place in you.' Thoresby at last met Owen's gaze. He smiled.

Owen was not fond of Thoresby's smile. It often meant trouble. 'You did not summon me to Bishopthorpe to praise my work.'

'No. I have more work for you. I must take you away with me for a short time.'

Owen clenched his jaw.

'You will accompany me to my manor of Sherburne.' The manor was south of Leeds, a good day's journey from York.

'What is at Sherburne?'

'The stones to complete the minster's Lady Chapel. The quarry has been depleted.'

'So I have heard. But I thought Michaelo and the master mason were inspecting alternative quarries.'

'None was of sufficient quality.'

'There is a quarry on the land at Sherburne?'

Thoresby's eyes narrowed, as if he thought Owen was being obstinate in not understanding. 'No. I intend to dismantle the house itself. The stones are well cut, of excellent quality.'

Owen stared at Thoresby, wondering how one responded to an archbishop who had lost his mind.

Thoresby chuckled, though he did not smile. 'You find the scheme impractical.'

Mad was more like it. 'That is a beginning, Your Grace.'

'A beginning?'

Enough of this courtesy. 'I think it folly to pursue such a scheme, Your Grace. I cannot but wonder at your motivation. Do you tire of the house? It is no longer to your liking? What of the next Archbishop of York? He might take exception to your wanton destruction.' As Owen spoke he watched Thoresby's cheeks puff out and redden.

'Wanton destruction?'

'Such a house took many men and much labour to create. And you would tear it down because you prefer using the stones for your tomb, when you assuredly have alternatives that would not entail such destruction.' Owen surprised himself with his vehemence.

'Had I an alternative I would pursue it, Archer. But the quarries near at hand do not offer such quality, and those far away will take too long and cost too much, and workers are difficult to recruit in the midst of pestilence. I would complete the Lady Chapel this year, before Martinmas.'

Owen closed his eye, considered. Even using Sherburne's stone, the archbishop could not expect the masons to meet that goal. Little more than three months. And whence came that goal? Did Thoresby think his death so close at hand? 'Why this year?'

'I have vowed to complete Our Lady's

chapel in return for her intercession on behalf of the people of York. I have prayed to her to spare them from the pestilence.'

Owen looked Thoresby squarely in the eye. 'Then you are too late, Your Grace. We have buried more than one hundred in the city these past two months.'

Thoresby's face was pinched, his eyes sad. 'I did not know it was so many,' he said, his regret clear in his tone. 'Still. I may save far more than that.'

Mayhap. But Owen would not leave Lucie at so perilous a time on such a fool's errand. 'Forgive me, but I am needed at home, Your Grace. And you need me to protect your interests in the city. The fear makes the crowds unpredictable. Think of the Lammas Fair.'

'You know full well there will be no Lammas Fair this year. Which is yet another reason to use the stones I already own. I shall have no revenues to spare. You will go with me to Sherburne.'

'Why? Of what use will I be to you there?'

'You question my orders?'

'This is a fool's errand, Your Grace. And hardly the work of either your captain or your steward.'

Thoresby slammed his palms on the table, and rose, leaning across, his face close to

Owen's. He reeked of ambergris, rosemary, wine, and sweat: unusual for the archbishop, who had a peculiar fondness for bathing. 'You shall obey me!'

Thunder did not intimidate Owen. 'I cannot leave my wife and the shop for so long, Your Grace,' he said quietly. 'Not in a time of pestilence. Each day the apothecary is filled with customers. I must help Lucie as much as I can.'

'What of her apprentice?'

'He works hard, Your Grace. But there is much to do.'

'You have managed well enough coming here.'

'That is not the same as being away for a long while, Your Grace, with no opportunity to return and see how they fare.'

'You are my man,' Thoresby stated, knowing full well how Owen hated such a claim.

'That can change, Your Grace.'

They glared at one another. The silence lengthened. Suddenly Thoresby rose, walked to the window, asked without turning to face Owen, 'What do you know of the troubles at St Leonard's?'

Who had won? Owen doubted he was the victor. But he meant to stand his ground on Sherburne, so how could he be the loser? 'Walter de Hotter stabbed and strangled in his house, odd wounds on two victims of a fire, one of them dead. A golden chalice missing, a valuable missal cover, some goblets. I know only what all in York know.'

'More thefts than that. Considerably more.' A moment of silence. 'My nephew will be called south as soon as the deaths from pestilence cease.'

Owen felt a shower of needle pricks across his blind eye. This did not bode well. 'Aye, he is an important man in chancery and the Queen's household. I should think he would have little time to devote to the hospital.'

'But he will not wish to leave until harmony is restored at St Leonard's.'

'They say he has an eager investigator in his cellarer.'

Thoresby turned round, smirking. 'Don Cuthbert? The man offends all to whom he speaks. He is not the man for the task.'

'Don Erkenwald is more suitable, and he has been uneasy about Hotter's death from the beginning.'

'I prefer that my own man see to it.' Thoresby held Owen's gaze as he emphasised 'my own man'.

'It has naught to do with me.'

'You wished to remain in York. I shall grant your request. On the condition that you assist my nephew in seeing harmony restored to St Leonard's.'

'It is not your right to arrange for my hire as a spy.'

'No? Mistress Wilton might feel otherwise.'

Owen paused. Had Lucie spoken to him in private? Recently? 'What do you mean?'

Thoresby resumed his seat, steepled his hands. The smirk still taunted Owen. 'As I recall, Mistress Wilton hindered our efforts to discover the truth about my ward's poisoning. How long ago that seems. And yet, even so, I intervened with the guild so that she might marry you and retain her standing as Nicholas Wilton's widow.'

Relieved to hear that Lucie had not betrayed him, Owen was yet disturbed. 'Surely my work the past six years has repaid you tenfold.'

Thoresby chuckled. 'It is you who has been well paid, Archer.' He closed his eyes, leaned his forehead on his steepled fingers. 'Why do you not wish to assist my nephew?'

'You know that is not the point, Your Grace.'

The head lifted. 'No?'

False surprise. It was these moments that kept Owen from liking the archbishop. And yet Thoresby was godfather to both his children. 'Sir Richard was a generous host when I was in Beverley. I have no quarrel with him.'

'Good. He learned to trust you.'

Perhaps this was not a matter of Thoresby's volunteering Owen, but of his communicating a request from another. 'Sir Richard asked for me?'

'He did.'

Damn the man. 'I do not know how much time I might devote to such a task. With so many coming to the shop, there is little time during the day to prepare the physicks; we work in the evening and early morning. And there is the garden, and my responsibilities as your steward here. Besides all that, there is another matter on my conscience.'

'Ah? And what is that?'

He told Thoresby about Tildy and Kate's loss. 'We promised we would send word to Tildy at Freythorpe if the sickness touched her family.'

Thoresby poured himself more wine. 'Freythorpe is on my way to Sherburne. I shall call there, deliver the news, see my godchildren.'

Owen did not know whether to be grateful for Thoresby's generosity or worried about the archbishop's motivation. 'Your Grace. It is a kind gesture. There are few willing to go abroad with such messages.'

Thoresby smiled. 'You see? There is nothing to keep you from the hospital.'

Owen tasted bile. 'Do you enjoy moving us all round like pawns?'

'I confess it is one of the pleasures of age. There are far too few, Archer. You would not know that, but someday . . .'

'You never meant to take me to Sherburne.'

Thoresby raised an eyebrow, but said nothing.

Later, after they had shared a meal, Thoresby mentioned Honoria de Staines. 'I warned Richard that St Leonard's was not the place for such a woman.'

'Why do you speak of her?'

'Two of the missing goblets were hidden in her bedchamber. She claims they were gifts but will say no more. See what you might glean from her.'

'Considering her reputation, the goblets were likely gifts from a lover.'

'Then why does she not name him?'

Owen wondered the same thing. But he was not in a mood to agree with Thoresby. 'Is it so difficult to imagine such a woman being loyal?'

Thoresby dismissed Owen's suggestion with a sniff. 'And while you are asking questions, find out why Don Cuthbert is her champion.'

Owen drained his cup. 'A fool's errand.'

'Sherburne or St Leonard's. Your choice, Archer.'

'I shall surely deserve Heaven when my time comes.' Owen pushed himself away from the table, rose.

'Let us pray that your time is not so near you have no more opportunity for sin.'

Owen crossed himself. 'Honoria de Staines is not the only subject of rumour. What of Sir Richard? Is he beyond suspicion?'

Thoresby suddenly took an interest in the bowl of fruit before him, spent a moment choosing a peach, sniffing it. 'No one is beyond suspicion, Archer. But his asking for you is the action of a fool if he has aught to hide.'

Was that meant as praise? Owen studied the archbishop, bending to the task of quartering the peach with his dagger.

'Is your nephew likely to play the fool?'

'From time to time.' Thoresby raised his eyes to Owen. 'See you watch your back. I would not lose you on a fool's errand.' He smiled.

At table, Lucie silently stared down at her

food as Owen recounted his interview with the archbishop. Thoresby was right, she was far more fearful of insulting him than Owen was. He was a powerful man, and though an archbishop, he was human enough to have a temper that he did not always bother to check. What might he do to them? And yet he could be so kind. But best of all was the love Owen had expressed through this refusal.

'You do not look at me. You are angry?'

Lucie glanced up, surprised by the question. Jasper also watched her, though less obviously than Owen whose hawkeye was fixed on her. 'Sweet *Jesu*, how could you think me angry, my love?' She rose, held out her hand to him. 'Come. Let us walk in the garden.'

The shrubs and trees rustled softly in the evening breeze. As they strolled past the rosemary hedge, Owen said, 'The archbishop had a fire of rosemary wood in his parlour on such a day.'

Lucie pressed Owen's hand. 'As you said this morning, we are all a bit childish at present. These are fearful times.'

'Not so bad as the previous two.'

'A death is a death, Owen.'

'Aye. But he is more than childish, Lucie. To destroy a house for the stones.'

'It is not such an odd idea to me, my love.

And for what better purpose?'

'I am wrong?'

Lucie stopped, turned to him, took both his hands. 'Perhaps to criticise his scheme so fiercely, my love. But not to insist on my need of you.'

'And what of involving myself in the troubles at St Leonard's?'

'Who better than you, my love?'

Owen was silent.

'Well? Who better?'

'Why do you think he is willing to stop at Freythorpe?'

Always suspicious. Lucie lifted Owen's hands, turned them palms upwards, kissed them in turn, looked him in the eye. 'Do not question it, just be thankful he will do it. He is proud of Hugh and Gwenllian. If aught is amiss, we shall hear quickly.' She could tell from his eye that he did not share her confidence. She was suddenly fearful.

Alisoun arrived at the farm long after sunset. She was relieved to find the nag in the enclosed field, sleeping under the stars. Alisoun gave her a spoonful of her aunt's facial concoction, having brought a goodly portion with her, and she promised to give the horse a brushing in the morning and to apply more salve to her wound. The nag whinnied softly as Alisoun slipped away: a pleasant, companionable sound in her solitude. Not like the crickets whose night song made the farm seem lonelier. The crickets' chorus was a sound the girl associated with heading out in the dark to relieve herself, or lying awake in the cottage unable to sleep.

As she entered the yard, Alisoun paused. She sensed company, not by sound or sight, but by a prickling at the back of her neck that her father had taught her to respect. Someone had come to rob them. Or take over the farm. It was just what Alisoun had feared. And her uncle was to blame with his silly idea of bringing her to his house. She stood as still as possible, studying the barn and house, seeking a glimmer of light that would tell her where she might find the intruder. But all was dark. Was she imagining it? Who but she could find their way round these buildings at night?

Unless the dead walked. Alisoun crossed herself. Not that her family had any cause to harm her from the other side of the grave, but to see them once they had passed to the other side . . . They would be different. She did not like to think of that. It frightened her that they would have been changed by death. Would she know them? Would they know her?

Alisoun felt her stomach going queer. She forced her mind from such thoughts, peered into the darkness. And then she saw it. A flickering light up in the barn's loft.

Whence came the light? Her stomach leapt and tumbled. The spirits of the dead might be wrapped in light. And angels: might they not glow? Like the stars?

Alisoun shook her head and considered the light. Surely angels, pure beings, would glow with white light. And they would not flicker because they would be perfect. This was a candle or a lantern, no spectre.

An intruder then. She found that comforting. She could deal with an intruder. Taking a deep breath to steady herself and quiet her stomach, Alisoun strung her bow, readied an arrow, and crept across the yard to the barn. The warped door to the barn was slightly open, so she might slip in without a sound. But would the intruder see her? She paused, considered. She could not call on her memory to predict how the light the intruder carried up there would fall on the floor below. Her father had never taken a light up to the loft because it was much too easy to spark a fire in the barn.

Alisoun crept close to the opening, peered inside, withdrew her head quickly, her heart pounding. God must be watching over her.

Had she crept in without first looking, the intruder would have seen her. He sat at the top of the ladder, his feet resting on the top rung, a lantern dangling from one hand. And he was watching the door. Had he heard her? But she had been as quiet as could be. Adults did not hear that well, unless they had trained themselves to hear. Hunters and soldiers had trained hearing. Alisoun knew he was neither. Or she was fairly certain he wasn't. But now that she thought of it, she was not sure what he was. Or who. All she knew was that her mother had tried to keep this man's visits secret.

It had been almost a fortnight since Alisoun had hailed the fisherman on the river. More than a week since the Riverwoman and the archer had been there. Folk never kept quiet. One of them or all three of them might have spoken of the deaths. Alisoun felt undeniably sick to her stomach now. It must be that he had heard about her family. He might not know she had survived. Or if he did, he would expect her to be with her kin.

Alisoun imagined him in the house, in the barn, walking round her land. She did not like it. She had never liked him. She did not like that he'd been through the house and barn, that he had touched her things. She hated him.

She would shoot him. But she couldn't while he held that lantern in his hands for he might drop it in the hay and set the barn on fire. So she prepared herself for a long wait.

Waiting was the worst part. The crickets seemed louder, the night sky darker and closer. She must not think about her prey else she might grow angrier and that would make her more likely to miss. She forced herself to think about the two who had come to bury her family. The old hag she had seen before, when her mother had given birth to her brother and sister. What Alisoun remembered about those events was how her mother had suffered. Especially after her brother's birth. Her mother had said that the Riverwoman was a trustworthy midwife. But her mother had been so weak with her brother's birth, and he had been such a troublesome, weak baby. Alisoun had decided that the Riverwoman had poisoned her mother, or put a curse on her. Yet when Alisoun had searched the loft after the Riverwoman and the one-eyed soldier had returned the horse and cart, certain that they had gone up there while she was hiding in the wood, she had found naught out of place. So the old woman and the archer were honest.

A rustle from within. Alisoun checked her

bow, slipped into the barn. Her patience was rewarded. The intruder had set the lantern down on a ledge near the nag's stall and was searching the nag's hay, his back turned. Nicely illuminated, he presented an easier target than Alisoun's usual coneys. She shot, hit the back of his leg just below the knee. As he cursed and stumbled, she drew another arrow, waited until he faced her, then shot him in the upper arm. Or had she hit his shoulder? She did not stop to make sure. She ran.

The moon shone on the quiet village. A barking dog rushed towards Alisoun. For a moment, her heart pounded. But she reminded herself that he knew her, had licked her hand a few days earlier when she had passed through with her uncle. As he reached her, he paused, ceased his barking, sniffed the air. Then he cautiously circled round her, sniffing. And again. And again. His circles grew smaller and smaller, but it took five for him to remember her. Then at last he stood in her path and barked once, his tail wagging, demanding her attention. Alisoun dropped to a crouch and patted him, hoping to quiet him.

'Who goes there?' a man shouted from a house.

Alisoun's head shot up. Could he see her? The moon was behind clouds, so she could not identify the vague form in the doorway. But that was good. If she could hardly pick out the man in the gloom, he could not see her well, either.

'Come, boy, come here,' the man called.

The dog hesitated, then ran to him, barking.

At that moment Alisoun took off. She knew that as soon as the dog reached his master, he would head back to Alisoun, barking for his master to follow.

She beat the dog to the church, let herself in, shut the door and slumped down against it, exhausted. Sanctuary at last. He could not come for her here. She could safely sleep, and in the morning she would pray God to forgive her for wounding the man. As she began to nod, she felt a chill draft from beneath the door, where it did not quite meet the stone threshold. Though the day had been hot, the stone church was damp and cool. She crawled away to a more sheltered corner and settled once more. Within moments she was fast asleep.

Twelve

Delirium

Alisoun woke with her heart pounding. The stench of pestilence was strong in the air. She looked round in confusion. Moonlight shone dimly through the windows, illuminating the altar. Now she remembered. She was in the village church. She had come seeking sanctuary after injuring the intruder in the barn.

But the stench. That had not been there when she'd arrived. Shivering with cold and fear, Alisoun probed her armpits, groin, behind her knees, her throat, behind her ears — all the places where pustules had appeared on her family. But she found nothing. Thanks be to God Almighty.

But whence came the foul odour? Perhaps there had been a burial today and the odour lingered? No, that could not be, not without a change of priests, for Father John would not allow the parishioners to bring the corpses into the church. He said they defiled the house of God.

Alisoun stood, looked round, but the

moonlight did not reach the floor. Slowly, inching down along the north wall, she made her way towards the eastern end of the church. As she moved, the stench lessened. At last she found the air more redolent of damp stone and stale incense than pestilence. She settled back down against the wall to resume her night's sleep.

At dawn a curious rat woke her as it sniffed her ankle. She kicked at it, sat up, clutching her pack to her. The stench almost gagged her. Once more she searched her body for signs of pustules, said a prayer of thanksgiving when she found nothing. But whence came such a stench?

She stood, blinked in the soft dawn light. But it was the buzzing of flies that led her to the west door of the church, the door through which she had entered in the night. A child and an elderly one-armed man lay naked on the stones, dumped unceremoniously, the old man's nose to the floor, the boy's arm pinned beneath him. They reeked of pestilence and decay.

Alisoun backed down the aisle to the altar, carefully, fearful lest she trip on yet another corpse. At the altar she knelt, crossed herself, then rose and searched for the sacristy door. It did not open at her first try, so she beat on it. No one answered, but her energetic hammering at last swung it wide. A high window in the dark room illuminated a couple beneath a pile of clothes. The man had opened his eyes.

'Who is there?' he cried out in a voice thick with sleep. Father John.

'What? Someone is here?' the woman squeaked, sitting up quickly, exposing her bare breasts.

After a moment's hesitation, Alisoun pushed past the pair, both now fumbling for their clothes. She did not care who they were, she wanted only to escape. But the room was so dark. She dropped to her knees and crawled round, seeking a draft from beneath a door. At last she found one.

A light suddenly flickered. A lantern that had been shuttered had been opened, and Father John, his clerical gown hastily donned, blinked in the raw light and rubbed his eyes. A village woman held the lantern, her gown now pulled up to hide her nakedness.

Before either of them could focus on her, Alisoun flung open the door and ran out into the dew-drenched cemetery.

She cursed all men — thieves, liars and fornicators — as she stumbled across the mounds and out on to the common fields surrounding the village. A dog barked, perhaps the same one as last night, but she kept running. She must retrieve her horse and leave this curséd place. But where could she go? Where might one find sanctuary if not in a church?

Alisoun sank down in the grass and stared at the empty field. She had searched everywhere — the barn, the surrounding area. She had called and called. But the nag had been stolen. And she knew who had taken her. And the saddle. She should go after him, hunt him down, finish the work she had begun.

But for now all she could do was stare at the empty field and wonder why God so punished her.

Dame Constance escorted Honoria into the waiting area of the infirmary. The young woman had been scrubbing floors, and her veil was tucked into the neckline of her gown, her sleeves rolled up revealing slender forearms. She gave Owen a quizzical look as she curtsied respectfully. He had forgotten how lovely she was. The rumours about her had tarnished his memory.

'Captain Archer wishes to speak with you, Honoria,' Dame Constance said. 'He represents His Grace the Archbishop. Look you show him respect.'

Two lay brothers bustled through the waiting room, eyeing the three with curiosity.

'Is there a more private place we might talk?' Owen asked.

Dame Constance pressed her hands together, glanced aside, thinking. 'There is the gaol. You might speak in Honoria's cell with a guard outside the door.'

'You think she might escape me, Dame Constance?'

The nun coloured. 'Her reputation, Captain Archer. I would not leave His Holiness the Pope alone in a room with her.'

Owen bit back a smile, nodded to Honoria to lead the way. Even the notorious Alice Perrers was trusted in a room alone with a man. What powers did they think Honoria possessed?

In her room, Honoria offered Owen the seat by the window. She perched on the edge of her bed, pushed her sleeves down, folded her hands primly in her lap, but her gaze was frankly curious, studying the scarred side of Owen's face.

'They say a *jongleur*'s leman did that to you.'

'Aye, that she did. They say that you own clothing and goblets far too valuable for you to afford.' Barker, the gatekeeper, had told him about the silks.

A grimace, but the eyes remained level. 'You are quick-witted, Captain Archer.'

'I try not to be so entertained by my wit that I forget my purpose.'

'And what is that?'

'To discover the truth about the recent thefts and deaths at St Leonard's.'

Honoria tilted her head, smiled slightly. 'You think I hold a key to these troubles?'

Too sly, Owen thought. 'Why did you hide the goblets?'

A surprised laugh. 'Is it not obvious, Captain? You see what has happened — precisely what I feared if someone saw them.'

'You might have confided in Don Cuthbert. He has championed you before.'

Now she dropped her head, sighed. 'You are right, of course. But I recognised my folly too late — after Dame Constance had asked us whether we had noticed anything unusual, and I said nothing.'

'Your silence was no lie.'

She met his eye. 'You heard what Dame Constance thinks of me. It is so with all the nuns here. In faith, they think all lay sisters base, with our partial vows and no education. But me . . .' She shook her head sadly.

'Don Cuthbert thinks differently.'

'He did. I fear he does not now.'

'You might have approached him. I should think it preferable to your present circumstance.'

'I did not wish to make trouble for someone who has always treated me fairly. Don Cuthbert is not fond of Master Taverner.'

'Taverner?'

'It was he who gave me the goblets. Long before the ones in the guesthouse disappeared. You may ask him if that is not so.'

If she had meant to surprise Owen, she had certainly succeeded. 'Julian Taverner gave you the goblets?'

'Four years ago. As a wedding present.'

If Owen had ever known she was married, he had forgotten. 'You are widowed, then?'

'A year after we married my husband went off to be a soldier. Whether or no I am a widow I cannot say.'

'You have heard nothing?'

Honoria shook her head. 'I believe he lives. I believe that I would know if he were dead. And so I wait.'

'As a lay sister?'

'I was sent home to my father and his young wife, who did not like my presence.'

'What is Julian Taverner to you?'

'I was a servant in his household when he was still in the city. He said I was much like his daughter. He was kind to me.'

How kind did she mean, Owen wondered.

'Are you wondering whether he bedded me, Captain?'

Owen deserved the discomfort he now felt. 'You are considerate of his reputation.'

'As I have said, he has been good to me.'

'And yet now you deliver him up to me.'

'You are a friend to Master Taverner's niece. I thought I might trust you.'

Owen thought her response much too tidy. 'You are so comfortable in gaol?'

'You do not believe me.'

'You are said to be a woman who likes her comforts.'

'I cannot also be loyal?'

'I shall consider that, Mistress Staines.'

Bess dropped her apron on the counter and hurried after the messenger. Her uncle was ill. Very ill. He had summoned her. Damn the selfish canons. They must have released him from his bed in the infirmary too soon. It was just the sort of neglect John Cooper had hinted about.

She found Julian in his bed, soaked in sweat, complaining of a raging thirst and yet pushing away the bowl of water his elderly servant Nate tried to hold to his lips. 'Find Anneys!' Bess shouted to the messenger, who had accompanied her to her uncle's.

'I sent for her,' Nate said. 'She was busy with a sick child.'

'Then Honoria.'

'I could not find her.'

'Sweet *Jesu*. Then tell Anneys Master Taverner is dying. That should stir her.'

The messenger hurried out.

'I have been —'

'Save what little breath God has left you, uncle. I said that to get her here. Now try to drink some water.'

She told Nate to fetch Brother Wulfstan from St Mary's Abbey.

'You see, uncle? I would not summon such help if I believed you to be dying.' Though she feared she was doing just that.

What frightened Bess as she held a cup of watered wine to her uncle's lips was the thundering of his heartbeat. It was as loud as if she had her ear pressed to his chest. 'Uncle, you must try to lie back, calm yourself. Your heart.'

He blinked and wiped at his eyes as if the sweat blinded him. 'Bess?'

'I am here.'

'Does he —' He shook his head, gasping for air. 'Does he live?'

'Who?'

Julian blinked, reached his bandaged

hands to his eyes. As Bess was about to restrain him, he dropped his hands to his sides. 'They died for him. Was that not enough?' He could manage only a whisper, but he seemed more coherent.

'Who died? For whom?'

Julian jerked his head up, blinking. 'Bess?' His bloodshot eyes did not seem to be focused on her.

'Can you not see me, uncle?'

He turned towards her voice, frowning fiercely. 'Beware.'

'Of whom?'

His bandaged right hand shot up, beat against Bess's shoulder. She grabbed him by the wrist and held him still so that he would not injure his burned hand.

'Or is it her?'

'Who?'

'I have been poisoned, can you not see that?' Julian broke out of her grasp and tried to rise from the bed, but he was so weak she was able to push him down on the pillows. The effort had exhausted him. He lay still, his breath ragged and shallow.

Bess had long ago discounted the popular notion that someone was inflicting the pestilence on enemies by poisoning wells. Not all who drank from the same well sickened; nor did she think that one person could hate so many and not be consumed by his own hatred. 'Rest, uncle. I doubt you have been poisoned. I am here to help you.' She filled a bowl with vinegar and now and then dipped her hands in it to keep her uncle's diseased sweat from seeping through her pores. But as she worked along his body she found no pustules. Neither did he cough. He burned with fever, his skin was flushed and dry, his eyes seemed to be failing and he went in and out of senselessness and panic, but only the fever seemed familiar to the pestilence. Might she be wrong about his ailment? 'What happened, uncle?' she asked gently. 'Why do you speak of poison?'

Julian shook his head. He stared at her with wild eyes while he drank water, gulped air, and at last managed, 'Penance. Not enough. Laurence. Me.' He shook his head. 'He waited so long. Or she.'

Bess was puzzling over those words when Julian sat up, clutching at his heart, tearing at his throat as if to open it for air. She threw herself across him to restrain him and was struggling to reach a sheet on the floor with which to bind him when Owen appeared. Between them they were able to restrain Julian.

'What has happened here?' Owen asked when Julian was quiet.

Bess was about to speak when Anneys appeared with the messenger.

'Is it true? That he is dying?'

Bess crossed herself. 'Listen to his heart. I do not know what causes it to pound so.'

Anneys sank down on a stool. She looked most pitiful. 'Dear God, if he dies I blame myself.'

'Now why would you do that? You have been good to him.'

'I hesitated when he needed me.'

As if she were the only one caring for Julian. 'I hope that my ministrations have not been without merit.'

Julian began to moan. Both women hurried over. 'Bess?'

'I am here, uncle. And Anneys with me.'

'God forgive me.'

'Come, uncle. Take some water.' Bess lifted Julian's fevered head.

Anneys handed her a bowl of water. 'His heart beats so loud.'

'I said so. Come, uncle. Cool water.'

But he shut his eyes and dropped his head to the side. Bess lowered him. And with a shudder, he ceased to breathe. The horrible pounding stopped.

Anneys let out a cry. Bess knelt down beside the bed, staring at her silent uncle in shock. He had been a robust man. His injuries had not been mortal. How could he be dead? She pressed her head to his chest. Silence.

Owen knelt beside Bess, closed Julian's eyes. 'He is with God.'

'Mistress Merchet?' A monk bent over Bess, his youthful face creased in concern. He made the sign of the cross over Bess and Julian. 'I am Henry, Brother Wulfstan's assistant. I came as soon as I might.'

'God bless you for coming,' Bess said, 'but you are too late. My uncle is dead.'

'Has he been shriven?'

'I had no time to send for one of the Austins,' Bess said. 'It happened too quickly.'

'His soul may yet linger.' Brother Henry bent to Julian, called out his name. When he received no response, he glanced up at Bess. 'Shall I say the prayers?'

'I would be most grateful.' She was not fond of the canons of the hospital.

Brother Henry intoned the prayers for the dead and anointed Julian.

'He must be buried quickly,' Anneys said when the monk stepped back from the death-bed. 'We must prepare him.' She was her calm self once more, shaking out a clean sheet.

'Why such haste? He did not die of the

pestilence. There is naught to fear,' Bess said.

'I think that it was pestilence, and so do you. Why else would you have had the bowl of vinegar by your side?'

Bess glanced at Owen, who shook his head. She stayed her tongue.

'I shall tell Don Cuthbert what has happened,' Owen said, hastening out.

As Bess entered St Helen's Square, her cap askew and the stench of her uncle's sweat all over her, his thundering heartbeat echoed in her head. What horror had pushed it to such an extreme? Poisoning. Penance. *He waited so long.* That had been no pestilential fit. Was it possible that he was right, that he had been poisoned? She had seen enough die of the great mortality that she knew it took its victims in many ways, but none like that.

'Good day, Mistress Merchet. Are you well?'

Bess had not noticed Alice Baker standing by Wilton's apothecary, eyeing her with interest. 'Forgive me. My mind was far away.'

'You look tired.'

'God help me, so I am, Mistress Baker.'

Alice Baker shook her head. 'I see you carry no protection.'

'I shall remedy that at once.' Bess nodded to the woman and stepped inside the shop.

Lucie glanced up from a customer, took in Bess's state. 'Jasper!' she called. The boy came through the beaded doorway. 'Forgive me, Master Tyler,' Lucie said to her customer. 'I must see to a friend in need. Jasper will finish this.' She nodded to Bess to follow her to the back.

Seeing the sincere concern in Lucie's eyes, Bess collapsed on to a chair and wept.

Lucie gently patted Bess's back and rubbed it as she would comfort Gwenllian. She knew it was serious, whatever had so upset Bess; she was not given to hysterics, yet now she shook with grief. At last, when Bess quieted, Lucie poured two fingers of brandywine. 'Drink this.'

Bess did so in one tip of her head, then took a deep breath, closed her eyes, pressed her eyelids, sniffed her hands. 'I reek of the death-bed.' Her voice broke on the words and she wept again, more quietly now.

Lucie waited until she quieted once more, refilled her cup. 'Whose death-bed?'

Bess drank, hiccuped. 'Uncle Julian. He is dead. I cannot believe it.'

'How can it be? Surely he did not die of his injuries?'

'He was in such pain.' The tears threatened. Bess blotted her eyes angrily.

Lucie sat down, put her arm round her friend's shoulder. 'Tell me all.'

Amidst much hiccuping, more tears, and three more doses of brandywine, Bess recounted the horror of Julian's last moments. 'Anneys called it pestilence. She is wrong. I am certain of that. And I saw in your husband's face that he doubted it, too.'

Wrong indeed. Lucie had never heard such a combination of symptoms from pestilence. 'Owen was there?'

'I do not know how he came to be, but I was grateful. I could not have quieted him myself.'

Lucie was curious to hear Owen's account. It seemed to her that the symptoms indicated something quite different, not a sickness at all. But she wished to calm Bess, not upset her further. 'Sometimes a head wound can cause troubles long after the injury. A seizure is not uncommon.'

'With such sweating and thirst?'

'I should think it possible.'

'I would have guessed it his heart, not his head.'

'Perhaps. He has suffered injury and the loss of a dear friend. All this might weaken the heart.'

'You are trying to comfort me.'

'I confess that I am. How can I know what brought him down of a sudden?'

Bess patted Lucie's hand, stood up with a sigh, pressing her lower back. 'I am calmer now. I can tell Tom the news without alarming him.'

That evening, as Owen filled squares of cloth with fragrant herbs and Lucie stitched them closed, they spoke of Julian Taverner's death.

'You cannot believe that was a seizure from his head wound,' Owen said. 'Not so long afterwards.'

Now there was a kind lie come back to haunt her. 'I sought the first lie that came to me. I did not wish to tell her what I fear.'

'And what is that?'

'He claimed he had been poisoned. And unless I am much mistaken, a mortal dose of belladonna would cause such a terrible death.'

Owen nodded as he handed her the last square. 'I had much the same thought.'

Lucie sewed the pouch closed, put the basket of work aside. As she went to the window for some air, she said, 'I do not like to think it, my love. Not with your business at the hospital. But Julian suggested it. And with Walter de Hotter's death, the attacks, and the thefts . . .'

Owen joined her, slid his arms round her. 'What trouble has shattered St Leonard's peace?'

Lucie pressed his hands. 'Whatever it is' — she turned in his arms — 'you must take great care, my love.'

'Why did you not tell Bess of your suspicion?'

'Your task will be difficult enough without Bess hounding you.'

'You are good to think of that. What is the thread that connects them, eh? Walter, Laurence, Julian, the thefts . . .'

'Have you seen Ravenser?'

'Tomorrow. I thought today to speak with Edward Munkton and Honoria de Staines.'

'Ah. Honoria. Everyone who comes into the shop has something to say about her, and none of it kind.'

'She claims Julian Taverner gave her the goblets. As a wedding present.'

When Bess disliked her so? 'What did Julian say?'

'He was dead before I could ask.'

Lucie crossed herself. 'Do you think her a thief or a murderer?'

'Both. Neither. I do not know.'

'Julian spoke of a man running from

Laurence's burning house.'

'Honoria's missing husband?'

A jealous husband suited the woman. 'She has been in gaol for several days.'

'But she has the freedom of St Leonard's by day to go about her duties.'

'Perhaps Bess will remember Julian giving the goblets to Honoria.'

'What was Honoria to Julian, I wonder?'

'You can be sure Bess has an opinion about that.'

Thirteen

Bess's Complaint

The master's house at St Leonard's, though merely of timber, was comfortably large and well appointed with several glazed windows. Bess's knock was answered at once by a round man in a plain clerical gown, obviously more than just a servant. Bess adjusted her beribboned cap and stated her intention to speak with the master.

The clerk looked pained. 'God go with you, Mistress Merchet. Your uncle was a good man. May he rest in peace.'

'I intend to ensure that he does. Now I must see your master.'

'Sir Richard is resting. Perhaps tomorrow would be more —'

'Not tomorrow, no. I spoke with your master a few days ago and he invited me to come when I would. And I am here today.'

'But on such a day, Mistress Merchet . . .' Ravenser had just officiated at Julian's burial.

'My uncle is at rest. I cannot be until I speak with Sir Richard.'

With a sigh, the clerk invited her to stand just inside the door. He disappeared through an archway, and, faintly, Bess heard a sharp greeting, murmured words, then nothing. She glanced round, noted some bags still lying in the middle of the hall, unopened. Good. Sir Richard deserved to be inconvenienced, neglecting her uncle as he had done. She had been polite to him in public, but she meant to give him a piece of her angry mind. And something to ponder. She wandered over to the bags, crouched down, felt the leather. Supple. Expensive. Of course. They said Sir Richard set his sights as high as his uncle Thoresby's standing. He must have many prebends as well as his posts in chancery and in the Queen's household to pay for such leather. Bess sidled back towards the door as footsteps approached.

The clerk bowed respectfully, but his eyes expressed his disapproval. 'Sir Richard will see you now. I pray you, come this way.' Turning on his heels, he proceeded to lead her whence he'd come.

Bess followed with a grim determination.

As Richard de Ravenser rose from his chair and came forward to greet her, Bess thought how much more like his uncle he looked now than when last they had met several years before. Ravenser's lips, however, were thinner than the archbishop's. Cold, prim lips. This man did not live life to its fullest as she suspected his uncle had in his youth.

'Mistress Merchet. I imagine you have come about your uncle's untimely death. I assure you that we had every confidence he was sufficiently recovered to return to his home.' Ravenser motioned Bess to a straight-backed chair beside a small table on which were set a flagon of wine and two cups.

How civilised. Not everyone treated an innkeeper so. Bess took a seat.

Ravenser nodded to a servant, who had silently replaced the clerk, to pour wine. 'You will share some with me?'

'I would be honoured, Sir Richard.' Bess passed the cup under her nose, noted the strong bouquet. Ravenser's palate differed from his uncle's, with which she was familiar, for they often traded barrels of Tom's ale for casks from the archbishop's excellent cellar at Bishopthorpe. But a taste reassured her; a serviceable wine.

'Forgive me for not advising Douglas to expect you.'

'Perhaps it was best. More warning might have given him more arguments.'

'I assure you that his reluctance was not meant to offend you. He knows that the heat has brought on one of my headaches. He believes I should rest.'

Bess noted with interest that Ravenser's hand shook as he raised the cup to his thin lips: more than an ordinary headache. Watching him taste his wine, she noted the studied grace and delicacy of his movements, set off well by his elegant garments. Perhaps he was more like his uncle than she had at first thought. He glanced up at her quizzically.

'Forgive me, but you look so like His Grace the Archbishop.'

'Many say so. Would that I had his wisdom as well as his features.'

A comment meant to soften her. But Bess was not about to let Ravenser's troubles overwhelm her purpose. 'Wisdom. Yes, well, perhaps not. Was it wise to send my uncle from the infirmary so soon? Has it occurred to you that his death might be the direct result of your haste to empty his bed?'

A flush darkened the pale face of the Master of St Leonard's. 'Master Taverner was still under our care. His house is not so far —'

'Oh aye. But when his servant sent for Anneys she did not come. Only after I sent word my uncle was dying did she answer the summons.'

Ravenser pressed his fingers to his temples, closed his eyes. 'Mistress Merchet —'

'Would it interest you to hear that my uncle believed he had been poisoned?'

The sunken eyes snapped open. 'What?'

'Poisoned. That is what he said.'

'By whom?'

She would not yet tell him she did not know. 'Your cellarer hounded my uncle, you know. Questioned him about why Master Warrene returned to his house instead of tending the fire. Don Cuthbert thought he might have been hiding the items that have been missed round the spital. Now what do you think of that? Tormenting my uncle, injured and mourning, with such dangerous nonsense.'

Ravenser dropped his hands to his lap and seemed to fall into a deep study of them.

'Much goes on here without your knowledge, Sir Richard. I realise that you are an important man in Westminster. But you should know your people. Laurence a thief?' Bess shook her head. 'A man wealthy enough to buy corrodies at your great hospital for both him and his wife. And what of these thefts? What do you know of them?'

Without raising his eyes or moving in the least, Ravenser said, 'We were speaking of Julian Taverner's death. What do the thefts have to do with him?'

'What had they to do with Laurence?'

'I shall speak with Don Cuthbert about his accusations.'

'What of Honoria de Staines? They say you have her in close confinement. What has she to say for herself?'

'She is not your concern, Mistress Merchet. But I assure you I mean to discover the truth of all this.'

Bess ignored the impatient note in Ravenser's reply. 'On the day of the fire my uncle and Laurence de Warrene were attacked. Have you any idea who the attacker was? Was it the thief? Might it not be wise to find the culprit? Must I —'

Ravenser lifted a hand. 'Mistress Merchet, I should like to reassure you that I am doing everything I can to learn what has transpired here. But before I tell you anything, I require your reassurance that you will say nothing to anyone.'

So, despite his earlier courtesy, he thought of her as a lowly innkeeper given to gossip. 'One's status does not make one more or less discreet, Sir Richard.'

Ravenser pressed his temples. 'Forgive my clumsiness. I merely meant to warn you that secrecy is necessary at present.'

'You might better worry when you have

some information to keep silent about.'

'I hope soon to have such information. Archbishop Thoresby has agreed that Captain Archer may assist me.'

'He has?' Bess was of two minds about that. Owen was the best man to see through the murk, and that satisfied her. But that the archbishop had offered him meant something was indeed amiss. Lucie would not like Owen's involvement. Would she blame Bess for it? Still, appointing Owen to the task proved that Ravenser meant to do something. 'St Leonard's is cursed at present.'

In a breathless voice, Ravenser said, 'I would not say so, Mistress Merchet. Cursed is a strong word. I merely wish to discover the truth. Now pray, forgive me, I have a pounding in my head that will soon drown out all sound from without. I apologise on behalf of St Leonard's for your uncle's death. If, indeed, we were at fault.'

Bess rose and bowed slightly. She had many questions, but the Master of St Leonard's was quite visibly in distress. 'God give you comfort, Sir Richard. You might send your servant round to Mistress Wilton for a physick.'

'I have one of her admirable medicines, Mistress Merchet. It awaits me in my chamber. God go with you.' Ravenser courteously led her to the door, opened it. Douglas came scuttling to help Ravenser away, then shortly returned to let Bess out into the dusty yard.

Bess stayed the door with her hand. 'I certainly did not think my mission so distressing as to make him ill.'

'Sir Richard needed to rest after the burial. The hot sun. Had you heeded my advice . . .'

'I should have as great a headache as he. God go with you.'

Fourteen

Complexity

At Lucie's urging, Owen walked out into the quiet streets of early morning, heading for Magda Digby's house. It was just dawn and the gatekeeper had to be wakened, but soon the Riverwoman would begin her day, going among the sick outside the city walls and in the countryside and Owen wished to talk to her about Julian Taverner's death before he met with Ravenser later that day.

'Perhaps Bess should tell the tale,' Lucie had suggested.

'And when Magda says it is likely he was poisoned, what then?'

Lucie had looked up from the unguent she was mixing slowly over a low flame and met Owen's gaze with a crooked smile. 'My effort to keep that from Bess would have been in vain. And she would drive you mad.'

'Just so. When I have problems enough, thanks to His Grace.'

'Do not pretend that you are not keen to

put an end to the troubles at the hospital.'

'You foresee that? I had hoped merely to understand them.'

'Where will you begin?'

'I depend on Magda having heard something that might show me where to look.' All rumours in York quickly reached the Riverwoman.

As Owen waited for the summoned gatekeeper he thought about Honoria de Staines, the butt of so much suspicion. Julian's death had made it difficult to judge her. Lucie was right — he must ask Bess what she knew of the gift. And whether there was animosity between Honoria's husband and Julian. A conversation he dreaded.

' 'Tis just dawn,' a voice muttered above his head. 'Who goes there?'

'Captain Archer on the archbishop's business.'

An oath, silence, then the clanking of keys beyond the night door, the grinding of the key in the lock. The door swung wide with a groaning protest. The gatekeeper was not much cheerier.

'Business could not wait?'

'No.'

'Go on with 'ee then, Captain.' Dan stepped back to let Owen through.

Owen remembered something Lucie had

said a few days past. 'Your little one. She has recovered?'

Silence. Owen glanced round as the door was closing, caught Dan wiping his night-creased face on his sleeve. 'May she rest in peace,' Owen murmured and hurried on his way, cursing himself for waking a man who much needed his sleep. Dan and his wife had other children, but little Angelique had been their youngest and dearest, a fair, sweet-voiced girl not much older than Gwenllian. When Owen was out of sight of the gate he crossed himself and said a prayer for his own children.

Smoke from Magda's cook fire rose through the hole in the upside-down Viking ship that served as her roof. Still here, then. Magda was never careless with her fire, though her home sat on a rock in the mud flats and so was isolated by water or at the least mud from the flotsam and jetsam houses clustered against the walls of St Mary's Abbey and the city beyond. Owen knocked. As he waited, he fancied he heard a whinny nearby. Peering round the corner, he came face to face with a horse.

'So Magda is to ride today, eh, beauty?'

'Thou'rt out and about betimes, Bird-eye,' Magda said from the doorway. 'Dost thou remember Mistress Ffulford's nag?'

'I did not recognise her.'

'The child groomed her better than her recent keepers did.'

Owen ran his hand down the horse's mane, discovered a sticky concoction near the shoulder. 'Injured?'

'Aye. But she will mend. Come within.'

Owen bent low to clear the lintel. 'The girl is here?'

'Nay. Only the beast.'

'Her kin sold it when they took her in?'

Hitching up her patchwork skirts, Magda lowered herself on to a stool by the fire, picked up a bowl and spoon. 'Thou canst play riddlemaster all the day, Magda will not stop thee. But which answer is true she cannot say. Hast thou broken thy fast?'

'I have. But I would not say no to a cup of ale.' He told her of his encounter with the gatekeeper.

'Fetch thy own drink. Thou knowst where Magda keeps it.' She chewed on her breakfast for a while.

Owen settled on the rushes by the fire circle, drank half the cup of ale in one tilt of the head.

'What brings thee to Magda at dawn, Bird-eye?'

He told her about the task he faced at the

hospital. 'I am wondering whether Julian Taverner's death has aught to do with the thefts.'

'Taverner. Aye. Magda heard of his death. Not the manqualm?'

When Owen described Julian's symptoms and his odd last words, Magda closed her eyes, nodded.

'Belladonna. Aye, 'tis fitting. Taverner was one to have enemies.'

'Enemies at the hospital?'

'That is for thee to discover.' Magda set aside her bowl, reached for a cup, drank. 'But mark this. Taverner's inn was small compared with the York Tavern. Yet he owned costly plate, paid dearly for a corrody at St Leonard's. Have the Merchets such wealth?'

'He was a smuggler.' Owen downed the rest of his ale. 'But so are they all in Scarborough.'

Magda barked in laughter. 'A goodly number is all, eh? Men are keen to make rules of such things. Seldom of use.'

'Even so. With so *many* about the same business in Scarborough, why would Julian Taverner be particularly likely to have enemies?'

'Now Magda makes a rule. A man with no enemies does not think of poisoning. But thou wilt find the truth.'

'I cannot see how it was done. He was tended by Bess, the lay sisters, and his servant, and had the walls of the hospital round him. How did the poisoner reach him?'

'Aye. Thou hast much work ahead of thee.' Magda put aside her cup, stretched as she rose.

'Honoria de Staines spends her nights in St Leonard's gaol, did you know?'

'Aye. For owning glass and silks above her station.' Magda lifted a pouch from a peg, carried it to her work table.

Owen followed. 'I wonder whether they have been right about her guilt, wrong about her sin. She was much with Julian Taverner.'

As Magda filled the bag with simples and such, she said, 'Honoria served him two years before she wed. She *would* be much with him.'

'Were they lovers?'

'And for that she poisoned him?' Magda crossed to her fire circle, crouched beside it.

'What of her missing husband?'

'She loved him. Fair poisoned herself trying to get with child for him.'

'She is barren?'

Magda wagged her head as she spread the embers and covered them. 'So many men and never quickening? Aye. He beat her, blamed her. But 'twas folk's grins poisoned him for her. She will not see him again.'

'You do not think he returned to have his revenge?'

Magda barked with laughter. 'Thou'rt so desperate as to believe that?' She began to rise, refused Owen's proffered hand. 'Away with thee. Magda must begin her day.' She closed the pouch, slung it over her shoulder.

As Owen stepped into the daylight, the horse greeted him. 'Where did you find her?'

'Tied without a tumbledown hut. Folk said a stranger abandoned the horse at the city gate when a cart tipped over, frightening it.'

'You believed them?'

' 'Twas too grand a catch for them. So Magda asked about the stranger. Clerk's gown, wounded in arm and leg, and in too much pain to calm the beast.'

'And he did not return for it?'

'Nay.'

'How do you come to have it?'

'Magda predicted they would have trouble trading it.'

'What will you do with it?'

'Climb upon the beast's back and ride upriver.'

'You are concerned about the child.'

Magda shooed him off. 'Thou hast thy

worries, Magda has hers.'

Tom Merchet glanced up from his work as Owen entered the dimly lit tavern. 'Any news of my godchild?' With the archbishop, Tom shared the honour of being godfather to Hugh.

'We may have some soon. His Grace is stopping there to tell Tildy of her brother's death.'

'He is good to do it. Few messengers on road these days.'

'Aye. Is Bess about?'

'In kitchen. Cook is ailing. A blistered hand. Much better thanks to Lucie's unguent. Wife tells me you mean to avenge Julian.'

'Holy Mary. Such a rumour —'

Tom silenced Owen with a slap on the back. 'Rest easy. She said nothing like.' His round face was jolly. 'But she did say you are to help Sir Richard with his troubles.'

'That I am. I must be off to see him midday. I thought I might speak with Bess about her uncle.'

'Keep up a chatter and she will be out here.'

Owen sat down across from Tom, touched the corner of the table the innkeeper had been smoothing. 'What happened here?'

'A bench brought down sharp on table.'

'And a customer?'

'Aye. He will live. And his attacker paid well for damage.'

It was a good thing Tom Merchet was well padded with bulk and muscle. An innkeeper could never be too strong.

'Tell me what you know of Julian Taverner.'

Tom sanded for a while, gathering his thoughts. 'Owned an inn at Scarborough harbour. Swan, he called it. And as all men from Scarborough, he was fond of ships grounded in foul weather.' Tom's prejudice had more to do with Bess's fond memories of her first husband, a clerk in Scarborough.

But there was perhaps some truth in what he implied; Magda too had suggested that Julian's money had come from somewhere other than the inn. 'He emptied the broken hulls?'

Tom laughed. 'Aye. Most like. While a taverner. But when his wife and daughter drowned in a storm, he changed. Blamed himself for the drowning, though he was nowhere near. Sudden storm, even the best get caught. He called it his punishment. And when pestilence came to Scarborough, he took it as his penance, went out and took care of folk left to die.'

'Punishment for what?'

'A leman, most like. What else? Though he never spoke of it.'

'Telling tales, husband?' Bess stood braced in the doorway that led out to the kitchen.

'You have a better answer, wife?'

Bess joined them at the table. 'Is it true, then, Owen? You have offered to help Sir Richard?'

'Offered? Nay. I have been ordered by His Grace.'

'No matter. However you come to it, I am pleased. You will put my mind at ease and that is all I can ask now he's dead.'

'I fear I might disappoint you.'

'Nay. You are too shrewd.'

'Then you will not mind if I pry a bit, eh? Do you know any of his old comrades from his smuggling days?'

Bess reared back. 'Smuggling? Who told you that?'

'He lived well in Scarborough, Bess.'

'The Swan is a fine inn now. It was grand when Julian ran it.'

'This is a fine inn. But could you afford a corrody at St Leonard's?'

'Nay. But you would do well to look elsewhere. John Cooper had somewhat to say about the deaths at the hospital.'

Owen waved away the rumour. 'I have heard it. Unholy and dangerous gossip, Bess. See that you do not repeat it. And none are to know what I am about, eh?'

'You can trust us,' Tom said.

Bess said nothing, but her injured expression reassured Owen.

'I have something else on my mind that you might help me understand, Bess.'

'Oh? And what might that be?'

'Honoria de Staines.'

Bess sniffed. 'Impudent harlot.'

Owen told her of his conversation with Honoria, though he did not mention it fell on the day of Julian's death.

'Goblets of Italian glass?' Bess shook her head. 'I knew the old man had been a fool about her, but goblets of Italian glass!'

'You did not attend the wedding?'

'I did not! Shameless hussy. I feared a child would arrive in short order with my uncle's eyes and nose, and our family's thick hair.'

Then Honoria's barrenness was not common knowledge. 'So he had bedded her?'

'I would think it more the other way. She lured him.'

'You have proof of this?'

'It is her nature, my friend. Why? Has this aught to do with my uncle's death?'

'No. Not at all. Just the goblets. They are very like the ones stolen from the master's house.'

'Ah. Well. She has no need to steal, that woman. She makes her money on her back, she does.'

'Your uncle witnessed their vows. Was he a friend of the groom?'

'Nay. He thought it a foolish match.'

'There was enmity between them?'

Bess made a face. 'He did not cuckold the young man, if that is what you are thinking.'

It was plain Owen could not rely on Bess's opinions in this.

The daylight burned his eyes as Brother Wulfstan stepped outside after a long vigil with the latest plague victim.

John Tyler, so recently bereaved, called from the doorway, 'Do you need an arm to steady you on your way?'

Brother Wulfstan shook his head, waved away the man's concern. 'See to your own, Master Tyler.' He had lost wife and infant, but he had yet a son and daughter to tend. 'You were a brave man to stay with them till the end. Many do not.'

'God bless you, Brother Wulfstan.'

The old monk turned down the alley that

led to Holy Trinity, Goodramgate.

'God go with you, Brother Wulfstan,' a nasal voice called in the dimness beneath the overhanging houses.

Wulfstan halted, squinted into the shadows. 'God go with you. Are you in need?'

A man limped out into the poor light. 'I am injured.'

An injury was a welcome change from plague sores. 'Come. Let us go forward into the churchyard. The light will allow these old eyes to examine your injury.'

They walked down the alley into the open yard.

'Feel the heat of this,' the man said, guiding Wulfstan's hand to a wound in his upper arm.

Wulfstan set his bag of medicines and bandages down, felt at the wound. 'Your sleeve prevents my examination.' There was but a small tear in the sleeve over the injury. 'Come with me to St Mary's. There I can remove your gown, clean the wound and bandage it.'

The man shook his head.

Wulfstan noted that the man's gown smelled strongly of horse sweat. He glanced up at the man's face, could match no name to it. 'You are a stranger in York?'

'Aye. I was attacked on the road.'

‘How do you come to know my name?’

‘I heard it spoken as you came out into the street.’

That might be so. ‘Why did you not go to St Mary’s?’

One question too many. The man lunged for Wulfstan’s bag of medicines and bandages. The old monk grabbed it, a foolish gesture. A yank and a push and he was on the ground clutching air. By the time Wulfstan struggled to his knees, he could see no sign of his attacker. Merciful God he was dizzy. And his heart pounded so. He dropped his head to his hands and knelt there quietly for a few moments until his heart slowed and he thought he might trust his balance enough to rise and walk. He felt a fool.

Once more the morning had been quiet in the shop. Lucie was about to send Jasper off to work in the garden when a form darkened the doorway. He was stooped with age, unsteady on his feet. Lucie did not at once recognise the infirmarian of St Mary’s, but Jasper dropped the powder he was measuring back into the jar and hurried to assist Brother Wulfstan to a seat.

‘Find the brandywine in the back room,’ Lucie ordered Jasper as she knelt to her old friend and dabbed at the scrapes on his cheek and forehead. 'Did you take a fall?'

'I did. And lost my bag.'

'When you have had some brandywine you must tell Jasper where you dropped it.'

'And then I shall help you back to the abbey,' Jasper said as he handed Wulfstan a cup of brandywine.

Wulfstan's hands shook too badly to hold it. As Lucie helped him lift the cup to his lips, she noticed blood on his left hand. 'You thought to catch your fall?'

Wulfstan said nothing, just drank.

Lucie wanted to weep, seeing him so weak. He asked too much of himself. Surely God did not require such sacrifice from a man who had spent his life helping others. When she lowered the cup from his lips, Wulfstan closed his eyes and smiled faintly.

'Better. I pray you, do not fuss. I would sit here and collect my wits is all. Brother Henry must not see me like this.'

'You must rest,' Lucie said. 'Let us help you to the pallet in the workroom.'

Fifteen

A Clash of Wills

Ravenser sat with elbows on the arms of his chair, hands steepled before his chest. So like his uncle, Owen thought. A deceptive likeness, for he found himself responding to the man as if he were Thoresby and then receiving an unexpected reaction. Ravenser was subtly different from his uncle. At the moment he was politely disagreeing with Owen.

'You waste your time trying to connect the thefts with the deaths of Hotter, Warrene and Taverner.'

Ravenser's uncle would have given it some thought.

'So much trouble erupting independently seems too much of a coincidence, Sir Richard. Not that I am at all certain one follows from the other, or which came first, or why. But so much trouble in so short a time in one establishment . . .'

A tilt of the head, a nod, as if seeing the point at last. Then a sharper nod. A decision. 'I trust you, Captain. I shall try to stay out of your way. You are most welcome, I assure you. But then I asked for your assistance, you know. His Grace was not keen when I approached him. He had other plans for you.'

So it was true. Ravenser had requested his help. Still, 'His Grace takes great pleasure in ordering my life.'

Ravenser gave a surprised laugh. 'You —' He shook his head. 'I am not accustomed to hearing my uncle spoken of in such a way.'

'I meant no disrespect. He is a great man.'

'But difficult when in a foul temper. Which he is of late.'

'He tells me the Queen is failing.'

Ravenser bowed his head. 'The realm will be the worse for the loss of Queen Phillippa.'

'His Grace particularly.'

'And adding gall to his wound, Mistress Alice Perrers gave birth to a daughter.'

'Has our King sired another bastard?'

'Perhaps not. Much is made of the fact that she is christened Blanche. They are quite certain she was named for the fair Blanche of Lancaster.' John of Gaunt's beloved wife had died the previous autumn. 'And if so, why? Might Lancaster be the father?'

Owen grinned. 'Mistress Perrers has a taste for power.'

Ravenser did not smile. 'And Lancaster a taste for beautiful women. I think it unlikely he would bed Perrers.'

'But His Grace thinks it possible?' Owen did. He thought there were few women in the kingdom who wove a more attractive web than Alice Perrers.

'He thinks it possible indeed. And he is furious. He hoped to enlist the duke's aid in ridding court of Perrers . . .'

'I should think that with Death reaching out for the Queen, the King would depend on Mistress Perrers more than ever.'

Ravenser massaged his temples. 'God might do better purging court than purging the city of York. Such petty jealousies.'

So he did not approve of Thoresby's interest in the matter. Owen thought it time to return to the matter at hand. 'How many know that I am assisting you in this?'

'Don Cuthbert, the cellarer. Have you been introduced?'

'We have met.'

Ravenser winced. 'He is a good man, I assure you, and he has agreed to assist you in any way you request. Within the rule of the hospital, of course.'

'Of course.'

'Don Erkenwald also knows. In fact it was he who alerted me to the problems.'

'He is a good man. So they are the only ones who know my purpose here?'

A sigh. 'And without the hospital, Mistress Merchet. I thought to reassure her that I did not disregard her uncle's claim that he was poisoned.'

'An appropriate gesture. Just the three, yourself and me, then?'

'Yes. And I should prefer to keep it from the others.'

Was the man a simpleton? 'I do not see how, Sir Richard. They will notice that I am about. Secrecy will make my task doubly hard.' He could see that Ravenser did not consider it his problem but Owen's. In that he was like his uncle.

'Perhaps if you spoke only of the thefts,' Ravenser suggested.

'And when I ask whether anyone remembers anything out of joint the day of the fire? Or whether Walter de Hotter argued with someone?'

Ravenser drummed his fingers on the arms of the chair as he considered that. 'Might we invent more thefts? Something missing from Laurence de Warrene's house? And something from Hotter's?'

'I do not advise a lie. Besides, there is the matter of Warrene's house being so thoroughly burned.'

Ravenser flushed, but attempted to hide his embarrassment with a brusque tone. 'I understand you spoke to Mistress Staines.'

Owen had wondered why Ravenser did not mention her. 'I did. And I am curious. Why confine her at night, but let her go about freely during the day?'

'I thought we might learn something by watching her — where she goes, to whom she speaks.'

'And if she is dangerous?'

'She cannot leave the hospital.'

'Some have died within St Leonard's, Sir Richard.'

A sharp intake of breath. 'I am aware of that, Captain. But neither you nor I believe Mistress Staines is a murderer, do we? She covets her neighbours' riches. How does she explain the goblets?'

'She says Julian Taverner presented them to her at her wedding four years ago. But he was dead before I could ask him whether she spoke the truth.'

'Why would she hide them if they were hers?'

'She says she heard about the missing goblets and feared she would not be believed. Dame Constance, for one, thinks Mistress Staines quite cunning.'

'What do you think?'

'Have you learned aught by watching her movements these past days?'

'As far as I know, no. Would you have me release her?'

'Not yet.'

'Ah.' Ravenser nodded. 'Good. As I said, I shall retreat into the shadows and allow you to proceed as you see fit. But I pray you, resolve this quickly and with as little information reaching the city as possible, or St Leonard's reputation may be destroyed. And without the goodwill of the people . . .'

'I have not yet begun and you are urging me to finish, Sir Richard? Then I ask you to pray for me.'

'I express myself awkwardly. But I think it advisable to be frank with you. It is an honour to be master of this hospital. Are you aware that it is the largest such institution in this realm outside London?'

'I have heard that claim.'

Ravenser drew himself up. 'It is not an idle claim. It is true. And to be the master of such a hospital, which gives solace to the ill, the elderly, the abandoned . . . I doubt that I need tell you that it lends a man a certain respectability. But where there is much to gain there is also much to lose. Were the hospital to fail . . .' Ravenser turned to the window and allowed silence to emphasise his last words.

Owen considered the man, trying to decide why he wished it were Thoresby sitting in that chair, not Ravenser. Perhaps it was because he sensed a secretiveness in Ravenser with which Thoresby did not bother. Even with his blunt acknowledgement of his ambitious motive in saving the hospital, the man still hid much.

He also exaggerated.

'Why should the hospital fail because of the thefts and, related or not, the odd deaths of several corrodians, Sir Richard?'

Ravenser reached for his cup of wine, sipped while studying Owen over the rim. A trick of his uncle's. Had he studied his uncle's techniques? 'Debt, Captain. And debt requires donors. I had been promised the receipts from the Lammas Fair this summer, but alas . . .' Ravenser set the cup down, leaned forward. 'Don Cuthbert has insulted the goldsmiths, a guild from whom I might have hoped for generous gifts; rumours are rampant in the city, which destroys my chances with other wealthy citizens; the late mayor and I quarrelled and the present mayor seems to know something of it. If this continues, we shall be ruined. It is that simple.'

'What of the possibility that there is a murderer in your midst? Does that not worry you at all?'

Journeys were seldom direct for the Riverwoman. Folk passing would mention a sick friend, a peculiar plant growing in the wood or on the riverbank, an animal lying injured on a track, and she would reorganise her day. Those awaiting her call knew not to expect her at a particular time, but they also knew that she would come, even if it were long after sunset. It was said she had better night vision than a cat.

It was mid-afternoon before Magda led the nag up the track to the Ffulford farm. She had no reason to expect the child to be there except that it felt right. Time enough to move on to Alisoun's kin if the farm was deserted. Magda tethered the nag to a branch out of sight of the barn, a nice grassy spot to entice her into quietly grazing. Then the midwife moved up the track on foot.

All was still. But someone watched her, she was certain. As she meandered round the yard, checking sheds and circling the barn and the house, she glanced at the area from which she sensed the eyes. A dark shadow against the trunk of an oak satisfied her. The child hid in the tree, observing Magda's exploration. It was not a tree from which Alisoun might glimpse the horse.

On her next circuit, Magda entered the house, checked that the child yet had food, admired Alisoun's cleverness. She came for the food stored within, but walked in the shadows so that the floor looked dusty, the house uninhabited.

Outside, Magda made her way to the barn, struggled with the door, opening it wide. Inside, she examined the hay, thought to pull some fresh hay down for the nag, but, remembering the child's defence of the loft, changed her mind. The child might be clever enough to fashion a trap. Magda had no time for that.

Satisfied that the child was present, and well enough to feed herself and keep her wits about her, Magda retrieved the nag, led her into her stall in the barn. Emerging into the bright sunshine, Magda sighed. It had been pleasant, having a mount for a day. But the gods had given her feet for a purpose.

Beneath the child's tree, Magda paused, shading her eyes against the sun as she peered up into the branches. A dirty foot confirmed her suspicions. 'Magda has returned thy property. Thou shouldst not be so generous, child, to loan a stranger thy horse, be he wounded or no. Magda lives beneath the dragon ship upriver from York.

Thou canst find her there.'

Her mission accomplished, Magda took her way home.

Owen held the dark red knight in his palm, felt its heft. 'Fine ivory. Heavy. How would a set of such pieces be removed without the servants noting it, I wonder? Where was the set kept?'

Ravenser had retired to his room with a headache. Douglas had been offered as a guide. The plump clerk indicated a trunk on the opposite side of the room, near the window. 'On that trunk, but the side farthest from the window.'

'I was not thinking the thief reached in for it. Standing so at a window, reaching in for each piece, a man would be noticed.'

Douglas ducked his head. 'Of course.'

Owen had not meant to embarrass the man. He liked Douglas. The man had so far dealt with him without guile. 'Be thankful you have no need to think of such things.'

'To be observant is a skill one might use for many tasks.'

'Where were the candlesticks?'

'By the door,' Douglas said, pointing towards a shelf conveniently placed for one entering the room to set down or pick up a light.

'Can you show me from where the other items were taken?'

'Some of them. A few the cellarer will need to show you. The blankets, for example. But I can show you where items disappeared from in the church.'

Vespers over, Don Cuthbert headed to his garden. That morning he had encountered two black rats on the path, their snouts twitching with delight over an early apple, a bruised windfall that should have been found long before it rotted and attracted the noxious creatures. Cuthbert had ordered a servant to search for any more rotting fruit hidden beneath the foliage in the vegetable bed. As he approached, he noted a dark-gowned figure hurrying away from him and bristled with indignation. Did she think to escape his inspection? No doubt she had idled away the afternoon. He strode into the garden, fists clenched, ready to give battle.

But it was the lay sister Anneys who turned as he called out. She clutched a dark bundle and looked ill at ease. As she should. Lay sisters were not invited to walk in this garden.

'*Benedicte*, Don Cuthbert.'

'*Benedicte*. Might I ask what errand brings you into the cellarer's garden?'

She held her burden out to him. It was a leather pouch. 'I noticed this as I walked past. Lying in the path. I thought someone had dropped it, but then I discovered no one about.'

Cuthbert held out his hands. 'I shall take it. Now if you would —'

Anneys withdrew the offering and took a step backwards. 'It is naught that might be of use to you.'

'You opened it?'

A smile meant to disarm. 'For a good cause, I assure you. I thought to discover to whom I should return it.'

'And who is that?'

'It contains medicines and bandages. Perhaps Master Saurian the physician dropped it.'

'Master Saurian fled the city at the first sign of pestilence, as you know. But in truth, were he here he would have no more business in my garden than you do.'

At last Cuthbert detected some discomfort. Anneys lifted her shoulders in a gesture of defeat. 'Someone in the infirmary?'

'I have no time for childish guessing games.' Cuthbert straightened to his full height, but the damnable woman still towered a head above him. No matter. He had the authority. He held out his hand. 'I will have it. And you will return to your duties.'

'But —'

'I will suffer no arguments.'

The woman dropped the bag in his hands and hurried away.

Medicines, she had said. Cuthbert had seen Captain Archer following the master's clerk across the yard earlier. Might he have misplaced this while he snooped in the garden? It tickled Cuthbert to think of the one-eyed spy searching for his pouch. It was wrong of the master to engage an outsider. The man had no right to be here, no right to question the canons and nuns. Or the lay brothers and sisters. So. His pouch. Cuthbert thought he might put it safely away and then forget about it.

Sixteen

Unsavoury Characters

Brother Wulfstan awoke confused. Had he moved his cot? The window should be above his head, not across the room. And so far across. His cell was not so long. He closed his eyes, felt his head. Often when he burned with fever he felt as if he were shrinking or the room expanding. He remembered that feeling from childhood. So long ago. Why could he remember that, but not whether he had moved his cot? But of two things he was certain. He had no fever, and his window was in the wrong place.

'Brother Wulfstan?' a low, gentle voice. Female. 'Brother Wulfstan, are you awake?'

He opened his eyes. Lucie Wilton leaned over him, her eyes dark with worry.

'Why has my window moved?' he asked.

Lucie frowned, obviously finding it puzzling, too.

'I knew it was not right,' Wulfstan said.

Lucie pressed his hand. 'You are in the workroom of the apothecary. Remember?

You fell in the street.'

Fell in the street? He remembered no — Ah. The stranger. He flexed his hand, felt the scraped flesh already tightening. 'Yes. I caught the fall with my hand.'

Lucie nodded. 'And cut your cheek.'

His right knee burned, too. 'He wanted my medicines.'

Lucie frowned. 'He?'

'The stranger.'

She glanced round to someone behind her.

Jasper stepped forward. 'Shall I help you sit up?'

'Bless you, my son. I would like that.'

The lad was strong, which was good, for Wulfstan found it was difficult for him to bend in the middle without much groaning, which would worry Lucie. He must have bruised half his body in his fall. When Jasper let him down he rejoiced in the plump cushions stacked behind him. Sinfully comfortable.

Lucie sat in a chair beside him, holding a bowl of fragrant broth. 'Shall I help you?'

An undignified way to eat, but far less embarrassing than spilling it over himself. The nourishment cleared away the cobwebs.

'You were attacked?'

Had he told her? Perhaps. Henry told him

he often muttered in his sleep. 'The stranger did not mean to attack me. I asked too many questions.'

'God help us if that is now the accepted response to curiosity.' Lucie poured a cup of watered wine, handed it to Wulfstan.

He was pleased to discover his hand was much steadier. As steady as it ever was at his age. Seeing the determined set to Lucie's strong jaw, Wulfstan launched into a full account of the incident. Soon his knee was covered with a soothing ointment and bandaged. And just in time. Simon, the Merchets' groom, waited without with a donkey cart to take Wulfstan home.

'I do not need that,' Wulfstan protested. How would he explain it without alarming Brother Henry and Abbot Campian?

'He will take you to St Mary's postern gate,' Lucie said. 'I shall not treat you like a child. But I urge you to take a companion when you next go out into the city, my friend.'

'I do not believe he meant to harm me.'

'But he did harm you.'

'I shall pray over it.'

At the door Wulfstan had another disturbing surprise. Magda Digby, the heathen midwife, stood in the entry. Wulfstan knew that Lucie and Owen often worked with Mistress

Digby and respected her. But a man of the cloth could not condone her pagan ways. Still, they did say she shared his work in ministering to the victims of the pestilence.

'Thou tookst a fall, Infirmarian?'

'I did, Mistress Digby.'

Lucie told Magda of Brother Wulfstan's accident.

'Wounded. Clerk's robe. Smelling of horse, thou saidst?' the old woman nodded thoughtfully.

Her eyes were sharp, her posture quite upright for her age. Wulfstan had to admire her. From all accounts she was older than he by far. 'I must not keep the donkey cart waiting.'

But Lucie was watching Magda with interest. 'This man has crossed your path?'

'Not in the flesh, but Magda has heard of him. What didst thou have in thy bag?'

'Vinegar, clean cloths, a sweating tisane, a softening poultice, a knife to lance the blisters,' Wulfstan frowned. What else? 'Holy oil, holy water, a crucifix . . .' He shook his head. 'I cannot recall all of it.'

'A heavy burden, Infirmarian,' Magda said. 'Hast thou no assistant?'

'I want none.'

The old woman pulled a pouch from her voluminous robes, took out a small bottle.

'A tonic for old bones, Infirmarian. Thou must keep up thy strength for the work ahead of thee.'

Wulfstan hesitated. Her remedies were said to be comforting; but did she say pagan charms over them?

'It contains naught harmful to thy Christian soul,' Magda said.

Wulfstan pressed his hands together and bowed towards her. 'Forgive me.' He reached for the offering. 'God bless you, Mistress Digby.' Surely God would forgive him.

As Owen knelt in the infirmary chapel, gathering his thoughts and praying for guidance, footsteps approached from behind, paused, and retreated in haste. A reaction to his presence that Owen found interesting. He slipped into the shadows and followed the footsteps down into the undercroft of the chapel. But instead of entering the room in which the children were at supper, the footsteps went out of the undercroft door. The early evening sun did not reach the walled yard, but there was enough light for Owen to recognise Don Cuthbert carrying a bundle the size of a blanket. Owen watched with interest as the cellarer disappeared into a storage shed built against the far wall. He emerged empty-handed. The behaviour of a thief?

Owen had planned to meet with Cuthbert on the morrow, but the circumstances changed that. He was about to step from the undercroft door when someone came up behind him.

'Captain Archer?'

Owen spun round.

'*Benedicte*, Captain.' The quiet voice belonged to the lay sister Anneys. She must have been one of the women sitting with the children.

He bowed slightly. 'God go with you.'

'And with you, Captain.' Anneys gestured behind her. 'Did you wish to see the children?'

'No. I was up in the chapel, I wondered where the stairs would take me.' *And where they had taken the cellarer, who is now lost to me by your courtesy.*

'They tell me you have your countrymen's gift of song, Captain. The children are fond of singing.'

Owen found the woman's forthright manner at odds with her humble station. One might mistake her for the nun in charge of the Barnhous. 'I have no time for such pleasant pastimes at the moment. Might we speak?'

'Now? I am sorry, but I am helping with the children tonight. One of the sisters is ill.'

'Pestilence?'

Anneys crossed herself. 'The first among the sisters, praise God.'

'She looked after the sick children?'

'Yes. I shall do so now.'

'May God be merciful.'

'I do it willingly. I sat with another victim and did not fall ill: Master Taverner.'

Should he tell her that Julian had not died of plague? Did it matter? Owen had buried victims and he was still healthy. 'Might I speak with you tomorrow, then?'

Anneys nodded. 'The children rest just before vespers. I could meet you in the minster yard. I often walk that way.'

'I shall be there.' Owen retraced his way up the steps. He was uneasy. Cuthbert might have seen them talking. An innocent pastime. However, if he was the thief he might now know that Owen had followed him. He already knew Owen's business at the hospital. It was most unfortunate that Anneys had interrupted him.

He noted that there had been no hesitation in the lay sister's arrangement to meet him on the morrow, no withdrawal to ask permission. It was plain she had not been a servant for long.

* * *

The sun was setting, the narrow city streets were dark and cool as Owen headed home. The lamp beside the door was lit to guide him. As he entered, Kate hurried across the hall towards him.

'Captain! We worried when you did not come home. I will fetch your food.'

Lucie and Magda sat at the table in the hall with brandywine and a bowl of fruit before them. Jasper sat on a bench by the window, mending a shoe.

Owen thought of his meeting with Magda in the early morning and the nag tethered by her house. 'Have you been to the Ffulford farm?'

'Aye.' Magda told him of her journey while he helped himself to brandywine.

'You think the child is safe there?'

'Aye. She is a clever one.'

As Owen ate his supper, Lucie told him of Wulfstan's attack.

God's blood, what next? 'The man who stole the child's horse attacked Brother Wulfstan for his medicines? Have you informed the bailiff?' He could tell by the look on Lucie's face that she had not. 'I have my hands full at the hospital. I cannot search the streets for this man.'

Lucie started, then dropped her gaze. 'I

shall inform the bailiff in the morning,' she said, her voice tight. 'It has been a busy day.'

Dear God, of course it had been. Owen grabbed her hand. 'Forgive me. I did not mean to give you an order.'

Lucie nodded, said nothing.

'Another is abed with boils at St Leonard's,' he said, changing the subject.

Magda looked up from her brandywine. 'A child?'

'No. The sister who cared for the children in the infirmary.'

'Thou hast reminded Magda of a task left undone.' The Riverwoman pushed her stool back from the table, rose with a grunt. 'A child awaits.'

'When do you rest?' Owen asked.

'When the manqualm passes.'

Kate saw Magda to the door.

In the morning, Owen stopped to see the bailiff Geoffrey before he went on to the hospital.

Geoffrey rubbed his forehead hard, shook his head. 'The old infirmarian? He should not go abroad is what I say. 'Tis the empty streets, eh? And the empty houses. No witnesses to trouble. Gives a knave courage. Bastard.' He spat in the corner. 'Twenty years ago we boarded up the houses. But folk leave and come back. Fearing the Lord's wrath, eh? Bury the dead. Stay for a while, then take fright and run off again. We cannot know who is gone for good.'

It was more than Owen wished to know. 'I will be on my way, then.'

'They say your children are with Sir Robert.'

'Aye. We thought it best.'

Geoffrey shook his head. 'These be terrible times, Captain. Unsavoury characters abroad. Old men should keep to their homes.'

Owen did not bother to comment. A bell tolled as he walked down Blake Street. He was surprised he still noticed.

Seventeen

Alisoun's Resolve

A weary Magda trudged home through warm summer rain in the middle of the morning. She had spent the night at the sick-bed of a child, making progress, with two of her boils lanced, when suddenly the mother forbade more. 'Hear her screams. You make it worse.' Worse, yes: if Magda could not lance all five large boils, the lancing of the two had been unnecessary torture for the tiny creature. 'Twas all or naught, but the mother would not hear reason. She could not understand why the path to healing should be through pain.

Still, Magda did not allow herself to despair. That brought weakness, and this was no time to feel the years upon her. Some food and a rest were all she could afford. That must suffice.

Magda was not pleased to see the Ffulford nag tied up before her door, and Alisoun sitting on the bench under the eaves.

'What wind carried thee here, child?'

The brown face peered up through a tangle of hair. 'You left the nag. *I* can hide from my kin, but I cannot hide *her*.' Alisoun chewed on the corner of her mouth, picked at the ragged edge of her apron with filthy fingers.

'Thou thinkst to stable her here?'

'I would let you ride her.'

Magda barked with amusement. 'Thou dost not understand the cost of feeding such a creature away from thy pastures. And where wilt thou be, Horsetrader?'

'I need an escort into the city. A lone child — they will think I am a beggar. Or a thief with the nag.'

'Aye, 'tis true. Thou'rt requesting something?'

The child dropped her chin to her chest, worked in silence on the unravelling of her apron. Rain pooled on the rock beside her. Soon she would be soaked.

As would Magda. 'Come within.'

Alisoun shook out her handiwork as she rose. 'Would you see me through the gate?'

Magda touched the child's matted hair, tsked. 'Thou needest tidying.'

'What does it matter?'

'What is thy business in the city?' Magda held the door wide, noted how the child glanced anxiously at the nag, particularly at a pouch hanging to one side. 'Thy nag is safe here. Come inside or stay without, 'tis no matter.'

The door was closing behind Magda when Alisoun grabbed it. Within, she eyed the roots and plants hanging in the rafters to dry, the rows of jars on shelves along the walls, the curtained alcoves. 'Why do you need to know my business?'

Magda sat down on a stool at the fire, stoked it, swung the kettle over it. 'No need.'

The girl stood by the fire, watching Magda toss herbs into the broth.

'Art thou hungry?'

'A little.'

Magda nodded at a stool. 'Sit.'

Alisoun obeyed, though she perched on the edge of her seat as if about to spring up and run. 'Can you get me through Bootham Bar?'

The Riverwoman rose with a grunt, poured herself a small cup of watered wine, sat down again to stir the broth. 'What dost thou offer in fee?'

'Fee?'

Magda took a mouthful of wine, tilted her head back, swallowed. 'The sick need Magda. Thou hast given no good cause for her to neglect them to escort thee into the city.' She set down her cup, ladled broth into a bowl, handed it to Alisoun.

'What do you want?' the girl asked as she sniffed the broth.

'What wouldst thou part with in exchange, that is the question.'

The child paused with the spoon almost to her lips.

Magda waited patiently.

'You can have my horse,' spoken just before the spoon delivered the broth. The child gasped at the heat, but was soon spooning quickly.

Magda kept her silence until the child's bowl was empty.

'Will you accept that?'

'Thou thinkst it a gift to present Magda with a creature so costly to feed?'

'I thought it was generous.'

Magda's barking laugh startled Alisoun. 'Generous, aye. Far too generous. Hast aught dear enough, but not so dear?'

'I have nothing else.'

'What of the pack on thy horse? Is there naught inside thou mightst part with?'

'What do you know of it?'

'Magda knows what she sees.'

The child put down the bowl, crossed to the door. 'I can sneak in.'

'Take thy horse. Magda has no need of it.'

Alisoun slipped out the door. Magda

dipped brown bread in her broth, sucked on it, chewed. In a little while the door opened.

'Would this be enough?' The girl stood in the doorway, holding out a folded cloth.

'Thou hast feet.'

Alisoun brought it to her. Magda put down her bowl, took some of the cloth in her hands. Even her calloused fingertips could feel the delicate embroidery, the gold thread. A ridiculously fine item to take in trade for a short walk to the gate, but the child must learn the price of what she asked.

'Aye. This will do.'

The gatehouse of Freythorpe Hadden was a wattle and daub structure meant to impress rather than withstand attack. It stood on a stone bridge arching over a stream. A young man stood before it, barring the way with a pike. 'Get thee gone, sir. We want no visitors.' As he caught sight of the livery, his expression grew uncertain.

Thoresby's man Gilbert rode forward. 'Tell your master that John Thoresby, Archbishop of York, has come with news from the city.'

The young man turned to Thoresby. 'Your Grace the Archbishop?'

Thoresby inclined his head in a slight nod.

The young man dropped his gaze, bowed while crossing himself.

'*Benedicte*, my son.'

'Forgive me, Your Grace. I have orders to turn away all strangers. But I am certain that Sir Robert did not mean you.' The young man lowered his pike, stepped aside. The company rode through the gatehouse. The lad mounted his own horse and rode past them to announce their approach.

Thoresby was pleased by the caution shown thus far.

Freythorpe Hadden was a substantial stone and timber house of two rambling storeys with a tower at one end. In the arched doorway stood Dame Phillippa, Sir Robert D'Arby's sister and housekeeper. Elderly though she was, she stood straight and proud, her widow's wimple stubbornly white. As Thoresby dismounted and approached, Dame Phillippa turned her head slightly, spoke to someone behind her. When she turned back, her eyes were anxious.

'Your Grace,' she said, making her obeisance. 'It is an honour to welcome you to Freythorpe.'

'*Benedicte*, Dame Phillippa. I bring gifts for my godchildren and news that all are well in their household.'

'God is merciful,' Phillippa said, crossing

herself. Her eyes brightened. 'I feared ill tidings.'

'Not all my news will be welcome. For Mistress Wilton's maid servant I bring news of the death of her youngest brother.'

Phillippa put one hand to her mouth, one to her stomach, closed her eyes and stood silently for the space of a prayer, then turned, led Thoresby and his company into the hall, where a servant was setting out wine and food. 'Please, Your Grace, take some refreshment while I gather the household.' She left a medicinal scent in her wake.

Thoresby settled himself, gave his full attention to the wine. It had been a dusty ride, with the sun beating down. The hall was cool, the wine soothing. In a short while, a young woman entered with the red-headed Hugh in her arms. Clutching the woman's skirt was a lad Gwenllian's age.

'Tola,' Brother Michaelo said. 'Granddaughter of Magda Digby, the midwife. And her son, Nym.'

Tildy, ashen-faced and hesitant, followed slowly behind carrying another baby.

'Mistress Tildy,' Thoresby said with a courteous incline of his head.

She was so pale, the wine-red birthmark on her left cheek seemed angry in contrast. 'Your Grace, they say you have news for me.'

A servant took the baby from Tildy.

As gently as he could, Thoresby told her. When her hands flew to her face, he excused her from the company. 'Grief is best first felt in private.'

Tola looked uncertain whether to follow after her stricken friend or stay.

'Stay,' Thoresby ordered. 'I would see my godson.' He glanced behind her. 'And Gwenllian.'

Sir Robert D'Arby bustled into the room with Gwenllian. The two were dusty and flushed with exertion. 'Forgive my delay, Your Grace. Welcome to Freythorpe Hadden.'

'You must forgive me for not warning you of my visit. You are all well?'

Sir Robert's grey eyebrows came together, he bowed his head. 'The pestilence has not touched this household, though it has taken my steward and the village priest, who also served as my chaplain.'

Thoresby motioned to the elderly knight to join him at the table. Gwenllian joined Tola and the other children.

Sir Robert sat down opposite the archbishop, nodded to the servant to pour his wine. 'What brings you south, Your Grace?' He quenched his thirst as Thoresby described his mission.

Dame Phillippa slipped quietly into a seat at the table. 'Is it necessary to dismantle that lovely house?'

'The Lady Chapel will be lovelier still.'

Sir Robert was shaking his head.

Thoresby nodded to him. 'You have something to say?'

White-haired and stooped, Sir Robert was yet forward with his opinions. He tilted his head and lifted one shoulder as if to say *Remember 'twas you who asked.* 'Whence will come the workers, Your Grace? Until the pestilence has passed over the north, they hide behind their shutters.'

'You believe they would ignore their archbishop's summons?'

'I believe they fear pestilence far more than the ire of any mortal man.'

'I might offer indulgences for the work.'

'That would help, but only for those resigned to death.'

Thoresby sat back and studied his wine. The old man might be right in that.

Phillippa shifted uneasily on the bench, her eyes worried. 'Your Grace, my brother boldly speaks of matters about which he has no knowledge.'

'Nevertheless, he may speak truth,' Thoresby said. 'But you need not worry that I shall blame Sir Robert if his prophecy proves true. And now I must ask after my godchildren. Do they mind you? Are they as well as they appear?'

Dame Phillippa gave a favourable report, to which Gilbert listened with great interest, as he was to relay it to Owen and Lucie.

As Owen passed under the statue of St Leonard, he noticed a child speaking with Dame Beatrice, the sister in charge of the orphans. A horse stood nearby, steadied by a servant. The child wore a gown fashioned from the pieces of cloth that Magda used to test dyes. Alisoun Ffulford and her horse. Sweet Heaven, what was she doing at the hospital? And dressed by Magda?

He decided it was best not to interfere.

Eighteen

A Riddle

With Simon, the York Tavern's groom, as an armed escort, Bess Merchet set forth from Bootham Bar, north through the Forest of Galtres, to Easingwold. She had delayed the journey, waiting for a day that dawned clear with a brisk north wind. Some said the south wind brought pestilence, so she had deemed it wise to stay within the city walls, which she believed afforded a goodly protection, as much as possible. Tom, always contrary, had pointed out to her that if the walls afforded protection then the southerly wind theory could not be true, else how were folk dying who never ventured from the city. As if Bess believed that God had chosen only one avenue by which His wrath might reach the people, or claimed that it was a proven cause! But she would be a fool to ignore any theory that struck her as possibly true.

Once in the village of Easingwold it was easy to find Peter de Hotter's shop. He sat outside, with his awning and counter down, rolls of cloth displayed. But rather than seeing to customers, of which he had none at the moment, he was mending a stool.

'God go with you, Master Hotter.'

The man glanced up, squinting into the sunlight. 'Do I know —' His face suddenly brightened. 'Mistress Merchet. What coaxed you out of the city? The fine day? A thought to escape the sickness out here in the countryside?'

'You bring me here.' She bent close to add softly, 'I would speak with you about your father's death.'

Peter dropped his tool on to the stool, placed both on the counter and rose. He was a square, fleshy man, about Bess's height. His eyes, so close to hers, were dark, wary points beneath pale brows. 'What is your interest in my father's death?'

Bess glanced round. 'Do you have an apprentice who might watch the shop for a time so that we might talk elsewhere? Where none might hear?'

The merchant moved not a muscle. 'What is your interest?'

'Well, now. I should think you would not mind remembering your dear father.'

'I do not mind. What I want to know is why you are so keen to speak of him with me that you leave your place of business and come through Galtres to do so. 'Tis not everyone's choice for a summer's day, and in these times.'

His surliness bespoke poor business. Peter had been much pleasanter in the city. Bess revised her approach. 'My uncle, also a corrodian of St Leonard's, died recently.'

Peter did not relax. 'So the count is at six corrodians now.'

'Aye.'

He shook his head, walked over to the counter, picked up the abandoned stool, resumed his seat. 'My father surprised a burglar is all. It has naught to do with the others.'

'You are tallying the deaths, all the same.'

'I have heard the rumours. Idle gossip, if you ask me. The canons were good to my father. I will not believe ill of them.'

'They say you found nothing missing.'

'We have finished our discussion, Mistress Merchet. I would ask you to buy something or leave.'

Bess fingered the cloth. Tattered at the edge, dusty. 'You should reopen the shop in York, Master Hotter. Even with the pestilence upon us our trade is better than this.'

Peter bent back to his mending. 'I shall bide my time, Mistress Merchet.'

Such discourtesy did not deserve reward.

Bess departed empty-handed, and angry to have risked her health and lost a morning for naught. It was no wonder Owen resented the archbishop for assigning him such tasks.

Ravenser crushed the letter from his uncle while muttering a few choice curses. How much of a fool did Thoresby think him? *See to your affairs . . . Remember your reputation and that of your family . . . The Queen's trust . . . Do all you can to assist Archer in his efforts . . . Dispatch this affair quickly, the Queen has need of you . . .*

That Thoresby should think it necessary to write such things to him, he who was trusted with Queen Phillippa's purse, and Queen Isabella's before her! Why had he ridden to York and asked for Archer's assistance if not because he understood the necessity of ensuring that the name of Ravenser be unblemished?

And yet . . . He had awakened in the night with the memory of something he had neglected to tell Archer. He shouted for Douglas.

A cup of ale in hand, Owen paced back and forth in Ravenser's garden. He had just wasted precious time with the master's servants attempting to draw out memories of an intruder, an unexpected visitor, someone who might have slipped away with the chess set and the candlesticks. But no one remembered anything out of the ordinary, which Douglas had implied was quite typical of servants. Magda would have laughed at the 'rule', but Owen had merely asked for some ale to wet his throat before he'd turned his thoughts to something that he hoped would prove more enlightening — the shed behind the Barnhous. When Douglas had seen him pacing the hall, he had invited him to stroll in the garden.

The master's garden was an enclosed herber, the stone wall almost Owen's height. Within, tidy herbal borders outlined lovingly tended roses and a small lawn. The sanded path that Owen strode lay between matching arbours, one of which at the moment framed Richard de Ravenser, looking livelier than he had the previous day. Perhaps it was his deep blue houppelande and green leggings. Owen thought it rather elegant dress for a hospital master.

'*Benedicte,* Captain. Fortune places you here in my garden.'

'*Benedicte,* Sir Richard. I fear it is frustration, not fortune that drove me here.'

Ravenser sighed in insincere sympathy. 'The servants were unhelpful. I have heard.

But perhaps I might ease your mood. I have remembered something that I am quite embarrassed to have neglected to tell you.'

'I am eager to hear something of use.'

'I cannot promise that it will be of use; but I am not the one to judge. Shall we sit?' Ravenser had paused beside a turf seat.

Owen accepted the invitation, his curiosity roused, and the pacing and the ale having done their trick of easing his mood.

Ravenser tucked the ends of his houppelande in his belt, sat down, glanced round with a proud smile. 'A lovely garden is it not? I understand that you have a physicks garden that apothecaries come to study.'

'Aye. It was my wife's first husband's masterwork. She has continued to collect seeds and cuttings from the continent.'

'Mistress Wilton's feverfew tisane has no match in all the kingdom.'

Owen knew Ravenser spoke from experience. He was one of their best customers for the headache remedy, ordering large quantities whenever he came to the city. 'I shall tell her you said so. What was it that you wished to tell me?'

Ravenser smiled. 'I see that you are anxious to continue. I shall be brief. It is about Laurence de Warrene. I often played chess with him when in residence at St Leonard's.'

Ravenser proceeded to tell Owen of the evening when Laurence had posed the riddle, and how worried Julian Taverner had been that Ravenser might have repeated it to someone.

How might one unwittingly commit a sin. If none suffer but the guilty, has a wrong been done? Owen had never heard a riddle quite like it — it had no rhyme, and it likely had no answer. 'Why do you call it a riddle?'

'What would you call it?'

'Questions, simply posed.'

Ravenser shook his head. 'Laurence seemed quite uninterested in my opinion. Besides, being a collector of riddles, I know they come in many forms.'

A collector of riddles? What idleness was this? But Ravenser awaited more discussion. Owen focused his gaze on a rose, thought a while. 'With two orbs shot wolves and men. With one reveals men's dangerous secrets,' he said.

Ravenser shook his head in puzzlement.

'That is a riddle, Sir Richard.'

The master frowned over it, then brightened. 'Owen Archer.' He nodded with approval. 'Delightful. Let me see —' Ravenser now gazed out across the garden. 'Image of a greater man, shared blood, yet melancholic where he is sanguine.'

Well, Owen had not meant to begin a game, but it proved an interesting exercise. 'You are melancholic?'

'My physician tells me that is the cause of my headaches.'

'But you do see the difference? How a riddle's key is a word, not a yes, or no, or a philosophical discourse on guilt?'

Ravenser was not convinced. 'Had Laurence desired advice, he would have asked more directly. Our evenings were quite companionable.'

Owen grew weary of Ravenser. 'I thank you for telling me of it, Sir Richard. Would you object to my looking round one of the sheds behind the Barnhous?'

Pursed lips, as if suppressing a smile. 'Do not tell me you suspect one of the children? Or Dame Beatrice?'

'I observed your cellarer in there last night. He went in with a bundle, departed empty-handed, and his behaviour was that of someone anxious not to be seen.'

Ravenser looked suddenly anxious. 'Don Cuthbert is troublesome but trustworthy, Captain. I have ever considered him so.' He paused. 'Still. Why would he use a shed so far from his cell?'

'That is what I should like to find out.'

'I pray you, proceed.'

* * *

Owen's request flustered sweet-faced Dame Beatrice. 'Do you fear someone has left something dangerous in there? Sweet *Jesu.*' She crossed herself, blinked rapidly. 'Shall I take the children to the yard?' Her colour was rising.

'I pray you, do not be alarmed. It has naught to do with the children, or danger. Is it a shed that you use?'

'Yes. Yes, indeed, we do. The children's possessions — gifts, some items their mothers brought to the hospital . . .' The sister broke off abruptly, frowning down at her folded hands.

'Then you do not mind —'

Dame Beatrice shook her bowed head. 'That odd child. Whatever shall we do with her?'

'About my searching the shed . . .'

The gentle eyes met his. 'Forgive me. But then, you might be of help with her. She tells me that she knows you.'

'Who?'

'Alisoun Ffulford.'

He had forgotten that he had seen them together in the yard earlier. 'I buried her family. That is all. She is giving you trouble?'

'She wishes to stay here. Don Cuthbert

has granted permission, though reluctantly.'

'But she has kin.'

'None with whom she chooses to live.'

'She is a wilful child.'

'Heaven forgive my saying so, but she is, she is, Captain. A pouch heavy with the Lord only knows what and she will not let me put it in the shed.'

'Two items will be a bow and a quiver of arrows, I have no doubt.'

The sister looked dismayed. 'And what is a child doing with such a weapon?'

'Defending herself.'

'From whom, for pity's sake!'

'Might I search the shed, sister?'

'Yes, of course. You are a busy man and I am keeping you. You are welcome to it.'

'Would you be so kind as to accompany me? You might quickly see whether anything is there that should not be.'

'Oh, indeed.'

When they stepped into the dark shed, Owen opened the shutter on the lantern he carried and despaired. Though it was a small shed, it was crammed from ground to sloping roof with barrels, crates, and on top of these bundles of cloth and leather, some hides. Don Cuthbert was short. Where might he have hidden something?

As if hearing his silent question, Dame

Beatrice reached into the darkness behind the door and dragged out a ladder. 'Are you looking for something as large as a barrel or crate?' she asked, suddenly all business.

'No. A pouch, mayhap. The size of a folded blanket.'

The nun squared her shoulders, gazed upwards. 'Catch me if I totter, Captain.' And up she went with the lantern in one hand, her skirt clenched in the other. 'Goodness, the cobwebs. Saint Antony, I pray thee guide me.' She poked about, then suddenly, 'Ah. This is unfamiliar.' She turned round, handed down the lantern, then a substantial leather pouch. 'Would this be it, then?'

Owen set it down on the ground, unbuckled the strap, discovered medicines, a crucifix, candles . . . Brother Wulfstan's stolen bag? He did not understand how it came to be here. 'I believe it may be. St Antony has worked a miracle.'

Dame Beatrice had climbed down and was brushing off her skirts. 'It is a rare day he disappoints me.'

Now to find out how the bag came into Don Cuthbert's possession. And why he had hidden it.

Owen met Don Cuthbert in the church nave. The cellarer glanced at the bag, sniffed, raised his protruding eyes to Owen. 'It is the sort of bag one might expect you to carry.'

'Aye, but it is not mine. It belongs to the infirmarian of St Mary's, from whom it was stolen.'

'Stolen?'

'Even so. And what I am wondering is how did you come to be hiding it in the shed?'

Don Cuthbert's delicate fingers fluttered as he rose to his toes. 'I have thought from the first she was trouble.' His pointed teeth were bared in a smile.

'She?'

The cellarer glanced round the shadowy nave, leaned closer. 'Anneys. One of our lay sisters. I found her clutching it in my garden.'

Anneys. The woman who had distracted Owen from his watch. 'She brought it to you?'

'No, she did not. Indeed she gave it me unwillingly.'

'Then you hid it in the shed behind the infirmary, by the Barnhous?'

'How did you know that?'

'I followed you when you crept away from the chapel.' And had Anneys also followed? Owen had assumed she had come from the children's refectory. But had she? 'Why did you hide it?'

'You know better than I how dangerous physicks can be in the wrong hands. I thought it best to hide them until I might discover to whom they belonged.'

'Anneys works in the infirmary, does she not?'

Cuthbert held himself very still. 'The lay sisters work where they are needed. But she is a favourite in the infirmary. Calm, with steady hands.'

'Is she not entrusted with physicks in her work?'

Owen watched with interest as the cellarer realised his faulty logic. A mere ripple in the brow, averted eyes.

'Yes. She is indeed entrusted with physicks in her work.'

'Then why did you feel these particular physicks dangerous in her possession?'

Cuthbert pushed his hands up his sleeves, looked down at the floor. 'You will think me a fool, Captain. But I see that I am not clever enough to dissemble with you. So I shall speak plain. I envied you when Sir Richard told me you were to help him discover what is amiss at St Leonard's. When I saw the bag, I presumed it was yours. And thus I hid it. To spite you.'

The candour silenced both of them for a time. They stood facing one another yet not looking each other in the eye. Owen leaned against a pillar, stared off into the shadows. Cuthbert rocked back and forth on his small feet and studied the floor.

And yet it seemed an oddly companionable silence to Owen. At last he said, 'Thank you for telling me. You have saved me from rushing down the wrong path.'

Cuthbert rose to the tips of his toes, then settled. 'I wish to help the master, Captain.'

'Dame Beatrice mentioned that you have agreed to take in a child, Alisoun Ffulford.'

'Ah, yes. The orphan.'

'But one with kin.'

'Her mother grew up in the Barnhous, Captain. The girl says her mother urged her to come here. How could I send her away? But you can be sure I shall alert her kin to her whereabouts.'

'Mistress Ffulford was an orphan?'

'I do not remember the details, Captain. But yes, she married from here.'

Interesting. 'I would speak with Anneys.'

'Shall I have her summoned now?'

'If you would be so kind. And while we wait for her, would you describe for me the wounds you saw on Masters Taverner and Warrene?'

Anneys had bold eyes and a confident

bearing. Once again she struck Owen as an unlikely servant. But she had evidently come at once, and she thanked Don Cuthbert most courteously for offering to leave them alone to talk. Owen had purposefully left Wulfstan's bag in sight. Now the woman gazed at it with interest.

'You have seen this before?'

She turned to Owen. 'Captain, it is obvious that Don Cuthbert told you he found me with this in his garden.'

Clever woman to begin so. 'He did.'

'He did not believe me when I told him I had found it there.'

'As simple as that? You saw no one with it?'

'I saw no one.'

'Don Cuthbert tells me you were reluctant to give him the bag.'

'Indeed. He does not work with the sick. I thought it best to take it to the infirmary.'

A familiar argument, though this time it seemed more likely to be true. Owen was about to release Anneys when something occurred to him. 'It would not be customary for a lay sister or brother to walk in the cellarer's garden. How came you there?'

Hands clenched, head bowed. 'I had been sitting with a child who is dying, Captain. Not of pestilence. A brain fever. I cannot tell you how difficult it is to watch a child sink deeper and deeper towards death.' She was silent a moment. 'I wished to walk somewhere lovely. I wished to be alone. I wandered into the garden.' She raised her eyes to him. Her cheeks were wet with tears.

'God go with you.'

It was difficult for Owen to think about his work as he walked to St Mary's postern gate. All he wanted to do was ride for Freythorpe Hadden and see with his own eye that his children were safe and well. He left Brother Wulfstan's bag with the porter, with a message requesting that the infirmarian examine the bag and let him know what, if anything, was missing.

And then, without planning it, Owen delivered himself to the minster, where he knelt down before the lady altar to pray for his family, for Lucie as well as the children. Each night she crawled into bed exhausted, yet she slept only fitfully, worrying about the children. Owen feared that in her weak state she would succumb more readily to melancholy, and thence to illness.

When prayer had quieted his mind, he left the great cathedral and headed home. As he walked, he wondered how he was ever to unravel all that he had learned and choose what was of use. As he went through the day, he discovered much to question. How had a stranger found his way into the cellarer's garden? Had Anneys been following Don Cuthbert? Why had Cuthbert not believed her? Why had Alisoun Ffulford chosen St Leonard's?

Kate greeted Owen at the door with the news that Gilbert awaited him in the garden, with news of the children.

Gilbert dined with Owen and Lucie, who plied him with queries about Gwenllian and Hugh, most of which he could not answer. After Gilbert had taken his leave, Owen asked Lucie to withdraw to the garden with him.

As they walked along the paths, he recounted his day, hoping she might see what he could not. The riddle play amused her.

'How clever of you. Do you mean to try that on all those you question?'

'Do you think that I should?'

'You learned something about Ravenser you had not known.'

'Melancholic. It is not difficult to see. But do you think Thoresby sanguine?'

Lucie squeezed his arm. 'I daresay few would be so quick to think of a riddle describing themselves.'

'I might silence them for good.'

They laughed, then grew quiet.

'Owen, my love. What of this child? Does it not seem that God is keen to cross your paths?'

'Or the Devil.'

'Is she that unlovable?'

'Do you not think it odd that they admitted her without a sponsor, a gift to the hospital . . .'

'You said she had a pack with which she was loath to part.'

'She carried something with which she might pay her way?'

'It is possible. Perhaps she sold the nag.'

Owen stopped, gathered Lucie in his arms. 'You are weary and I have burdened you with my troubles.'

'Not at all, my love. You have distracted me with riddles. I am grateful for that. It is far too quiet in our home at present.'

Kate found them after sunset, Owen sitting with his back against a tree, Lucie with her head on his lap, both soundly asleep.

Nineteen

Too Many Coincidences

As the sun sank behind the hulk of St Mary's walls and the monastic buildings beyond St Leonard's, Dame Beatrice supervised the laying down of six tidy rows of pallets, blankets and pillows. When Alisoun had first arrived she'd wondered where the children slept — she had foolishly imagined individual cells, as for monks. Instead, the undercroft served as the day room, refectory, and bedchamber for the children of St Leonard's. And if one counted the curtained areas far back in the corners, it also served as their infirmary and bathhouse — to which Alisoun had been subjected on the first day. The Riverwoman had not been the only one who'd thought she'd stunk. She had submitted without argument, as long as she was allowed to keep her pack beside her. Now the pack lay beneath her feet, covered by the blanket. No one could pull it out from under her without waking her.

A full hour of anxious bustle ensued, with Dame Beatrice and her lay helpers herding the children to their beds and making certain they were down for the night. At last the only lights in the long, high-ceilinged room were at the doorways. All the sisters had withdrawn except for one lay sister who sat beneath the light farthest from Alisoun. In time, the whisperings and rustlings of her fellows ceased, and Alisoun drifted into a dream.

It was night, a cool spring evening. Alisoun slept in her own bed with the babies. Her mother stood in the doorway, clutching her elbows as she did when she worried, facing out into the night, waiting for her father who had been too long at the market. Her mother at last turned away from the door, a slow, heavy-hearted turning, and crossed over to Alisoun and the babies. Alisoun drifted back to sleep, woke to find her mother's face bent close to hers, wetting it with her tears. She reached for her mother's hand, but her mother shook her head and backed away.

Alisoun woke on the narrow pallet, chilly beneath her itchy blanket. No babies surrounded her for warmth. Her eyes were drawn to the light that shone over the nodding sister, then to a figure who stood in the shadows at the foot of her pallet. Alisoun blinked.

'Mama?'

Whoever it was took a few steps backwards, then turned and hurried off into the darkness. Alisoun stretched out slowly, searching for her pack with her feet. Nothing. She ducked under the covers, crawled to the foot of the pallet, searching. Searched the floor round her. It was gone.

Of course it had been him. The figure had been too tall for her mother. And her mother was dead.

How had he discovered she was at the hospital? Had he followed her? Or had the Riverwoman told him? Alisoun should have known better than to trust the heathen midwife.

Now he had her treasures. Some of them. The ones she had not buried. Alisoun's face was hot, her eyes tingled with tears. The Riverwoman had betrayed her. She could trust no one.

Dead blossoms to trim, rosehips and mint to harvest. Lucie kept herself busy in the garden till mid-morning while Owen helped Jasper open the shop. It was Owen's gift to her in gratitude for her patient attention in the evenings, despite her long days in the shop. Lucie's cat, Melisende, stayed close to her, rolling in the path beside her, sniffing the plants she had trimmed, now and then insinuating herself beneath busy hands for a scratch. Jasper's orange tabby, Crowder, watched from the workshop windowsill. The morning grew warm, and as she tired Lucie fought thoughts of her children.

'Thirsty work on such a hot morning.'

'Magda!' The elderly woman crouched beside Lucie in the path, scratching Melisende's long ears. Lucie had not even noticed the cat's movement. 'How long have you stood there?'

'Long enough to see thee blot thy neck and forehead. Hast thou no work in the shade?'

Something of import must bring Magda here so soon after her last visit. 'Come,' Lucie gathered her tools, stood up. 'Have a cool drink with me in the kitchen. Then I must free Owen from the shop.'

In the kitchen, as they waited for Kate to bring water from the cellar, Lucie and Magda bent over the embroidered cloth spread out on the table.

'An altar cloth. The Ffulford girl gave it to you?' Lucie wondered whether it could be the cloth missing from St Leonard's. But how might it then have come to the child?

The Riverwoman folded the cloth with thoughtful care. 'Aye, the child traded it for Magda's help at Bootham Bar. Thou sayest an altar cloth. Magda thought it had the look of a church ornament.'

'You must wait here for Owen. He might know something of this.'

Owen rubbed the scar beneath his patch. Douglas had described the cloth in enough detail for him to recognise the chalice of gold thread lifted in delicately embroidered hands. He did not like this development. 'What mischief has that child got into?'

Magda shook her head. 'She says little. Thou hast seen this piece before?'

'I believe this to be the altar cloth stolen from St Leonard's.'

Magda snorted. 'A child who cannot pass the guards without escort has not been thieving at the spital.'

'I would agree. But whence came this cloth to her, eh? And why has she asked for the protection of the hospital?'

'That is what she sought in the city?' Magda frowned as she folded the cloth, handed it to Owen. 'Mayhap her kin fear her. All in her house died but Alisoun. They wonder how she came to be saved. Fools oft see evil in good.'

Owen placed the cloth in his pack. 'I must show it to Don Cuthbert.'

'Be patient with the child, Bird-eye.'

Cuthbert lifted the cloth in his spidery hands. 'Alisoun Ffulford, you said?'

'Aye.'

The cellarer held the cloth close to his bulging eyes, examining the fine needlework. 'I am certain it is ours, Captain.' He put down the cloth, tucked his hands up his sleeves, rocked back and forth on his heels. 'What do you think it means?'

Owen wished he knew. 'Have you learned any more of her mother?'

'She was sponsored by a wealthy Yorkshire family who wished to remain anonymous. Two children were left in our care. One died of sweating sickness: a boy.'

'So Judith Ffulford and the boy were from a wealthy family?'

'I think it unlikely. Such people take care of their own.'

'But sponsoring means they paid well for the children's care?'

'Well enough.'

Owen felt the prick of trouble beneath his patch. 'Where is the child?'

'You will question her about this cloth?'

'I will indeed.'

* * *

All dressed alike in undyed gowns and leggings, a group of small children sat quietly on stools or on the floor listening to a lay sister who told a story about Christ and St Christopher. A group of older girls sat in the yard by the shed, frowning over a sewing lesson. Three tall boys were at work on the roof of the storage shed. Owen did not see Alisoun at once; Dame Beatrice pointed her out among the needleworkers. She was a lighter shade of brown now that she was clean. Her hair was neatly tucked into a kerchief, her legs were covered, her feet shod. 'You have transformed her.'

Dame Beatrice made a face. 'Outwardly, yes. But God forgive me, her soul is intractable.' She clapped her hands. 'Alisoun!'

Owen recognised the scowling brown eyes raised to the nun. The child forced a smile, but it faded when she glanced at Owen.

'Captain Archer is here to see you. Come along.' Dame Beatrice's brusque tone was so unlike her usual manner it effectively discouraged argument. The child put down her sewing, rose and followed quietly. Dame Beatrice led them up the stairs to a small room next to the chapel, then left them alone.

Owen pulled the altar cloth from his pack.

'Did you give this to Magda Digby?'

Alisoun sat with her feet twisted round the rungs of her chair, her hands gripping the seat on either side of her. She stared at the cloth in puzzlement, then lifted her eyes to glare at Owen. 'It was mine to give.'

'Don Cuthbert disagrees with you. He says it disappeared from St Leonard's church.'

For a moment, the brown eyes revealed confusion. 'He lies.'

Owen crossed his arms, leaned back against the wall, allowed a silence to make the child uncomfortable.

She began to fidget, clenching and unclenching the edge of the chair. 'May I return to my lesson?' she asked at last.

'No.'

'What do you want?'

'I want to know where you found the cloth.'

'In my mother's things.'

'Your mother stole the cloth?'

'No! How could you say that?'

Owen leaned forward, hands on knees, brought his face close to the child's. 'Tell me about the man who stole your horse.'

'What does he have to do with the cloth?'

'I am the one asking the questions today.'

The child chewed on a fingernail. 'Do you

think the man who took my horse stole the altar cloth, too?'

'Did he?'

'How would I know?' Her voice rose to an unpleasant pitch.

But though she was upset, Alisoun was becoming more rather than less stubborn, much like Gwenllian when pushed into a corner. Owen rose. 'Forgive me for wasting your time. I had hoped to discover whether the man who stole your horse was the one who attacked the infirmarian of St Mary's and stole his bag, which was later found within the hospital walls. But I see you know nothing.' He took a few steps towards the door.

'So he *was* here.'

Owen spun round. 'You saw him?'

The brown eyes froze. 'You are not as clever as you think.'

'None of us is.'

Owen waited.

Alisoun fidgeted. Finally, 'My mother learned to embroider here. She embroidered cloths for the village church.'

'This one belonged to St Leonard's.'

Silence.

Owen shook his head. 'God go with you.' He stepped out of the room.

Anneys was just coming up the stairs. 'I

shall see to her, Captain,' she said, breathless from the climb. 'Come, Alisoun.'

The child stood in the doorway, twisting a lock of hair that had escaped her kerchief and staring down at her shoes. Owen thought she might be more helpful the next time they met.

Geoffrey the bailiff unlocked the door to Walter de Hotter's house. 'What do you seek, Captain?'

'Something that looks as if it should not be here,' Owen said. 'Where was Walter lying?'

Geoffrey indicated the spot by the overturned stool. 'I tried to leave it as I found it, but I cannot say whether his apprentice shifted aught. He said nay, but he was shivering and babbling.' Walter's apprentice had discovered his master's body the morning after the murder, when he had come for his breakfast.

Owen noted the bloodstained rushes. 'Were the doors ajar?'

'Not the street door. But that one. To the garden.'

Owen stepped out into the garden, an oblong of weed-choked herbs and flowers surrounding a pear tree. The tree would survive, but many of the plants had already died from lack of water and neglect. The sight saddened Owen.

'Walter's son is in Easingwold,' Geoffrey said, as if to explain the untended patch.

'I had heard.' Owen stepped back into the house. 'Pass me the lantern now.'

The bailiff opened the shutter, but held it beyond Owen's grasp. 'I would accompany you, Captain.'

'You do not trust me?'

'I would watch and learn from you.'

There were better ways to learn than to watch a man think, but Owen could see Geoffrey was sincere. 'Come then. We will walk slowly through the house, noting all we see.'

It had been a comfortable household. Once brightly painted cushions, now faded, softened the benches by the table. On the walls, ochre stripes and dots danced against a yellow background. In the chest beside the table, two silver spoons nested among horn ones. Other costly articles included a pearl-handled knife, three pewter platters and a plain silver cup. Another chest in the bedchamber at the top of the ladder held several finely embroidered sheets, a heavy woollen blanket, and two down cushions, all carefully stored with sachets of sweet-smelling herbs. The walls and the bed curtain were painted with white flowers. On a hook by the bed hung a cloak lined with beaver and a good leather belt with a silver buckle.

'A thief might have found something of interest here,' Owen commented as they climbed back down to the main room. 'And much of it easy to hide on his person.'

'Aye, but his son's wife missed naught.'

Owen returned to the garden to consider what he had seen. While he thought, he idly pulled at the invasive weeds. Perhaps not such an idle activity. With a bit of clearing, one patch towards the centre was noticeably bare, and the soil crumbly as if recently disturbed. He found a small spade in the shed, dug down into the centre of the patch. Nothing. He moved his attention to the edge, beneath an encroaching patch of chickweed, dug deep. At last the blade hit something hard. He probed, dug up something small, held it up to the fading light. 'What have we here?' he muttered as he brushed earth away. It was an ivory pawn dyed with ochre.

Excited by Owen's find, Geoffrey knelt down beside him, picked up the spade and began to dig at the opposite edge of the patch. 'I feel sommat!' He unearthed a white rook.

The two men took turns digging, but found no more.

'Why would Walter have buried these?' Geoffrey wondered aloud.

Owen pushed himself up out of the dirt. 'Not Walter. His murderer. Unless I am much mistaken.'

'But why?'

Owen glanced round at the buildings bordering the garden. One had two shuttered windows overlooking the garden, another had one. 'Come within.' Inside, he settled down on a cushioned bench, set the two pieces on the table before him.

Geoffrey took a seat opposite him, tugged off his hat, scratched his head. 'You thought we might be overheard?'

'Risk is foolish in this game.'

Geoffrey picked up the pieces one at a time and looked at them closely. 'A fine set, this was. I should like to see the whole set.'

'With luck, you will.'

'What are you thinking, then, Captain?'

'That when there are too many coincidences, there are no coincidences.'

Geoffrey frowned. 'Word games?'

'Nay. Consider. Walter de Hotter had been two days at St Leonard's with an injured knee. His house was empty. Suppose someone who had been robbing the hospital saw him there, knew his house would be empty, buried the chess pieces in Walter's garden. He returned for them when he was ready to sell them or hide them elsewhere, but was surprised by poor Walter.'

'The thief is someone who is often at the hospital, then?'

'I think so.'

'Had these chess pieces just gone missing about the time of his death?'

'They were not missed until the master returned. But consider this. Walter was often at the hospital. The thief might have buried them during one of Walter's earlier visits, then returned this time to remove them.'

'Would Walter not have noticed the disturbed earth?'

'They were buried deep. Perhaps it was done before the spring planting, when most of the bed would have been bare, perhaps the soil just turned over for planting. He may have seeded over them in spring. Mayhap the entire set was buried here and the thief missed these when removing the others.'

'Which means he might return.'

Owen would like that. 'Can you spare a man to watch the house?'

'Nay. But I might find a lad to do it.'

'Good.' Owen rose, walked over to the garden door. 'One building behind has a window facing the garden. Who lives there?'

Geoffrey joined Owen in the doorway,

peered out. 'Widow Darrow and her crippled son.'

'Who lives next door? Two windows face this garden.'

'Master Saurian, the physician.'

'Indeed?'

Twenty

Alisoun's Secret

As evening shadows spread in the garden, Lucie put aside her work, drew Owen outside. 'I cannot bear the silence. Come. Walk with me and tell me what you learned today about the child and the altar cloth.' She led him down the path between the lavender and the santolina.

But the beauty of the garden was lost on Owen at that moment. He, too, found the evenings too quiet. He put his arm round Lucie, pulled her close. 'Shall we send for the children?'

Lucie pressed her head against his shoulder for a moment. 'How lovely if it were that simple. But three children died in the city today. And they say animals are falling in the fields round us. It is not yet time to bring Gwenllian and Hugh home.'

'I had not heard about the beasts.'

'Tell me of your day. Speak of anything but the sickness.'

Owen began with Alisoun and continued

with the treasures in Walter's garden. 'Saurian the physician is often at the hospital, is he not?'

'Yes. And he is a gossip. He would be delighted to tell you all he knew were he in the city. But he accompanied the master of Davy Hall to his manor when the pestilence reached the city.'

A convenient escape, and perhaps for more than the obvious reason. 'How is his business?'

'His —' Lucie suddenly stopped, turned to Owen. 'You think he might be the thief?'

'Is it possible?'

A little laugh. 'Only if he is remarkably greedy and stupid. What of the Yorkshire family who sponsored Judith Ffulford? Is there truly no record of their name?'

'They paid well for their anonymity.'

'They could not be from York then. Someone would remember them.'

'I have not asked all at the hospital.'

Lucie bent to pet Melisende. 'I would not bother. Doubtless the children were moved far from their home because they were an embarrassment.'

That left Owen with something to ponder.

This time Alisoun knew in her dream that

she must awaken, that it was not her mother leaning over her. Her heart racing, she woke. The figure stood at the foot of her pallet. Alisoun lay very still, trying to hold her breath. Was it him? The figure wavered because a wind had the night sister's light flickering. Alisoun could see only that it was a tall figure in a dark hooded gown. It might be almost anyone at the spital — a canon or lay brother, a sister or lay sister. Or the man from the farm might have crept in in disguise, which seemed most likely to Alisoun. Who else had reason to frighten her? He meant to hurt her as she had hurt him. And he was looking for the treasures she had buried.

Alisoun closed her eyes, then opened them just enough to catch any movement through her lashes.

While she waited she prayed.

At last the watcher moved. Alisoun opened her eyes. He had his back to her. She slipped on to the floor and began to crawl after him. It was difficult watching him and picking her way carefully among the pallets. She lost sight of him. He must have made it to the doorway to the chapel stairs. She rose to a crouch and hurried towards the doorway, heard footsteps above her, started up the uneven stone steps, tripped on her hem.

* * *

Owen was still lingering over his early morning bread and cheese when Kate opened the door to a messenger from St Leonard's. Owen heard the lad asking for him. Fearing it was bad news, he hurried over.

'God go with you, Captain. Dame Beatrice prays you to come to her as soon as you are able. Alisoun Ffulford has been injured.'

'What has that to do with me?'

'Dame Beatrice begs you to hurry.'

Owen arrived to chaos. A child had fainted in the midst of play and though they had hurried him off to the infirmary it had frightened the rest of the children who cried and clung to the skirts of the sisters. Dame Beatrice had a cluster of children about her.

'*Benedicte*, Captain,' she gasped. 'I pray you, go to the room by the chapel. The child awaits you there.' She bent down to the children clutching at her skirts.

Don Cuthbert hurried from the room to greet Owen.

'What are you doing here?' Owen asked.

'The sisters are busy with the children and the sick. But after what happened last night Dame Beatrice rightly thought the child should be guarded.'

Alisoun sat in the middle of the room, head down, hugging herself. She showed no sign of injury.

'What happened? What did Alisoun do?'

Cuthbert glanced back at the child. 'That is for her to tell you, Captain. I know only that she was found at the bottom of the chapel steps just before dawn with a swelling behind her ear that was first feared to be a boil.' He crossed himself. 'But it is merely a bruise, thanks be to God. The child says she tried to follow someone who had awakened her and she tripped in her haste on the stairs.'

'Someone awakened her?'

'She says they stood over her as she slept, and when she woke they ran — a fantastic story.'

'A child telling tales. Why was I sent for?'

'The child asked for you.'

Owen wondered for what sin he was being punished. 'I suppose you must leave us alone.'

Cuthbert began to leave the room.

'Stay just without, if you will,' Owen requested. 'I want no one to overhear.'

'Gladly.'

Owen walked over to the child, who had not looked up from her examination of the floor since he'd arrived. 'Alisoun?'

Still looking down at the floor, the child said sullenly, 'Dame Beatrice says I should trust you.'

'I see.' Pulling a bench over so that he might sit opposite her, Owen sank down, crossed his arms. Still she stared at the floor. 'Are you likely to listen to her?'

A deep breath. 'I wounded the man who stole my horse.'

'Ah. What else might you tell me?'

As if a dam had been opened, the child told Owen of the night she had run from her uncle's house and found the man in the barn. 'I shot him in the arm and the leg, I think.'

'With your bow?'

Alisoun nodded. 'Then I ran.'

Owen did not speak at once, thinking what might have happened to the child had she been a poor aim. But what had this to do with her accident?

His silence drew her eyes up to his. 'Yesterday you were full of questions.'

It was his first view of a bruised eye. 'What happened last night?'

'I tripped on the steps.'

'But your eye.'

'I fell forward, didn't I?'

'Someone watched you?'

'He wants revenge.'

'Are you saying the man you injured was here last night?'

'And the night before. I hate him.'

Hatred took time to develop. 'You have seen him before.'

'Did the Riverwoman tell him I was here?'

'I am certain that she did not.'

The child sighed, looked down at her hands which were twisting a handful of the fabric of her skirt. 'He took my bag.'

The one Dame Beatrice said she would not let out of her sight? 'When?'

'The night before last. I had it under my feet. He got it while I was sleeping. Then he stood there watching me. He came back last night.'

'Did you wake the others?'

'No.'

'Why not?'

'The treasure was my secret.'

He would come back to that. 'You did not cry out?'

'I thought it was my mother at first. And last night I tried to follow him.'

'Tried to?'

She bent her head, lifted her hair to show him a knob behind her ear, on the same side as her bruised eye. 'I *told* you I *fell*.'

'Are you certain it was him?' Where was he hiding? Owen would have liked to have begun a search, but he deemed it wise to try first to ascertain whether the child was telling the truth. She might have walked in a dream. One of her comments had given him an idea . . . 'Your treasure. What was it?'

'A silver missal cover.'

'How did you come to possess such a thing?'

The sullen child dropped her head. 'It was one of the treasures my mother hid in a chest in the barn.'

Owen remembered their first meeting — she had been guarding the barn, not hiding from them. 'Hid? From whom did your mother hide these treasures?'

'From folk who would steal them.'

'Were they gifts from your father?'

Alisoun shook her head.

'Tell me about these treasures. What were they?'

Alisoun described many of the items missing from the hospital: silver candlesticks, tapestries, the golden chalice, the pearl and silver cross, the missal cover, the saddle.

'Sweet *Jesu!*'

'I buried everything but the tapestries and the saddle before I went to my uncle.'

'And the embroidered altar cloth?'

'That was in the pack. I used it for a pillow.'

'The pack also contained the tapestries and saddle?'

Alisoun shook her head. 'Just the missal cover.'

'Where are the tapestries, the saddle?'

'The man who stole my pack stole them, too.'

'You had them with you at St Leonard's? Dame Beatrice mentioned nothing but the pack.'

'He stole them at the farm.'

'When you injured him?'

The child squirmed. 'Yes.'

'Who is he?'

Alisoun dug at the floor with the toe of her soft shoe. 'I do not know his name.'

'Whence came these treasures?'

'I do not know.'

'How did your mother come to have them?'

'I do not know.'

'Then how do you know they were not from your father?'

'I think she hid them from him.'

'But she let you see them?'

Alisoun shook her head.

'I see.' Owen wondered whether she knew all the treasures had been stolen from the hospital. He decided not to mention it. 'Why would she hide things from your father?'

'He called mother a liar when she spoke of her father.'

'No doubt because she had been abandoned at the hospital.'

'It was her mother abandoned her.'

It was an odd logic that only the mother abandoned her. 'How did she know of her father?'

'She never said.'

'And you never asked?' Owen found that unlikely. 'What did she say of him?'

'He was a rich man. She had been born to a better life than the farm.'

'Did your mother ever mention her father's name? His family name?'

Alisoun shook her head.

Perhaps the tale had been meant to enchant the child. But if so, whence came the items? 'Why did you have the missal cover in the pack?'

'I thought they might want something for my keep at St Leonard's.'

'Has anyone spoken to you of items missing from the hospital?'

'You mean he stole other things? Not just my pack?'

'How much of what you have told me is true?'

'All of it.'

Owen shook his head. 'What am I to think of a farmer's wife possessing such a hoard, child?'

'They are my grandsire's treasures and

that man wants them.'

'How did he know of them?'

Alisoun wiped her nose, lifted one shoulder, let it drop.

'You tell an odd tale, child.'

'You will believe it when he's killed me.' She glowered at him.

'No doubt. You say you buried the treasures. Will you tell me where?'

'You would dig them up.'

'Does that not seem a wise thing to do?'

'They are mine.'

'Perhaps not.'

'My mother was not a thief.'

'Doubtless she was a good woman, Alisoun.'

'I hate all of you.'

Owen rose. The child would tell him no more today. Best to let her think about it. 'We shall search the hospital for the man. Meanwhile, a sister must be near you at all times.'

'Let Anneys stay with me. She is nice to me.'

Ravenser's clerk had taken Cuthbert's place outside the room.

'The cellarer was too busy to wait?'

'I offered to relieve him, Captain. I have learned something that might help you.'

Douglas looked pleased with himself as he handed Owen a parchment.

It was a deed of gifts to St Leonard's. Owen glanced at the bottom. Signed by Laurence de Warrene and Julian Taverner.

'Read the list, Captain.'

Amongst other items were the majority of the goods lately missing from the hospital. 'This must be significant. How did you discover this?'

'A speck of memory. Something Sir Richard once said in jest when Master Warrene won a game. "And why would you not play chess well on your own board, with your own pieces?" They played, you see, on Master Warrene's board, which he had given to the hospital.' Douglas looked smug. 'It seemed of little import, but I thought it worth searching to see if other gifts had also been bequeathed by Master Warrene. And I came across this list.'

But what did it mean? 'Why did Sir Richard not tell me of these gifts?'

'I doubt he knew.'

'He knew of the chess board.'

'He played chess with Master Warrene is why. But this deed was written before Sir Richard was master.'

Twenty-one

More Than Friendship

Up on a ladder, nailing a loose shutter in place, Tom Merchet paused to watch a hunched, obviously weary man pushing an overloaded cart through St Helen's Square. He wore a light tunic over his leggings, but even from Tom's perch, circles of sweat were visible around the man's neck and under his arms. Piled haphazardly in the cart were bedding, several chairs, pots — one of which was jarred loose as a wheel rode up on to a grave at the edge of St Helen's cemetery. Someone fleeing a plague house? As the man lowered the cart handle to go after the rolling pot, a chair began to slip. Tom hurried down the ladder to assist. He caught the pot with his foot before it gained speed on Coney Street. As he handed it to the panting man, Tom recognised him. Julian Taverner's former servant. 'Nate! You would leave York without a farewell?'

With a half-hearted curse, Nate yanked the toppling chair from the cart, set it down on the square, sat down on it, took out a dirty cloth and wiped his sweaty, dusty brow. His hands were knobbly with swollen joints. 'I am too old for this, Tom Merchet. I thought to die in my master's service. Happy to do so. And now he is gone. What am I to do?'

A good question. 'Did Julian leave you any money?'

Old Nate blew his nose, sat a moment catching his breath. 'Oh, aye, the master gave me a fair sum. 'Course he did. He was a fair man, Master Taverner was. And he left me all his furnishings. But where am I to put them? I have nowhere to go. What am I to do now? Who would hire a man as bent as old Nate?'

Tom considered. They had no need for an extra pair of hands, nor had they accepted lodgers since the pestilence began. The tavern was open only to those the Merchets knew, and only those with no pestilence in their households. Which meant they had precious little business, certainly not enough to warrant hiring Nate.

And what of his having lived at St Leonard's? Might he carry pestilence? No more likely than Bess herself, Tom thought. She had been with her uncle at the last and was still standing and able. It might even be true he had not died of pestilence.

'You might rest a while with us, Nate. Long enough to think what you will do.'

The man's large nose grew red and his sad eyes glistened. 'You are sent by the merciful Lord, Tom Merchet. I'll not forget this kindness.'

As Tom helped Nate pull the cart into the tavern yard he wondered what Bess would say about his kindness.

Hands on hips and foot tapping, Bess was not pleased. ' 'Tis not the pestilence worries me, Tom Merchet. Nate is old, that is what worries me. Not a man to find work easily. What then? Do we give him a room for life? Have him underfoot until he wastes away?'

'Sweet Heaven, wife, I want but a few years to match his age. Am I wasting away?'

Bess peered out of the window of her parlour to where Simon was helping Nate unload the cart. 'Look at his joints. See how he hobbles. You are healthy. Nate is not. 'Tis all the difference.'

'You owe it to your uncle.'

'I owe my uncle nothing. A soft heart is what you have, Tom Merchet.' Bess sat back down at the table where she had been working on her books, picked up her quill.

Tom leaned on the table. 'Which of us is to tell him then, wife?'

Bess snapped her head up, her eyes round as if he had just said a most ridiculous thing. 'Tell him what? He is here now. Naught to do but make the best of it. You always make such a muddle of things.'

Leaning down, Tom gently kissed his wife's hot forehead. 'Rest easy. Nate seems a man wants something to do. He'll not burden us.'

Bess patted her husband's hand. 'He reminds me of Uncle Julian is all. I've neglected him. He will not rest in his grave until his murderer has been brought to justice. I must get to work.'

'I thought you had journeyed to Easingwold. That was not work?'

'Precious little good it did.'

'Have you told Owen about your journey?'

'Aye. A chiding I received for it, and not a word of thanks.'

'Owen's not one to behave so. What did he say?'

'That he could not undo the harm I did.'

Tom's eyes grew round. 'He said that?'

Bess sniffed and waited for sympathy.

'Well, that should teach you to stay out of his business.'

The cur. 'I came to that decision on my own, husband.'

* * *

Bess rose from her work as Owen entered the tavern in the late afternoon. 'What brings you here so early?'

Owen glanced round the room. 'I never thought to see it empty at this time of day.'

'You have not come to see how we fare, friend,' Tom said. 'You have some news?'

'I have come with more questions about Julian Taverner and Laurence de Warrene.'

'Oh?' Bess did not like Owen's tone.

'None of the servants can hear us?'

Bess shook her head. 'They are all about their business.' She leaned closer. 'Tell me, for pity's sake. What have you learned?'

'You know of the thefts at the hospital?'

'Of course I do.'

'Did you know that many of the missing items were originally given to the hospital by Julian and Laurence? A gold chalice inlaid with precious stones, a silver filigree missal cover with gems, a saddle inlaid with gold leaf . . .'

'Uncle Julian?' Bess sat down. 'He had such things to give away?' He had never given her any evidence of such wealth. 'Was it these things bought his corrody?'

'No. The gifts were an additional payment. "For our sins", the deed read.'

Bess pressed her eyelids, forced down her

disappointment. He might have left her such treasures and instead he had given them to St Leonard's. Had he ever thought what Bess and Tom might have done with such wealth? 'Ungrateful old man.' A deep breath. 'Tom, pour four ales. Owen might profit from a word with Nate.'

Owen glanced from one to the other. 'Your uncle's servant?'

'He is lodging here until he finds work.' Bess found Owen's obvious pleasure a nice reward for her trouble with old Nate. 'Tom will fetch him for you.'

'I feel a servant myself,' Tom muttered as he put the four tankards on the table. 'Shall I assist Simon with Nate's things, wife?'

Bess shook her head at him. 'And who else will do it?'

It was a sweaty, breathless Nate who sank down at the bench and greedily gulped at his ale.

'You will have a head feels it has been pressed for wine if you drink so,' Bess warned.

Nate set his tankard down, eyed the pitcher with interest. 'I'm that thirsty, Mistress Merchet. I loaded the cart myself. Pulled it all the way from St Leonard's. You cannot imagine how hot that sun is.'

'Precious little sun reaches Blake Street,'

Bess muttered. Pray God he did not drink them into debt while he was here. 'This is Captain Owen Archer. He is helping the Master of St Leonard's with a problem.'

The old man turned his attention to Owen. 'Thieving and such, eh?' A knowing wink. 'My master and his friend dying so suddenly. And poor Walter de Hotter.' Nate nodded. 'Things are not as they should be at spital, 'tis plain. I know about you, Captain. There are many at spital glad to hear you will put an end to the troubles.'

'I confess I am a long way from doing that, Nate.'

Bess chuckled into her cup at Owen's modesty.

'I cannot think what I know that might help,' Nate said.

'You were with him when he became ill. Who helped you with him?'

'Honoria, though she could not stay. She had other chores. She sent for Anneys when she saw how quickly he was failing. And then we sent for Mistress Merchet.'

'Did Honoria or Anneys give him any physicks?'

'Nay. Well, naught but what he was taking already.'

Bess interrupted the muddled old man. 'His headache had gone, Nate. He took no more physick after the first day home.'

Nate shook his head. 'He was drinking sommat for quick healing and strength, Mistress Merchet. It smelled most foul. I would not forget such a thing.'

Owen turned to Bess. 'You had taken him physicks from the apothecary?'

Bess stared at Owen as she realised what he was about. 'I did. But none of them foul-smelling, I am certain of that.' He believed her uncle had been poisoned. Holy Mary, Mother of God.

But Owen, with a grim sigh, changed the subject. 'Your master had money and treasures when he came to St Leonard's, Nate. Too much to have made it all at the tavern.'

'Aye, that he did. He made a goodly sum outside the tavern, as do many who live on the North Sea. Were a fool otherwise, eh?'

Bess did not like this turn.

'So he was a smuggler,' Owen said.

Nate wrinkled his nose. 'Now where would he find the time to go to sea? Nay. He waited for the goods to land, the master did.'

'He emptied ships foundered on the rocks?'

'To be sure. Not a soul along the coast did not take advantage of others' misfortunes, Captain. But among so many the rewards are small. The master and his friends, they thought of something better. Looted the caves of the smugglers, they did. And who could bring them to justice? Thief blaming thief.' Nate chuckled.

Bess groaned.

'Dangerous business,' Owen said.

'Oh, aye. One of their partners paid for it with his life, he did. They did not risk so much after that. And when Master Taverner's wife and child died at sea . . .' Nate shook his head. 'The master could not be persuaded it was not God's vengeance. But why would the Lord punish the innocent, is what I want to know?'

'Did your master sire any other children?'

Nate snorted. 'Bastards, you mean? Is it bastards you seek? Now, that I cannot say, Captain. He was a man for the ladies, truth be told, even at the end. But I did not ask and he did not say, eh?' The old man chuckled and shook his head.

Bess wondered why her uncle had trusted the man.

'What made him choose St Leonard's?'

Nate grew serious. 'In truth, I cannot say. My master had the habit of secrecy, Captain. We travelled round, he spoke with the wardens and masters, and at last chose St Leonard's. 'Tis all I know.'

'From whom did he steal in Scarborough?'

'The big smuggling families. Ones who would not miss the income, you see. He was honest in his own way.'

Bess held out her tankard to Tom, who had just settled beside her.

He grinned as he reached for the pitcher behind him. 'You are learning much about your Uncle Julian.'

'Stealing from his neighbours. I would not have believed it of him. I don't know as I do yet.'

'His partner,' Owen said to Nate, 'the one who died. What was his name?'

Nate closed his eyes, pressed a knotty fist to his forehead, whistled through his broken teeth. 'So long ago. Sometimes they called him "that bastard". I recall that.' The old man grinned, wagged his head. 'They were not always gentlemen.'

Well, that did not surprise Bess.

'Was Laurence de Warrene involved?'

'You can be sure. 'Twas his idea to do it. Always a clever one, Master Warrene. Mistress Taverner never liked it much. Nor Mistress Warrene.'

'They are all dead now. Who else might remember those times?' Owen asked.

Nate stared into his empty tankard. 'I cannot say as I know which of them might still be alive.'

Tom refilled the man's cup. 'One of his women?' he suggested. 'A man oft confides to a woman what he tells no one else.'

'Oh, aye. The master might have done.' Nate tilted back his head and drank down his ale as quickly as the last.

'He had women here?'

'That he did, I can say. Who they were, I cannot.'

Owen drained his cup, stood up. 'I thank you. You will be silent about what we have discussed?'

'Aye, Captain.'

Bess straightened up as Owen turned his hawk-eye on her. What must he think of her now? To have had a thieving uncle.

'I must search the hospital and go out to the Ffulford farm,' Owen said. 'I've no time to sift through your uncle's lemans. Have you the time?'

Bess's heart leapt. 'Are you asking for my help?'

'I have always said you were the one should spy for the archbishop.'

'You do not know how right you are,' Tom muttered.

But Bess paid her husband no heed. 'Would you step without?' she asked Owen.

'I have a matter to discuss.' She led him out into the yard just beyond the kitchen. 'You believe Uncle Julian was poisoned.' She could tell by the set to his jaw that he was sorry she had realised his intent. 'Do you think me an idiot? Do you ask for my help to keep me out of your way?'

'Bess, for pity's sake. I hoped to spare you the pain until I knew for certain. I do think it likely, but I do not know. And as for your help, I need it. I can trust few people with such business.'

Well, he looked sincere, he sounded sincere . . . 'Lucie thought all along it was poison, eh?'

'She did.'

'You would use me now? After my failure in Easingwold?'

'I regret my words to you.'

Bess patted his hand. 'No matter. But I shall help you only if you swear you will keep no more from me.'

'I swear, Bess.'

He almost choked on the words, but Bess could ask for no less.

Later in the evening, as Owen helped Lucie hang a new crop of mint sprigs from the rafters of the workroom to dry, she asked whether he had told Bess about the riddle.

'Do you think it important?'

Lucie handed him a bunch. 'Does it not fit with his smuggling activities? "If none suffer but the guilty, has a wrong been done?" He stole from the guilty.'

'But what of the first part? "How might one unwittingly commit a sin?" '

'By neglect? I find that part puzzling. But you might tell Bess. Now you have asked her to help, you must tell her what you know.'

'Am I a fool to involve her?'

'You would be a fool not to. Bess would take part whether you wished it or no — you have seen that. Far better to give her tasks than have her surprise you.' Lucie shook out the basket. 'Finished. You might have a last ale with Bess tonight. Perhaps she already has a plan.'

St Helen's Square was quiet as Owen stepped from the shop. No bells tolled, no mourners knelt by fresh graves in the cemetery. Pray God it meant the pestilence had run its course. He would have his children safely home.

The York Tavern was not as crowded as in better times, a dozen folk, no more. And they were oddly quiet, watching the door with uneasy eyes as Owen came through. Then they resumed whispering among themselves, shoulders hunched forward towards their tankards.

The innkeeper stood near the door, his face red and glistening with sweat, his legs firmly planted, muscular arms, bare to the elbow, crossed over his stomach, his eyes wary.

'What's amiss, Tom?'

'A bit of trouble. Wife's in kitchen seeing to Simon's eye.'

'An unwelcome customer?'

'Aye. A stranger with a bad look and smell to him. Sickening, I would say. Sent him to spital.'

'And he blackened Simon's eye?' The groom was tall and strong, a good fighter. 'A sick man with such energy?'

'His friend gave Simon trouble.' Tom relaxed his stance. 'They are gone from here. Did you come to drink?'

'I came to talk to Bess.'

'You will need drink, then.' Tom turned, pulled Owen's mazer off the shelf, filled it with foamy ale. 'That should keep you a while. She is in kitchen, as I said.'

'You will call out to me if they return?'

'Oh aye. But my gut tells me they will not be back. 'Tis a queer time when an innkeeper sends a man with coin on his way.'

'No bells tonight. A good sign, I think.'

'Pray God it is so.'

Simon sat slumped against the wall holding a compress to his eye. Bess invited Owen back into her little room off the kitchen.

'It will be quiet here. I see Tom has already seen you have something to drink.'

'I forgot to tell you something. A riddle your uncle wanted Laurence to keep to himself.'

'A riddle? What good is a riddle if you keep it to yourself?'

'Fortunately, Sir Richard also heard it.'

'Will it help us?'

Owen drooped over his cup. 'I cannot think what it means. Lucie thinks it has to do with their smuggling.' He recited the riddle.

Pouring herself a small brandywine, Bess held it up to her nose while she considered. ' "How might one unwittingly commit a sin?" Sounds like clever words to me, showing off. Laurence thought himself a bit of a wit, you know.'

'Ah well. It might come to you.'

'I am off to see Nell, the laundress, in the morning.'

That brightened Owen's mood. 'Lucie said you would already have a plan.'

Alisoun had made a mistake coming here. No one cared for her. The children were herded like sheep, constantly shushed, as if their voices disturbed the sisters, disturbed God. Why had her mother told her to come here if she ever needed help? Why had she spoken of the spital with affection? Alisoun felt she had been better off in hiding. She had been hungry and lonely, and that would have become worse as winter approached and she had no crops, no livestock — her uncle had taken it all, for safekeeping, he had assured her — but she could practise shooting, watch the birds, sit by the river and listen to the cries of the boatmen, eat when she wished, sleep when she wished, and never be scolded. All her own choices . . .

So once again she plotted her escape. She would go by night. It frightened her a little that the watcher might be somewhere in the shadows, but it was worse to lie on her pallet and wait for attack. She had attempted to walk out of the spital in the middle of the day, casually, but the gatekeeper had sent her back — with a promise that he would say naught to Dame Beatrice, a kindness Alisoun had not expected, but still he had sent her back. So the night was her best chance. She had noticed that the gate had a small door with a latch on the inside, but not without, and therefore the gatekeeper might not see the need to lock it. She hoped to sneak through, just barely opening the door, while he was drowsing.

Alisoun tiptoed through the rows of sleeping children. Lord, how some of them snored. And stank. If she could only reach the blessed night air and get out of this midden where no one wanted her. She yearned for the clean stench of horse sweat. But she would not enjoy that by escaping. She had given the horse to the spital. For safekeeping, they had said. How would she get the nag now?

She tripped as a voice whispered from the shadows. 'Who goes there?' A woman's voice.

Alisoun kept walking.

The woman grabbed her arm. She had a strong grasp. Alisoun could not pull away.

'You would leave the Barnhous?' the woman asked.

She must be one of the sisters. She would be satisfied with an untroublesome reply. 'I must relieve myself.'

The woman stepped into the moonlight, pulling Alisoun with her. It was the lay sister, Anneys. 'Ah. Young Alisoun. You mean to escape?'

Alisoun hesitated. She had made note of the woman, thought her different from the others. Was it possible she might help Alisoun?

'Why would I escape?'

'I have watched you. You are unhappy here.'

'I was wrong to come here,' Alisoun said. 'I have kin. This place is for children with no one.'

'You would sneak from the gate with your horse?'

'I must leave him here.'

'I might bring him to you at the Water Gate.'

'Why would you help me?'

'Of what use is it to us to force you to stay?'

'They stopped me when I tried to walk out.'

'Not all of us feel the same.'

'The Water Gate is locked.'

'I have borrowed a key.'

Anneys offered too much, too readily. Alisoun did not trust her. 'What do you want from me?'

'Mayhap God gave me a sign to watch over you. Come. We cannot stay here. Someone will hear us.'

'You will go with me?'

'I, too, tire of this place.'

Twenty-two

A Sleuth and a Samaritan

Bess's day began earlier than usual, and so did Tom's. She had wakened him to give him instructions regarding the maids, the cook and his assistant, and Simon the groom. 'I depend on you to see that they complete their work today, Tom. I must go out.'

Tom rubbed the sleep from his eyes. 'What do you mean to do — ask every woman in York if she lay with your uncle?'

What was wrong with him of late? 'You will see, Tom Merchet. I am not the silly woman you think me.'

'I was teasing, for pity's sake. I did not mean it.'

'You are not a man enjoys hearing himself chatter, Tom. You think Owen foolish for asking my help. But you will see. And you will have me to answer to if all is not as it should be when I return.'

'I told you I was teasing, and I'll not say it again.'

'What has been said has been said.'

'Had I known helping Owen would put you in such a mood, I'd have begged him to reconsider.'

As if he had any say in it. Men thought they ruled the world.

They broke their fast in silence. Bess then donned her second-best gown and one of her ribboned caps and set off to seek out Nell, a sometime laundress at the hospital. A woman might note much as she scrubbed other's clothes and bedding. Nell had oft provided Bess with important insights into her neighbours.

As Bess hurried past the crier, he shouted good news: a day had passed without a plague death in the city. Praise be to God. Mayhap they were safe now. Bess pressed two pennies into the crier's palm.

Nell lived off Lop Lane in a tiny wattle and daub house in the shadow of larger buildings that faced the street. Little light meant a scraggly kitchen garden, but it was imperiously guarded by a hen who eyed Bess with distrust and clucked her disapproval of the early morning caller. Bess found Nell round the corner of the house, preparing to lead her cow out of the rear gate.

'Good morning, Nell. Off to the strays?'

Nell wore a much mended gown and a cap stained by the morning's milking. The peaceful look on her round, freckled face quickly changed to worry. 'Bess Merchet? What trouble brings you here so early in the day? I have had my share of trouble.'

'What trouble?'

The laundress lifted a rough, chapped hand to her opposite shoulder, clutched it as if protecting herself. 'My son's baby died the day before yesterday. And now his daughter burns with fever.'

Sweet Heaven, that was a heavy sorrow. 'The crier gives us hope, Nell. None died yesterday.'

'I cannot see how that will save my grandchild.' Her eyes filled with tears. 'This pestilence is a curse on my house.'

Bess wished she had not spoken. Nell had every right to feel the pestilence as a personal curse. She had lost her husband to it in the last outbreak, now one grandchild — two most like. 'Come. I shall walk with you to the strays.' The fields where the cow grazed were just without the city walls. Bess could spare the time.

As they led the cow out into the quiet street, Nell gave a great sigh. 'Not all are dying. In faith, far fewer than the last two times. But still my family is taken one by one.' She blotted her eyes on her sleeve, took a deep breath. 'Forgive me. I have never been one to complain. I do not wish to start now. You have not told me why you sought me betimes.'

'You will have good ale tonight if you help me, Nell.'

The laundress glanced over the lumbering cow at Bess. 'I am sorry about your uncle. Is it sommat to do with him? I have not been to spital in a month. I know naught of his death.' She patted the cow and coaxed her to turn on to Petergate. 'He was a good man, Master Taverner.'

'Amorous, I am told.'

A twinkle in the tired eyes. 'There was talk of that. I envied his women. But he did not fancy me.'

And no wonder. Nell was a lumbering woman in movement and wit, much like the beast they led. Though she was blessed with an unscarred, unmarred face and most of her teeth. 'Did my uncle have a leman at the hospital?' Bess asked.

'There were rumours — one of the servants. Or a lay sister — and what are they but servants who do not know their place?' Nell sniffed.

So they were impatient with Nell. Bess might be, too, if forced to work alongside her.

'But most of the gossip was of someone

without,' Nell added.

'Who?'

'Some said Felice Mawdeleyn. But I could not swear to it.'

Well. Her uncle had had an eye for a pretty face, that was for certain. 'Sly Felice. How did she keep such straying from Will?'

'They do say Will Mawdeleyn lost more than his leg when that horse came down on him.'

'Do they now? Who might know for certain about my uncle's women?'

'Barker the gatekeeper.'

'You are a good woman, Nell. Come to the tavern when you will. I shall see you feast well.'

They had reached the grassy strays. Here no trees or buildings hid them from the sun. Bess could feel its warmth. It was easy to forget the pestilence on such a day.

Nell nodded to Bess. 'You are kind. I have told you naught you could not hear from another.'

'I trust you, Nell. You are no idle gossip.'

'Never idle.' Nell turned and slowly led her cow towards the river, where the grass was high.

In Spen Lane, near St Andrew's Church, Brother Wulfstan noticed a red cross on a house that was one of the abbey's properties in the city. He had thought the house vacant. But that meant nothing; many abandoned houses in the city were at present home to those escaping the ill in their own households, and sometimes it was the sick who were shoved through loose shutters and left to die, the shelter considered a kindness.

After a long night watching at the bedside of a dying child whose mother was too terrified to comfort her, Brother Wulfstan's head and bones ached, his eyes burned, his tongue was woolly, and he yearned to sit on a bench in the shade of his garden sipping watered wine freshened with mint leaves. But if there was a body within he must say prayers over it and arrange for its removal. With Gog and Magog abroad in the land, he could not desert the needy. How much worse must it have been in the first visitation, when half the city's inhabitants had died? Half his brothers had died also, but they had been cared for in their suffering, no one had been sent away.

Wulfstan took a deep breath of what little fresh air there was in the street, preparing himself for the stench of the plague dead. Holding a sack of herbs to his nose, he pushed open the door.

Light filtered weakly through shutters at

the rear of the main room. Dust danced in the light. A rat ran over the monk's foot and escaped out into the street. Wulfstan blinked as his weak eyes adjusted, took his scented bag from his nose, sniffed. He coughed violently as the stench hit him. Dead or dying. But there was no one in the main room. He opened a shutter better to see the room. A ladder led to a solar or loft. The thought of climbing it made him ache all the more. But he must. He opened another shutter to let in some air. It hung crookedly and banged against the wall.

'Who is there?' someone called weakly from above.

'God go with you,' said Wulfstan. 'I am the infirmarian of St Mary's, come to help you. I saw the cross on the door.'

'Leave me. I am better dead.'

'Do you have water up there?'

A brittle laugh. 'Neighbours do not bring gifts when the red cross is on the door.'

Pressing his aching lower back, Wulfstan let himself out by the back door. Across the rear yard he explored the kitchen. A lidless jug half filled with water smelled musky. Best not to chance it. Beneath the table he discovered a bottle of wine. It was turning, but it would be useful for mixing a salve if he should need to. He put the bottle in his pack.

Returning to the house, he climbed the ladder, slowly, gagging on the stench which grew stronger with each step.

'I am a sinner, Father.' The man's voice was hoarse from fever and thirst.

Wulfstan had made it to the top of the ladder and was too short of breath to reply. He put the herbs to his nose, clutched his side and waited until the room stopped spinning, then walked round the screen which shielded the sick man from view.

The room in which he lay was large, with shuttered windows facing away from the street. The man was naked, curled up on a filthy pile of straw. A mouse sniffed at his clothes, which had been thrown over a stool. Wulfstan shooed the mouse away. The stench of plague mingled with urine and sweat. Wulfstan approached the pallet. 'Was it for you they put the cross on the door?'

'No. I took it as a sign I would not be disturbed.'

'And then you fell ill?'

The man lifted his arm, revealing an oozing boil the size of an egg. 'One has burst.'

And thus the intensity of the smell. 'Praise God. It is a good sign, my son.'

The man curled up, facing away. 'I do not need lies.'

'It is no lie. Some whose boils burst live.'

The man turned his head. There was a flicker of interest in his wet, red eyes. 'You speak true?'

'I have no reason to speak otherwise.' Wulfstan felt the man's forehead. A fever, but not so high as to be dangerous. 'It was painful when it burst?'

'More painful before.'

'How long ago?'

'Dawn.'

The sickness might already be abating. Wulfstan noticed a boil in the man's groin, almost as large as the one under his arm. 'Your other arm?'

The man lifted it, revealing a small black knob.

'Could you bear my lancing the burst one? And the others?'

The man closed his eyes. 'Will it save me?'

'If God wishes.'

'And if He does not?'

'It sometimes hastens the end.'

A deep breath. 'Do it.'

Wulfstan noticed another blemish on the man. On one arm a red-lipped wound oozed puss and was hot to the touch. 'How did this happen?'

'A bitch bit me here. And there.' He lifted his leg to display a scabbed thigh wound.

Wulfstan touched it, gently pressed it.

'They do not look like bites.'

'Forgive me, Father.'

Wulfstan glanced up. The man watched him with the eyes of a frightened beast. Wulfstan remembered him now. 'Both wounds would have closed had you returned with me to St Mary's. Why did you take the bag and not the man with skill to use the medicines?'

'You will leave me now.'

'No. It does not matter.' Wulfstan opened his pack, handed the man a small leather flask of brandywine. 'What is your name?'

'Why?'

'I must call you something.'

'John.'

Wulfstan did not believe the man's name was John, but it did not matter. 'There is not much left, John, but drink what there is.' While the man drank, Wulfstan knelt and prayed God to give him strength, a steady hand, and clear vision. And if it was not John's time, that he might live and repent.

'I left your things in a safe place.'

Wulfstan nodded as he knelt awkwardly on his aching knees, drew his knife from its leather scabbard. 'Be as still as you can bear, my son. There will be pain, but the more you move, the worse it will be.'

First he probed the burst boil. John cried

out. Wulfstan sat back on his heels, watched as the putrid blood flowed faster. He wiped the sticky poison from his hands with a cloth. In a small dish he mixed powder of hemlock with a few drops of wine, stirred it, poured more wine. With the edge of a square of cloth he applied the salve to the boil. 'To ease the pain.' He then folded the cloth into a thick compress. 'Hold this over it with your other hand.' The man's breath was uneven. Wulfstan prayed God he was not killing him. He would like to see one man survive after watching so many die. 'Are you ready for the other arm?'

A silent nod.

Wulfstan said a prayer, leaned back and squinted, drew the knife across the boil. Nothing. He had not pressed hard enough. Sweat blinded him. He wiped his eyes, said another prayer, tried again. As the blade sank into the skin, black poison shot out and John cried out in pain. Wulfstan hurried to the window and gulped the air. The rooftops swam before him and he clung to the windowsill as his legs threatened to fold beneath him. He was too tired. He should have gone back to the abbey. But if he saved the man . . .

John moaned.

Wulfstan turned, steadied himself, and

keeping one hand on the wall crossed back to him. 'Forgive me, my son.'

'I can bear it,' John whispered.

'I shall lance the one below and let it drain while I mix the salve. Are you ready?' Wulfstan wiped his hands, dried the sweat on his brow, knelt to the last boil. It lanced with ease. Now the dirty straw on which John lay was saturated with the poison. It would be good to move the man, but where to? And how, with Wulfstan's head spinning and his legs so unsteady?

His hands shook as he mixed the salve, smoothed it on the boils. 'I must leave you now. I will be back. Or one of my brothers.'

'You will not say the prayers over me and shrive me?'

'I must rest. I promise you someone will come.'

'You never meant to save me.'

'God help me, John. I am ill.'

The man turned away from him.

Wulfstan managed to make his way to the ladder. As he descended, he could not grasp the ladder tight enough with the bag in his hand. He let it drop to the floor. The loss of the burden helped, but his knees threatened to buckle on each rung. By the time Wulfstan had struggled down, he had forgotten the bag. He pushed open the front door, took a step backward. The bright sun-light burned his eyes and made them water so badly he could not see. He withdrew, finding the dark interior comforting. He set-tled down against the wall. A nap might strengthen him.

Twenty-three

A Day of Diplomacy

Owen discovered the physician's house locked, the windows on his ground floor boarded up. He had hoped to look at the house, see whether someone might have stayed there and spied on Walter de Hotter. But the boards were well fastened. He moved on to the hospital to speak to Honoria about the foul-smelling physick that Nate said Julian had been taking the day he died.

But the sight of the almoner playing gatekeeper put all else out of his mind for a moment. Owen was accustomed to seeing the canon going among the poor, not guarding the gate. '*Benedicte,* Don Erkenwald. Where is Barker?' In truth, the muscular, scarred almoner looked more at home in a gatehouse than among the poor.

'He is assisting in the search,' Erkenwald said with a grave nod.

Owen understood the nod as an invitation for questions. 'You have found something?'

'Nay. Lost. Two members of our community disappeared in the night.' Erkenwald sank down on to a bench with a sigh, rested one elbow on his knees, his eyes level with Owen's. A soldier's pose, not a canon's. 'Matters have gone from bad to worse.'

'Who has disappeared?'

'Anneys, one of our lay sisters, and a child from the orphanage, Alisoun Ffulford. Did the boy not explain why Sir Richard sent for you?'

'I must have been gone when he came. I had hoped to search the house of Master Saurian. But it is boarded up.'

Erkenwald sniffed. 'And so it will be until the first frost. The physician fled the city.'

'I had heard.'

'I always counted him a coward.'

'Some find it unbearable to work among the dying.'

Erkenwald looked at Owen askance. 'A physician? Pah! I pray you, go to Sir Richard. He awaits you.'

As Owen crossed the yard, he wondered what new mischief was afoot. Had Alisoun's lurker taken action? But what had Anneys to do with it?

A servant showed Owen into Ravenser's parlour, where Owen was greeted by not only the master, but also Don Cuthbert, Dame Constance and Dame Beatrice. Ravenser rose to greet him, an unusual gesture. His expression echoed Owen's anxiety. 'We are guarding all gates to the hospital, and the lay brothers have begun a search with Barker in command. But I fear the man has fled with the child and the woman.'

'Barker did not see them pass last night?'

Ravenser looked to Dame Constance.

'Anneys lives in the lay sisters' house in the city. Barker would have noted nothing unusual in her passing through, and he does not remember a child,' Dame Constance said.

'You have found no sign of the man?'

Don Cuthbert shook his head. 'They have been searching since matins and have found no strangers amongst us.'

'Tell me how you discovered they were missing, Dame Constance.'

'Alisoun was not in her bed this morning, nor anywhere a child might roam. And when the lay sisters arrived they were without Anneys. Not that she is always prompt.'

'You have searched for Anneys?'

'We do not know where to begin.'

Nor do I, Owen thought. But it was not the sort of thing he cared to admit aloud.

Ravenser dismissed Don Cuthbert, Dame Constance and Dame Beatrice. When the others had departed, the master drummed his fingers on the arm of his chair. 'The situation is worse than it was when you began, Captain Archer. Why is that?' At that moment he looked more like his uncle than usual.

And had the same effect on Owen. 'Have I kept aught from you, Sir Richard?'

'Not to my knowledge.'

'Have you kept aught from me? What of your argument with William Savage. Should I know the details?'

Ravenser's colour heightened; his uncle knew no blushes. 'You presume —' He shook his head. 'No. You are quite right. I attacked you for no reason.'

'And William Savage?'

A sudden interest in arranging the items on the table. 'Savage. It is quite simple. I refused his wife's mother as a corrodian, though the terms promised to be generous. The discussion grew heated, we both said things we should not have.'

'Such as?'

Ravenser paused in his fussing, frowned up at Owen. 'You truly think it important.'

'As you say, the situation grows worse. I am obviously missing vital pieces of the puzzle.'

A nod. 'Savage mentioned the rumours of our financial straits, the corrodians dying conveniently, and then crowned it all with a new rumour, that Honoria de Staines was sleeping with corrodians of the hospital.'

'A rumour? Or a fact, I wonder. With whom did he say she was sleeping?'

Ravenser looked alarmed. 'It is of some import, then?'

'It might be,' Owen said.

'He would not say. Hence I believed it was a bluff.'

'Why was Savage so angry?'

'I accused him of fearing his wife's mother would take over his household. She is known to be most unpleasant.'

'Sweet *Jesu.* His Grace could hardly be more tactless.'

'My uncle would not have put himself in this situation, Captain.'

True enough. 'Is there aught else you have not told me?'

'I have bared my soul to you. Now make something of it.'

Owen rose. 'Patience, Sir Richard.'

'I am impatient only because I have been called south. The Queen is failing rapidly. But I do not like to leave until I know that the reputation of St Leonard's is saved.'

'Then pray that my day is fruitful.'

As Owen crossed the yard he met Don

Erkenwald. Hands on hips, he looked militant despite his robes and sandals. 'They have searched most of the area, Captain. No strangers.'

'It tells us nothing. He would have been a fool to stay.'

'The lay sisters mentioned a deserted house next to them, one that has seen trouble.'

'Aye. And many another house emptied by the Death.'

'Quite right. Where will you look?'

'First I must speak with Honoria de Staines. Where might I find her?'

'At the Barnhous. She is watching the sick infants. Then what?'

'If I learn nothing from her, I have a mind to travel to a farm.'

'Would that I had an excuse to accompany you.'

'How are you with a shovel?'

Erkenwald grinned. 'Very good. But that is not a unique skill.'

'I might also need you to take up a weapon.'

'What of your men?'

'They will be busy searching the city. I would welcome your help.'

Erkenwald nodded. 'Come for me when you are ready.'

* * *

Wulfstan woke once to feel someone brush by him. Then a child's voice cried out, 'Here. Is this the one we seek?'

A woman leaned close. 'You have saved my son. I shall do what I can for you.'

'Sweet Mary, pray for me,' Wulfstan whispered.

Someone lifted him and carried him into a bright place. Wulfstan's eyes could not yet open before the Divine Light, but his heart was filled with joy to know that he had reached his Heavenly reward.

By the time Bess arrived at St Leonard's, Barker was once more in charge of the gate. 'Do you remember my uncle, Julian Taverner?'

Barker brushed off the seat of a chair, beckoned Bess to sit. 'Master Taverner. He was a man respected all, no matter their station.'

'He did that, Barker,' Bess said as she settled down. 'And he was a fair man, was he not?'

'Oh, aye.'

Bess kept her eyes downcast as she said, 'He left me with a delicate problem, my uncle.' Now she peered up, pretending embarrassment.

The man's bulbous nose twitched. 'Oh, aye?'

'As he was dying, he said to me, "Swear you will take care of her." '

'Who?'

Bess threw up her hands. 'There. You see the problem. He died without breathing her name. But I have a thought it might have been his — his leman. And, well, you can see the care I must take in enquiring about her. I must avoid those who might talk to others afterwards. Ruin a good woman's name.'

Barker made a sympathetic face.

'Still, I feel a duty to find her and discover what I might do. What needs doing. And I thought — I *hoped* that you might have seen him walk out now and then. I know you would not be gatekeeper were you not a trustworthy, *discreet* man, and yet one who *notices*.'

Barker pulled himself up to his full height. ' 'Tis a delicate matter indeed, Mistress Merchet. And you are a good woman to wish to see justice done. Many would not feel so obliged.'

'I would not think of ignoring my uncle's last request.'

'Surely. He had a honeyed tongue, your uncle. Any of the women might have been with him one time or another.'

'Were there none he saw more than others?'

'That would be Felice Mawdeleyn. And, well, there was a lay sister of late. But Mistress Mawdeleyn and your uncle were longtime friends.'

'Will Mawdeleyn's wife?'

'Aye, the very same.' Barker shook his head. 'Will should have beaten her when she was contrary. 'Tis ever the problem.'

Bess bit her tongue. She had better things to do than argue with a thick-headed man. 'And one of the lay sisters, you said? Who was that, Barker?' Knowing of Honoria's attachment to her uncle, Bess asked the question as a test, to see whether the man's information was accurate. Many a gossip filled in the gaps in their knowledge with rumour.

Barker frowned and rubbed his shoulder. 'I should say no more, Mistress Merchet. Felice Mawdeleyn is more likely to be the one you want, eh?'

Very likely. Felice was the sort to inspire confidence. Yes, it was very likely. Still. 'You can trust me, Barker. I have no reason to make public my uncle's sins.'

'True enough. 'Twas Anneys, the one who has disappeared.'

Bess almost nodded, so certain had she been about what he would say. It took a moment to realise he had not said it. 'Anneys. Not Honoria de Staines?'

'Anneys. He was fond of Honoria, but like a daughter.'

'How do you know?'

The chest puffed up. 'A man can tell such things of another man, to be sure.'

'You say Anneys disappeared?'

'Aye. Last night. With the Ffulford child.'

Well. That would keep Owen occupied for the day. 'Bless you, Barker. You have been most kind to me. Come to the tavern some evening and we shall treat you well.' She walked slowly away, searching her memory for all she knew of Felice Mawdeleyn. Of Anneys she knew nothing. But Anneys was Owen's problem now.

Owen found Honoria de Staines folding laundry at a table outside a curtained alcove in the Barnhous. She nodded to him, put a finger to her lips and opened the curtain to show him three sleeping infants.

'God go with you, Captain Archer,' she said softly as she stepped away from the curtain. 'What would you ask me today?'

He chose first to broach the unpleasant topic. 'Forgive me, Mistress Staines, but I must know whether the late mayor, William Savage, spoke the truth when he claimed you were sleeping with corrodians at this hospital.'

The pretty woman coloured. 'William Savage said that?' She snapped the blanket she was folding. 'So that was his revenge.'

'Revenge?'

'Let us speak of William Savage, Captain.' Honoria placed the blanket on the table and took time to smooth it. When she turned to Owen, her eyes glittered with emotion. 'God forgive me for speaking ill of the dead, but William Savage played false with me. Oh, at first he was generous and kind, assisted me in my petition to work here as a lay sister. And then he demanded I lie with him. I refused.' She glared at Owen's questioning look. 'For fear of his wife, Marion, Captain.'

'Go on.'

'But she had already condemned me. She is a woman who believes the worst of everyone, and she was certain that he helped me because he had bedded me. She ordered him to make amends by purchasing a corrody for her mother so that she might be free of her.'

'How do you know this?'

'He told me. And he said she meant to blacken my name at the hospital. Can you guess why he told me, Captain? So that I might agree to enjoy the sin for which I was to be condemned.' She was finding it difficult to keep her voice low.

An ugly story, if true. 'Did you tell anyone of this?'

'Don Cuthbert. He believed me.'

Easy enough to confirm. 'And you had no relations with the corrodians?'

Honoria bristled. 'I am not a fool, Captain. I wished to stay here.'

One of her charges had begun to whimper. She disappeared through the curtains, emerged rocking a boy of Hugh's age in her arms.

'Is that all, Captain?' Her eyes were cold.

'Just one thing more. Julian Taverner's last illness. Old Nate mentioned a foul-smelling physick.'

'There was one with a bitter taste. Master Taverner complained of it.'

'It was one of the physicks Mistress Merchet brought?'

'I could not swear to it, Captain. Anneys had charge of his care. And now if you will excuse me, I must change this little one.'

'God go with you, Mistress Staines.'

Owen strode away with mixed feelings. A part of him pitied her; he knew that men treated women so. But he would have thought such a man as Savage above that.

Only a man who had earned his comrades' respect attained a position as mayor. Or was Owen naïve? Even so, why would Savage risk spreading a rumour that could return to bite him?

It was past midday by the time Bess made her way up Spen Lane towards Mawdeleyn's house, and a good thing it was that time or she might not have seen the black-robed monk slumped in the doorway. But with the sun overhead he lay in a pool of light, his hood pulled up to shield his eyes. It was not the sort of thing Benedictines did, sleep in doorways. And why should they with such a lovely abbey? Still, here he was. Bess stepped closer, then backed up when she caught the unmistakable odour of pestilence. The monk had sensed her presence and struggled to sit up. As he clutched the doorway, his hood fell back.

'Brother Wulfstan!' Bess pressed her scented sachet to her nose and mouth and crept forward.

Wulfstan gazed round, confused. 'I am yet on mortal soil?'

Bess knelt down, touched Wulfstan's forehead with the back of her free hand. He was on fire. Sweet Heaven, how was she to get him to the abbey?

She stood up, looked round. The normally busy street was deserted. No doubt all feared walking past the monk in the doorway. Still, it was disgraceful, with churches to either side, that no man of God had offered help or sought it for him. 'I am going to find a horse or a cart, Brother Wulfstan. I shall return quickly.'

Down Spen Lane she hurried and out on to St Saviour gate. In a short while, Seth, the ragman, came down the road, leading his donkey cart. 'Mistress Merchet. A queer place to find you of an afternoon.'

Bess was disappointed to see the cart almost empty. The rags would have made a nice cushion for Wulfstan. But no matter. 'I have found a soul in need, Seth, and you are a good Samaritan sent by God. I must get Brother Wulfstan to St Mary's. He is ill. He cannot walk.'

Seth's eyes grew big as he crossed himself. 'The Death?'

'I shall purchase every rag in the cart.'

'He will die, whether or no he makes the abbey.'

'A free tankard of ale each night for a week? 'Tis more than you deserve. You should do it for love of the man who has sat with so many who would have been abandoned.'

'Two tankards.'

'You will be the ruin of me.'

'I give you the rags.'

Wulfstan stood with Bess's help, and with Seth's aid she eased him into the cart. As she let go of him, Wulfstan touched her sleeve. 'I promised . . . shrive . . . must go back.'

'We are going to St Mary's. Do not try to talk,' Bess said, arranging the rags around Wulfstan, who shivered though the day had grown warm. She pulled the hood down over his eyes. 'Rest now.'

As they led the donkey cart through the streets to St Mary's, folk fled before them. Bess felt as if she were Moses parting the Red Sea. And it came to her that this plague with which God punished them for their sins made greater sinners of them all. Or most of them.

Brother Henry knelt in prayer at Wulfstan's bedside while the novice Gervase kept cool compresses on the old infirmarian's brow and sponged his face, neck, and arms with strawberry and sage water.

'John,' Wulfstan whispered.

Henry glanced up from his prayers. 'Who is John?' he asked again.

Wulfstan's eyes fluttered open. He put a trembling hand on his assistant's head. 'My attacker. He did not have the sacrament.'

'I do not understand, Brother Wulfstan.'

Wulfstan closed his eyes, asleep once more. Brother Henry wiped his own eyes and bent back to his prayers.

Twenty-four

Owen's Suspicion

Lucie studied Owen's back as he reached into the potting shed and pulled out the shovels. He cursed as he looked them over. 'Where is the old one?'

It was ever so, he missed nothing until he needed it, and he always behaved as if he had not been privy to its disposal. And always when Lucie was busy. 'We gave it to Magda. She knew of someone who would be grateful for it. *You* gave it to her.'

It was unclear whether his scowl was meant for her or himself.

'Then I must risk one of the better ones.'

'Apparently.' But Lucie knew that Owen's temper was not about the shovel. 'You expect to find more than the child's treasure,' Lucie guessed.

Owen took his time choosing a shovel, picking up one, then another. At last he put two aside and hung the others back on their hooks.

'Turn round, husband. I will see your face.'

Owen turned. His jaw was set in anger.

Lucie traced the tension with her finger. 'What is this? Angry with me for guessing?'

His jaw relaxed a little. But the scar that spread from beneath his eyepatch was livid.

'Are you angry with Ravenser and his men for letting Anneys and Alisoun slip through their fingers?'

'At myself. I am the one let them slip away. I have been so blind.'

'No, my love. You see quite well with one eye. Ever better,' Lucie teased, trying to cheer him.

Owen did not smile. 'Anneys was one of the first to arrive at Laurence's burning house.' He paced to the linden tree, turned. 'She was present when Julian died, and she had charge of his care — and no doubt control of his medicines.' He headed for the house, his long legs scissoring through the late summer garden. Lucie followed, wishing to hear the rest of his tirade. 'She had Brother Wulfstan's bag and followed me when I watched Cuthbert hide it. She may have overheard me questioning the child.' He stopped, turned his head round to see her with his one good eye. 'I have been such a fool!'

'Perhaps. But . . .' Lucie tilted her head, raised her eyebrows, waited for him to ask her to go on.

'But?' Arms folded in front of him, he glowered in the kitchen doorway.

Lucie chose her words to soothe, if possible. 'Each time, Anneys has had reason to be there. She may yet prove guilty of nothing more than a foolishly conceived plan to protect Alisoun.'

'I do not believe it.'

Lucie lost her patience. 'Do you believe she is guilty of everything? What of Alisoun's story of the man? And Wulfstan's attack?'

'Two are guilty, and Anneys is one of them.'

'Heaven help the woman if she is innocent.'

'Have you met her?'

Lucie closed her eyes, cursed herself for opening her mouth at all. 'I have been kept from all this by my work.'

'You are well away. Anneys does not look the innocent is my point. She has hard eyes, now I think of it. A bearing too confident for a lay sister.'

'And that makes her guilty?'

'You will see, Lucie.'

'I shall indeed. Come. You must help me move the jars to the workroom.'

They reached the hall as Kate showed Bess in. As soon as they saw their neighbour's face, they both forgot the jars. She told them about Wulfstan. When she was finished, Lucie did not speak at once, nor did Owen.

Kate set a beaker of water before Bess.

'Bless you, child. Bad news dries the throat.'

She had drained the beaker before Lucie spoke. 'It is what we have all feared. Jasper most of all.'

Bess pressed Lucie's hand. 'We do not know it is pestilence. He might merely have exhausted himself.'

'It is not like you to hide from the truth,' Owen said. 'A man does not burn with fever when he is weary.'

'Other maladies cause fever,' Bess said. 'There is more. The lay sister Anneys is missing, and Alisoun Ffulford.'

'I know,' Owen grumbled.

'And Barker says Anneys and my uncle were lovers.'

'What?'

Lucie rubbed her shoulders with a sudden weariness. 'You see, my love? It is unlikely she would have wished him dead.'

Bess's eyes widened. 'You thought *she* was the murderer?'

'I know nothing,' Owen said. 'Tell me of

Wulfstan. He had been alone?'

'He had been with a dying man, I think. He kept saying that someone must shrive him.'

'Wulfstan?' Owen asked.

'Shrive the man he had been with. In that house, I suppose. He called him his attacker.'

Owen rose. 'Tell me where it was.'

Lucie sensed an urgency in him. 'What is it?'

'Wulfstan's attacker. The one who stole Alisoun's horse. He has crossed my path too often for coincidence. I shall fetch Erkenwald and pay the stranger a visit.'

'But he is dying,' Bess said.

'Then we shall take a stretcher.'

Lucie pressed her cool hands to her hot cheeks. 'I do not know how to tell Jasper.'

Lucie returned to the shop intending to speak with Jasper when they had a quiet moment. It was difficult working beside him, trying to hide her feelings. Suddenly Alice Baker rushed into the shop, pushed aside old Jake, who had been ahead of her, leaned on the counter.

'Mistress Baker, I pray you, wait your turn,' Lucie said, motioning to the elderly man to step back up to the counter.

Alice Baker grabbed Lucie's hand. Her eyes were red-rimmed and frightened. 'I beg you. My youngest, Elena, she coughs and coughs. Since this morning. It is the pestilence, I know. What can you give me to protect her?'

Old Jake needed to hear no more. He crossed himself and scuttled from the shop. The form of pestilence most quickly spread was the one that began and ended in a bloody cough.

'Does she cough up blood?' Lucie asked.

The frantic mother tightened her grip on Lucie's hand. 'Is that what is to come?'

'Not necessarily, Mistress Baker. Now calm yourself. She is not coughing up blood?'

'Nay.'

'Is her nose running?'

'And her eyes, too.'

'It may not be the pestilence.'

'She burns with fever.'

'That does not mean pestilence.' Lucie struggled to keep her voice even.

Jasper came from the workroom, where he had been refilling jars. 'Brother Wulfstan might tell you quickly. Send one of your children to the abbey. They will know where he meant to go last. You might find him.'

Lucie touched Jasper's hand. 'No. Not today, Jasper. Pour Mistress Baker the cough syrup for children, and mix boneset and nettle to bring down the fever and dry the child's chest so the cough will cease.'

Jasper gave Lucie a puzzled look, but moved to obey.

Alice Baker let go Lucie's hand, pounded the counter. 'That is not enough!'

'That is the best I can do,' Lucie said, rubbing her hand. She wanted to slap the woman. Day after day she came in with her theories and remedies, but now, when a child was actually ill, she was so ridiculously helpless. 'If the child has pestilence, you have a house full of remedies, surely.'

The woman reared up. 'But my Elena is dying!'

'She is coughing. And if you give her the syrup and a heaping spoonful of the boneset and nettle in boiling water,' Lucie picked up a spoon to show her the proper size, 'Elena might quickly show improvement.'

'And if it is pestilence?'

Lucie dropped her head, pressed her temples. Jasper handed the bottle and package to Alice Baker. 'Bless you, my son,' the woman murmured, tossed two groats on the counter and hurried from the shop.

Lucie sank down on the stool behind the counter and pressed her fingertips to her hot eyelids. She must not cry. It would make it worse for Jasper.

'Mistress Lucie?'

She took a deep breath, raised her head, wiped her eyes. 'I must tell you something, my love.'

'It is Brother Wulfstan,' Jasper guessed.

She took his hand, recounted all that Bess had told her. Tears glistened on the boy's freckled cheeks. She touched them, pressed his hand. 'We do not yet know that it is pestilence.'

'How can it be otherwise? He has sat with so many of the dying, he has breathed their air, touched their bodies, their sweat, their —' Jasper's voice broke. He twisted out of Lucie's grasp, strode across the shop to the door.

'Where are you going?' A silly question.

'To see him,' Jasper shouted as he stepped out into the street. 'Do not try to stop me.'

Lucie wanted to run after him — not to stop him, but to join him. But he had not invited her. And she had the shop to watch.

Down Blake Street Jasper marched, hands pumping, teeth clenched. He was trying to keep himself angry. As long as he was angry about Brother Wulfstan's illness he would not do something that might embarrass him.

So to keep his mind on his anger he debated the target of his anger — God or Abbot Campian. He thought the abbot a good choice because he might have forbidden Brother Wulfstan's sacrifice; he had the authority. But Jasper had learned enough about debating to know that a solid, unassailable argument must stand up to generalisation. This particular argument, extended, would have supported Mistress Lucie in using her authority over Jasper to order him to Freythorpe Hadden with the children. And prevent him from his present mission. God, on the other hand, had authority over everyone and had brought this curse on mankind. But it was dangerous and possibly sinful to be angry with God.

The debate delivered Jasper to the postern gate of St Mary's Abbey still fuming. He rang the bell for the porter.

'Jasper de Melton. *Benedicte,* my son,' Brother William said, his fleshy face distorted in a frown that split his forehead in half with a deep groove. 'You rang with such energy I feared the chain might not hold.' He relaxed his face, but did not smile. 'You have come to see Brother Wulfstan?'

Jasper nodded.

'You may find it difficult to get past Brother Henry. But God has sent you here,

I cannot turn you away. And I know that Brother Wulfstan would like to see you.'

Jasper's anger had begun to dissolve with those kind words, and disappeared entirely as he ran through the abbey gardens, where memories rushed at him. By the time Jasper reached the infirmary, he had wiped his eyes on his sleeves several times.

When the door opened, Brother Henry looked in much the same state as Jasper. Only he had been wiping his eyes far longer, Jasper guessed.

Henry stuck his hands beneath his scapula and shook his head. 'It is the pestilence, Jasper. I cannot in good conscience allow you within.'

'If God has already chosen me, what can you do, Brother Henry?' Jasper asked.

The subinfirmarian did not move. 'You are apprenticed to an apothecary. Surely you do not believe we are to do naught to help ourselves?'

Jasper stood firm. 'I must see him, Brother Henry. My mother did not keep me from my sister when she lay sick with it.'

'And how might she have kept you separated? This is not your home. You have no need to be here.'

Jasper's eyes prickled once more with tears. 'I beg you, let me see him.'

'Do not think me unfeeling, lad.' Brother Henry touched a cloth to his nose. 'Does Mistress Wilton know you are here?'

'She does.'

'And she did not try to prevent your coming?'

Jasper shook his head.

Henry opened the door and stood aside. 'So be it. The odour will be unpleasant. I lanced a boil in his groin.'

The infirmary was dimly lit with oil lamps beside the beds of the ill. There were three patients present: Brother Jonas with an ulcerated sore on his foot; Brother Oswald, who was in the last stages of the Death, his breathing rattling deep in his chest; and Brother Wulfstan. Their beds were at far corners. As Jasper crossed the room, Brother Henry motioned to the novice who sat with Wulfstan to step aside. Jasper's steps faltered as the odour of the pestilence grew stronger.

Wulfstan lay with his eyes closed, his hands folded on the coverlet in prayer. The skin on his face was like netting folded up; there was no flesh to smooth out the wrinkles. Jasper knelt beside Wulfstan's bed, bowed his head, and whispered prayers. Soon he felt what seemed a feather on his head. Brother Wulfstan's hand. The monk was gazing on him.

'I am glad to see you, my son. But Lucie — does she know you are here?' Wulfstan's voice was but a whisper.

Jasper kissed the old monk's hand. 'She did not stop me.'

Wulfstan pulled his hand away. 'Have a care.' His eyes fluttered closed.

As Jasper waited for Wulfstan to make note of him again, he told him of his day, the remedies he had dispensed, how oddly Mistress Baker had behaved. He had no idea whether Wulfstan could hear and understand. It was not really for Wulfstan that he chattered on. It was for fear he would hear the death rattle in the old monk's breast. Jasper had recounted his activities of the past three days before Wulfstan opened his eyes once more.

'Has someone gone to John?' Wulfstan asked in a voice ever weaker.

'Who is this John?' Jasper asked. 'Was he in the house where you were taken ill?' He knew Owen had gone there.

Brother Henry stepped closer. 'Thus have I queried him also. Again and again he has mentioned John.' He bent to Wulfstan, lifted his head and helped him drink. Little went down. His tongue was swollen.

'Remember,' Wulfstan whispered, his eyes on Henry as the monk lowered him and fussed with his pillows.

'What must Brother Henry remember?' Jasper asked, bending his head close to the old monk's lips. 'Tell me all you can, Brother Wulfstan.'

Wulfstan's words were unconnected — the medicine bag, the attack, Spen Lane, lancing, growing too weak to shrive the man.

'I must go to Captain Owen and tell him this,' Jasper told Henry.

'Have a care. And return in the morning, if you will.'

'If he —' Jasper took a deep breath, rushed the words, 'I do not want to come back and find he has gone.'

'I promise you I shall send word if he seems to be failing quickly.'

Twenty-five

The Guilt of a Father

The Mawdeleyns lived near the King's Fishpond. The muddy banks from which the water receded in high summer stank on hot, sunny days. Bess was thus delighted to be greeted with the scent of meadowsweet when the Mawdeleyn's daughter opened the door to her. The pleasant scent grew stronger as Bess entered the house, crushing the herb beneath her feet.

Felice, her wimple and apron snowy white against her olive complexion and russet gown, rose from her spinning to greet Bess with a warm smile. She was a comely woman, graceful in her movements, even-featured, with perhaps more colour than men cared for — except her uncle. 'I have expected this visit ever since your uncle died,' Felice said when her daughter had withdrawn after carrying in a flagon of wine and two lovely Italian blue glass goblets.

Having prepared a speech that would draw Felice out, Bess found herself momentarily at a loss for words. And curious about the goblets. Were not the missing ones blue?

'You have come about Julian, of course?' Felice asked as she poured.

'I have, Mistress Mawdeleyn, yes, I have. Forgive me. I did not think you would be so . . .' She searched for the right word.

'Shameless?'

'Oh, dear me, no! I thought you would fear trouble if we spoke openly, is all.'

'Trouble? Now he is dead? The trouble happened ten years ago.'

Ten years. An enduring affair. 'Your husband knew?'

Felice blushed, but did not lower her eyes. 'A husband knows when his wife has been bedded, Mistress Merchet. Unless he sleeps in another house and never gazes upon his wife.' She stood up. 'I will get his things.'

'His things? What is this? Is that why you thought I came? To collect —' Bess shook her head. 'What things?'

'His gifts to me.' Felice lifted one of the Italian goblets. 'These were part of a set. He gave the rest to St Leonard's, but he said he wished to surround me with beautiful things.'

She and Honoria de Staines. Still, Bess had not known her uncle could be so tender. 'And so they should remain. I did not come to rob you, Mistress Mawdeleyn, neither of your memories or your gifts. Whatever he gave you he meant for you to have. I came because I hoped you might help me. To be frank, Uncle Julian believed he had been poisoned.'

The generous lips rounded in surprise, the dark eyes seemed darker yet. Felice slipped back down in her chair with hand to throat. 'Dear God.'

Bess believed the emotion to be sincere. 'Forgive me for distressing you. But I hoped he might have confided in you.'

'Confided?'

'He spoke little of the past to me. I know of naught that might support his accusation. Do you know of any enemies he might have made?'

Felice lifted her cup to her lips daintily, then took a decidedly undainty drink, head tilted back. When she set down the goblet, Bess saw that it was empty. A clean linen cloth appeared from a sleeve to dab at the full lips. 'Enemies. Blood enemies, for someone to poison him.' Felice frowned up at the ceiling. 'He once told me of something for which he had done penance for many years. But he begged me to keep my silence. Indeed, this spring he reminded me of the need to keep his secret.'

'Surely now he's dead . . .'

Felice considered her hands. She held them so a gold and silver ring caught the light. Undoubtedly another of Uncle Julian's gifts. 'If he was poisoned,' Felice said, 'I would have his murderer found and punished.' She raised her head, her chin forward, her eyes sad. 'In Scarborough, before the death of his wife and daughter, Julian was a smuggler.'

'So I have heard. But it was more like he thieved from the smugglers.'

'I am glad you knew that Julian was not always honest. I did not wish to be the one to tell you.'

'But that was long ago. To what end would any of them come to York at this late date and murder him, as well as Laurence de Warrene and Walter de Hotter?'

'I can think of no cause. And I know nothing of Master Hotter. Julian never spoke of him. I do know that Julian and Laurence de Warrene worked with others from time to time. One in particular was someone who had knowledge of the families from whom they stole. Adam Carter. And it was his death for which your uncle did penance for many, many years. He believed that his own wife and child died for his sins.'

'A Carter? One of the Carters of Scarborough? Thieving rogues all of them. He was likely stealing from his own. But why?'

'He called himself a Carter, but he was a bastard. His father would not acknowledge him — though he thought to ensure Adam's future by employing him. Which to a proud man was applying vinegar to the wound.'

'And so he stole from his father?'

'With Julian and Laurence.'

'What happened?'

'He took ever greater risks. Julian and Laurence had families. They were more cautious. One night the tide caught them still struggling along a cliff with a barrel. Julian and Laurence abandoned it. Adam began to follow them, but turned back and tried to save it. He was caught by the tide. Julian and Laurence did not realise what had happened until Adam's body washed up on the shore.'

'Faith, a terrible thing. But I cannot see how his greed was their fault.'

'Julian did not at first either. But when his wife and daughter were lost at sea, he saw it as a sign from God. That is why he worked among the victims of the pestilence. It was his penance.'

Bess did not speak for a time. She had known of their deaths, had known of her uncle's penance, but she had not understood why he blamed himself.

Felice poured more wine, then sat twisting the ring on her finger round and round. 'What made it all the worse was that Laurence had kept Adam's booty in his house. The Carters would have grown suspicious had Adam openly owned things he could not afford on his pittance of a wage. He had planned someday to leave Scarborough, taking the lovely things he had hoarded with him. When he died, Julian and Laurence shared his spoils.' Felice lifted her goblet. 'These were Adam Carter's. When I first heard the story, I urged Julian to give the rest of the man's treasures to St Leonard's.'

Bess found it a disturbing tale. 'And did my uncle give them to the hospital?'

Felice's eyes were sad. 'I believe he did. He was a good man, Mistress Merchet.'

'I had always thought him so.' Of late she had not been so certain. 'Adam Carter's hoard. Would it have included altar cloths and an ivory chess set?'

'Why? Do they have something to do with Julian's death?'

'Mayhap.'

Felice ran her finger down the side of the goblet, seemingly studying it with great intent. After a long pause, she returned to Bess. 'I remember nothing about an altar cloth. But Julian once offered me a chess set. I know not whether it was ivory. Or if it was part of Adam's things. I told Julian my family had no leisure to learn such games.'

'I must tell you, it was a relief to learn it was you and not Honoria de Staines my uncle cared for.'

The full lips twitched, then broadened into a smile. 'He cared for both of us, but in different ways. He thought of Honoria as his daughter. And she broke his heart.'

'How?'

'He was scandalised by her affairs — she knew a goodly portion of the town council. I believe it is why her husband left her.'

'I had no idea.'

'Her lovers have good reason to be discreet, Mistress Merchet.'

Bess rose, feeling she had imposed on the woman long enough. 'Mistress Mawdeleyn, you have been patient with me. I am glad that my uncle has someone like you to mourn him.'

'I do mourn him, Mistress Merchet.'

When Bess had taken her leave, she walked back through the city with no eye for the folk round her. Her thoughts were with her uncle. So many years he had lived in the city, so many times they had shared an ale and talked of this and that. And never had he told her of Honoria, Felice, or Adam Carter, or offered her an ivory chess set. She wondered what other treasures he had shared with his women.

Twenty-six

Tidal Waters

Staying well back in the shadow of the poor people's shacks near the bank, Anneys and Alisoun studied the Riverwoman's rocky island. No smoke rose from her chimney, the door was shut, and, most importantly, Magda Digby's boat lay becalmed in the mud beside the rock. But it would not be for long. The incoming tide surged up the Ouse and already the tops of the waves broke on the rock on which Magda's house sat.

Anneys made a disapproving noise deep in her throat. 'Not much of a boat. Is it watertight?'

'The Riverwoman rowed it upriver with Captain Archer to bury my family,' Alisoun said. 'Wait here while I make certain she is away.'

Anneys sank down on to a piece of driftwood, wiped her forehead. 'You will need me.'

'What if she is there? How do I explain you?'

'And if she is there, what will you do?'

'Find another boat.'

'We have no time!' Anneys's voice was a weary whine.

'Then we shall wait until the next high tide. You sound as if you need a rest.'

Anneys slapped Alisoun's face. 'Stubborn, insolent child.'

Alisoun rubbed her cheek. 'Stay here.'

She cursed the woman under her breath as she crossed the water. Anneys behaved as if she were sorry she had helped her. But it was Anneys who had offered. It was Alisoun who should be sorry she had accepted Anneys's help. Would she have stolen the boat before Magda's eyes? Alisoun would not. She liked Magda Digby. She had no intention of keeping the boat. Her plan was to take it upriver, collect the treasures, and return the boat to Magda. They must come back to see whether Finn still lived, and take him with them if he did.

Alisoun made a circuit of the strange house of the Riverwoman. The upside-down dragon gave her pause; it seemed coiled to strike. But she was not so silly to believe it could. When she had listened at the door and peered in one of the small windows, she was satisfied that the boat could be taken without incident. Already the rising water rocked it back and forth. Soon it would be afloat.

Jasper raced to St Leonard's, but Owen and Erkenwald had already left with stretcher-bearers. His heart was beating hard as he raced down Petergate to St Saviourgate. It was just outside the house on Spen Lane that he found them. Panting, he told them what he had gleaned from Wulfstan about the sick man.

Don Erkenwald turned to Owen. 'Perhaps you will have need of me as a canon as well as a digger.'

'Aye. And a fighter, mayhap. The day is young.' Owen pressed Jasper's shoulder. 'Go home to Lucie. Tell her all you have learned.'

'I could help you.'

'At the moment, she needs you more, Jasper.'

Jasper thought of her alone in the shop, worried about Wulfstan, about Owen, about himself. 'All right.'

Erkenwald adjusted the girdle that rode beneath his barrel stomach, squared his shoulders. 'Best that I enter first. If he is there, he will perhaps be grateful to see a man of God. At least he might pause before attacking.'

Owen slipped his dagger out of its sheath.

'We shall wait just without the door.' Two lay brothers accompanied them with a stretcher.

Erkenwald also unsheathed his weapon, then, with his left hand on the latch, he turned. 'It is many years since I tested my courage in such a way, Captain. God grant that I do not fail you.'

A slight smile on the man's lips reassured Owen. 'You will not.'

The canon opened the door quietly, slipped within, leaving it ajar.

It was the waiting that was difficult. Owen strained to hear, but a noisy cart rattled down the lane, then a woman shouted for her child. At last, Erkenwald's almost bald head poked out. 'A man lies asleep up in the solar. The house is vile with pestilential vapours. Yet his blankets are clean, he has food, wine and water. Someone has cared for him.'

Wulfstan had been too ill to do so much for the man. 'Are you certain he is alone?'

'He is alone in the house,' Erkenwald said. 'I did not search the kitchen behind the house. Do you want to do that while I pray over the man?'

'You will wake him?'

'If he can be waked. How else is he to confess his sins?'

'You might need my help.'

'As I said before, I think it best he is certain of my peaceful intentions before he sees your scarred face.'

Owen looked at the canon's partial earlobe and the scar that puckered his chin. 'You think your robes hide your scars?'

Erkenwald touched his earlobe. 'A patch is easier to see.'

There was no denying that. 'Go up. Steps or a ladder?'

'Ladder. I shall carry him down.' Erkenwald pushed the door wide, retreated to the ladder.

Owen motioned for the lay brothers to follow him within. 'Wait below. I shall search the kitchen.'

As he stepped into the dusty main room, Owen smelled the stench of pestilence. Out of habit, he pulled his scented pouch from his belt. But that gave him no free hand. He put it away with a prayer for his safety, listened to Erkenwald climb. The floorboards creaked and groaned as the canon stepped off the ladder and moved across the solar. Then silence.

Owen made a circuit of the room, memorising the placement of windows and doors, the few pieces of furniture. Then he stepped out of the back door. The kitchen was a conical building with two unglazed windows and a flimsy door in need of repair. It was shielded from the house by a pear tree heavy with green fruit. Crouching down, Owen crept across the packed mud and gradually rose beside one of the windows, peered in. Little light, but he neither sensed nor saw any movement. He dropped down, crossed to the other window. Again, nothing. He eyed the door. It was so crooked on its hinge it would be difficult to open. He studied a long gouge in the ground at one edge of the doorway — where the door would swing out. Until recently the door had stood ajar.

He decided to slip in through one of the windows, a quieter entrance. Bread baskets brushed his head from the rafters as he eased through, something small skittered across the floor. The room had a layer of dust as thick as the one in the house and a sickly sweet stench of rotten meat. Not a room in which he wished to linger. He did see one useful item. A rope coiled in a corner. He lifted it, shook out a mouse, and slipped the coil up his arm to his shoulder. Near a trestle table, just visible in the light from one of the windows, was a dark, damp area in the rushes where something had spilled of late. But the hearth was cold, no smoke lingered in the air. Satisfied, Owen climbed back out.

A whinny stopped him halfway to the house. It had come from behind the kitchen. Drawing his dagger, Owen crept back to the kitchen, flattened himself against the wall, moved round until he saw the horse. It was tethered to a thick vine that climbed the wall at the back of the property. Alisoun Ffulford's nag. Owen crossed himself. He began to feel as if the horse haunted him. At least it seemed to be alone here at present. He noticed a bulge in the vine to which the nag was tethered. Parting the vine, Owen whistled at his discovery — a tooled leather saddle and a pouch containing a chess board and chessmen. At last things were adding up. He left the items where he had found them for now.

As he returned to the house, one of the lay brothers told him that Don Erkenwald had called for Owen to join him.

Dagger in teeth, Owen climbed the ladder. The stench was worse as he rose. Once up, he crept with care round the brightly painted partition. Erkenwald knelt on the floor holding the hand of a sickly pale man who lay on a blanket, with another covering him, his eyes wide in his bony face as he caught sight of Owen.

'Who is this? I asked for sanctuary.' His voice had the querulous timbre of the ill.

Erkenwald patted the man's hand. 'Captain Archer is Brother Wulfstan's friend. It was he brought me here to fulfil the good monk's vow.'

The man shrank into himself as Owen moved closer, but he did not take his eyes from Owen's. 'The monk is ill?'

A nod. 'Pestilence. I pray God for a miracle.'

'God grant him health,' the man whispered. 'He saved me.'

Owen considered the man. A long face, made longer by a tonsure. 'You are a cleric?'

The man fought to keep his drooping eyelids open. He was yet weak. 'I took minor vows. I wish to serve at St Mary's.' Owen had to lean close to hear the man's fading voice.

Erkenwald met Owen's eye, raised an eyebrow in question.

Owen shook his head.

Erkenwald bent to the sick man. 'The captain and I have no right to make such a decision. We must take you to St Leonard's Hospital. But we shall tell them your wish.'

The man clutched Erkenwald's habit. 'No.'

'It is best for you. We can care for you there.'

'Why do you prefer St Mary's?' Owen

asked. 'Is it because you stole from St Leonard's?'

'Trade with me. I know where you can find the woman and child.'

'He has Alisoun Ffulford's horse out in the yard,' Owen told Erkenwald. 'And he has tucked away an ivory chess set and a saddle fit for a king.'

'Has he now?'

'I must ask you some questions, John,' Owen said. 'Telling me where they have gone is not enough. I had already guessed they would go to the Ffulford farm.' He nodded at the flicker of disappointment in the man's eyes.

'He is very weak,' Erkenwald said.

'Not so weak he cannot think to bargain. Who is Anneys to you?'

'Swear you will take me to St Mary's.'

Erkenwald nodded.

'We journey together. Sometimes a woman is a help to me, sometimes a cleric or a man is a help to her.'

'You thieve together?'

'We live as we can.'

'What does she want with the child?'

'Anneys says she is her grandchild.'

'Do you believe that?'

'Anneys does not lie to me.'

'What do you know of the three corrodians

of St Leonard's who have been murdered?'

'I know nothing.'

'Come now. That chess set has passed time in Walter de Hotter's garden.'

The man turned away from them.

Owen smelled guilt on him. It was enough for now. He did not wish to spend any more effort questioning the man at this time. Rising, Owen shrugged the coil of rope from his shoulder. 'We can lower him to the men below.' He handed Erkenwald an end.

When the lay brothers had John on the stretcher, Erkenwald knelt to him with the rope and trussed him up. He fought, but feebly.

Owen grinned. 'A nod is not your word?'

Erkenwald glanced up as he secured the knot. 'I was nodding at my thought — once a thief, ever one, eh?'

The lay brothers looked confused.

'We shall accompany you to the top of Lop Lane,' Owen said. 'You will take him to the hospital, explain to Don Cuthbert or whoever needs to know that he is to be guarded. The hospital gaol is the place for him, I have no doubt.'

'And we?' Erkenwald asked.

'We take shovels, arms, and ride to the farm.'

On Petergate they met the bailiff Geoffrey.

'I thought you should hear, Captain. A woman and a girl stole the Riverwoman's boat.'

'How long ago?'

Geoffrey looked up at the sun. 'Long enough to be well away.' He nodded at the man on the stretcher. 'Restraining the sick?'

'He may be one of our murderers. And a thief.'

'You have done a good day's work.'

'It is not over, Geoffrey. Will you escort them to the hospital?'

'That I shall do, Captain. You need not worry that he will be brought there.'

'The men know what to do with him.'

'You are off to catch his partners?'

'Aye. And to return the Riverwoman's boat, God willing.'

Twenty-seven

Painful Truths

Bess Merchet was sitting with Lucie in the kitchen when Owen rushed through in search of the shovels he had packed.

'You must listen to what Bess has learned,' Lucie said.

'I must hasten to catch Anneys and the child before they slip through my hands again. Did Jasper return?'

'He did. He is in the shop.'

'Good.'

Bess jumped up to follow Owen. She would not be brushed aside when she had worked so hard. But she was mindful to be brief.

Owen sat a moment beside the pack of shovels. 'You give me much to think about.'

Bess did not think he was sufficiently impressed. 'Do you not see? Honoria and Uncle Julian were at odds. Sir Richard's clerk says my uncle made a new will. Perhaps she thought to murder him before he had the chance.'

'When did Douglas tell you of the will?'
'When he told me of my share.'
'Do you know that Honoria received less in the new will?'
A pox on his reasoning. 'No.'
Owen nodded. 'I am more intrigued by Julian's remorse over Adam Carter's death. It seems more than the thieving bastard was due.' And with that, Owen rose, threw the pack of shovels over his shoulder, and rushed out.
'That is the last time I assist your husband,' Bess declared.

Alisoun paused in her hunt for shovels to watch Anneys, who sat in the doorway of the house alternately wiping her brow and drinking from a jug of well water. What had she done that made her so hot? The day was mild for summer, and Alisoun had done most of the rowing. They would have made more progress by now if the woman had helped more.
It was mid-afternoon. There might yet be enough light to dig up the treasures, but by then it would be too late to return to York. When Alisoun mentioned this to Anneys, the woman assured her that they had left ample food and drink for Finn.
'But what of us?'

'We can sleep in the house, child. It was good enough for you once.'

'I shall sleep in the barn.'

'Why not the house?'

'It is full of ghosts.'

Anneys made the sign of the cross and told Alisoun to go find the shovels.

Lame John and his son Rich lay in the tall meadow grass at the far end of the field watching Alisoun and Anneys work. They had retreated after creeping close and seeing the wealth the two were collecting.

'What devilment is this?' Lame John muttered. 'Where did my brother's child get such things?'

'They brought no horses,' Rich said. He wriggled backwards until he could stand behind a tree. His father joined him more slowly.

'A boat, then?'

'Aye, that's what I'm thinking. And if we see to it, they might stay long enough to explain what they're about.'

Lacking customers and unable to keep his mind on his lessons, Jasper shut the shop for a while and went in search of Lucie. He found her up in the solar, kneeling over a small chest, lifting items from it: toys, a child's gown . . . He knew that it had been her mother's chest; in it she kept her memories. Jasper's mother had had such a chest.

'I have nothing of his in here. Nothing,' Lucie whispered.

Jasper knelt beside her. 'Brother Wulfstan means as much to you as he does to me.'

Lucie gathered the items she had spread on the floor, placed them back in the chest. 'I have never known a gentler soul than Wulfstan. I cannot say that I have always been good to him.' She blotted her eyes on her sleeve.

'I should have asked you to come with me.'

Lucie hugged herself. 'I feel frightened. Fearful of what will take the place of such goodness.'

Jasper did not know how to comfort her. 'I must return to the shop,' he said.

'I will come with you.'

Lame John backed away, shook his head. 'I cannot.'

His son lifted his hand over the boat, was about to bring the jagged rock down on the curved prow when his father caught his hand. Rich dropped the rock as he yanked out of his father's grasp. Lame John lunged for the rock.

'What is this?' Rich hissed. 'You have

changed your mind?'

' 'Tis the Riverwoman's boat.'

'And what if it is? She was not with them. You think she loaned it to them? Those two?' Rich spat in the grass.

'I would not be cursed by her.'

'How will she know? 'Tis that changeling, Alisoun, stole it. She damaged it. Who is to say otherwise?'

'The Riverwoman might know otherwise.'

'A midwife? Herb-gatherer?'

'She is more than that.'

'She is a good woman. She would think us in the right. Alisoun is our kin. We must protect her from that woman.'

Lame John laughed. 'You want the gold and silver.'

'Did you see it? When are we to see the likes of that again, eh?'

Lame John handed his son the rock.

When the prow had been sufficiently splintered, Rich tossed the rock aside, brushed off his hands.

'You've taken the skin off your palms. Down to the river with you, wash them off.'

'What then? Do we await them here?'

'Nay. We must see what they are about.'

Lucie and Jasper found no customers in Davygate, but they opened the shop door in the hope of distraction. Jasper sat on the bench by the window; Crowder climbed up on his lap, and as the lad absent-mindedly stroked the cat, Lucie told him of her first visit to Brother Wulfstan's garden.

The trussed man on the stretcher attracted much interest at the hospital — until word spread that he stank of pestilence.

'The gaol? And keep him under guard? But what has he done?' Don Cuthbert found them puzzling suggestions.

'Captain Archer did not say,' replied one of the stretcher-bearers.

Cuthbert tucked his hands up his sleeves, considered the alternatives. He had so far managed to keep the deaths from pestilence quite low by separating the sufferers from the other infirm. The hospital was not crowded, but to place him in a room that might be secured would require inconvenient shuffling.

'The gaol it is, then. Put him far from Mistress Staines.' In truth, she should be released to the house of the lay sisters, but he was not about to do so without the master's order. He must tread lightly for a time.

Twenty-eight

Rich as the Master

Alisoun stared into one of the crimson bells of the tall foxglove. Might the plant have grown in this spot after she'd buried the treasures? Had it been long enough since she'd disturbed this earth for a weed to seed itself and grow? Perhaps she had sped its growth by loosening the earth round it. That had been her principal task each spring, to loosen the soil round her mother's older herbs.

She did not wish to ask Anneys whether it was possible that the treasure lay below the plant. Alisoun was not yet ready to admit to her that she could not find the last of the treasure. Anneys did not seem patient with failure. They had dug up the trench that Alisoun remembered digging: from the second post in the fence beyond the tree from which she'd fallen when she was small to the old ditch. This plant was growing at the edge of the ditch. Alisoun might have gone that far, though she did not think so. It was a measuring point on the property. She had feared her uncle would notice if it was disturbed. But she had been weary on the evening she had buried the goods. Perhaps she had gone farther than she had intended.

'We have not the time to stare at flowers.' Anneys's voice was hoarse with exhaustion, though she had done precious little of the digging. In fact she had stopped after losing her balance and slipping into one of the holes shortly after they had begun. 'A moment ago you feared we would be interrupted,' Anneys reminded her.

It was true. Alisoun had sensed someone watching them, but the feeling had gone away. She had stood very still, trying not to breathe. Only the insects and the birds disturbed the afternoon, and, farther away, the river. Whatever Alisoun had heard, she did not hear it again. Still, she had bent back to her digging with more energy, and in a short while she had retrieved all but the cross.

Was it under the foxglove? Alisoun pushed herself up from her crouching position, retraced her steps to the spot at which they had begun their dig, crouched over the hole, dug a little beyond, until she reached hard, undisturbed soil. It was indeed the end of the trench.

'Where is the rood?' Anneys asked from above.

Alisoun took a deep breath. 'Under the foxglove . . . I think.'

'You think? You do not know?'

Alisoun flinched at the tone, and the foot that tapped impatiently, perhaps even angrily, beside her. 'It is the only part of the trench we have not tried.'

'Meaning?'

Alisoun rose, faced her interrogator. The tall woman leaned on her shovel, glaring at Alisoun with dark eyes. Soil smudged her face and made her even more malevolent. 'Meaning I hope it is there, because if it is not, someone has been here before us.'

Anneys straightened. 'Foolish child. That was the most valuable piece.'

'I did not take it.'

'But you let someone else take it.'

Alisoun ran down to the foxglove, sank down beside it, began to dig with her hands, plunging them into the soil, which was rough with pebbles that stung her with scratches.

Anneys knelt beside Alisoun, caught her wrists and pulled her hands from the soil, shook her head at the torn fingernails. 'You have hurt yourself. Let me dig.'

But Alisoun was not listening. Anneys's hands were hot and clammy. Alisoun withdrew her left hand, touched the woman's forehead, then her right cheek. 'You are sick.' Her eyes were bloodshot and heavy-lidded. 'Grandame, you are sick!'

Anneys pressed Alisoun's hand. 'What does it matter? Tomorrow we shall float downriver as rich as the Master of St Leonard's. Come. Use the shovel. Try this last place.'

And at last, much to Alisoun's relief, she found the pearl and silver cross. But by then Anneys's breath was coming in gasps.

'By Christ's thorns, these are riches indeed,' Lame John muttered to his son. 'I told you we would do well to watch the farm.' They lay in the tall grass beyond the old ditch, hidden by more foxgloves growing wild in the field, gazing upon the items heaped on the cloth beside the woman and Alisoun.

'Do not rejoice yet,' Rich said. 'Listen.'

Lame John tensed and listened, heard horses approaching. On hands and knees he crept backwards into the wood, an awkward, jerking motion with his uneven legs. Rich followed.

Anneys and Alisoun heard the horses. As one they gathered the corners of the cloth on which they had placed the treasures, pulled them together. Anneys slung them over her shoulder and stumbled. Alisoun put an arm round her and helped her walk beneath the load. Past the barn, the house, through the meadow with its clutching and clinging weeds, and at last to the bank and the boat. Anneys dropped the bundle and sank down beside the boat to catch her breath.

Alisoun was uneasy. 'Someone has been here.'

Anneys wiped her face with a cloth dipped in river water. 'How do you know?'

'We left the boat on its side. It now sits upside-down.'

Anneys turned it over, placed the bundle in the prow. 'Come. Our pursuers are behind us on horseback.'

Alisoun stood firm. 'Take out the bundle. We must see whether someone damaged the boat.'

Paying no heed, Anneys pushed the boat down the bank. 'Come along or stay behind, all the same to me.'

It was not all the same to Alisoun. With misgivings, she joined the woman. 'Climb in. I will pull you on to the water,' she said as an offering to win back Anneys's favour.

With a satisfied nod, Anneys picked up the oar, climbed into the boat and settled herself in the stern. Alisoun pulled the boat down into the river. At once it began to take on water and list drunkenly. She grabbed the bag of treasures. 'Jump out,' she shouted to Anneys.

Paying her no heed, Anneys clutched an overhanging branch to steady herself as she grabbed for the bundle. 'Where do you think to go with them? Get into the boat.'

'Can you not see the hole?' The water gurgled into the prow. 'For pity's sake, sit down and I will try to guide you back to the bank before you sink.'

'Do you think me a fool?' Anneys let go of the branch and lunged for the bundle. The boat twisted as it caught the current and began to drift from the shore, dragging Anneys with it.

'Kick yourself loose while you are in the shallows,' Alisoun shouted. She watched helplessly as the current pulled the listing boat down and away, into the deeper water. Anneys could not swim, nor, it had been plain as they'd rowed upriver, had she much experience in handling a boat. And weakened with fever . . .

Alisoun dropped the bundle on the bank and ran back towards the farm, hoping that the riders had reached the yard.

Don Erkenwald reigned in his horse and

pointed to the shadows at the edge of the wood.

'They heard us,' Owen said. 'Pity.' He had hoped that Anneys and the child might be making enough noise with their shovels to mask the sounds of their approach. 'Ride on as if we have not seen them. We shall tether our horses on the fence near the trees in which they hide.'

With a grin, Erkenwald urged his horse forward.

Owen made note of the trench of disturbed earth along the fence. So the child had buried the items there. And already dug them up?

'Captain Archer!' Alisoun Ffulford ran across the yard with an awkward gait, her hem heavy with mud. She waved her arms and shouted, 'Ride to the river! She is drowning!'

The child had come from the river; so who hid in the wood? An important question, but there was no time for it at present. The river took its victims quickly.

When Owen reached the bank, he saw no sign of Anneys or a damaged boat, heard no cries for help. All he heard was the river lapping the bank and the insects buzzing near his ears. He had played the fool. The child's story had been a ruse to lure him and Erkenwald away from the trench where presumably the stolen items had been buried. Anneys was no doubt hiding in the wood by the barn with another accomplice, and the boat hidden somewhere in the brush on the riverbank.

As he resolved to turn back, Owen heard a faint cry. He turned round, thinking it was Alisoun running up behind him. But the cry came again, clearly from behind him now, out on the water.

Erkenwald shouted, 'Look you! By the rock downstream, near the bank.'

There it was, a battered boat caught in a tangle of weeds and saplings.

Alisoun had reached the bank. 'Help her! The prow has been damaged and Mistress Anneys cannot swim.'

'She is in the boat?' Erkenwald asked.

'Yes. Hurry!'

'She may yet be safe. The weeds seem to be holding it afloat.'

Alisoun grabbed Owen's foot in the stirrup. 'She is weak with fever, Captain. Please. Hurry. She will die.'

Owen dismounted. 'Come. We may need your help as well, child.' He led his horse down along the bank. Erkenwald dismounted and followed.

Twenty-nine

Shattered Plans

After a brief burst of activity, the shop grew quiet once more. Lucie left her work and stood in the doorway gazing towards Stonegate, hoping to see Owen step out into St Helen's Square. As the afternoon shadows lengthened, she grew more and more concerned about Owen's safety, Wulfstan's condition, Jasper's silence. And beneath that was the painful yearning for Gwenllian and Hugh. Jasper came up behind her, slipped his arms round her, pressed his head against her back. Lucie turned and hugged him.

'Come,' she said, 'let us close the shop and go to Brother Wulfstan.'

Bess tried to busy herself in the tavern, but the thought of the man in St Leonard's gaol was finally too much to resist. She marched to the hospital and demanded to see Sir Richard.

'You might prefer to speak with Don Cuthbert,' Douglas said, his hands folded on his comfortably padded stomach. The corners of his mouth fought an urge to smile; his eyes were not so successful in solemnity.

Suppressed laughter annoyed Bess. Cheer that must be hidden was at someone's expense. 'What amuses you?'

'Amuses me? By Christ's rood, Mistress Merchet, I am merely happy to be leaving York.'

'How can you be leaving?'

'It seems we have caught the thief and shall shortly also have the murderer.'

'Captain Archer has returned? I had not heard.'

'No, not yet. But Sir Richard is confident.'

'Sir Richard is a fool to act on expectations.'

'We do not leave at once. His Grace the Archbishop arrives tomorrow and will dine here. But we hope to depart by the week's end.'

'Ah. Archbishop Thoresby returns. Does he arrive with his dismantled house?'

'A portion of it, yes. He rides ahead of the slow-moving barge.'

'People are dying all round and the nephew entertains, the uncle plays with his lavish tomb. No wonder God is punishing us. 'Tis a pity He is punishing the wrong people.'

'Mistress Merchet, you tread dangerously.'

'I shall leave you to your packing, Douglas. Where might I find Don Cuthbert?'

Brother William directed Lucie and Jasper to Abbot Campian's house. 'My lord abbot has moved Brother Wulfstan to his quarters.'

Lucie caught her breath. Of course she had known there was scant hope Brother Wulfstan would survive the pestilence, but to have withdrawn Brother Henry's care seemed a premature admission of defeat. Lucie reached for Jasper's hand, clasped it firmly for comfort as she led him through the abbey grounds to Campian's house.

They were met at the door by Brother Sebastian, Campian's secretary, his pale, ageless face solemn as he bowed and led them to the abbot's parlour. Even before they reached it, Lucie could smell the incense of burning juniper wood. As Sebastian opened the door the smoke drifted out, an aromatic but unhealthy, too heavy fog. The room was also too hot for the summer evening. The abbot had placed Wulfstan's bed before a briskly burning fire. It was no wonder the infirmarian struggled for breath. 'Give him some air, I pray you!' Lucie said as she moved towards a casement window.

Sebastian stopped her. 'I pray you, Mistress, I know what you think, but Brother Wulfstan's breathing was as laboured in the infirmary. It is neither the smoke nor the heat of the fire causing it.'

Of course not. It was the pestilence. Lucie turned back towards the bed.

'Brother Henry thought a good sweat might help dispel the poisoned humours,' Sebastian added in a voice that trailed away uncertainly.

Lucie touched his forearm. 'Forgive me. You are very good to him. I do not mean to interfere.'

Abbot Campian knelt at Wulfstan's bedside, a string of paternosters flowing through his hands as he prayed in a low murmur.

Lucie hesitated to approach. She had lost so many she loved, and yet each one was as if the first, the pain as sharp and deep, the desire to deny the possibility of death as strong.

'Is he awake?' Jasper asked Sebastian.

The monk nodded solemnly. 'His breathing is more evenly measured when he sleeps.'

Abbot Campian turned an ashen face to the visitors. 'Come. I know he wishes to speak to you, Mistress Wilton.'

* * *

Don Cuthbert rocked back and forth on his sandalled feet, his hands tucked up his sleeves, and listened to Bess's tirade with a blank expression.

'I know nothing of the master's plans, Mistress Merchet. He asked me to talk to the prisoner, discover who he was, what wrong he had committed, and I have done so.'

'You have spoken to him?'

'More to the point, he has spoken to me. The threat of lying naked on the stone floor without food or water eased his tongue.' Cuthbert sniffed smugly.

Bess found his satisfaction disturbing; but she must humour the little torturer. 'What have you learned?'

'His name is Finn. He has admitted to assisting in the thefts, and — how did he describe it?' Cuthbert dropped his head, searching his memory, lifted it suddenly and smiled, showing his teeth. 'He admits to "being surprised by Walter de Hotter and in my panic mortally wounding him". He seems to dislike the word "murder".'

Perhaps she was too kind to those she questioned; the canon had learned much from the prisoner in a short time. 'What of my uncle and Laurence de Warrene?'

'For that, he suggests we speak to Anneys, lately a lay sister of this hospital.'

'I know who she is.'

'I never trusted her, God knows that I did not. And I warned Dame Constance about giving her too much responsibility.'

'What has that to do with my uncle's murder, for pity's sake?'

'No one watched her.'

'What will you do with him?'

'He pleads benefit of clergy and asks for sanctuary at St Mary's.'

'Sweet *Jesu!* How can he expect such a gift?'

'He believes that God had some purpose in curing him of the pestilence.'

'He did indeed. So this Finn could be properly punished.'

'Indeed. But that awaits Captain Archer.'

'I must speak to the prisoner.'

'No, Mistress Merchet.'

Well, she would find a way.

At high tide the bank was as treacherous as a marsh with flooded pools hidden by underbrush. Owen lost his footing once and frightened his horse. He moved even more cautiously after that.

His slow gait made Alisoun impatient. 'She will drown before we get there. Why did you not leave your horses back on the high ground?'

'She may be far from the bank, but the weeds on which she is caught tell me that the water is shallow enough there for a horse to walk. I can put her on the horse.'

'Oh.'

'Do you have a better plan?'

'No.'

Abbot Campian rose, invited Lucie and Jasper to take his place at Wulfstan's bedside.

Lucie reached for Wulfstan's hand. He pulled it away, but not before she had felt its heat.

'I would not have you ill, my friend,' Wulfstan whispered.

'Are you in much pain?'

A trembling smile. 'It has passed.'

'But you burn with fever.'

'God purifies me.'

'I did not believe He would take you. How can He withdraw the comfort you have given to the sick?'

'He answers to no one, Lucie. Not even my lord abbot.' Again the weak smile.

'Forgive me, Brother Wulfstan.'

'Forgive?'

'I once asked for your silence. You almost

died then because of me.'

Now he reached for her hand, pressed it with the little strength he had. 'Good has come of it. I forgave both of us long ago.'

Erkenwald turned his head. 'There is someone back in the clearing.'

'The treasures!' Alisoun cried. 'I left the bundle of treasures back there.'

'Who is behind us?' Owen asked.

But the child was already crashing back through the brush.

Owen continued downstream; Erkenwald followed.

Owen could now see the boat and the woman clutching it. She was halfway in the boat, her legs floating on the current. Owen could not tell whether her head was in water. But surely it had been she who shouted just a while ago, so he still hoped to find her alive.

When they were as close to Anneys as they could get on the bank, Erkenwald took a rope out of his saddlebag, tied it round a sturdy trunk, and Owen pulled the rope through his horse's harness. Then he and his horse waded out.

Alisoun dropped to her hands and knees and crept through the tall weeds to the edge of the farm's landing-point. She saw no one. Nor did she see the bundle. She rose and moved into the trees, heading for the farm. There was no easy path upriver from the landing-place, so whoever had taken the treasure must have gone inland.

The water swirled round Owen's legs. It was cold, even in the shallows. He soon felt the cause of the shallow area as his feet discovered an uneven, rocky bottom. He worried for the horse. But the beast picked its way with care until it reached Anneys's bobbing feet. Then it shied, but it quieted and stood still when Owen waded past and moved the legs into the broken boat. He felt for a pulse. Anneys moaned.

'Do not be afraid. I am going to lift you on to my horse. He will carry you to the riverbank.'

Near the barn, Alisoun's uncle and cousin stood arguing.

'This load will slow us,' said Lame John. 'I say we bury it in the hay, return tomorrow with the cart.'

Rich laughed. 'Oh, aye. They will ride away with the woman and child and never think to watch for us.'

Lame John crossed himself. 'You heard

the child. The woman has drowned. I told you we should not damage the boat. We killed her.'

Alisoun crept into the house and retrieved her bow and arrows.

Anneys clung to the horse, shivering. Erkenwald had taken his blanket from his saddle, spread it on dry ground. As soon as the horse reached the bank, Erkenwald lifted Anneys, carried her to the blanket, rolled her up in it.

'God watched over you,' the canon said, shaking his head. 'I cannot think why.'

Owen crouched by Anneys's feet. 'Come. We shall lift her to the horse, return to the farm for the child.'

Alisoun sat in the doorway of the house. 'You should see to my uncle. Out by the barn. He is injured. And my cousin Rich. I shot them for thieving.'

'You injured your kin for that pack of treasures?' Owen asked.

'They have my hen and my cow. I'll never get them back.'

Was there ever such an accurséd child, Owen wondered as he headed for the barn in his clothes heavy with river water. Why was she his particular penance? What had he ever done to a child to deserve this? He loved his own, he had taken Jasper in when he was in danger, he always took particular care to instruct customers on the small doses children required.

An elderly man sat with his back against the wall of the barn, his eyes closed, head hanging down, chin on chest. Another man lay on his stomach, but propped up on his elbows so that he might spew forth curses. Owen knelt to the latter, found a wound behind the man's left knee that bled freely.

With a choice curse, the man shoved a small, bloody arrow at Owen's face. 'I have removed it, but I cannot stand on the leg.'

He would live. And walk again. The older man's wound was in his left arm, near the shoulder. A graze, nothing more.

Lame John lifted his eyes to Owen. ' 'Tis God's punishment for damaging the Riverwoman's boat.'

'So it was you ruined Magda Digby's boat. She will not thank you for it. Many sick folk must go without her help until another boat be made.'

'I told Rich we should not do it,' Lame John said.

'Stop your whining, old man,' Rich shouted. 'I have paid more dearly than you. Is that not enough?'

'What of the woman?' Lame John asked.

'She survived the river.'

Owen rose as Erkenwald approached, leading the horses and holding tight to Alisoun's hand. Anneys still lay across Owen's beast. 'Is there a cart we can use?'

'At our farm,' Lame John said.

'Aye,' Alisoun muttered. 'They kept that, too.'

Bess found Honoria in a curtained corner of the Barnhous, with the ailing infants. The young woman darned while her three charges slept.

'I have no doubt Captain Archer will allow you to return to your house in the city,' Bess said, settling down beside her.

'And why is that?' Honoria asked without lifting her eyes from her work.

'Another woman my uncle held dear also has a pair of Italian goblets. It seems you spoke the truth.'

'I am not the one who needs to be told.'

'I confess I was surprised to learn that my uncle was bedding Anneys and not you.'

Now the head raised, the dark eyes met Bess's. Honoria was laughing. 'Anneys bedded? Oh, I think not, Mistress Merchet. I do not know what her game was with your uncle, but she did not mean to lie with him.

She flirted with him, but she had naught but scorn for him behind his back.'

'Scorn?'

'I know not why. Nor why she quizzed him so. As if she must know everything about him. Yet she was quiet enough about her own past.'

'What do you know of her?'

'She was widowed three years ago. Had three children, none of whom could offer her a home. Or would, more like.'

'She asked my uncle questions?'

'Oh, and he bragged to her. About all the treasures he had given to the hospital, the work he did among the plague-sick when the Death first stalked the land.'

One of the children woke and began to fret. Honoria put her work aside and lifted the child on to her lap, smoothed her damp hair from her forehead, held her until she slept once more.

'You are good with children.'

'So says Dame Beatrice. Do you have more questions?'

'What do you know about my uncle's penance? Captain Archer thought it strange, all that guilt about the death of a thief who died thieving.'

Honoria shook her head. 'Not for him, for the children. Master Taverner learned that

Carter had two children by his mistress — a mistress your uncle never even knew of — and when he died she was without means of caring for them, so she abandoned them to the family.'

'The Carters of Scarborough?'

'They in turn sent them far away. So it was said. And Master Taverner swore that had he known of them he would have given the children their father's share of the spoils.'

'Did he search for the children?'

'Where would he search? He could not discuss this with the Carters, for pity's sake. He was not a man to destroy himself.'

'The penance he undertook was severe,' Bess said.

Honoria kissed the child in her arms. 'No more than what we do here every day, Mistress Merchet. Do not fool yourself that your uncle was a saintly man. He was no better than he should have been.'

'I, for one, shall miss him,' Bess said, rising. She was anxious to escape into the untainted air.

'There are many will miss him,' Honoria said softly.

Bess had much to ponder as she headed for home. So Anneys had not been Julian's leman. But had she murdered him? The man Finn seemed to suggest that. She prayed

God Owen found the woman and brought her to justice if it was true. The city could use a good hanging.

But as she walked Bess thought more of Honoria's tale of Adam Carter's leman and his bastards than of vengeance. Poor Uncle Julian. It did him credit that he had felt such remorse for neglecting his partner's family. She could feel proud of him once more.

Thirty

Jasper's Despair; Wulfstan's Request

Shivering in his damp clothes, Owen jounced about on the wagon seat as he guided two horses unaccustomed to pulling a wagon. Alisoun sat beside him; Erkenwald rode in the back with Anneys. Owen felt cursed. Pestilence had touched his house this day — for he had no doubt Jasper and Lucie had gone to Brother Wulfstan, and he himself had breathed the poisonous air surrounding two victims, 'John' and Anneys. It did not help that in addition to his worries and discomfort, he had the irritating Alisoun as companion.

'She is my grandame, you know,' the child suddenly announced, leaning close to make sure Owen heard. Her breath was stale and her hair stank of sweat and horses.

But she got his attention. 'Your grandame?' So Anneys had told 'John' the truth.

'She came to York to get back her treasures.'

'How were they *her* treasures?'

'Because they were her husband's.'

Was it possible? Had Carter been married? 'Was Adam Carter your grandsire?'

'If you know the tale, why are you asking me?'

'Because that is what I do.'

'Oh.'

'What else did your grandame say?'

'Why should I tell you?'

' 'Twas you began it.'

A brief, sullen silence. 'They murdered my grandsire and took all he owned and vanished. My grandame had to give up her children because she could not feed them. And then a farmer married her and she had another son, Finn — the one I thought was stealing from me.'

'The man you wounded?' So his name was Finn, not John.

'I did not know who he was. My mother never told me.'

'So then what happened?'

'She was widowed again, and she had nothing again.'

'Why?'

'Because the sea rose up and turned the farm into a salt marsh, didn't it?'

'Of course. And then what happened?'

'And so she and Finn thought to find the men who had murdered her first husband

and stolen his treasures.'

'An impressive tale.'

'You never believe me.'

'I am a cautious man.'

For a long while the child was silent. Owen tried to organise what he had learned this day. According to Bess, Anneys was Julian's lover; and yet according to the child, she blamed him for her poverty and thought him a murderer. Alisoun's story made his original casting of Anneys as Julian's murderer plausible; Bess's did not. And Honoria had been bedding the town council, but not corrodians. A tangled mess, it was, and he felt little nearer the truth than at sunrise.

'Quite a coincidence, your mother and the men your grandame was after both being in York, or nearby.'

'My grandame says she did not know my mother was here. But when she learned it, she saw it as God's sign that she was in the right.'

'In the right?'

'To avenge my grandsire's death.'

'And how did she do that?'

'Stole back his treasures.'

'And murdered Taverner and Warrene?'

'No! They died of plague and fire.'

'Ah. Why did you tell no one at the hospital that Anneys was your grandame?'

'I did not know.'

'Your mother did not tell you?'

'No.'

'A queer thing.'

'Grandame said Mama punished her for abandoning her in Scarborough.'

Owen wondered who had been punished more — Anneys or Alisoun. The child was silent for the rest of the journey.

The gatekeeper at Bootham Bar stopped Owen. 'Abbot Campian prays you hasten to his house.'

'Brother Wulfstan?'

The man bowed his head, made the sign of the cross.

'I can take them from here, Captain,' Erkenwald said. 'Sir Richard's squire Topas will stand watch with me.'

'I thank you. You have been a great help to me.'

'God forgive me, but it has been my pleasure, Captain. Now hasten to your friend.'

A time-consuming task that did not require a clear mind was Lucie's way of surviving the horrible evening of worrying about Owen and dreading word of Wulfstan's death. A farmer had delivered swine gall the day before. Lucie and Jasper had transferred it to their own jars earlier, but now she must seal the lids with wax or the odour would foul the storeroom. It was hot work melting wax in the workroom. When Lucie came to a point at which she could pause, she stepped out into the garden.

The evening had grown cool, with a welcome breeze. As she sat on the bench, she fought sleep, and was drifting off when sounds in the shop caught her attention. She had asked Jasper to tidy up, but he should have been finished long ago. Fearing an intruder, she picked up a knife and moved through the workroom towards the shop. Through the beaded curtain she saw light; an oil lamp flickered on the counter. That relieved her. A thief would not be so bold — unless he had not heard her in the next room. How long had she dozed on the bench?

She stood against the curtain and waited for the intruder to come into sight. Praise God, Jasper crossed behind the light. He carried a leather pouch. Lucie slipped through the curtain.

Jasper looked up, startled, then swung the pouch behind him, out of sight. 'Mistress Lucie. I thought you slept.'

Sweat beaded on Jasper's upper lip and glistened at his temples. Was it the heat from the workroom? Or was he nervous, Lucie wondered.

'I must have slept. You should have waked me. The spirit lamp is lit in the workroom.'

'I saw. I was watching it.'

'From in here?' Lucie took a few steps to the left.

Jasper moved so that his body still hid the pouch.

'What is in the pouch?'

'What —'

'No, Jasper. Do not play the fool, or mistake me for one. I saw you carrying a pouch. What is in it?'

He set the pouch on the counter.

Lucie did not look into it. Not yet. 'What are you doing?'

Jasper tossed his head to clear the hair from his eyes. 'I mean to continue Brother Wulfstan's work.'

'You are no physician.'

'Neither is he.'

'Jasper.'

'I can apply ointments, make a tisane to ease pain, lance boils.'

'No.'

He grabbed for the pouch, but too late; Lucie already clutched it to her.

'Come to the house with me,' she said.

'I mean to do this.'

'You will obey me, Jasper de Melton. You are my apprentice and you live under my roof as my son. Come to the house.'

He followed.

The warmth of the sickroom soon dried Owen's clothes and soothed his joints, particularly the knees on which he knelt beside the sick-bed. Brother Wulfstan was near death, his breath rattling in his shrunken chest. But he opened his eyes, recognised Owen.

'I am comforted. Lucie and Jasper are in your hands, and God's, and both of you are trustworthy.' Wulfstan signed a blessing over Owen, then closed his eyes. 'Peace, now.' He smiled slightly.

Owen bowed his head and prayed. Not so much for Wulfstan's soul; he had no doubt the infirmarian would die in a state of grace. Rather he had recognised the smile, one he had seen on the mortally wounded after battle, when they wearied of fighting for life and welcomed the peace of death. Owen prayed that Wulfstan's suffering would soon be over.

When at last Owen rose, Abbot Campian asked for a word. Merciful Mother, what now?

The abbot looked as if he would be the

next victim, his face pale and shadowed from lack of sleep and food, his eyes red-rimmed.

'You must rest, my lord abbot.'

'Soon enough. While my old friend still breathes, I shall stay with him. I ask a favour for him, Captain. I do not like it. Nor will you. But it is Wulfstan's wish that I intercede for the man John, save his life so that he might dedicate himself to God. Brother Wulfstan believes there was a reason the man survived the pestilence, that he is to devote his life to praying for the victims of the pestilence in York.'

Owen did not like it. Not at all. But when he looked into the abbot's grief-ravaged eyes he could say only, 'I shall present the case to Sir Richard on the morrow, my lord abbot.'

'Jasper means to return at first light. You will not prevent him?'

'I would not try.'

Some wine and a quiet talk with Lucie, perhaps some bread and cheese. Owen did not ask for much. His heart sank as he walked into the hall and heard Bess's voice up above. He sat down on a bench and rubbed his knees. 'What are they about up there, Kate?'

'I do not know as I ought to say, Captain,' Kate whispered, her eyes bright with worry.

'Perhaps it is best you go up.'

Slowly he climbed the stairs; he had left his shoes below.

Bess was saying, 'All those churches right there, in Spen Lane or near, and not a priest came out to help Brother Wulfstan. I tell you, Lucie Wilton, it —'

'For pity's sake, be quiet!' Lucie snapped.

Owen wished he could back down the stairs and let them be, for he knew such behaviour from Lucie meant trouble. But he would not be able to rest below for wondering. He stepped on to the landing. From a chair placed before the door to the children's room, Lucie looked up, startled. Her eyes were swollen. Had she begun her mourning for Wulfstan? Bess stood against the rail of the landing, arms folded over her middle. Though she had not been crying, she looked grim. He thought to cheer them.

'Fortune smiles on me this evening, to find two beautiful women at the door of my chamber.'

'Jasper's chamber,' Lucie said.

'It does not sound as poetic.'

Neither woman smiled.

'Why are you sitting there?'

'The door has no lock, so I am barring it.'

'Who is within?'

'Jasper.'

'What has he done?'

'It is what he meant to do.' Lucie told Owen how she had discovered Jasper in the shop.

Bess nodded. 'He is a good lad. He means well. But she is right, you know, it is not the place for a young boy, working among those dying of pestilence.'

Were they both mad? Did they truly think the boy would disobey Lucie? 'Why are you here, Bess?'

'To hear what happened at Ffulford farm.'

'I have brought Anneys, the child, and the stolen items to St Leonard's. That is all you shall hear tonight, Bess.'

Her face as red as her hair, Bess turned from him with a little gasp and sought a sympathetic look from Lucie.

'I pray you, leave us,' Lucie said.

When Bess had snapped her skirts and marched with a good bit of noise down the stairs, Owen said quietly, hoping to control his anger, 'You cannot be doing this, Lucie.'

A cold stare. 'Do you disbelieve your eye?'

'You have stood back and let him grow as he would. Why do you stop him now?'

'Do you want him dying of pestilence?'

'No.'

'Do you want him out on the streets at night, stumbling among the sick?'

'You exaggerate —'

'Do you?'

'Come away from there. Let me talk to him.'

'He was stealing from *me,* Owen. He meant to disobey *me,* his master.'

'It is not the master apothecary who sits so, it is the mother.'

Lucie folded her arms and turned away from him.

Owen went down to the hall, calmed himself with wine, filled the empty pockets in his stomach with bread and cheese. When at last he climbed the stairs once more, he found the chair moved aside, the door open. Within, Jasper slept on his cot, fully clothed. Lucie sat beside Hugh's cradle, staring at nothing.

'Come to bed, my love.'

At some god-forsaken hour of the night Owen woke to find Lucie pacing the room. His first thought was of Jasper. He sat up sharp. 'What is it? Has the boy disappeared?'

Lucie turned, hurried over. 'No. He still sleeps.' She sat at the edge of the bed. 'Poor Bess. She had much to tell you.'

'It did not seem the time to talk.'

'No.' Lucie played with the edge of the light mantle she wore over her shift. 'I know she would prefer to tell you herself, but . . .'

Owen took one of her hands in his. 'Does it involve Anneys?'

'Yes.'

'Please, my love, tell me. The woman is dying. If there is aught I need ask her, I must do it soon.'

'The man in St Leonard's gaol is called Finn. He has confessed he murdered Walter de Hotter. And he has suggested that Anneys can name the murderer of Julian Taverner and Laurence de Warrene.'

So Owen had guessed right. Anneys was the murderer. She had to be. 'Mother and son murderers. It explains much about that unpleasant child.'

'Finn is Anneys's son?'

'Aye. And Alisoun is Anneys's granddaughter. Charming family. According to the child, Anneys claims to be a Carter.'

Lucie squeezed Owen's hand. 'That is the key! Adam Carter had two bastard children. When he died, his leman abandoned the children to his family, who sent them away.'

'To St Leonard's.'

'So it seems.'

Owen embraced Lucie. 'I shall make it up to Bess somehow.'

'Let us pray that matters with Jasper are as easily solved.'

Thirty-one

Remorse

In the morning, Jasper apologised and begged to go to St Mary's as he had planned. When Owen saw Lucie's haunted eyes, he offered to escort the lad and entrust him to Abbot Campian until he returned from St Leonard's. Lucie accepted.

When they arrived, they found the door to Abbot Campian's house ajar.

'Wait here, Jasper.' Owen stepped into the hall, listened, heard nothing, made his way to the sickroom. Within, Abbot Campian knelt beside Wulfstan's bed, head in hands, weeping. Owen withdrew. He had no need to tell Jasper of his loss; St Mary's bell had already begun to toll for Brother Wulfstan.

'We must go back, Jasper. Tell Lucie.'

Eyes wide to fight tears, Jasper nodded. His face was chalky beneath the dark freckles. 'I should go to her. You go on to St Leonard's. I promise to go straight to the apothecary, nowhere else.'

'Your word is good enough for me.'

It did not make Jasper smile, but he stood a little taller as they made their way back to the postern gate.

When Owen arrived at Finn's room in St Leonard's gaol, the man was sitting up in a chair, drinking a cup of ale. Owen leaned against the door and stared at the man who had survived the pestilence. Why him and not Brother Wulfstan? God's purpose in this was difficult for Owen to understand.

'Perhaps God spared him so that we might know the truth,' Don Cuthbert had suggested.

Owen thought it a paltry reason.

Finn began to fidget. 'Why do you stare at me?'

'Is it true Anneys is your mother?'

'Is that why you refused me sanctuary?'

'You murdered a man who had done you no harm.'

'I am in minor orders; I demand benefit of clergy.'

'And you shall no doubt be granted it if you can read a passage from the bible. But if you think the Church's justice will be gentler than the King's, you are a fool.'

'At least I would live.'

'Perhaps. And perhaps you will regret that.

So. Is Anneys your mother?'

'She is my mother in fact, though little in feeling.'

'And yet you assisted her, did you not?'

'What do you know?'

Owen prayed God would not punish his family for the lies he intended to tell. 'Your mother is ill, so I did not force her to speak too long. I know that she came to York seeking Julian Taverner and Laurence de Warrene, and the goods she believed they had stolen from her. And that you assisted her in this, which led to the death of Walter de Hotter by your hands.'

'That is all?'

'That is your response? You feel no remorse?'

'She told you naught else?'

'What else is there to tell?'

'What of the deaths of Taverner and Warrene?'

'Pestilence and fire, she said. Is she lying for you?'

Finn spat on the floor. 'The day she lies for me, for anyone — Oh, aye, she tells you of my mortal sin, but confesses neither of hers. Unnatural mother. She cares for no one.'

'She searched the north for her daughter.'

'That, Captain, was God's doing, not my mother's. She sought her treasures, not her daughter.'

'Do you accuse her of murdering Taverner and Warrene?'

'I have no need. God knows.'

'The Master of St Leonard's wishes to know. On the orders of His Grace the Archbishop.'

'I can be loyal.'

'You would have her look worse than you. But it is a fool's lie. She had the goods, why would she need to murder them?'

'She hated them is why. She did not arrive with that intention, but watching them living in such comfort. On her wealth. Matilda de Warrene never knew a hungry day and was pampered by those thieves. Worse was Taverner bragging of his saintly work among the sick, and all the riches he had given to the spital.'

'Taverner thought he saw a man in Laurence's burning house.'

'Mother is tall for a woman, eh? I never set foot in the spital grounds till I left the monk's bag with her. She cursed me for that.'

'So it was she who stole the items and brought them to you?'

'Aye.'

'Then you took them to Judith Ffulford

— all that you did not put aside for yourself. Did you not trust you would get your share?'

'Share? I deserved half. How did Judith deserve aught? What did she do but try to hide it from us?'

'She was your sister.'

'She was but my half-sister, what did I know of her? She would stand there with the items, never moving until I departed, sneering at me. *You need me,* she liked to say. That child will be just like her.'

'What would you do at St Mary's? Spend your life feeding the hatred in your belly?'

'I took minor orders.'

'We shall see about that.'

Anneys lay propped up on pillows. Sweat glistened on her face. She stank of plague. Owen drew his scented sack from his belt, pressed it to his nose.

A lay sister gave Anneys a sip of wine. Much of it dribbled down her chin. 'Her tongue and throat are swollen, Captain. She should not talk long.'

'What does it matter?'

With a frown of disapproval, the young woman withdrew to a corner of the room. Owen sat down at Anneys's bedside.

'You condemn me before I am tried?'

'I meant that you are dying.'

Anneys touched his hand. 'Promise me that a new deed of gift is drawn up, that the treasures are returned to St Leonard's in *my* name.'

'I can promise you nothing.' In truth, he did not know what Ravenser would do with the items. Nor did he care.

'You give me no comfort on my deathbed?'

'You? Who took two men's lives because you lusted for the riches your lover had stolen?'

'Who told you I took their lives?'

'Finn.'

Anneys turned her head away. 'God blessed me with such loyal children.'

'Judith and Finn both helped you.'

'Greed inspired them, not love. Finn ruined it all. Hiding the chess set in that man's garden. But for that, no one would have questioned the deaths at the hospital.'

'Why murder Julian and Laurence? You had what you wanted.'

'Send Don Erkenwald to me. I would be shriven.'

'I thought God had allowed you this vengeance.'

A shadow of uncertainty in the red eyes.

'It *was* a sign from God that Judith was here.' Anneys coughed, pressed her head back into the pillow. 'Leave me.' Her breath was ragged.

Owen bowed to her. 'This death is far gentler than the execution you deserve.'

The lay sister, who had hurried over to give Anneys some wine, begged Owen to go.

He did so, gladly. Even on the battlefield one saw remorse in the faces of the enemy — but he had sensed none in either the woman or her son.

Don Erkenwald stood without, making a show of speaking with Topas. He quickly broke away from his conversation and joined Owen. 'Did she confess?'

'She wants you to hear her confession.'

'But she is excommunicate. She murdered within the hospital.'

'She does not seem to know that.'

'I cannot reveal what she says.'

'She is guilty, I have no doubt. A cold woman.'

'You are weary of this.'

'I am sick at heart. This is when I most miss soldiering. A practice yard is what I need. A straw man to attack until my arms give out.'

'Have His Grace's retainers no such place?'

'They do. But Sir Richard awaits me.'
'And His Grace.'
'Jesu.'

Thirty-two

Honouring the Dead

Douglas opened the door to Owen. 'Sir Richard paces his parlour awaiting you.'

'I have much to tell him. Is it true His Grace also attends your master?'

'Yes. And he is in a rage.'

'You have heard the cause?'

'A barge with stones for the minster's Lady Chapel arrived at St Mary's dock, as is customary for work on the cathedral. But permission to unload has been refused until the day after tomorrow. His Grace and Abbot Campian had words. Apparently the abbot said the city had no need of His Grace's "self-serving gesture", that the pestilence was withdrawing from York because of Brother Wulfstan's selfless work among the dying. And that Wulfstan had given his life for the people — You see the thrust of the insult.'

Owen wished he had witnessed it. 'Tomorrow they bury Wulfstan. I understand the abbot's wish to halt such activity until afterwards. His Grace did not?'

'To be fair, His Grace arrived already in mourning. Queen Phillippa is dead, God grant her peace.' Douglas bowed his head, as did Owen. 'His Grace has vowed to complete the chapel in her memory, and by Martinmas.'

'That was ever a foolish goal.' Owen took a deep breath. 'This is my purgatory, Douglas. Announce me.'

Ravenser spun round when Owen was shown in. The master's dress was not so gay as was his custom, his eyes were bright with tension. 'So? Is it true? You have the pair who tried to destroy this hospital?'

Owen bowed to him, then Thoresby, who stood with his back to the window that looked out on the garden. 'I have much to tell, Sir Richard.'

'You are thirsty?'

'I am in sore need of brandywine.'

Ravenser nodded to Douglas, who slipped from the room. The master motioned to Owen to sit. Owen glanced at Thoresby, who was still standing.

'Sit, Archer. Forget that I am here.'

Not something Owen thought possible, but he settled into a cushioned chair; the wagon seat had been far less comfortable than a saddle.

Ravenser settled across from him. 'I understand Judith Ffulford was the daughter of the woman Anneys. Was it the death of the woman's son at the orphanage that turned them against St Leonard's?'

'Their purpose had naught to do with the hospital, Sir Richard.' Slowly, in detail, Owen repeated what he had learned about Anneys and Finn.

Ravenser shook his head and drummed his fingers throughout the report, but saved his comments till the end. Such as they were. 'Faith, she seemed a respectable widow. And he is a clerk, you say? He might have found honest work.'

'Some folk find thieving easier, Sir Richard.' Would he not comment on the grim single-mindedness of Anneys, a woman so poisoned with hatred, and the children who accepted it?

'How did it further their cause to spread scandalous reports of the hospital's finances?'

Indeed, he was like his uncle, concerned only about his career. 'That had naught to do with them. I believe it was Honoria de Staines gossiping with her . . . admirers.'

A sniff from Thoresby's direction reminded Owen of his presence.

Ravenser glanced at his uncle and reddened. 'Continue, Captain.'

So the Master of St Leonard's was embarrassed to discuss this in front of his uncle. Then why had he not seen Owen in private? Puzzling, but distracting. Owen wished to make his report and be done with the wretched business. He told Ravenser of Honoria's problem with the late mayor, and Cuthbert's sympathy.

'So she has kept her vows?'

'I cannot say that, Sir Richard. She apparently kept company with much of the council at one time or another.'

Ravenser had sunk down into his chair and pressed his temples. 'Don Cuthbert said she wished to change, to devote herself to God. How could I have believed that?'

Thoresby took a comfortable chair beside Owen, steepled his hands, and proceeded to stare at his nephew.

Ravenser bowed to him. 'You warned me. I might have been ruined by that harlot. I shall send her back to her father's house.'

'And what of Don Cuthbert?' Thoresby asked.

Ravenser looked startled. 'What of Cuthbert?'

'Surely he is no longer to be left in command in your absence?'

'He is a good man.'

'Are you blind? Do you not see how all this is the result of the canon's poor judgement? Neither Mistress Staines nor the woman Anneys should have been accepted into this hospital.'

For a long moment, Ravenser stared at his uncle. Then he said simply, 'We shall discuss this later. Cuthbert is not the captain's concern.'

Thoresby grunted, but settled back in his chair.

Owen thought it a remarkable victory for Ravenser.

'What of the woman's health, Captain?' Ravenser resumed. 'Is she likely to die of the pestilence?'

'Aye. There is little hope for her.'

'Good. But what of this Finn? The city gallows? The minster gallows?'

'I must speak to you about that.' Owen relayed Wulfstan's request.

Ravenser shook his head. 'Impossible. The man is excommunicate, as is the woman: such is the fate of any who enter any property of the hospital to do violence, or to loot or burgle.' He almost smiled.

But Owen could not allow Ravenser his comfortable response, even to help him save face with his uncle. 'I think not, Sir Richard. It seems he entered the hospital grounds only to deliver Brother Wulfstan's bag to Anneys.'

'He murdered Hotter in the man's house, which was deeded to us when he became a corrodian.'

'Ah. Then you are right, it is impossible.'

'Perhaps not,' Thoresby said. 'It depends on the wording of the deed. The property may have remained in the corrodian's possession until his death.'

Ravenser did not acknowledge his uncle's interruption. 'I do not like this scheme, Captain. Walter de Hotter's family will not like it.' He took a deep breath, rose and walked to the window.

Owen gladly allowed him time to consider. The brandywine was easing his aches, and the drama playing out between Ravenser and Thoresby was lightening his mood.

At last Ravenser turned. 'Given Brother Wulfstan's years of selfless work for this city, I cannot disregard his wish. But it is not enough that Finn can read; I do not trust that test. I shall look into it, see whether anyone will come forward and support his claim. If so, and if the wording of the deed proves to be in his favour' — he nodded once in his uncle's direction — 'Brother Wulfstan's wish will be granted. But if the man ever sets foot outside St Mary's, his life is forfeit.' He paused. 'And if there is no proof of his taking orders, or if the deed proves against him, he will hang for breaking the King's peace. Douglas will write up my decision.'

Owen thought Ravenser more than fair, and said so.

'You have done well by me, Captain Archer. I am grateful.'

But Thoresby plainly could not believe what he had heard. 'You would grant the man a comfortable life at St Mary's in exchange for his prayers? You are no nephew of mine. Of what possible value are the prayers of a thief and a murderer? It is as much an abomination as your allowing harlots to live under your protection as lay sisters. If this man is not excommunicate it is only because of a poorly composed deed.'

Ravenser did not flinch. 'I have restored peace here in St Leonard's.'

'Owen Archer has restored the peace.'

'Very well. And I am grateful to you for his help. Nor will I go forth with Brother Wulfstan's wish if I find no proof that Finn is due benefit of clergy.'

'Benefit of clergy. Every snivelling coward in the land memorises the lines we use as proof.'

'I have said I shall not accept that.'

Thoresby waved him silent. 'What of the

child's part in this?'

'She is a child, uncle. She is to return to her kin, though not the family she lately left.'

'What a kind man you are. At least Anneys will presumably have the good grace to die before you reward her for her considerable sins.' Thoresby rose from his chair. 'Come, Archer. Let us retire to your house and leave Sir Richard to one of his headaches.'

Ravenser held out a hand to Owen. 'I am grateful, Captain. I shall make it worth your trouble.' He turned to his uncle, who was already at the door. 'You will return to dine with me?'

'Tomorrow. I dine with Archer and Mistress Wilton today.'

Dine with them? It was news to Owen. As he followed the archbishop he wondered how to tactfully ask *Who invited you? What do you want?* Much puzzled him. It was out of character for Thoresby to allow Owen to witness a family squabble. But most he worried about Thoresby dining at his house. Kate would be frantic. And the household was in mourning. What sort of cheer might they offer His Grace?

He was slightly relieved when Thoresby turned to him at the East Gate and said, 'Good work, Archer. Godspeed. I have some business to attend to in the city, but I shall follow you shortly.'

Lucie slumped on to the stool in the shop. 'He could not choose a time when he would be more unwelcome.'

'I had the same thought. But how does one refuse hospitality to the great John Thoresby?'

'One does not.'

Jasper, still pale, turned from his customer. 'Go to Kate, Mistress Lucie. We are not so busy today I cannot manage the shop.'

Lucie pressed his hand, slipped away with Owen. But she did not immediately go to Kate. She pulled Owen down on to a bench along the path to the roses. 'Come. Tell me all you learned. I would know the outcome of all these troubles. Thoresby's feast can wait.'

Owen had little desire to repeat what he had just reported to Ravenser, but Lucie had listened so patiently to his worries. And it might distract her. He did not like the shadows beneath her eyes and the tremor in her hands. So he told her all he had learned from Finn and Anneys, and amused her with the conflict between Thoresby and Ravenser.

'Think how much greater a burden it is to be Thoresby's nephew than it is to be his steward and spy.' Lucie rose, pressed her fists into her lower back. She still looked weary, but she smiled. 'You might take comfort in that.'

'Small comfort. But, aye, it was good to see him abuse someone else today.'

Lucie's smile faded. ' "How might one unwittingly commit a sin? If none suffer but the guilty, has a wrong been done?" I understand the first part now. They could not know Adam Carter would turn back. Nor did they know he had two children. How did Laurence de Warrene and Julian Taverner become involved with such a man?'

Owen put an arm round Lucie's shoulder. 'They were younger and hungrier than when we knew them.' They slowly walked towards the house. 'Strange that it was Laurence who posed the riddle, but Julian who seems to have felt the strongest guilt.'

'It seems so to us, but we have only Julian's account. Laurence may have felt his wife's poor health was a terrible penance; Matilda took a long time dying.' Lucie's voice was sad. She and Matilda had enjoyed trading seeds and clippings from their gardens.

Owen thought to cheer her. 'They are tending Matilda's garden at the hospital. She would be proud of it.'

'I am glad of that.' Lucie was quiet a moment. 'You know, in the end, the second part of the riddle was wrong. Not only the guilty suffered. And think what that woman almost did to the hospital that raised the daughter she abandoned.'

'And what of the penance? Were they responsible for Adam Carter's death? Or the fate of his leman and children?'

'That, my love, is a question for our dinner guest.'

'I think I shall leave it for another day.'

Epilogue

From dawn onwards, all employees of the York Tavern felt the brunt of Bess's frustration. If perfect cleanliness was possible, they would achieve it this day. Scrubbing, dusting, sweeping, polishing, and Bess herself doing the work of three. She could not believe the ingratitude shown her the previous evening by Owen and Lucie. Shoving her out of the house as if she were any old busybody. For pity's sake, it was her uncle's death and his claims about Laurence's death that had made folk see that something was amiss. And all the days she had sacrificed to assist Owen. Small thanks she received for it.

By midday, she was exhausted. 'I shall have a rest now, Tom. See that they don't slacken their pace.'

Up in her bedchamber, she flung open the shutters to get a breeze. It had all begun here, when she had smelled the fire. The sky was blue today, and but for the tolling of St Mary's bell, it was passing quiet. That was another frustration; after all her effort, Brother Wulfstan had passed away. What was God about these days?

And what was that? She leaned farther out of the window. Merciful Mother, it was His Grace the Archbishop of York coming out of Stonegate into the square with a dark-haired child clutching his left hand, a babe in his right arm. Brother Michaelo walked behind him carrying a large basket. She squinted. The babe had flame-red hair. Bess turned and hurried down the stairs.

'Tom! You will never guess what the archbishop has returned to us. Stop that noise and listen to me.'

Tom paused with a wooden mallet in mid-air; he was trying to hammer a pewter plate flat once more. 'What is it, wife?'

'Gwenllian and Hugh. His Grace has brought them back from the country.'

'There is a tale to tell in that, I would guess.'

'I should attend them. See whether they have enough food.'

'You would do better to wait until summoned.'

But she was already mounting the stairs. A splash to her face, neck and hands, off with the apron and on with one of her be-ribboned caps and she would be presentable, even to an archbishop.

She arrived in time to witness tearful greetings. Lucie's were not entirely tears of joy as she clutched Hugh to her.

'Sir Robert is ill,' Thoresby was telling her, 'and thus your aunt and I thought it best the children be brought away from him.'

'Pestilence?' Lucie asked in a whisper.

'No. A chill brought on by a tumble into the pond. It seems he was jousting with Gwenllian.'

The dark-haired two year old sat in her father's lap, solemnly listening. Owen stroked her hair, curly and wiry as his own. 'That does not mean you are to blame, Gwenllian.'

She said nothing, but grabbed Owen's hand and held on tight.

'Is he very ill?' Lucie asked.

Thoresby motioned to Michaelo to take the basket to the kitchen. 'At his age, any illness is difficult, Mistress Wilton. Dame Phillippa seemed anxious, but I think it was the children worried her.'

Perhaps it was not the time to interrupt, Bess thought. She was backing out of the doorway when Owen noticed her.

'Come in, Bess, come in.'

'Your Grace,' she bobbed a curtsey. 'I had to come see whether my eyes tricked me.'

She gave the children hugs, glanced over the well set table. So there was to be a feast.

'She has sharp eyes, Your Grace,' Owen said. 'And was a great help to me in finding the truth about her uncle's death.'

'Which I have yet to hear, neighbour,' Bess reminded him.

'You are a woman of many gifts, Mistress Merchet,' Thoresby said. 'I shall remember you if ever I need another spy.'

Bess shook her head until her ribbons bobbed. That was the last thing she wished. 'I pray you, think not of me for such work, Your Grace. Managing the tavern is more to my liking.' But it was pleasing to be praised for something other than her housekeeping. 'Though I do admit I have a certain knack for it.'

Author's Note

The concept of a hospital in fourteenth-century England differed from the modern concept in a critical way, perhaps best defined by Rotha Mary Clay in her classic 1909 work: 'the hospital . . . was an ecclesiastical, not a medical, institution. It was for care rather than cure: for the relief of the body, when possible, but pre-eminently for the refreshment of the soul . . . The staff . . . endeavoured . . . to strengthen the soul and prepare it for the future life.' Not that survival was unheard of. St Leonard's ordinance stated that those cared for within the hospital were not to be discharged until convalescent and able to work.

Along with the concept, the meaning of the word 'hospital' has changed, and one might almost say contracted, over time. St Leonard's, York, encompassed most of the definitions provided by the OED: 'A house or hostel for the reception and entertainment of pilgrims, travellers, and strangers; a hospice. A charitable institution for the housing and maintenance of the needy; an asylum for the destitute, infirm, or aged. A charitable institution for the education and maintenance of the young. An institution or establishment for the care of the sick or wounded, or of those who require medical treatment.' St Leonard's was, additionally, a monastic house, and it daily provided alms to the poor of York and fed the inmates of the York Castle prison. Hence, it was of tremendous importance to the city. There were other hospitals in York, but none was so diverse in purpose, none touched on so many aspects of the people's lives. Most were more specialised, caring for lepers, ailing clergy, wayfarers, the poor and, increasingly, guilds provided care for their own ill and elderly. A specialty not found was pestilence.

The pestilence of 1369 was the third visitation of the plague. Records of this outbreak are sketchy, but most agree that it took mostly the elderly or infirm and children, which suggests to our modern way of thinking that people were building up an immunity. Rosemary Horrox sums up fourteenth-century theories of the plague's causes: 'Scientists were agreed that the physical cause of plague was the corruption of the air — or, rather, since air was an element and could not change its substance, the mixing of air with corrupt or poisonous vapours, which when inhaled would have a detrimental effect on the human body. Where they differed was in the explanations they gave for the corruption. Some causes were obvious. Everyone agreed that the air could be poisoned by rotting matter, including dead bodies, or by excrement or stagnant water. Naturally enough, suspicion was extended to anything which smelt unpleasant . . . [thus] suggested precautions against plague always include a recommendation to surround oneself with pleasant smells.' Yet day to day life had to go on, so people became creative about portable sources of positive scents. Some of their preventatives might have had the incidental effect of repelling fleas or creating an environment unappealing to rats, which may have accidentally saved some people.

Gathering the victims together in an infirmary was absolutely contrary to the wisdom of the times. The sick were isolated, as far as was possible, and the healthy were advised to avoid crowds. I thought it an interesting situation in which to study St Leonard's, to show how the role of a hospital in a community has changed. Richard de Ravenser goes to York not to give moral support to his people working among the plague victims but to see to the hospital's finances and shore up its reputation. The plague had no particular significance to the Master of St Leonard's.

One of the few charitable institutions that survived the Conquest, St Leonard's was popularly said to have been founded by King Athelstan in 936 as a hospice, or guesthouse for wayfarers (not the canons of the minster). It was known as St Peter's Hospital until the late twelfth century, as it was administered by the canons of York Minster, or St Peter's. An estimated 300 people populated the precinct, which extended from Footless Lane almost to Petergate, and from Lop Lane to the south wall of St Mary's Abbey. The full complement of staff of the hospital included a master, at least thirteen brethren, lay brothers, eight sisters, plus clerks, servants and lay sisters. In the fourteenth century, the mastership of the hospital, by then known as St Leonard's, was in the King's patronage, although Richard de Ravenser, being the Queen's Receiver, may have owed his appointment to the Queen. Of course, he was also the nephew of John Thoresby, Archbishop of York.

The work of the hospital was financed by the Petercorn, a grant of thraves (or a measure of grain, roughly twenty-four sheaves), one from every plough (or about every 120 acres) in the diocese of York. After the first visitation of the Black Death, the income from the Petercorn did not keep pace with prices and wages; poor harvests such as that of 1368 aggravated the problem. The hospital received endowments of land, churches and mills, which brought additional income, but the dwindling of the Petercorn had encouraged former masters of St Leonard's to sell corrodies for quick cash. A corrody was rather like an investment in a retirement home — a sum of money paid in return for not only room and board but also medical and spiritual aid. Difficulties arose when corrodies were sold for flat fees; many corrodians lived longer than expected, and thus cost the hospital. The King, being the hospital's patron, also used St Leonard's and other establishments as repositories for ageing servants; and the King paid no fee for these corrodians.

As Keeper of the Hanaper and Queen's Receiver, Richard de Ravenser proved himself adept at finance. In 1363 the King promoted Ravenser's Keeper status to a clerk of the first grade. Also in this year, the King gave Ravenser as the Queen's Receiver, the task of clearing the queen's considerable debts. So it is not surprising that during his mastership of St Leonard's (1363–84), Ravenser placed priority on improving the hospital's financial situation. He refused to sell corrodies for flat fees; instead he sought to increase the hospital's valuable and appreciating property holdings in the city in the form of messuages and tenements in return for corrodies and obits (offerings for annual memorial masses on behalf of the deceased).

I thought the issue of corrodians outliving their welcome a situation ripe for a murder mystery. And had Ravenser not been a real historic figure, I doubt I could have resisted implicating him in some convenient deaths. But the more I read about Ravenser the more I felt that his flaw was more likely to be an obsession with balanced ledgers and good reputation and a lack of intuition concerning the people in his charge.

But one evening in 1995, during a congenial dinner in York, Patricia Cullum mentioned the lay sisters who began to appear, perhaps in the late fourteenth century, at St Leonard's. And slowly Anneys began to form in my imagination: a widow taking minor vows as a lay sister in order to move about the city and the hospital without bringing much attention to herself. It was convenient (for me) that the lay sisters lived outside the hospital, in the city. And as they were little more than servants, I thought it unlikely anyone would be terribly interested in their backgrounds or their activities when they were not on duty.

Plague and the Queen's death were interesting complications. It is unclear when John Thoresby dismantled Sherburne for its stones, but I thought it fitting that he would have done something so drastic at this time, with his city in turmoil and the Queen on her death-bed.

Queen Phillippa did not die of plague; she had been ailing for years, and in the summer of 1369 she took a turn for the worse. Many say that when Phillippa died, Edward III lost his anchor. Unless, of course, one considered Alice Perrers a fitting substitute. Froissart reports that on the Queen's death-bed she asked the King to grant three wishes: that he would honour her debts, and her bequests, and that when he died he would be buried beside her at Westminster. The King tearfully agreed. By tradition, her death-bed was donated to the clergy. The hangings and coverlets were made into vestments for the clergy of York Minster, in memory of her wedding in the cathedral. Her subjects had loved her dearly, and she was deeply mourned. Her body was taken down the Thames as far as the Tower so that her funeral procession would move through the crowds in London on its way to Westminster. She was buried in earth brought from the Holy Land.

By many accounts, the infamous Alice Perrers did indeed give birth to a daughter christened Blanche in this year. A tribute to John of Gaunt's late wife? Or a not-so-subtle clue as to the father? Interestingly, not all accounts of Alice's life include a daughter by this name. She remains ever the enigma.

PASADENA PUBLIC LIBRARY
1201 Jeff Ginn Memorial Drive
Pasadena, TX 77506-4895

Bibliography

The Black Death, Rosemary Horrox (translator and editor), Manchester University Press, 1994.

Cremetts and Corrodies: Care of the Poor and Sick at St Leonard's Hospital, York, in the Middle Ages, P. H. Cullum, University of York, Borthwick Paper No. 79, 1991.

Hospitals and Charitable Provision in Medieval Yorkshire, 936-1547, P. H. Cullum, unpublished doctoral thesis, University of York, 1989.

The Mediaeval Hospitals of England, Rotha Mary Clay, Frank Cass and Co. Ltd, London, 1966; reprint of 1909 edition.

'St Leonard's Hospital, York: the spatial and social analysis of an Augustinian hospital', P. H. Cullum, in *Advances in Monastic Archaeology*, eds R. Gilchrist and H. Mytum, BAR British Series 227, Oxford, 1993, pp. 11–18.

The employees of Thorndike Press hope you have enjoyed this Large Print book. All our Large Print titles are designed for easy reading, and all our books are made to last. Other Thorndike Press Large Print books are available at your library, through selected bookstores, or directly from us.

For information about titles, please call:

(800) 257-5157

To share your comments, please write:

Publisher
Thorndike Press
P.O. Box 159
Thorndike, Maine 04986